Beverly Cochran live[s] ... with her lawyer husband, Hugh. For several years she taught English at Peterhead prison. This is her first novel.

The Housekeeper

Beverly Cochran

First published in 1994
by HEADLINE BOOK PUBLISHING

First published in paperback in 1995
by HEADLINE BOOK PUBLISHING

A HEADLINE REVIEW paperback

10 9 8 7 6 5 4 3 2 1

ISBN 0 7472 4731 5

Typeset by CBS, Felixstowe, Suffolk

Printed and bound in Great Britain by
Cox & Wyman Ltd, Reading, Berks

HEADLINE BOOK PUBLISHING
A division of Hodder Headline PLC
338 Euston Road
London NW1 3BH

For Pat and Kenneth Boyd

PART ONE

Mary Ruth's Story

Chapter 1

I was sixty last year. My cousin Verity swam across Lochfearn on her sixtieth birthday. I've never swum across anything except the local swimming bath. My name is Mary Ruth Findlater. I was the housekeeper at Fionn-glass House for Lord Fionn-glass of Fionn-dhruim. No one doubts that Miss Eliza Potts, heiress of Stoke-on-Trent, was impressed with her future husband's new Scottish title in 1860, but it is not easy to pronounce or to spell. Happily Angus, our postie, is adept at interpretation.

The house is lovely. Well worth keeping. It was designed by Thomas Smirke and built for the first viscount's grandfather in 1830. It has a big entrance hall which soars up to a gallery. It's all wood-panelled and smells good. The fireplace is eight feet high and there are huge sofas and Chinese and Indian rugs and the dining room looks west along the river to the hills and — this is no way to explain. I will begin with the events of January 1991 . . .

It was Monday the fourteenth, and I was feeding my hens. A weasel had been in the run. The young blonde chicken lay beheaded and with her guts eaten out. Feathers, soft, blonde, pinky feathers lay in a line along the edge of the feed trough. The other hens were grouped together at the back of the pen. I opened the wire netting door and carried the big jug of hot food across the green. Clucking energetically to encourage the poor frightened creatures to follow me, I spooned the mash on to the frozen ground in a patch of sunshine. The hens gathered busily and started to eat. I went into the run, scooped up the head and picked up the dead body. I walked round the woodshed to the manure heap and dropped the head and body on to it. The dog appeared and began sniffing. I shooed him away and looked round for the shovel. It was not leaning on the shed where I had left it.

Murmuring 'Nothing's easy', I set off round the house to the side door. Perhaps Douggie had moved it when we had been expecting the heavy snow in December, or rather when the weather forecasters had been expecting it. In our part of Scotland they never seem to get it right. We're too far east and too sheltered by the Cairngorms for the westerly storms to reach us; too far west for the North Sea storms to hit us, and when a northern gale blows in we're all too busy to listen to the forecast. The shovel wasn't on the veranda hanging by the woodpile either. At this point I heard the postie's van so I walked round to my back door to greet Angus.

'There's terrible mole heaps you have, Mary Ruth. It's a colony, surely? Why don't I ask Donald Molloch to come across and see to them for you?'

'Kill them you mean, Angus.' We have this conversation all year round. We have very energetic moles.

'Ach, he'll only put a smoke bomb down and frighten them off. Unless you ask for the strychnine. And that's not everyone he'll do it for.'

'Douggie and I tried smoke bombs. We thought we'd driven them off, but the heaps reappeared. They do no harm anyway and we use the soil in the garden.' That's where the shovel will be, I thought. Last time Douggie was here he'd been shifting mole hills from the front lawn. 'Isn't poison illegal, Angus? I know traps are.'

'You'll find poison is allowed for moles. I'll tell Donald.'

'And I'll tell the moles,' I replied. 'They'll be pleased to hear that I can poison them after all.'

'Well, Donald Molloch will know. He'll be over soon.'

'I hope so, but since he told me how strychnine works in a mole run, is it any wonder I don't want it?'

'They're cannibals right enough,' said Angus, 'but they do say it works fine well.'

'There's enough killing going on, Angus. Leave my moles alone.'

'It's Armageddon right enough,' he went on. 'Do you think there will be war in the Gulf?'

'I'm afraid so. It's becoming a question of pride.'

'What a world. Here's millions dying for want of food while money is turned into weapons. It doesn't bear thinking about.' He sighed and added, 'Here's your post. I must be on my way.'

'Thank you, I must get on. I'm looking for the shovel.'

'You'll not get it in the ground the day. Earth stands hard as iron.'

'I'll have to cover the henlet. The dog's interested. There's been a weasel in the hen run.'

'Or a mink. Ach! Any more signs of the fox?'

'No, he's taken the hint since I've kept them penned in. Cheeky thing. I saw him one night in November, scooting off with his tail stuck out behind him.'

'Devils they are. Fair enough if they are feeding young, but they kill for fun too.' He levered himself back into the post van saying, 'Well take care, Mary Ruth.' Then off he went, doubtless to tell the neighbours what an old softie of a toonser I was – I was born in Edinburgh – because I didn't want Hairy Donald to honour me with strychnine and poison the moles of Fionn-glass. Like me they lived here and I wished them no ill.

I pushed my mail into my pocket and set off to the greenhouse. Sure enough, the big shovel was there resting on the wheelbarrow. The ground was 'hard as iron', Angus was right. I took the shovel into the greenhouse, prised up a heap of earth, carried it round to the manure heap and put the earth on the little hen.

Mrs Inglis will be sad. She comes on Wednesdays to help clean the house. Not that it is used, the Laird lives in London, but we keep it swept and dusted. It's hard on her because she is a perfectionist. She was taken with the blonde henlet. The dog sat a little way off, regarding me with reproach. Perfectly good food there, he was thinking.

'Come on Napper,' I said and threw a stick for him. He bounded off at once. If not forgiving, at least prepared to forget.

I hung the shovel by my back door on the hefty hook my son had made for me in metalwork. Douggie will have to look for it now, I thought. I wouldn't mind, but we've five of the things, too many perhaps and never one where you want it.

In my kitchen the cats lay in their places on either side of the Aga. I put the kettle on and the radio. It was the morning service. 'Dear Lord and Father of Mankind Forgive our Foolish Ways' rolled out. I looked at my mail with interest before I opened it. Kenneth still teases me about this, but I enjoy working out who has written to me. One from His Lordship, one from Rentokil, one from Elgin and one from Kenneth in France. A catalogue about an imminent silver sale from Carter's, the Edinburgh auctioneers, and an appeal from War On Want. What a haul.

I made a cup of tea with a tea bag. Disgusting things. I must sort out another teapot. There are umpteen of them in the house. I hoiked the soggy bag out with a spoon and dumped it in the garden bin. Then I sat with my back to the Aga and opened the first letter. It read:

2, Baltic Mansions, Knightsbridge, London

Dear Mary Ruth,

A happy new year to you. Please send my best to Kenneth. We spent Christmas with Dorinda's family in Firenze. Tadeus is over the moon about the Iron Curtain going. He was romancing about his father's estate, now alas beneath eighty feet of water near Cracow, in the municipal reservoir.

I've now got three granddaughters. Lizzie's first effort was premature, but she's fine now. She looked like a skinned rabbit.

Anyway, the news is that Dorinda and I are coming for

Easter. April Fool's Day is actually Easter Monday, I know it's early in the year, but thought it might be warming up a bit. Or am I the April Fool? Anyway, can you get it all teed up.

There'll be nine of us. Four couples and Dorinda's brother from the States, sans wife and two ladies' maids. We'll need a cook and extra help in the house. Don't spare the firewood or the stone piggies or the food. They'll all complain they're freezing to death whatever we do, but I do want to pre-empt trouble. We'll need bedroom fires. Real ones if poss. They always take a trick with visitors. So I'll leave it in your capable hands. Money no object, within reason.

Why not sling some of the spare fish-knives and forks down to Carter's as per usual. Family parties do lap up the port somewhat. The things we do for England! See you at the end of March.

Yours aye,

Donald

PS We'll arrive Friday 29th, leave Wednesday 3rd. Giles and Marina Nichols-Gordon and Bimbo and Freddie Massingham are making up the party by the way. Don't for God's sake put Bimbo at the top of the stairs, remember what happened last time.

Cheers, D.

Mrs Inglis will be glad, I thought, and it will add zest to our spring-cleaning. It'll be good to have some company in the house too. Lord Donald's new wife, Dorinda, is an Italian contessa; she has only been to visit once, for two days, after their marriage in 1989. How times have changed. As the Hon. Donald Findlater he used to come regularly for the shooting and his first wife, Mary, 'our Mrs Findlater', used to come every summer for two months with the children.

I thought hard. Nine of them and two more backstairs. We were going to have a lot of work to do. I drank my tea and opened the letter from Rentokil. It began: Dear Satisfied Customer and then asked me if I was satisfied with their services. I'd had a twenty-year check last year. I didn't want another. What a commotion it was; all the attics had to be cleared. That reminded me, there were some good dining chairs up there, Hepplewhite I think. They'd been up there since the war. Perhaps Lord Donald would like me to sell them. I'd have to sell a lot of fish-knives and forks to pay for the entertainment of such a crowd. I put the letter down and opened the one from Elgin. It was headed:

Youngson, Dean and Field, Solicitors and Notaries Public,
North Street, Elgin

It was from Mr Field, my mother-in-law's solicitor. She had died at the beginning of December. He'd sent me a copy of her will just before Christmas. She'd left everything to my son, except her jewellery, which was for me. Mr Field had kept it to be valued for probate. As far as I could judge this would have taken five minutes. She had a silver bracelet, which I had given her, a little antique pearl ring of her mother's, her dress ring, a few pairs of ear-studs and a jet necklace. I'd left them with him. He wanted me to come to the office so that he might *discuss certain matters arising.*

Bless him, he's been retired for years, but as an old friend he had wanted to execute her will himself. He'd want to talk about her. Well, I could do with an excuse to go to Elgin and I could go to see my uncle Alec too. He's my mother's youngest brother and he'll be eighty in December. We're all getting on. Napper raised his head and pricked his ears. The back door opened and Douggie came up the passage and slowly opened the kitchen door.

'I see you,' he said to Napper who had dashed to greet him. 'Thought I'd put the roofing felt on the hens,' he said to me. 'Too frosty for digging.'

'There was a weasel in the run. Little blonde hen.'

'Poor thing.'

'Will you have a cup of coffee?'

'Later,' then as he turned to go he said, 'I see the shuffle's back on its hook.'

'There's no answer to that,' I said. I stood up and filled the kettle, put it on the slow ring and opened Kenneth's letter. Napper went out with Douggie. Like all Jack Russells he prefers to be outside if there's anyone going.

Polzac, Auvergne, 5 January 1991

Dear Mum,

Good news. I am coming to Edinburgh to see the director of the Black Gallery. He's interested in my street market paintings. I'm hoping for an exhibition at Festival time. I'm leaving here on the 14th of April with some friends who are driving north.

All well here. Marie-Claire is blooming, the doc's very pleased with her. The date seems to be the 3rd September so when you come for your annual inspection there will be three little ones for you to spoil. Everyone here sends love. I still can't believe Granny isn't there. You must miss her terribly.

Must stop. Hope to be with you 17th or 18th. Will ring.

All love,

Kenneth

I do not spoil my granddaughters, but I was pleased to hear from him and that his visit was to be after the family invasion. Carter's catalogue would keep. I had sold valuables before for Lord Donald at their salerooms. I was in Edinburgh quite regularly to see my sister, in fact I was there far more than His Lordship was in Scotland.

Certainly some money for entertaining the Easter visitors would be required. Everyone who came to stay seemed to develop gargantuan appetites. It was the country air I reckoned, though Kenneth always maintained it was the country cold. I'm rather ashamed to say that I left the War On Want envelope unopened. I feel increasingly helpless in the face of famine and floods and starving refugees and my widow's mite wouldn't be much help to the poor. I moved the kettle to the side of the slow ring. It was ready. I put two mugs on the Aga and went outside to find Douggie. We often had our coffee outside, but not when there were ten degrees of frost.

I went round to the hen-house. The roof had been leaking. Douggie was almost finished re-covering it, balanced on our old ladder. 'Shall I find some nails for you?' I called.

'I'll get a new ladder to you,' he said. 'This one's like me. Needs pensioning off.' I picked up the nail tin. He held out his hand. 'Two-inchers,' he said. I poked about in the tin, sorted one out and handed it up to him. Then I put the tin on the food-bin lid and started sifting through for some more.

'Apart from that it's a terrible weight,' he said.

'Not as bad as that long one we used to use for the gutters.'

'Right enough.' He held out his hand again for a nail. 'That was made for three men.' He held the nail steady and tapped it in. All his movements were slow and deliberate. He held out his hand for another nail, leaned forward and placed it carefully. 'In the old days there were five gardeners, so Joe told me. Before the war,' he added.

'I can't think what they did,' I said. I thought Douggie and I did well.

He gave me a slow look, full of reproach, like the dog. 'Cutting the lawns with a pony? Edging? The walled garden, the greenhouses, the pond, the flower-beds, the shrubberies, planting out, manuring?'

'In the winter?' I tried. I have never won an argument with Douggie.

'Right enough, but they'd have repairs, creosoting, painting, ditching, woodcutting.'

'I give up. Ready for coffee?'

He gave a final tap and climbed slowly down. Then he moved the rickety ladder along and slowly climbed up again. 'Finish this first.'

Later, as we sat in the kitchen warming up and sipping the black instant coffee we had grown to like when the milk was still in its crate at the bottom of the east drive, I told him about the letter from His Lordship. He didn't say anything at first.

Douggie came to do the gravel hoeing, general maintenance and grass cutting to help me. He had never been a worker on the estate. He had dug a vegetable patch in the garden to the south of the house and I helped tend the flowers. Old Lord Fionn-glass's mother, who was English, had wanted a flower garden, but eight hundred feet above sea level it is not easy. The season is short and we have to rely on all the old perennials: catmint, lupins, columbines, pyrethrum, 'peeny roses' and later marguerites, Michaelmas daisies and golden rod.

Plants have too many enemies in exposed hillside gardens. Rabbit wire keeps rabbits out, but not moles, mice, woodpigeons or deer. Sudden frosts in June and heavy rains in July don't help either, but it is the wind which kills all but the hardiest. My old faithfuls come up very slowly each year, but even the humble, native potentilla dies back to a few skimpy sticks in our garden.

'It'll make a power of work for you and Mrs Inglis,' Douggie said after a while. 'How long are they coming for?'

'Friday to Wednesday,' I said. 'Over Easter, including All Fools' Day.' I grinned at him. 'It won't be warm.'

'Easter's early this year. Hunt-the-gowk's Easter Monday. They're the cuckoos, April is too early for this house.' Then he paused and added, 'It's a pity to have a house this big and not use it more. Houses need living in.'

'At least they are coming. It'll cheer us all up.' But he wouldn't agree.

He set off after thanking me for his coffee muttering, 'A power o' work, a power o' work.' As we reached the back door he looked at me and said, 'You do a lot for them, Mary Ruth. It's not many that can find an honest housekeeper prepared to live alone in a big house like this and take care of it so well.'

'I'm happy enough, Douggie, and at least I can work at my own pace and read in peace.'

'Hmmph!' he said and went to his car. I don't think he disapproves of reading, so perhaps for once I had scored a point. I watched him drive off slowly in his old Saab. He's getting old too. I couldn't imagine life here without him. Who else would help me? We are isolated.

I reread His Lordship's letter and it cheered me up. After all I am his housekeeper and it's my job to keep the house. I have a roof over my head. I have nothing to complain about. I'm perfectly happy, but I felt sad for all that. Douggie was right, houses need living in, not just keeping.

'Well this won't get the boat launched,' I said to Napper as I rinsed the mugs. I lifted the broth into the simmering oven, put on my long duffle-coat and went through into the house to start planning for the visit.

My greatest ally was Mrs Inglis. She was a wonderful worker, but there was a lot to do. His Lordship's suggestion of extra help was fine, but who was there to ask? I knew Helen from Knockglass would be glad to come to cook and as it was a holiday weekend there was a good chance she'd bring Jean, her niece, who was saving every penny towards her wedding. I'd have to ask Helen at once. She was in demand in the season at all the hotels as relief cook. I'd better ask Mrs Inglis to find someone to help in the house. She would have to work with her.

It was bitterly cold in the house. I stood in the hall, numb. I'd need a notebook and pencil. I went back to my own kitchen and fetched them and put on my navy woollen fingerless gloves, my tammy and my woolly scarf before I went back through the green baize door. No wonder no one had ever lived in the big house in the winter. Whatever Douggie said it wasn't a house for living in. It wasn't really a home but an investment, like so many of the summer houses built in Scotland after the Clearances. It was lovely though, unlike some of the later Victorian monstrosities built by the hastily ennobled rich.

Now, which rooms? The galleried hall was always popular, but it was only usable when the log fire had been lit for three or four hours. So the little sitting room would need turning out, and the dining room for the evenings. We would have to do the drawing room, it was the showpiece of the house, but I didn't think they'd want to sit in it. Not in April.

What about the billiards room? It had been added to the house in the 1920s. It was as cold as a tomb even in high summer. Then upstairs. Sheets and blankets would need airing, and beds. Would the sweep come in the winter? The roof was dangerous enough in the summer. Had we enough electric fires? Safe ones? Downstairs again. Was the big freezer still functioning? It had been off for years. Wood, mountains of it, would need fetching nearer the house from the old bakehouse. Who could help Douggie with that? Some of it could be stored in the conservatory, unless he decided to put plants in there. Highly unlikely. It made the billiards room feel cosy.

Towels, bath mats, hand towels. Cleaning stuff. Vacuum bags. The floor-polisher. The silver cutlery, candlesticks, tureens. The family china, glasses, napkins, tablecloths. It was never-ending. By Tuesday evening I had a working plan sketched out. Helen and Jean had promised to come and by bedtime I felt I was ready to face Mrs Inglis with a calm mind and a monumental list.

For the next ten days I worked with Mrs Inglis. She came once a week unless I had extra jobs for her and she had the time. She worked for the County as a home help and they often ran out of money towards the end of the financial year. This was hard enough on the home helps, but it was devastating for the elderly who relied on them. Most of the housebound were women and all of the helpers were. The organizer was a man. We didn't talk much as we worked, but over the years I had built up a picture of this man and I was glad I didn't have to rely on him for my bread and butter.

I was also glad of Mrs Inglis's help. She knows how to do everything in a country house from removing stuck glass decanter stoppers to sexing day-old chicks. She can light a fire without a fire-lighter and she only uses one match. She puts me to shame for all my schooling.

Chapter 2

By Friday the twenty-fifth of January, Burns Night, we had prepared all the main bedrooms. I'd managed to find enough safe electric heaters. Lord Donald's idea of real bedroom fires was impossible because the sweep had blocked off the upstairs chimneys to stop the jackdaws nesting.

They are determined birds. They will fill up six feet of stack with bits of stick before they build their nests. After a few years the damp created by the birdlime, rotten eggs and dead chicks seeps through into the house. Then you need scaffolding and men with crowbars to break through the wall to clear the lum. The sweep has wired old oven shelves over the ones we use.

I made a note, *No upstairs fires possible.* As we had long ago lost the upstairs fire makers, it was as well. Douggie's face, when I told him how many wood fires we were preparing to use downstairs, would have curdled the milk as it was. He is reliable, hardworking and he never complains. When totally disgusted with a suggestion, he ignores it.

After Mrs Inglis had gone I took a walk round the bedrooms, closing the shutters and admiring her faultless work. One of the idiosyncrasies of the house is that there are no double beds in it. There were rose, mauve, blue, green, apricot and purple silk curtains, bedspreads and eiderdowns for each of the six main bedrooms. They are old-fashioned now, but they are beautiful. The pine floors were gleaming like mirrors and so was the mahogany and cherry-wood furniture. There is no substitute for the genuine thing. It's like real blonde hair. It has a glow, a sheen, a bloom which cannot be produced artificially.

In the big airing cupboard the barrel heater was warm and the monogrammed linen and the blankets lay airing. The bathroom taps shone and the big bath mats were ready to hide the worst of the pock-marked lino.

I went downstairs feeling pleased with our progress and with Mrs Inglis's company, though after all the years I had been in the big house I was happy to be alone in it too. I went through to my quarters and had a cup of tea. Then I had a bath, put on my best and set off for The Commercial hotel in Balessie for the Burns supper, which promised as ever to owe as much to John Barleycorn as to Robert Burns.

The Commercial in the village is typical of our north-eastern pubs. Off the tourist trails, they have an apologetic air and are cold, gloomy and none too clean. The landlord-owner dodges into the barren lounge from the public bar where a few stalwarts stare at the television and down their pints as if they were that nasty brown medicine we all hated as children.

Behind our pub there is a cold hall, with stone-flagged pink-painted lavatories which are even colder. The stage, just large enough for a three-piece band, is backed by a dark brown velvet curtain twenty feet high. How it was put up no one knows and it has certainly never been taken down in living memory. If you bump into it a cloud of stale dust bellies out and settles slowly to the floor.

When there is to be a dance, always preceded by a meal, long trestle-tables are pulled out from under the stage and placed lengthwise down the hall. A popular function like Burns Night is always well-attended and there is little room to move when all the tables are up. Once you have shuffled along between the folding chairs to your place, negotiated with your neighbours and the person behind you and then wormed your way into your seat, that's you settled till the meal is over.

I was welcomed by Douggie and Stella, her brother Fred and his wife Helen who was coming to cook for me. Fred was the gamekeeper and chief stalker at Knockglass and a friend and neighbour of Donald Molloch, part time mole-catcher, from the Mains of Knockglass. I hadn't seen them since Hogmanay. They wanted me to sit between them. It was not easy. I'm well-built and they are both well over six feet.

We were all talking at once, greeting the rest of the table which included Sandy from the shop and Ina, his permanently cheerful wife, said by some wag to be the cause of Sandy's gloom – though Douggie maintains that Sandy was bullied into staying in the shop by his mother after his brothers went to Canada. Whatever the truth, he is a soured man.

Angus our postie, on the other hand, is always cheery as is Bella and his uncle Angus who was the last full-time gardener at Knockspindie till he retired. They were just inquiring after Kenneth when Mr Rennie, president of the Burns Society, called for us to be upstanding to welcome the haggis.

Mr Rennie, still called the dominie locally, was the head teacher of Balessie Primary. He'd encouraged me to let Aunt Connie pay Kenneth's fees at the Edinburgh Academy. She was Dad's oldest sister, childless, rich and bossy. She was certain I was eccentric for living in the country with my humble in-laws and said so. I hadn't much choice. I didn't want to live with her in Morningside and though I could have shared our family home in Edinburgh with my sister and her husband, they were newly married and both out working during the day. Anyway, Kenneth had a good education and Aunt Connie was able to hold her head up in her social circle.

It was a help to us all in the end, for as Kenneth started in Edinburgh, my parents-in-law were offered a council house in the village. There was no room for us and Mrs Joe's job as housekeeper was offered to me, on condition that I moved into the big house from the garden cottage. The insurance company argued that anyone could come and load the furniture and drive off without being seen. A neighbouring laird had a house cleared overnight, after some long-term tenants had left. Even the finger-plates and doorknobs had gone. No one noticed a thing.

Malcolm Malcolmson, the village policeman, began piping as we struggled to our feet. He entered the hall blowing hard followed by the cook from the hotel carrying an enormous haggis on an ashet. There was a narrow passage down the middle of the hall and they processed with much dignity, considering the difficulties. The cook put the ashet down, the pipes swirled to a climax, Malcolm downed his dram of whisky and we sat down again with much jostling to hear Mr Rennie address the haggis.

When the rustic virtues had been extolled and the haggis slit with a great flourish of his dirk, he called on Dr McPherson, the minister, to say the Selkirk grace. In solemn tones he roared:

Some hae meat and canna eat, and some wad eat that want it,
But we hae meat, and we can eat, sae let the Lord be thankit.

We then began handing the obligatory bowls of broth along the table to those remote from the kitchen. 'Helen tells me there's a great muckle party coming for Easter,' boomed Fred into my right ear, as Donald said with equal force into my left, 'I'm hearing from Angus that you are fairly surrounded by mole heaps, Mary Ruth. I'll surely be needing over to you when lambing's by.'

Everyone laughed. 'She'll be under siege on all sides,' said Douggie.

'It was good to see our Mrs Findlater,' said Ina in a burst, 'Helen and I were just saying how nice it was to see her again.'

'She's a real lady,' said Douggie.

'There's not many would come all the way from Bristol in December to an old housekeeper's funeral,' Ina went on.

'She was close to Mrs Joe years ago, remember,' I said.

'I was sorry not to be able to speak more to her,' said Helen. 'Fred had to get back, but I did manage to say hello. She recognized me,' she added with a little smile, 'and we talked about the fun we had when you used to come to Knockglass for picnics. Dear me, it's a long time past now.'

'They were good times,' said Ina, 'when the children were young. Our Jamie was always welcome at the big house. He and Malcolm used to go off on their bikes and spend the days with your Kenneth and her Julian. There was never any side to Mrs Findlater.'

'They boys had the best time of their lives fishing with Joe and eating Mrs Joe's scones,' said Uncle Angus. 'Boys like eating,' he added and began to chuckle. 'I mind the night Joe and I took them to watch for the big badger. They ate all their provisions and fell asleep afore he come.'

'And on wet days we used to teach them to dance in the big hall,' I said as everyone began to laugh. 'We had an old wind-up gramophone and we used to roll up the rugs and do the Dashing White Sergeant and the Eightsome, Mary and I and her girls and the four boys.' I felt quite sentimental. Mary had been a good friend to me. Though I seldom see her now, we write regularly. She is always trying to persuade me to visit.

'She was wonderful with the children,' said Ina. 'Just like Mrs Joe. They were lucky boys.'

'Mrs Findlater was good to Ellen too,' Douggie reminded us.

'Oh, yes,' said Stella. 'I was working for the council then and she was in over and over again until she managed to get a place for Ellen.'

'Every time I go past thon North Lodge I think about poor old Ellen,' said Angus, 'and what a cheery soul she was, considering.'

I thought about the cold, damp, tree-shrouded North Lodge and felt a shudder run down my back. Ellen had been housekeeper once at Fionn-glass House.

'I enjoyed my news with Mrs Findlater,' said Stella. 'That's the best of funerals, you meet all the old friends. She was telling me about her granddaughters. She's enjoying being a granny.'

Douggie smiled at her and said, 'You grannies are all the same. Power without responsibility.'

'Oh! Douggie,' said Stella who hardly ever sees her two grandsons who live in England.

'Mrs Findlater, though I suppose we ought to call her Lady Mary now, is a sad loss to this community,' said Bella as she finished her broth. 'She seemed happy enough to me, but it's changed times for her.'

'She was aye a fine woman,' said Angus. 'It was a sad day for us all when he put her aside.'

'Ye need money tae pit yer wife aside, never mind takin' on a new een,' said Uncle Angus, 'and from what I've heard the new een's a real handful. He niver hud any common sense, thon Lord Donald.'

'Now, Uncle,' said Angus, admonishing him, 'dinna speak ill.' The old man cackled and dug into his broth. He knew we all agreed with him.

'She seemed happy enough,' said Ina. Everyone nodded and began speaking at once about Lady Mary, her kindness and assumed happiness. We were all enjoying ourselves when Sandy looked up from his plate and said solemnly, 'Guid folk are scarce!' This made us all quiet again.

'She did enjoy her visit to Fionn-glass,' I said, trying to lighten the atmosphere. 'After the funeral I took her up before I drove her to the airport. We closed all the drawing-room shutters to find where we used to hang the dartboard. The marks of the misses are still there.'

'Happy days,' said Ina smiling at me.

'And now no one ever comes to the big house,' said Sandy, and after a pause added, 'I don't know how I keep going at the shop.'

Douggie, who can be relied upon to rise to the occasion, said, 'Hundreds of moles come, Sandy. You could make a pair of trousers if you could catch the Fionn-glass moles.'

'Strychnine will clear them, Mary Ruth,' said Donald Molloch at the mention of moles, 'but maybe you are thinking it is cruel,' he went on, mopping up the last of his broth with his bread.

'It is,' I said, 'and they're not doing any harm, Donald. Couldn't you just come for a visit? It seems a terrible way to die to me.'

'Now Donald Molloch,' said Helen firmly, 'I'm not come out for the evening to hear you talking about killing things, no matter how you do it. He and Fred never stop talking traps and snares and poison. It fair turns my stomach to listen to them,' she turned to the company with an appealing smile, 'don't you agree?'

Happily the summons for the empty soup-plates came and in the confusion of passing them one way and plates of haggis and serving dishes of tatties and neeps the other way, we managed to avoid any more talk of death and destruction. 'I must say,' intoned Sandy, 'I must say, Mackie does a good haggis.' He sounded disappointed.

'Oh, Sandy!' said Ina. 'You say that every year,' and she broke into a great peal of laughter which everyone joined in.

Bowls of ice-cream came along the table next, followed by coffee and glasses of whisky. Then we settled ourselves to hear 'The Immortal Memory'. The speaker was from Inverness and first he made us laugh, then he spoke of Burns's determination to speak the truth about society and after a pointed reminder that the Arabs were our brothers too, delivered 'Is there for honesty poverty'. I like the second verse best:

What though on hamely fare we dine
Wear hodden grey, an' a' that?
Gie fools their silks, and knaves their wine,
A man's a man for a' that.
For a' that, an' a' that,
Their tinsel show, an' a' that,
The honest man, tho' e'er sae poor,
Is king o' men for a' that.

He finished with a flourish and as the applause broke out and we struggled to our feet again for the toast, Donald Molloch beamed down on me and said, 'I wonder what Rabbie wid hae made o' the tinsel show o' oor consumer society, eh Mary Ruth?'

'It's thon television has brought temptation tae the country folk,' said Fred before I could answer. 'The loons are aye wantin' central heatin' and fitted carpets,' he added with disgust. 'They don't want tae bide in the country ony mair.'

It's not only television that's encouraging the young to move. In the last forty years I've seen machines replace men, and the army doesn't take the numbers it did, but farmers and gamekeepers enjoy being gloomy so I just nodded.

The toast to the Lassies, the reply and the singing followed and it was after ten before the call came to clear the room for the dancing.

'You're not giving us "Tam o' Shanter" this year,' I said to Mr Rennie when we met at the bar which was squeezed up at the back of the hall.

'No, Mrs Findlater,' he replied, 'I've persuaded Donald Molloch. He's performing in the interval.'

'So he was telling me. He says it's a long time since he was called upon and he hopes he can remember it.'

'He'll be fine. Once you've learned "Tam" you never forget it.' He bought me a whisky and said, 'Cheers! How's Kenneth and his family?'

'They're all well, thank you. He's coming home in April.' I felt a sudden desperate longing to see him. Whether Mr Rennie noticed my distress I don't know.

'Mind and tell him to come to see us,' he said as we were swept apart by the crowds. It was half past one before I left to drive home and they were still dancing.

Recovering the following morning from the many whiskies bought for me by generous neighbours who still can't accept that an Edinburgh woman can be happy staying 'oot by', I looked at my mail as I drank a third cup of tea. Littlewoods pools were enticing me, but I have never been able to understand how to fill in the coupon, so that wasn't much good. Help All Children had sent me a gift catalogue and there was a note from my sister, offering me a bed when I took the silver to sell for Donald.

The Household Account was in need of a boost. The wages I had already paid were eating up money and I knew he'd want Helen to prepare roasts, game, fresh and smoked salmon for his guests and have fresh fruit and exotic vegetables brought in from the Fruit Basket in Nairn.

No one could describe Sandy's vegetables as exotic. He has sacks of local potatoes and carrots, tough kale and big yellow neeps in the winter. Requests for mange-tout, avocado pears and baby corn would be considered an 'imposition'. It's the lack of competition that gives him the power over us all and we need the man with his little tubs of margarine and his small packets of cornflour, Bisto and soap powder.

I did ask him once why he didn't stock economy sizes and the ensuing lecture on cash flow and the economics of small shopkeeping, albeit subsidized by the Post Office counter, had taken half an hour. Now, like everyone else, I was just grateful that he was there.

I spent the rest of Saturday checking the china and glass store cupboards and making a list for Mrs Inglis who was coming on Monday with Mrs Gordon, a young widow whose husband had been killed in the Piper Alpha disaster. She had moved back to the village with her two boys and liked to be busy. I knew how she felt.

When my husband was killed in Malaya I had worked harder than at any time in my life although I was expecting Kenneth. I polished furniture for Mrs Joe all day and knitted all night. I was lucky though, as my mother-in-law left me to bring up my son. Mrs Gordon has a mother eager to 'sacrifice herself' and raise her grandchildren, leaving her daughter to find ways of occupying herself.

I was looking forward to going to Elgin: my uncle had promised to take me to evensong at St Drostan's priory. He'd taken early retirement from teaching and trained as an Episcopalian priest and he still works two Sundays a month. The isolated communities on the Moray coast were strongholds of Catholic and Episcopal people. Now two or three churches are under one charge and there are still not enough priests to serve them. These old Scottish churches held on to their beliefs even more staunchly because they were persecuted, I think. It's easier to drive habits in than it is to drive them out. It makes me sad to see them close from neglect, but Alec manages to rejoice that some of them have become community centres.

Sunday was lovely, cold, but with brilliant sun and a blue sky. I arrived in time for lunch. As always Alec had prepared a splendid meal. All the bachelors I know are good cooks. I wonder sometimes about the so-called general truths. All the women I know are competent drivers too.

From his sitting room window there is a view of the ruined cathedral. While I sat looking at it, a generous whisky in my hand, he pottered in and out of the kitchen adding more dishes to the table. He had cooked a hot beef curry with apricots, and a creamy cauliflower one, prepared poppadums and made bowls of cucumber raita and lemon sambal. We talked all through our meal, washed up together and settled down to read the *Sunday Times* until it was time to go to St Drostan's.

The priory was founded as a refuge for the dying, and perhaps because it was never a house of great wealth or scholarship it survived all the Jacobite troubles. It is still a place of refuge today, offering retreats to busy people. The brothers earn their living running a market garden.

We arrived in good time and as the words of the appointed evening psalm began I thought about Fionn-glass House. 'Except the Lord build the house, they labour in vain that build it,' sang the voices in the cold still air. We had a lot more work to do before Lord Donald came. The simple unaccompanied singing and the old familiar prayers reminded me how far so much of the world is from rest and quietness. We drove home without talking through the frosty countryside, but as Alec put his key in the lock he said softly, 'I pity the poor souls sleeping out tonight.'

'It's knowing how to help that's so hard,' I said as we climbed the stairs and went in to have supper away from the perils and dangers of the night.

Chapter 3

The next morning I walked along in the sun to my appointment with Mr Field. There was a new Pets Palace on the High. I stopped for a minute to look. *Snakes*, it said on a card, and sure enough there was a tank with some sad-looking grey snakes lying coiled in it.

'Is that you, Mary Ruth?' said a powerful voice behind me. Turning, I recognized Martha Bold. Her husband had been the head cattleman at Knockglass estate for forty years before they retired to Elgin. Before I could speak, she went on, 'I said to Arthur, "That's Mary Ruth Findlater, or I'm a Dutchman." What are you doing here?'

Martha always asks questions when she speaks. I had long ago found a way of dealing with it. 'Looking at the snakes in the window,' I replied truthfully. She smiled grimly. She was only half convinced that I was as simple as I pretended.

'Disgraceful!' she boomed. 'All part of this yuppy trend. Children were happy enough with a kitten in my day. What are you doing in Elgin?'

'Oh!' I said, as though I had just realized what she meant. 'I've been to visit my uncle.'

'At this time in the morning? What time did you leave home?'

'I came over yesterday. How is Arthur?' You have to fight back with Martha.

'Dyspeptic. I've found him a wonderful herbal remedy, but you know what he's like. Will he take it? Will he take it? That man is thrawn, Mary Ruth, thrawn. He's over there,' she said suddenly and pointed. Arthur stood patiently waiting for her on the other side of the road. He acknowledged me with a gentle bend.

'I must say hello to him,' I said and crossed the road. Martha followed me, calling out to Arthur.

'There you see. I was right. It is Mary Ruth. I told you.' Arthur smiled at me and pulled off his cap for a moment. Martha continued over the noise of the street. 'She came last night and stayed with Alec, but I don't know where she's bound now.'

'How is he?' asked Arthur. 'I haven't seen him in a long while. I'd like fine to see him. Tell him we were asking for him. Has Martha told you where we are going?'

'Not yet.'

Martha obliged. 'We're going out with the walking group. We are very busy in our retirement. It'll not be long till you are retiring, Mary Ruth. Have you put your name down for a house?'

Really, I thought, she is insufferable. She'll be asking me about my pension next. I opened my mouth as she went on, 'It's essential to keep busy. I have my little flock here on Mondays. We walk five miles most times. It keeps us fit. Doesn't it, Arthur?' She gave a quick look at her watch and gasped. 'Twenty past nine. We must get on. I'm the leader. Won't do to be late.' She turned to her patient man, dismissing me with a nod. 'We must get on, Arthur,' she said clearly and firmly as though he had been arguing.

And dear old Arthur, after forty-five years of being interrupted, ordered about, ticked off and accused of slowing down their progress smiled and said, 'I'm ready Martha,' in the same pleasant voice he'd used to his beasts all those years. Some said he should have beaten her for the first year of their marriage. Arthur never even smacked his dog. 'Martha brings out the worst in everyone, but the best in Arthur,' my mother-in-law used to say.

'Do you enjoy walking?' I asked Arthur, as a farewell gesture of solidarity.

'He enjoys all the chatter, that's for sure. Which way are you going?' she darted at me. 'We could walk along together.'

'I must just pop in the pet shop,' I said, and so arrived five minutes late at Mr Field's office, clutching an unwieldy brown-paper parcel of cat food. The receptionist smiled at me and offered to take it and I handed it over gratefully. I have quite a selection of folding bags at home. I never have one with me when I could do with it.

The receptionist, who can't have typed because she had fingernails as long as those of any Chinese empress, was very smart. She wore a shiny brilliant blue suit with a short-sleeved jacket and her skirt had a slit in it which showed her thighs as she walked upstairs. As I followed her I marvelled at the changed times. When I had first been in this office it was under the eye of a Miss Burnett, who must have sucked Pandrops all day because she reeked of peppermint. She wore hand-knitted Fair Isle sweaters and her tweed skirts hid most of her legs. She used to sigh as she led the way upstairs. Clients are an unnecessary interruption of the day, was written all over her.

This glamorous young lady swept ahead of me along the back corridor past shining rubber plants and framed etchings. She was fragrant with expensive perfume and assured me that Mr Field was expecting me. I suppose she was thinking I was a funny kind of client in my old green jacket and sensible lace-up shoes. Not at all what we are used to nowadays, her jaunty back seemed to say. She didn't ask me if she was going too fast for me, but I sensed she was about to offer me a hand at the shallow steps down into his room.

'Thank you,' I gushed in my lowest voice, giving her my best smile. Perhaps she'll think I'm an eccentric millionaire, I thought, hoping there was nothing stuck in my teeth.

'Mary Ruth, my dear, how lovely to see you. Come in, come in.' Mr Field, tall, slim, soft of voice, rose to his feet and walked round his desk, holding out his long slender-fingered hand to me. We shook hands. He pulled out a red leather chair for me and I sat down and slipped my jacket off. He went round the tidy desk and sat down, carefully adjusting his immaculately creased trousers. He put his hands together and looked hard into my face.

'You are well?'

'Very well thank you. And you?'

'I have nothing of which to complain. My digestion is good. My wife and I have many interests and many friends. We have taken to playing cribbage in the evenings. It is difficult to make up a bridge four nowadays: few elderly people like going out at night, we find.'

'Mary and I played cribbage. I miss it. And her.'

'You must. You were good friends; you must miss her very much.'

He opened a drawer and brought out three brown envelopes. He pushed one of them across the desk. 'Here is the jewellery you left with me. It is not valuable, though I'm sure you will value it.' He picked up the larger of the other two envelopes. 'Before I show you this, Mary Ruth, may I ask what arrangements Lord Donald has made for your retirement?'

'You're the second person this morning to ask me that.' I told him about Martha.

'She is not wrong, my dear,' he said. 'Though it was neither the time nor the place to be talking of it. Has he paid your National Insurance? Where will you live?'

'I'm a long way from retiring,' I said. 'I have a small army pension. My stamps are paid. I'll probably go to live with my sister. She and her husband live in our old house.'

'Does any of it still belong to you?' He sounded puzzled.

'Well, no, I sold my share to them when Kenneth went to Glasgow, but it's always been understood and anyway, I could go and live with Kenneth in France. Why does all this matter?'

'Your mother-in-law thought it mattered. She told me you had no home of your own, that's what puzzled me. She didn't have as much faith as you seem to have in your employer. It's convenient for him to pay you so that he can insure everything, but you'll have to retire sometime. I shouldn't wonder if he doesn't sell the house. Anyway, that is why she asked me to keep these for you.' He drew a worn navy jewel case out of the envelope. 'And here,' he picked up the other envelope, 'are the other items.' He tipped two smaller matching cases on to the desk. 'Open them up.'

I did so. In the larger case there was a sapphire and diamond choker. In the other cases were two sapphire and diamond bracelets and a pair of pendant earrings also of sapphires and diamonds.

'Where did she get these from?'

He handed me an envelope. I read the note inside. It was dated the fifteenth of June 1931. It said:

> I, Donald, Third Viscount Fionn-glass of Fionn-dhruim do give this collar, these bracelets and these earrings to Mary, Mrs Joseph Findlater of the Garden Cottage, Fionn-glass House, by Balessie to be hers entirely to do as she likes with them.
>
> Fionn-glass

Mr Field smiled. 'They were legally hers, as you can see. They belonged to old Lord Fionn-glass's mother and he gave them to your mother-in-law, here in this very room. It was my father's office then. They will be yours on your sixty-fifth birthday or if you die before it, they will belong to Kenneth. That was Mrs Joe's bequest. She wanted you to have them as security for your retirement. She came to see me last year, when she knew she was terminally ill. I've had them valued. If you wish to sell them in five years' time they will fetch at least ninety thousand pounds.'

'Ninety thousand pounds! Why ever would he have done such a thing?' I asked.

An hour later, sitting in Alec's kitchen drinking coffee, I told him about the jewellery and asked the same question.

'What did Mr Field say?' asked Alec cautiously.

'Well, nothing really, but Alec, she never mentioned the jewels. She could have bought a house for their retirement or used the money to educate Kenny. It might have kept him out of the army.

He could still have been alive. It just doesn't make sense.'

'Did Joe know about the jewels?'

'No, Mr Field said no one did. No one but Mary. I asked him.'

'Well,' said Alec rubbing his hand up and down his cheek. 'Well in that case, Mary Ruth, she obviously felt she couldn't sell the jewels until after Joe died. The question is, why?'

We looked at each other across the kitchen table. Then I realized. 'Oh Alec! Was old Lord Fionn-glass Kenny's father?'

Alec moved his coffee-cup about in its saucer. 'It had been noted, Mary Ruth, how like Donald your husband was. I was teaching in Knockglass in those days. As boys they looked like brothers, or cousins.'

'Which they were if my theory is right.'

'I think,' he said gently, 'there really is no other explanation. Why else would Lord Fionn-glass have given ninety thousand pounds' worth of family jewels to what was, dear, sweet, lovely creature though she was, only a twenty-year-old housemaid who had just married his gardener? Joe was a good deal older than she was and she was a bonny girl, she could have had her pick of the young men. Charity begins at home, they say, and I've never heard of a rich man giving away money for no good reason.'

'Kenny was born on the fourteenth of May 1931,' I said slowly, 'I've Mary's marriage certificate at home. I can check. What a story!'

'It is indeed. How sad that she never enjoyed her good fortune,' said Alec. 'How old was Joe when he died?'

'Ninety-two.'

He shook his head. 'Still, she loved him. Followed him within the year, but she did right by you.'

'Not till I'm sixty-five.'

'She knew you better than you know yourself. You'd be giving it all away and have nothing for your retirement, if you had it now.'

'Everyone keeps talking about my retirement. First Martha Bold, I met her in the street. Damn! I've left the cat food at Mr Field's. He showed me out of the side door.'

Alec raised his eyebrows. 'Cat food?' he queried.
I began to laugh.

Driving home later on the Monday afternoon I thought about my mother-in-law. My parents had been killed in a road accident when I was twenty and Aunt Connie had immediately considered herself the head of the family. She said our parents respected her. It was true she came for lunch every Sunday, and they did call me Mary Ruth on her advice to distinguish me from my mother. Mum's names were Mary Ruth Catherine and she had wanted three daughters, one for each name. She used to tease me, saying if she hadn't given me two of her names Jim would have been a girl. Aunt Connie, however, was not entrusted with our care.

A widow for most of her life, she lived in wealth and great comfort on the life rent of her husband's fortune. She was used to her own way as no one who did business with her ever disagreed with her. I wanted to marry Kenneth and I did. It's just as well too because we only had three years together before he was killed.

We had gone to visit his parents in the summer and when he was posted to Malaya I stayed on. I was in my first weeks of pregnancy and I didn't feel like travelling. Just as we were preparing for Christmas the news came that he had been killed in an ambush with three of his men.

I could not believe it and for weeks I was in shock. We had a memorial service which helped, and my sister and brother and Uncle Alec came to see me, but it was my mother-in-law who helped me the most. Whatever she may have thought about my Atholl Crescent-taught ways of housekeeping she kept it to herself and gradually I recovered. We all enjoyed Kenneth. He was a happy baby. Mary said she had never seen Joe so happy since Kenny was a baby.

Joe was a gentle man who loved his fiddle and his garden. He was the youngest of five brothers. The others went to what he always called the 'Kaiser's War'. Three were killed in the first year in the trenches and one was blinded and lived in an institution near

Stirling till he died. When he was ten, Joe's mother had died and he'd been put under the care of the head gardener's wife at Fionn-glass. She had a reputation as the meanest woman in the valley. Many a tattie bogle was better dressed than young Joe and scarecrows here are not smart, but he had plenty of porridge and she refused to let him go to the war. He always said she was 'a guid woman', so that was that.

Joe was always generous. Mrs Joe used to say, 'It's just not in his nature to be unkind.' It wasn't. It wasn't in her nature either. She could have made a comfortable life for herself if she had sold the sapphires, but she would never have hurt Joe. I never suspected her secret. I was longing to see Kenneth's face when I told him. We had never had any spare money. Now, I thought, I'll be able to send something worth while to charity. To all the charities. Alec's words came back to me. Mrs Joe had understood me better than I knew.

As I drove along the familiar road in the dusk I realized how sheltered I had been. I'd left my parents' home for army quarters, then I'd shared with my in-laws and now I was in Lord Fionn-glass's house. I'd never had to worry about accommodation. I had an army pension and Donald gave me fifty pounds a week. He paid for my Aga fuel and my car tax too. I saved a thousand pounds a year for my annual trip to France.

Martha and Mr Field were right. I was not practical. I'd never thought about retirement. How good of Mrs Joe to think of me. I would be independent. I must tell Catherine and Allan. They might be relieved for all their repeated offerings of a place for me. I had been thoughtless.

As I turned in at the east gate, I wondered what Lord Donald would think if he knew that his housekeeper was the widow of the direct descendant of the Fionn-glass family and was going to inherit his granny's sapphires and diamonds.

When I reached home it was six o'clock and dark. The wind was getting up and it was very cold, but Mrs Inglis had lit my little sitting room fire for me and my cats were glad to see me. They showed their affection by winding round my legs and mewing for food. 'Cupboard love,' I said to them as I fed them, 'that's all this is.'

Napper sat nervously at the door of the kitchen while they ate. We have had words before about his speedy assaults on their dishes. I like to think I've trained him, but if I leave the room when the cats are at their bowls he moves in like a missile and they leap on to the table. Nature, I suppose, but it must be bad for their digestion and it wastes cat food. I made his meal and put it by the door.

'There you are,' I said, 'now perhaps I can make my own supper.'

Chapter 4

The end of January continued cold, and I looked in vain for my first egg. Mrs Inglis and Mrs Gordon tackled the downstairs and I helped Douggie wheel enough firewood to the side veranda to fill it. By the seventh of February we were all very pleased with ourselves and then the snow started.

I can never remember so much snow falling so quickly. Overnight there was a foot of it and no one came the next morning. I spent an hour digging the old Land-Rover out of the stables. I like to have it at my door in snowy weather. In four-wheel drive it is as dependable as a shire-horse, once I have encouraged it with WD 40 and given the pump a tap with the spanner.

It went on snowing over the weekend. The hens refused to leave their perches and once the cats came in they settled down with their backs to the Aga, wound their tails over their noses and went to sleep. Napper made a few dashes into the snowy yards, but lack of smells and his cold feet soon brought him in to sit in his basket, shivering and restless.

I spent the weekend reading and listening to the radio. Tibby, from the Mains farm, came up on Saturday evening and on Sunday in his big snowplough, and I went down the east drive on Monday to collect my milk and visit the village shop. Here I heard that the new coal lorry had skidded gently across the road and demolished the village bus shelter. The driver had foreseen such an accident as the new lorry had power steering which he had advised against. It was with something like glee, Ina had told me, that he had driven off to report it to his boss.

The snow melted very suddenly, but then the temperature dropped and though the roads were clear and gritted, my drives were packed ice. Angus walked up through the wood twice with my post, but no one else came. It was far too cold to work in the house and after a miserable week on my own, I was really looking forward to going to Edinburgh when an unexpected telephone call came from Lord Donald.

'Mary Ruth,' he said, 'I'll be in Edinburgh tomorrow for a meeting and I was wondering what the weather was like, looks ghastly on the telly. I'll hire a car and come up and see how it's all going for Easter, if you think I can get through.'

'I'm sure you can get to Balessie,' I replied, wondering why he needed to come and check the housekeeping arrangements all of a sudden, 'and I could come down in the Land-Rover for you, but I shan't be here tomorrow. I'm going to Edinburgh with the canteen for Carter's.'

He didn't seem to know what I was talking about.

'I'm going to Carter's on Wednesday,' I explained, 'with the silver.'

'To Carter's?' he repeated. Then after a pause, 'I'll meet you there. What time are you going?'

'Ten.'

'Right, I want to tell them as well.' I was wondering what he meant when he added, 'If I'm not there, I'll meet you at the North Hotel, at twelve, for lunch. All right?'

'It's called The Princess now,' I started to say, but he'd hung up.

On Tuesday morning I went to the store cupboard and selected a big oak canteen with about a hundred solid-silver forks and spoons in it. I knew from past experience it would sell for at least fifteen hundred pounds. I left Mrs Inglis and Mrs Gordon polishing the table silver in my kitchen where it was warm. The house was shining and smelled of wax polish and pine wood.

When I pulled up at Catherine's front steps in the New Town it was just five. I rang the bell hurriedly, watching out for the traffic warden, and bundled my luggage and the canteen in through the door. Catherine beamed at me and hugged me.

'Come in,' she said. 'Come in, come in.'

'I'm going to park first.' I'd been caught before.

'Leave it there,' she said, 'it's past warden time.'

'I'm on double yellow lines.' My sister doesn't drive. Car parking must be one of the main topics of conversation in Edinburgh. I once said this to Catherine, but she replied that all we country folk talk about is the weather.

As we drank our tea I marvelled at the big, newly-created basement kitchen which had been a damp cellar in our childhood. 'School gets worse and worse,' she said, 'but you're right, the kitchens in this house get better and better. Mind you, had we known the council was about to slap an order on us to reface the outside of the building we would never have started this.'

'It must have cost an arm and a leg,' I said.

'It's mad anyway,' she went on as she began to prepare the meal, 'all the years when the children were at home and I was always in the kitchen I used the long narrow one upstairs just like Mum did. It required a work of art to extract anything from the fridge.'

'More a feat of gymnastics, but I take your point,' I said and looked with interest at the panelled ceiling, the spotlights and the parquet floor. 'This is wonderful and warm and it doesn't even smell damp any more.'

'That's because we spent a fortune on a damp course and we have to keep the central heating on all year, but it is splendid and in the spring I'm going to set to work on the area at the back and create a hanging garden. Will you root some honeysuckle cuttings for me, in August?'

'It's a bit spindly.'

'The spindly bits won't show if I plant it up in the garden and let it hang down. Have you still got the Dorothy Perkins by the walled garden? I'd like a cutting of that too. Ours died, and it's my favourite rambler.'

'Dorothy Perkins never dies.'

'Well, ours did. The one Granny planted.' She pointed up with her vegetable knife. 'It was in that bitterly cold spell about four years ago.'

'Now who's talking about the weather?' I said.

Later, after our home-made cream of celery soup and stuffed pork fillet, I told them about my windfall. I was touched at their delight and we had, in Aunt Connie's words, 'a good and useful discussion' on our several retirement plans. Allan had thought to take early retirement, but didn't want to lose some bonus and Catherine had two more years of teaching left. They were thinking of splitting the house in two and selling one half.

'Hours of discussion and argument, as you may imagine,' said Allan, hauling himself up out of his big armchair and taking our glasses to refill them. 'It's a forbidden subject now when the kids are home. Just about ruined last Christmas. Considering who does all the work in the garden, I find their arguments for not selling it, specious.'

'Well, I'm not entering the lists,' I said, 'but why do you want to sell half the house?'

'So that we can buy a boat to live on in the summer in Brittany.'

'What a lovely idea,' I said, 'but why not the South of France? I thought that was where all good northerners went.'

'Too hot and too expensive,' said Allan, 'and you can get Radio Four in Brittany. Cheers.'

'What about you, Mary Ruth?' said Catherine. 'There'll always be a room here for you, but . . .' They both looked at me.

'I am not thinking of retirement at all,' I said. 'I'm cosy where I am and when I'm sixty-five I'll be inheriting Mrs Joe's sapphires, then I'll be able to buy myself somewhere to stay. Sufficient unto the day! You sound like old Mr Field who suspects Lord Donald of untold chicanery, but he's coming for Easter with a big house party. I'm meeting him at Carter's tomorrow to discuss the arrangements. Little does he know about mine. Oh!' I added, remembering, 'Martha Bold practically held a public meeting about my future in the street in Elgin a couple of weeks ago.'

At the mention of Martha, Allan said, 'We must get on, Arthur,' in a fair imitation of Martha which made us all laugh, and we sat and gossiped about family and friends until we'd finished our nightcaps.

The next morning I set off to Carter's in Heriot's Place carrying what I later found to be two and a half thousand pounds' worth of Georgian cutlery which was to fund Lord and Lady Fionn-glass's jamboree.

I love Edinburgh especially in the winter. There is something about the pinky-grey buildings which pleases me when the skies are grey too, and the absence of tourists peering into closes and reading earnestly from little books, helps. I trudged the three hundred yards up the hill to Carter's, clutching the oak canteen to my bosom, enjoying looking down into the areas for signs of life in the pots and barrels which would soon have bulbs and azaleas flowering in them. Thanks to the gloom there were lights in the ground-floor and basement offices. I looked shamelessly through the windows every time I stopped to readjust the canteen. There seemed to be a rubber plant in every office. I was beginning to wish I had ordered a taxi as the box was very heavy.

Carter's, despite its international fame, is in a small side street. There is a single brass plaque next to the door which says *Carter's*, otherwise the place is unremarkable. I was shifting the canteen into a more comfortable position and half leaning on the handle when the door was opened for me by a tiny, fragile, softly spoken man who murmured, 'Good morning, madam.'

I reeled in, grunting 'Ooh!' and dumped the canteen on the highly polished oval drum table which stood in the middle of the entrance hall. Happily I did not damage the 'Wemyss Basket with Rope Twist Overhead Handle' which was set in its exact centre. I did not feel like a dignified emissary from His Lordship. I tried to make amends.

'Good morning,' I said when I had my breath back. 'I am Mrs Findlater from Fionn-glass House, I wrote to you. I have brought some silver for the next sale. Here it is.' I pointed. 'Lord Fionn-glass is coming to meet me here. He wants to speak to someone,' I added uncertainly.

The little doorman smiled and said softly, 'I quite understand. Please have a seat, Mrs Findlater,' and disappeared. The receptionist was sitting at a mahogany secretaire and speaking in a low voice into the telephone. I looked at the paintings of gun dogs on the walls until a panelled door opened noiselessly and the tiny door-keeper reappeared. Bowing to me slightly he whispered, 'Miss Wauchop is just coming, Mrs Findlater.'

It was some time since I had been to Carter's. There used to be a sensible young woman with a cheerful and audible voice who sat behind a sturdy oak table and dealt with simple matters like receiving a canteen of cutlery for sale. I was already bewildered by the changed aura when a tall, beautifully groomed woman wearing a scarlet poncho over skin-tight black leggings and a golden ankle bracelet like a slave-shackle, swept through the doorway. Her long frizzy hair rose in a black mane above her head and stuck out behind her.

She extended a scarlet-tipped hand to me and whispered huskily, 'Mrs Findlater. Do come, please, into my room.'

Without shaking my hand she turned abruptly and moved off. I looked round to see if Donald was coming through the door. There was no sign of him. I made a grab for the canteen, but a discreet cough stopped me. The tiny door-keeper picked it up. Thoroughly uncomfortable by now, I followed the swaying scarlet poncho into a room about forty feet long, lit by three blazing crystal chandeliers. I was directed by a graceful gesture to a tiny Regency chair upon which I sat with great care.

I was wondering whether or not to tell her that I was expecting Lord Donald when the canteen was carried in, effortlessly. The little man was tougher than he looked. He laid it reverently before Miss Wauchop on a piece of felt which she whipped out of an unseen drawer before he lowered it on to her table. This was an early Victorian walnut sofa table. They don't have ordinary desks at Carter's and after forty years of polishing them I can tell one table from another.

Inclining her head in thanks, Miss Wauchop dismissed the doorkeeper and opened the canteen with such excessively arched wrists and delicate fingering that I was about to giggle. On closer inspection the very elegant Miss Wauchop was well past forty and her girlish gestures did not impress me. I'm too old to posture, myself.

Naughtily perhaps, I said in a business-like voice, 'It's only a canteen of cutlery, Miss Wauchop. I expect it will fetch about fifteen hundred pounds. Maybe more if someone's especially interested. The ladle and the sugar sifter are particularly fine. There are twenty-two more sets at Fionn-glass. I chose to bring this one because it is incomplete. Lord Donald wants me to sell it. Can you let me know when the next suitable sale will be?'

Women like Miss Wauchop don't glare or pull faces. She looked up and said courteously, 'Of course, Mrs Findlater. I'll fetch your file.' She rose gracefully and went out of the room which was panelled and painted in white and gold. There were three magnificent dark blue Persian rugs with borders of soft green on its gleaming maple floor. It was an intimidating place. I wondered how people felt who had to sell their family heirlooms in such an atmosphere of luxury and elegance. Belittled, I should think, rather as I did. Miss Wauchop returned with the Fionn-glass folder.

'Now,' she murmured, opening it with more elaborate hand and finger movements, 'I see you have sold a considerable number of items for His Lordship over the years, through us, Mrs Findlater. Mostly silver, I see. Aha!' She pounced with a delicate little gesture and took up a paper. 'Here is His Lordship's authorization letter.' She held it out at arm's length and cast an eye down it, then as she put it down she said, 'I see that the cheques are made out to you and marked Household Account and sent to Fionn-glass House. That is all I needed to know. I'm sure you will understand that I wish to be entirely conversant with the procedure for such an eminent client as His Lordship.'

I nodded.

'Well, Mrs Findlater,' she went on, closing the file and opening a drawer with more exaggerated hand movements. 'Let us see when the next silver sale is, shall we?'

I smiled.

She smiled. 'The next sale will be on the twenty-eighth of February.' She put her hands together, gave me another mirthless smile, then added archly, 'I think, if I may say so, that the canteen will fetch rather more than you think, Mrs Findlater. Well over two thousand, I'd say, but we shall, as they say, see. Shan't we?'

'We shall,' I said simply. Her punctuated style of speaking left me breathless.

She signed the receipt for the canteen and we wished each other a gracious good morning. Donald wasn't in sight as I left, so I went to Waterstone's for some books for Mrs Gordon's boys. Then I walked along Princes Street and was in the downstairs lounge of The Princess, watching the door for Donald, by five to twelve.

It was half past before he came, and I twice had to tell the waiter I was waiting for someone and didn't want a drink or a cup of coffee. I was beginning to think he thought I was just there for a free sit-down when Donald appeared. 'Mary Ruth,' he called loudly down the room. I was so pleased to see him that I nodded when he asked, as he peeled his coat off, 'What'll you have, dry Martini?'

I would have preferred a whisky like his, but at least the waiter had stopped eyeing me and we thoroughly enjoyed our chat, though at five past one when we had caught up with family news I still had no idea what he really wanted to talk about. We moved to the dining room, clutching our winter coats and our bags, to be told there was no table available for half an hour as we hadn't booked. Donald had to leave for the airport at two, so we went back to our seats in the lounge and ordered a sandwich and a cup of coffee. The waiter gave me another funny look.

I chose chicken and salad sandwiches. There were four of them with no crusts, and the chicken was paper-thin slices off a roll of pressed meat and not hefty chunks off a roasted bird, which I had expected in such a big hotel. The salad was a lettuce leaf. It was over three pounds too. Donald had broth with crusty brown bread and a prawn sandwich which was twice the size of my chicken one, which didn't make me feel any better either.

'What do you want to talk to me about?' I asked him when we were drinking our coffee and he was lighting a cigarette.

'How did you get on at Carter's?' he asked, leaning forward to pull the ashtray towards him.

'Fine. It seems to be under new management. I had to see a Miss Wauchop. A formidable lady.'

'Still a good firm,' he said, but whether it was a statement or a question was hard to tell. 'Would you like an ice-cream?' he asked all of a sudden, without looking at me.

'No thanks, it's cold enough.'

'Do you think the house will be warm by Easter?' he asked me next.

'Well, it will be aired and there's seasoned firewood piled up in every available place and Mrs Inglis is forever trotting upstairs with hot bottles for the beds.' I paused and waited for him to speak. He was tapping the ash off his cigarette with great concentration. 'It's all beginning to look lovely,' I began, but he didn't want to hear any more.

'Good,' he said, 'we're all looking forward to coming.' Then he looked at his watch, snapped his fingers at the waiter and as he picked up the bill said, 'I must go now, Mary Ruth. Sorry not to have had longer to talk.' We parted on the front steps.

On my way back to my sister's I went into Jenner's and had a Danish pastry and another cup of coffee. Donald wasn't mean, but he was thoughtless and I still didn't know what he wanted to tell me. I was cross with him for delaying my start homewards. I had to wait until Thursday now, to be sure of making the journey in daylight.

I was glad to reach home and went in to a storm of barking and jumping from Napper. He can jump nearly three feet high when he's excited. Mrs Gordon was washing dusters at the sink and Mrs Inglis was making tea. It was just three and would soon be dark.

'Napper's glad to see you,' said Mrs Gordon as the happy dog continued jumping up at me. 'How was the road?'

'Not too busy, but I am glad to be home. I think it's going to snow again. Get down you silly beast, here I am. Is everything all right?'

'We're all fine,' said Mrs Inglis. 'Napper's been good. He likes coming to stay with me, don't you Napper?' The dog rolled over and wagged his tail. He does like Mrs Inglis. He never rolls over for me.

'We've finished the silver,' said Mrs Gordon as she let down the rack to hang the dusters to dry.

'We're coming along nicely. We've only the maids' rooms and the windows to do now,' said Mrs Inglis. 'Come and have your tea while it's hot.' We sat round the table and she poured, saying, 'Oh, and Lady Fionn-glass rang to tell you to buy new duvets and pillows for one bedroom. One of the guests is allergic to feathers. For both beds, she said.'

'Thank you,' I said, wondering if that was what Donald had been going to tell me. His preoccupation and awkwardness were not typical. He probably had some business on his mind.

It was good to be in the warm kitchen eating big slices of fruit loaf and drinking hot tea. I gave Mrs Gordon the Roald Dahl books for her sons and Mrs Inglis a bottle of cochineal which Sandy does not stock. She is a regular baker and over the years I've brought her vanilla pods, cinnamon sticks and green colouring when I've been to Edinburgh. She disapproves of my bringing her anything, though she's always bringing gifts to me, notably jam, dried flowers and well-rooted cuttings. The difference between us is that I like receiving presents.

They told me all that they had been doing and asked after my sister and her family. I did my best to describe Miss Wauchop, but I knew they thought I was exaggerating. I told them that I'd had lunch with Lord Donald, if you could call it lunch, and that he was looking forward to Easter. As they set off for home, the first big flakes of snow began to fall.

'Here we go again,' said Mrs Gordon at the door.

'It'll be clear by Monday, I hope,' I said. 'I shan't expect you tomorrow if this keeps up.'

'Away in out of the cold,' said Mrs Inglis, 'and there's a stew in the bottom oven for you. I nearly forgot.'

'Thank you,' I said. 'I shall enjoy it.' I did too. Mrs Inglis is a first-class cook. It's as well she remembered to tell me about the stew though. There is one certain thing about an Aga, if something is burning in the oven you can't smell it.

It did snow all night again and was over a foot deep by morning. I went to inspect what they had accomplished. The dining room, with all the table silver sparkling, was ready. Even the intense cold could not diminish its beauty. I closed the shutters to check that they had been cleaned behind. The catch needed mending, I noted. What good workers Mrs Inglis and Mrs Gordon were. They had set the fire and filled the log baskets too.

I checked my list. The curtains. Taking them down was just possible for one. Putting them up again was teamwork. I spent the rest of Friday alone with the rickety ladder, unhooking the heavy velvet curtains in the drawing room, the little sitting room and at the end of the hallway. I'd take them to the cleaners in Elgin when the road was ploughed.

I took Napper for a walk in the snow on Saturday, and then settled down to listen to the radio while I wrote to Kenneth. Mrs Inglis had found some oil-paintings in the little sitting-room cupboard. I'd helped her hang them. I knew Kenneth would be interested. It was something to write about, anyway. I was keeping the news of the sapphires and his ancestry for when he came home.

[illegible] and that he was [illegible] forward [illegible]
[illegible] as soon as [illegible]

[illegible] the door.

[illegible] said. [illegible]
opinions [illegible]

[illegible] today.

[illegible] too [illegible]

[illegible]

[illegible]

[illegible]

[illegible]

[illegible]

Chapter 5

On Sunday morning, as I was scraping the hen-mash into their trough, Tibby arrived in the big snowplough. 'Thought you might be wanting to the Kirk,' he shouted as he climbed down from his high seat and crunched through the snow to bring me my milk. 'It's fairly frozen,' he said. We stood and looked at the two snow-encrusted bottles, their silver tops raised by the frozen cream.

'How is the big bad world?' I asked him.

'There's fearsome bombing in the Gulf, but you'll have seen that on the television.'

'I meant the big bad world of Balessie, Tibby,' I said. 'I know about precision bombing and the build-up of ground assault troops and what Schwarzkopf and co. are up to. It is the pressing matter of whether the road to Elgin is clear that I was meaning.'

He threw back his head and roared with laughter. 'Mary Ruth, you are the limit. Here's the whole world worrying about Saddam Hussein and you stand asking if the road to Elgin is clear.'

'Oh, come on Tibby. I have no control over the Gulf War and little hope that all this wicked waste of money will help the ordinary Kuwaitis. It's not that I don't care. I keep getting charity mail shots, that seems to be the new name for begging letters, but I can't begin to help them all.'

'Aye, and some charities are wasteful from what ye hear. We should support local causes which we can check on,' he said, adding, 'or so the minister was saying.'

'Talking of which,' I said, 'I suppose I've no excuse now for not going to church. It's only half past nine. Thanks for the ploughing.'

'You'll manage fine,' he said. 'The main roads are clear. I'll go down the west drive; thon north drive must have been put in for show.' He was right, it doesn't join either main road directly.

My efforts to reach church were well received by the eight others who were there. Dennis, our rector, has three churches to care for and lives twenty miles away, but he is never late. St Andrew's is lovely. It has a small tower and its bell is clear and sweet. We have a fine organ and a red Turkey carpet in the chancel which is unceremoniously swept with an old Ewbank at the end of every service, by Mrs Smart.

She is an aged Englishwoman, the widow of a convalescent soldier who died of the flu in Balessie House, just as the war ended. She has lived here ever since and would have us all out evangelizing amongst what she calls, with no tact at all, 'the poor Scotch people round here.' She means the local Presbyterians. The rector keeps her occupied with everything but evangelism. She organizes the flower rota, cleans the brasses, unlocks and locks the doors, rings the bell and knows when you last came to church.

'I haven't seen you since before Lent, Mary Ruth. The rector took a beautiful service on Ash Wednesday, though we were only four. He's always at his best at the great feasts,' she said and handed me my books.

I can't say I see Ash Wednesday as a great feast, but I knew what she meant. I moved into my usual pew and knelt down briefly. Then I sat in the quiet and the cold and read the Collect, the Epistle and the Gospel for the day in the Prayer Book. I love the language of the Prayer Book and I like to think that for over four hundred years the same words have been used at services all over the world. I'm not sure I'm much of a Christian. I really don't believe in the resurrection of the dead, or the virgin birth. I dare say if I'd been born in an Islamic country I'd have been a lover of traditional Islamic prayers, but so many of the new transla—

My thoughts were interrupted by a chord. The rector came down the aisle and welcomed us. After a patchy rendering of 'Forty days and forty nights', we made our confession and were absolved, listened to the Collect for the day and then settled into our seats, tucking our coats about us to preserve what body warmth we had left.

Meanwhile, with smart ringing footsteps, his Sunday kilt swinging, Colonel Fraser-Gordon of Knockspindie strode purposefully to the lectern. He has a deep, strong voice surprising in so short a man. 'The Epistle is written in the fourth chapter of Saint Paul's First Letter to the Thessalonians, beginning at the first verse,' he announced firmly.

As I listened I sympathized with St Paul. His letters sound to me like a mother's. 'I love you, remember to clean your teeth.' 'It was lovely to see you, remember to write to Granny.' Most readers bark them out like orders. The colonel is no exception. He finished the exhortation to be pure, to abstain from fornication, concupiscence, whatever that is, and from defrauding our brothers, and we rose to sing the gradual hymn.

The Gospel, read by the rector, was the story of the Woman of Canaan who asked for mercy for her daughter who was 'grievously vexed with a devil'. Jesus was only sent for 'the lost sheep of the house of Israel', she was told. I wondered if this was the first recorded closed shop. 'It is not meet to take the children's bread and cast it to the dogs,' came next, but she countered with, 'Truth, Lord, yet the dogs eat of the crumbs which fall from their master's table.'

'And her daughter was made whole, from that very hour,' came the soft voice of the rector.

'Thanks be to Thee, O Lord, for this Thy glorious Gospel,' we said, and waited for him to turn to the altar, genuflect, cross to the pulpit and mount its steps. Holding up his cassock he revealed his walking-boots and scarlet woollen stockings. Very sensible, the chancel has no heater at all.

'May the words of my mouth and the meditations of our hearts be alway acceptable in Thy sight, O Lord, our Strength and our Redeemer.'

'Amen.'

We sat down to listen. It is a rare treat nowadays to hear a sermon which makes you think for the rest of the week. We are lucky, Dennis is a scholar. He spoke of the waste of money on armaments, the Gulf War, the plight of refugees. He commented on Matthew's known twisting of the stories to make them fit in with the words of the prophets. He argued that even the crumbs that fell off the rich western man's table were enough to feed the poor of the world. Our prayers were not only to be for ourselves, he said, but for all God's children, especially for the people of Iraq who were under bombardment now.

He said categorically that it was not enough to give away unwanted or unused possessions. We had to sacrifice ourselves and work for others in any way we could. We had no right to a reward, but, like the Woman of Canaan, we had an urgent duty to care for the helpless.

I began to think of all the appeals for medicines, vaccines, bandages, old spectacles, vans and bicycles, water purifiers, tents, blankets, clothes, food, seeds and skilled people, and could only think of the vast field hospitals the Americans had taken to the Gulf. We can do it when we try. It's the will to help others that we lack, not the means. That canteen I had taken to Edinburgh would restore the eyesight of thousands.

There was a great snort behind me. Miss Roland had her own way of warning the rector of the time, of the cold and of any wanderings into what she called 'rampant socialism'. The snort was followed by a nose-blowing of such vigour that I suspected she was making the noise with her mouth, as it was hidden behind a man's handkerchief.

It served its purpose, as it always did. The rector smiled down on us and said, 'We must learn to recognize the dragons of greed and of neglect and find the strength in prayer and in our faith to destroy them, for the sake of our Lord Jesus Christ. Amen.'

'You were in fine voice,' Colonel Fraser-Gordon said to me at the end of the service.

'Thank you, I do my best,' I answered.

'Jolly good!' he said, and moved on to speak to Mr Phimister, our treasurer.

Miss Roland, who ignores the animal rights groups' injunctions on fur coats, was swathed in her Canadian beaver coat and wearing a flying-helmet with the ear flaps down. She said to me confidentially but loudly, 'He was off again today, you will have noticed. Can't do with disloyalty in time of war. Not fashionable nowadays, I know, but charity begins at home.'

I find it difficult to know what to say when she starts on this tack. I smiled, feeling a hypocrite, and asked after her cats. Her mornings are spent cooking chicken breasts for eight Siamese. The treasurer fawns on her as there is much repeated promise of a legacy which we shall receive, she says, 'When I am gathered'. She has left her fortune to the Society for Cats and Kittens because, she tells us, 'there's quite enough namby-pambying of people'.

Her maternal grandfather made his money in a sugar refinery in Liverpool. I don't think there was much namby-pambying of the workers there. She carries on the family tradition, I suppose. She did lose both her brothers in the First World War, but she inherited the bulk of her grandfather's estate as well as her father's huge, fussy, late-Victorian house, The Laurels. In its cramped, sunless lodge live her man, Connal and his long suffering wife, Maureen, who cleans the house and makes jam from the soft fruit grown in the sunny walled garden behind the big house.

'Anyway, my darlings will be well provided for when I am gathered,' Miss Roland was saying. 'Look after your own, my grandfather always said. Look after your own.' She then left me with a nod, wrung the rector's hand and set off. She walks to church unless it is pouring out of consideration for Connal. 'Needs some time to himself,' she says.

I called at the pub to see what papers Mackie had. 'There's a *News of the World*, a *Sunday Telegraph* or a *Sunday Post*. Take your pick.' It was such a miserable day I wouldn't have minded buying all three to while away the afternoon.

'I'll take the *Telegraph,*' I said. 'Thanks, Mackie. They have the best clothes by post of all the papers.'

'And you so fashion-conscious, Mary Ruth. I'm afraid it's all war coverage today. And it'll be worse yet. It'll be summer in the Gulf soon, heat, sandflies, stench, lack of water, no sewers.' Mackie had been a Desert Rat. 'These days it's all high tech. Soldiering isn't what it was.' He was rubbing a damp and grubby piece of towelling slowly over the counter as he spoke. He wiped a soiled ashtray with it as I was counting my money out, then he dipped the cloth into the dirty sink-water, squeezed it briefly and put it by the pumps.

I passed Miss Roland just as she reached her gate. She raised her stick in greeting and I waved my fur glove at her. I still wear my fur gloves. I've no business thinking she should abandon her beaver-skin coat.

As I drove along the main road in the wake of the snowplough I thought about her cats. Better fed than most children in the richest countries let alone the poor ones. Perhaps when I retired and had my jewels I should start a cats' home and launder the money left by the likes of Miss Roland. If drug barons can launder money surely I could do it. Anyone can be a criminal. I'd send the money to the charities which wrote so often asking for my help. I remember reading once that more money is left to animal charities than to charities for children.

Through the window of the cleaner's in Elgin the next morning, the young assistant watched me struggling to unload the first bundle of curtains. She smiled cheerfully as I carried it across the pavement, felt for the door handle and shoved the door open. I dumped the mass of dusty velvet on the counter in front of her and went for the next pile, leaving the door open. Some assistant.

'Ready next Monday,' she said brightly. 'What name is it?'

I told her, and went to Super Store. How times change. No one twenty years ago would have believed there would ever be such a place in Elgin. It is a huge warehouse with an acre of concrete car park. Lulled by the music and the warmth inside, I wandered down an aisle of electrical equipment. I passed banks of television sets all tuned to the same programme and with the sound turned down. I felt *they* were watching *me*.

There was a garden section with bags of 'smell-less' manure, 'Grecian' urns and 'Tudor' bird houses. There were fountains supported by fat little cherubs in a grey pumice-like material which I thought most unpleasant. I found a rack of signs with 'Dun Romin', 'Oor Hame', and for the subtler minds, 'Emahroo', carved on them. In one enclave there were vividly painted garden gnomes with inane grins. Some were holding spades and some fishing-rods, a few were perched on mushrooms, others wheeled little barrows. They were designed for different-sized gardens and the disparity in their size was unnerving.

I had almost forgotten what I had come for when I came upon the bedding department. I don't know what a tog is, but I do know we need high ones at Fionn-glass. I collected two single duvets and four pillows, all guaranteed non-allergic. They were difficult to carry and I was not making good progress when I heard my uncle's voice.

'There's shopping trolleys for loads like that, Mary Ruth. Put them down. I'll fetch one for you.'

'Thanks, Alec. I'm mesmerized by this place. I'll wait here for you.' He went off, and when he returned with a trolley we loaded it and went along to the bedlinen bins.

'Nothing's easy,' said Alec as we sorted through higgledy-piggledy packets of covers with footballers, snooker tables and dartboards printed on them. Others had spots, stripes, zigzags, checks, all in crude colours.

'You'd have a sore head waking up to this lot,' said Alec. 'I know the times they are a-changing, but there must be some people left who want plain white bedlinen.'

At last we found some peach-coloured covers. 'These will do,' I said. 'Have you finished, Alec?'

'I came in to see if they had any small tins – and I mean small – of magnolia, as they now call cream. They haven't. I only want to paint a strip about two inches deep along the top of the new tiles beside the bath.'

'Let's get out of here then and have a coffee. I'm beginning to suffer brain damage. The assistants must be tough. That muzak is terrible. I couldn't work in it all day.'

Alec laughed. 'I was thinking that, but I have the radio on all day and fondly imagine it's improving my mind.'

In The Coffee Jug he asked if he could come on Monday the eighteenth of March, as he was bidden to his friend Martin's eightieth birthday celebrations in Deeside. 'I'd like to break the journey and I could admire your great works,' he added. I was pleased. We could do with a few compliments.

When I reached home there was a note from Mrs Inglis about a Chinese jardinière they had found, full of broken cues, in the cloakroom off the billiards room. Intrigued, I went to have a look before unwinding my woolly scarf and undoing my coat. Despite the wood fires we had been lighting every day it was still bitterly cold in the house. Standing in the middle of the round mahogany breakfast table in the big hall was the new-found Kangxi jardinière. Sparkling.

It was three feet high, decorated with exotic fruit, birds, trees and flowers on a green background. It had a wide beaker top, didn't appear to be chipped or cracked and was certainly wasted as a container of games equipment. Mrs Inglis, right as usual, had suggested it would look good in the dining-room window. It did.

When I thanked her for rescuing it, she said, 'You know, Mrs Findlater, if you don't think I'm speaking out of turn, there really ought to be an inventory of the valuables in this house. It won't be the only one where no one really knows what there is. My cousin found a chess set once, in the old nursery amongst some toys. Her employer had it valued and it was sold for over four thousand pounds.'

We digested this in silence as we went to the cold back regions.

Although I had lit the Aga in the big kitchen its warmth didn't reach the pantries and stores. Outside it was below freezing. Mrs Inglis went to the flower room. There are four high cupboards there with at least eighty vases, bowls and baskets of every shape and size.

Mrs Gordon was in the glass-pantry scrubbing the shelves before an orgy of glass washing. I had promised to dry for her. Until she was ready, I went to select the decanters we would need from the fifty locked in the store cupboard where I also kept the silver canteens. On Friday we tackled the big Royal Doulton dinner service. It has twelve hundred pieces, and it took us all morning to select a suitable number of plates, bowls and ashets, carry them through to the big kitchen, wash and dry them and arrange them on the dresser shelves.

'After all this,' said Mrs Gordon with feeling, as she put her coat on, 'I hope they enjoy eating off them. What a week!'

'I'll take these glass-cloths home and wash them,' Mrs Inglis offered quickly. She never likes to hear any criticism of the family.

On Saturday the thaw set in. It came as fast as the snowstorms, and by Monday we were all working under Helen's direction in the big kitchen and grumbling about the dirty, wet conditions outside.

Helen is a very experienced cook and knew exactly what she wanted. We chattered as we trotted about under her orders, putting the newly cleaned and burnished saucepans, steamers, fish-kettles, roasting tins, colanders and bowls in place. 'That little scullery was for the vegetable maid,' Mrs Inglis told us. 'The only good thing about it was the slatted wooden rack which kept her feet off the stone slabs. She used to prepare for fifty sometimes.'

'Mrs Joe told me there used to be twenty indoor servants,' I added.

'My auntie was a housemaid here in the twenties.' This was Helen. 'She had to carry jugs of hot water up to the dressing rooms before dinner and then go up and empty all the slops during dinner.'

'So this is where you all are,' said Douggie opening the outside door. 'My, it's dreich today. Dreich!' He shuddered and went on, 'There's a raw wind too.' He sat in the big Windsor chair by the Aga to warm himself. 'I've put a new ladder to you in the big hall,' he said to me. 'You'll want to hang the cleaned curtains without breaking your neck, I doubt.'

'Thanks, Douggie.'

Napper jumped up on to his knee. 'I see you,' he said and tickled his ears. 'It's a pity they're coming so early in the year, there'll be nothing in the garden. I'm hoping the primulas I've potted up will be ready. They'll look bonny on the terrace, but there'll not be many lilies. We could have had a good show,' he paused and added heavily, 'if we had had more notice. You've more sense nor ony,' he added to the happy dog.

'Mrs Inglis has promised to do the flowers in the house,' I said to change the subject.

'They'll be done right then,' he acknowledged. 'I know your reputation, Mrs Inglis. Great rival of Stella's you are. The bulb show at the Rural brings out the *beast* in the womenfolk.' He chuckled at his old pun.

When I had made the coffee Mrs Gordon said to him, 'Will I give you a hand with your chair?'

'Mercy no, lassie,' he replied. 'I'll see masel' by the hens' trough. Thank you for asking,' he added as he pulled the big chair to the table. 'I was hoping you'd made shortbread, Helen,' he added slyly as he took his coffee.

'Away with you, Douggie Robertson, do you think I've had time for baking?' She had brought some from home in a tin, though and we ate it all up as we laid our plans.

'Will you order the flowers for me next time you are in Nairn, Mrs Findlater?' asked Mrs Inglis. 'All my lists are ready.'

'Of course. I'm due there on the eleventh, for the dentist.'

'Have them all out,' said Douggie. 'Much less bother.'

All the women turned on him and shouted, 'Douggie!'

Mrs Gordon sneezed suddenly. 'Oh, excuse me.'

'Bless you,' we chorused.

'You want to take care. It's cold in these back regions,' said Douggie.

'Designed by men,' Helen said to him, 'for women to work in.'

'Designed by the rich for the poor to work in,' he replied dourly.

'The billiards room is even colder,' put in Mrs Inglis quickly. She doesn't like talk about class either.

'Good job we've no time to play then,' said Douggie.

'I hope there's no more snow to hinder us,' said Mrs Gordon.

'There'll be no more snow,' said Mrs Inglis firmly.

'And if there is, it won't lie!' Douggie said, finishing the old local saying and raising a laugh.

'I've nearly done my vegetable and fruit lists,' said Helen. 'I've bits of paper all over the house. Fred and Donald Molloch were teasing me only last night. They asked if I was writing a book. They've no idea how much organizing there is to do. They think meals prepare themselves, I think. By magic.'

All the women laughed.

'Nothing to cooking,' said Douggie as he stood up. 'It's the eating that needs the stamina.'

'Get out of my kitchen!' said Helen.

'That's a week's honest wages,' I thought, as I paid the cleaners a hundred and eighty-five pounds for the curtains. Helen had gone to order the meat and fish. We met in The Coffee Jug before we went to Allison's for the groceries.

I hadn't been there for a while and found a new section with mixes for Indonesian satay sauce, Mexican taco, biriani and koorma dishes. When Kenneth comes home he wants mince and tatties, haddock and chips and my home-made steak and kidney pie. Of course in France he's used to marvellous food. I'll show him, I thought, and chose a taco set. Looking for the hot chilli sauce I heard Helen's voice. 'Martha, how are you?' I toyed with the idea of staying out of sight, but she went on, 'Mary Ruth's with me. We're laying in provisions for the family visit at Easter.'

'You are not forgetting to get from Sandy, I hope?' said Martha.

She never misses a trick and I felt I had to take over so that Helen could get on. I walked around the pickles unit to greet her.

'What visit is this you are having? Is Her Ladyship coming this time? How many of them are coming? How long are they staying?' Then, before I could answer her catalogue of questions, she stared into my wire basket and demanded, 'What's all this?'

'I'm trying a new dish for when Kenneth comes next month.'

'It's good Scotch food you should be giving him,' she announced. 'He has enough foreign food I'd have thought. All those greasy sauces. I've never understood the French and furthermore, I'm surprised at Mr Allison. This used to be the finest old-fashioned grocery shop in the north-east and now look at it.' She gestured with a dismissive wave of her shopping basket. 'Shelves of stir-fry sauces and packets of dry mixes, all designed to disguise bad meat, if you ask me.' She gave another glare into my wire basket. 'I'm surprised at you, Mary Ruth, I always thought you had plenty common sense.'

'A change is nice,' I said weakly. 'I think Mr Allison knows what he's doing, Martha.' I felt on firmer ground here. 'This is still the best grocery in this part of Scotland.'

'He's still in business,' she grudged. Helen smiled as she passed with an assistant. Martha returned to the attack. 'So when are they coming?'

'Good Friday.'

'Far too early. They'd do better to come in June. Much the best month here. I'm surprised at Lord Fionn-glass. His new wife an Italian too. That house is perishing in April,' she announced.

'Well, it's their house and that's when they are coming.' To pre-empt any more interrogation I told her who was coming and what we had been doing to prepare for them.

'How long are they staying?' she asked, frowning.

'Until the Wednesday—' I was cut off with an explosion of disgust.

'Ridiculous!' she spat the word out. 'Typical! Hardly here and they're away again. Absentee landlords are all the same. They live down in London and as long as there's an old retainer to keep the house for them, they think they can come on a flying visit whenever it suits them. That's no way to run an estate.'

What really annoys me about Martha Bold is that she's usually right. Happily, before I could think of anything to say which might have been disloyal, we were greeted by Mr Allison himself.

'Welcome, Mrs Findlater, we haven't seen you for a long time, and Mrs Bold.' He smiled at us both. He is a big cheerful man with a mind like a razor. He looked into my basket. 'I see you have some imagination.'

'I'm looking forward to trying tacos,' I said.

'Have you seen our new goat cheese and yoghurt?'

Martha sniffed, but even she didn't start extolling the virtues of winter cabbage and mealie puddings in front of the master himself. Excusing myself, I went to find Helen.

We were shown out with great courtesy by Mr Allison.

'Yours is one of the last big houses still belonging to the family, Mrs Findlater. Please tell Lord Donald I was asking for him. I mind years ago when you used to bring the boys in the holidays. I could never tell which was which.' He laughed heartily. So did Helen. I smiled to myself. So Mr Allison thought the cousins' sons looked alike too, I thought, as I started the engine to drive us home.

Chapter 6

It was windy when Alec arrived on the eighteenth. Ten days to go and all the cleaning finished. After I'd taken him on a grand tour everyone came into my kitchen for coffee. We had no sooner sat than the phone rang for Mrs Inglis and then Helen had to go to take delivery of goods from Sandy.

'No peace for the wicked,' she said, bustling off.

'Ask him if he wants a coffee,' I called after her.

'It's going like a fair here today,' was Alec's comment.

'Has been for weeks. Hope it'll be appreciated,' was Douggie's.

'The flowers are coming first thing next Wednesday,' said Mrs Inglis sitting down again. 'I can't remember having so much to organize since my aunt went into hospital.' She went on happily, 'What a business that was. She was taken in twice and sent home again before they did her op. Her cat was dizzy with all the changes. Back and forth from her house to mine, the poor thing didn't know whether he was coming or going.'

'Sounds as though he was doing both,' said Alec, and we all laughed.

'Sandy's to get back to the shop. Ina's a hair appointment,' Helen told us as she came in, 'but he said to say thanks anyway.'

'I must tell you all how lovely the house looks,' said Alec. 'It takes me back a long way to see it looking so beautiful. It's perfect!'

Everyone was delighted.

* * *

After supper Alec and I were trying to watch the nine o'clock news on the television. The reception was dreadful.

'There's a storm brewing,' I said as I turned the telly off.

'It's here,' he announced as the lights went out.

'Well,' I said, lighting the candles, 'we might as well go to bed. It'll be a branch on the wires.' In my kitchen the windows rattled and the Aga whistled in the dark.

'This will soon blow itself out,' Alec said. 'It's too strong to last.'

In the morning, however, it was still blowing hard though the lights were on again. Mrs Inglis arrived and went through to the house. She rushed back only seconds later calling for help.

'The dining room window has blown open. Come quick!' We left our half-eaten breakfast. There was a gale blowing ash from the fire all over the hall and the cold was intense. I ran with her into the dining room. 'The shutters missed the jardinière, thank goodness,' she gasped as we grabbed them. 'I can't shut the casement, the bolt's buckled.'

'Go and ring five-five-two,' I shouted to Alec, 'and tell Mac to hurry.'

He went, but was back almost at once with Mrs Gordon. 'The phone's off. Must be the wind.'

'Tibby and Mac and Douggie are clearing a fallen tree on the drive,' said Mrs Gordon, 'I'm sorry I'm late.'

'Go and tell Mac we need him,' I said to Mrs Gordon, 'before he goes.' She ran out and Alec went too.

We hung on to the shutters and waited. 'If I hold both the shutters, do you think you could reach the jardinière?' asked Mrs Inglis.

'I'll try.' Mrs Inglis frowned with determination and put her back against the shutters. I left her to it and picked up the lovely pot.

Alec came back. 'When sorrows come,' he declaimed, 'they come not single spies, but in battalions.'

I put the pot out of harm's way and went back to help Mrs Inglis, saying, 'I wish you weren't so educated, Alec. It makes it hard for us normal folk, but for once I do follow you. What else has happened?'

'Half a chimney has come through the conservatory roof.'

'And that's not all,' said Mac, striding into the room carrying his tool-bag. 'The big woodpile on the veranda has toppled over and the garden seat has blown into the lily pond. Now what have we here?'

What we had was a mess. Mrs Inglis, Mrs Gordon and I cleaned up the mud and the glass shards, vacuumed, dusted and repolished the dining room and the hall, stairs and gallery. We relit the fires and then we set about the conservatory. There were bricks and slates, rubble and broken glass everywhere. Douggie helped us and it took until three on the Friday to put it all to rights.

'We could have done without this,' he said.

We all roared, 'Oh, Douggie!'

'The worst is over,' said Mrs Inglis, pacifically. 'Nothing else can go wrong now.'

Monday and Tuesday sped by. As I lay in the bath on the Tuesday night, thinking how pleased Donald would be, I heard the phone ringing. I do not know what to do when I'm in the bath and the phone rings. The passageway from my bathroom to the back stairs is long and draughty. Furthermore, experience has taught me that when I rush, inadequately draped in a towel, it's either a wrong number or the phone stops ringing as I reach it. I lay back and consoled myself with the thought that if it was urgent, whoever it was would ring again.

The flowers arrived at eight-thirty the next morning and Mrs Inglis and Mrs Gordon began scuttering about the house muttering about alabaster tazzas. I stoked up the fires and went to feed my hens. Lying inside the hen-house I found my favourite bantam with her head ripped off. It must have been a tiny mink or a weasel. Damn things.

I was back in my own kitchen listening to the radio and finishing my ironing when the phone rang. It was Lord Donald. We didn't speak for long. I put the phone down, filled the kettle and sat down next to the Aga. Napper came over to me. I patted my knee and he jumped up. I was sitting there scratching behind his ears when Douggie came in.

'Well?' he said, looking at me across the kitchen. 'You don't look very cheerful. I've brought you a jar of Stella's jam. We found some in the cupboard. It's maybe a bit foosty, but you can scrape the top off.' As I sat silent he went on: 'I'm going to wheel the primulas round to the terrace.'

'Do as you want, Douggie. It doesn't really matter. They're not coming. I've just had himself on the phone. She's not feeling well or some such. They're not coming. Not one of them. I can't believe it. Why wait so long to tell me? He says he tried to ring last night, but even that was Tuesday. I was in the bath. I didn't answer, after ten that was, too.'

'No time to be ringing anybody, or so I was taught. Well, what now? Does Mrs Inglis know, or Helen?'

'I've just put the phone down. I don't know how to tell them and Oh! Douggie,' I began to cry, 'something's been in the hen-house and my little tufted bantam's dead.'

'I'll go and take a look,' he said and went out.

I blew my nose on a piece of kitchen roll and put six mugs on the table. It was nearly half past ten. The back doorbell rang. It was the delivery man from Allison's with the drink I had ordered for the visitors. I directed him to the main kitchen door and signed the delivery note. It was for six hundred and seventy pounds. I hoped he'd drop the lot.

Fifteen minutes later we were all sitting round my table. 'But what did he say?' asked Helen, wiping her eyes on her pinny.

'He said, "I'm sorry, but I'm afraid I have a disappointment for you."'

'Tcha!' Douggie went, and gulped at his coffee.

'He said, "I'm afraid Her Ladyship isn't very well."'

'Her Ladyship!' Douggie again.

'Is she . . .?' asked Mrs Inglis hesitantly.

'Is she what?' asked the innocent Jean.

'Expecting,' said Mrs Inglis. 'I mean if she's suffering from morning sickness . . .' she trailed off.

'That's no reason for them all not to come. I mean all that food and the flowers.' Now it was Mrs Gordon's eyes that needed wiping.

'What am I to do with the food?' asked Helen.

'He said I was to share out anything I couldn't return. So it's flowers all round for Easter, not to mention fish and meat and fruit and vegetables. We shan't need to go shopping for weeks.'

'Let's not get hysterical,' said Douggie, 'and drink your coffee everyone, it's getting cold.'

'Well, there's one thing certain,' said Mrs Inglis drinking up her coffee and rising to her feet, 'all those fires upstairs need turning off. It's a waste of electricity. I'll go and do them and Mrs Gordon can come and help me. Then we'll divide up the flowers and take them to Balessie House for the old people and take some to the hospital. The churches might like some of them, too. After all, it is Easter.'

'Yes, you're right. We mustn't sit here girning,' I said, glad of her common sense as always.

Persistent Helen asked again, 'What exactly did he say?'

'He said he had a disappointment for me. His wife was not very well. They would not be coming, and please thank everyone and to share out anything that could not be returned.'

'Will I be paid for the weekend?' asked Jean. 'I was offered another job, but I turned it down and it's gone now.'

'You most certainly will, Jean,' I said firmly. 'You'll all be paid. That was the first thing I said to His Lordship.'

'He must have money to burn,' said Douggie, rising to his feet. 'I'm not best pleased. You don't deserve this, Mrs Findlater, nor do any of you.'

'You've done as much as any of us,' said Helen.

'Well, Jean,' said Helen wiping her eyes and blowing her nose,

'Let's go and start the food parcels. At least there are some who'll be glad of our baking in the village, but ring up the butcher's and the fishmonger for me, Mary Ruth. I am too upset to start phoning,' and she burst into tears.

'Now, now, Helen,' said her niece putting her arm round her. 'I'll help. Come along. More fool them for calling off. Don't greet.' Tenderly Jean guided her weeping aunt out of my kitchen. Looking back over her shoulder at me she said, 'Thank you for our coffee.'

'That girl's showing more sense nor ony of us,' said Douggie putting his mug on the draining board. 'I'll away and chop you some nice little logs for your fire,' he said to me. 'I've a tidy little pile of the Queen of Woods put by, for emergencies.'

I smiled. 'Thank you Douggie,' I said. 'I'll ring the shops for Helen now. I don't know what they'll think of me.'

'It's not your fault,' chorused Mrs Inglis, Mrs Gordon and Douggie and it was my turn to be tearful.

That evening Douggie's Stella and Ina from the shop came to see me. I was touched by their thoughtfulness. I offered them a drink, and as we sat by my fire we had a good laugh about Douggie's gift of the foosty jam.

'All I said to him,' Stella insisted, 'was mind and warn her to check the surface. He wasn't supposed to tell you it was covered in mould.'

'It isn't anyway,' I said and we all burst out laughing again.

'That's a nice bit of beech, Mary Ruth,' Stella said as she looked at the logs on the fire. 'More heat than the old pine and far less sparks.'

'It's a little treat Douggie brought in for me this morning,' I said.

'When is Kenneth coming?' asked Ina quickly. 'I am looking forward to seeing him. Mind and tell him to come by.'

'Everyone's saying that to me, the dominie and the police.'

'The police?' Ina asked in surprise. Then she chuckled and said, 'Oh! Mary Ruth, that's only Malcolm. He's always wanting to see our Jamie too, when he comes home.'

'Well, no wonder,' said Stella, 'those boys were aye the best of friends, and Malcolm's life here isn't very exciting. There's no crime here.'

'Only the odd salmon poacher and old Doddie's cows climbing out over his top park every second week,' said Ina, and as we began to laugh again she added, 'and there must be a limit to the fun to be had out of driving up that dreary glen to Daldrum Castle, even in a panda car.'

'They're called jam sandwiches nowadays,' said Stella to our astonishment. 'Or is that just the speed cops?'

We didn't know, and we whiled away the evening talking about anything that had nothing to do with Lord and Lady Fionn-glass and their abandoned visit.

After Easter, what Douggie still calls the 'lilies' came out. There were daffodils all around the policies and I filled every jug I had with them. I spent the mornings putting away the family china, the silver and the bedding and in the afternoons I took Napper walking and then worked in the greenhouse. Douggie was planting the vegetable patch and had begun edging the lawns. On Wednesdays Mrs Inglis came and did her normal work. She carefully carried all the wood ash out and placed it round the fruit bushes. 'May as well get some use out of all that wood,' she said.

Two days before Kenneth was due to visit I went to Amy for my twice-yearly haircut. My hair is very thick and springy and she tells me that if I went regularly and had it thinned and tapered I could be very chic. I don't believe it, though she is a wizard with the scissors.

Ina from the shop was sitting under the drier next to me.

'I want Kenneth to recognize me,' I said, watching great sheaves of hair falling to the floor.

'When does he come?' asked Amy, ignoring my caution as she removed a clip from the top of my head and replaced it deftly over my ear.

'Thursday. He's going to Edinburgh to see a gallery director about a potential exhibition. There's an awful lot coming off, Amy.'

'Trust me,' she said. 'He'll sweet-talk him, if I know Kenneth. How are the little girls?'

'Blossoming, I hear, and there's a new baby due in September.'

'I'd heard that. Hoping it's a boy this time, I suppose?'

'I don't know about them, but I am. How is Pamela? When does she finish at Leeds?'

'In the summer. She's applying to do research. They think she'll get a first. I don't know where she gets it from, but she is a clever girl.'

'She's a good worker, Amy, always was. She's a credit to you.'

'Mmm! Keep still, Mary Ruth, or you'll have it short whatever you say. She's her father's girl though, is Pam. He's full of ambitions for her. I'm afraid she won't be coming home to work.'

'Nor will Kenneth,' I agreed. 'Leave me some fringe.'

'If you had your way you'd look like an Old English sheepdog. Now keep still while I do your neck.'

She bent her head and in the mirror I saw her nod to her junior, Christabel, a pretty blonde girl with a mass of carefully untidied hair who fetched the brush and swept my locks aside. Then she released Ina from the drier. A voice on the other side of Ina said, 'Have you seen this, Ina? Show Mrs Findlater. She'll be interested, I'm sure.' It was Mrs Phimister, our treasurer's wife, her wet head draped in a towel. She has recently become the president of the Lifeboat Committee, the pinnacle of social achievement in our community.

To my surprise, Ina cast only a swift look at the proffered magazine and handed it back. This surprised Mrs Phimister too who said, 'Haven't you understood? It's not just the photograph.' She handed the magazine back to Ina and pointed to the front page.

'I see, er, yes,' said Ina.

'What's that then, Ina?' asked Amy.

'It's about a charity ball in London, at the Dorchester. For Help All Children,' said Ina brightly. 'It's Lady Fionn-glass with the Princess of Wales and the Duchess of York. Very nice!' She handed the magazine back to Mrs Phimister who wouldn't accept it.

'Look again, Ina,' persisted Mrs Phimister, 'look again.'

'Let me see,' I said and leaned sideways to take it from Ina.

She was reluctant to let it go and Amy said, 'Mary Ruth, if I cut your ear off it'll be your own doing.'

I managed to take the magazine from Ina and, while Amy continued snipping, I looked at the photos. The first thing I saw was the tiara which Dorinda, Lady Fionn-glass, was wearing. It was an arc of sapphires and diamonds, part, I had no doubt, of the set of which I was to inherit the choker, earrings and bracelets. I read:

> 'It was a surprise present from my husband, for my birthday,' Lady Fionn-glass told me. 'He found it in the vaults last October when he collected his robes for the State Opening of Parliament. The tiara hasn't been worn since Queen Victoria's jubilee.' Pictured talking to the Princess of Wales, who is wearing an Empire-line dress by Paul, and the Duchess of York who is sporting one of Miriette's creations inspired by a toreador's costume, Lady Fionn-glass is wearing a white satin Yatsuki kimono, especially designed to show off the family sapphires.

'She looks very elegant,' I said, looking into Ina's mirror.

'Yes,' she said avoiding my eye, 'very.' She reached over to take the magazine back.

'Look again, Mrs Findlater,' called Mrs Phimister. 'You'll find it's very interesting.' I was puzzled, so I looked at the main article again.

'Read it out,' said Amy. 'I've nearly finished, but keep still.'

I started to do so. It was by one Crispin Topp.

> On All Fools' Day, the Dorchester Hotel, Park Lane was the venue for the HAC Ball, organized by Lady Deirdre Plunkett Gall, who took over the presidency of Help All Children after the sudden and untimely death in February of

Lady 'Pud' Simonson. You will remember my telling you recently of her tragic and fatal fall while hunting with the Gloucestershire Fox-hunters.

I remember it well, I don't think, I thought and read on.

The Committee had feared that the ball would have to be cancelled after the sad demise, at only 49, of Lady Simonson. However, thanks to the ever-game Deirdre, 'Dodo' to her friends – or should I say 'Do! Do!' – who sportingly took over the reins (oops!) the situation was saved by a miracle.

'The miracle being money,' said Amy.
Ina laughed, but Mrs Phimister was silent.

The tickets, a cool £500 each, were being sold on the black market I heard, but the guests certainly had their money's worth.

I paused and asked, 'Do you really want to hear what they ate?'
'Why not?' said Amy. Ina nodded, so I read on.

Lady Deirdre, a cordon bleu herself, went to Mrs Beeton for her inspiration. Eight top-class chefs gave their time as their contribution.

'Mrs Beeton would not have been amused,' said Ina.
'This is all rather nasty,' I said looking ahead down the page. 'Are you sure you want the menu?'
'Yes, go on,' said Ina, 'it's an amazing meal.'
'Well, I can see at a glance it's very English.'

The hors d'œuvre consisted of Nantucket oysters, Portuguese sardines and anchovies, Norwegian herring fillets and Kenyan radishes.

Everyone laughed. 'Nae buckies?' asked Ina.

'Look,' I said, 'this is bad enough without bringing whelks into it.'

The clear soup was French, the thick German, the fish course was Scotch salmon and the entrée consisted of quenelles and kromeskies.

'That'd make a nice change,' said Amy. Christabel started giggling. She was slowly unwinding the rollers from Ina's hair.

The remove was a sirloin served with Chile corn buds and the roast was Welsh pheasant.

I skipped the *entremets* and the savoury and finished.

Dessert was crystallized fruit.

We were still laughing when Amy said, 'You'd need more than a Rennie's after that lot.'

Ina leaned across and took the magazine from me. 'That's a charity for starving children too.'

'And that's you, Mary Ruth,' said Amy. 'I'll let Christabel blow-dry it for you.' She began to brush out Ina's set. She nodded encouragingly at Mrs Phimister, still waiting with her head shrouded.

'You still haven't taken the point,' Mrs Phimister shrilled and snatched the magazine from Ina. 'Listen,' she searched through the pages, then gave up, waved the magazine at us and said, 'The ball was on Easter Monday which was the first of April this year. Hunt-the-gowk, we called it when I was a girl.' She leaned round Ina, fixed me with her eye and said to me in a penetrating voice. 'Were you not expecting Lord and Lady Fionn-glass and company for Easter, Mrs Findlater? As my husband has said repeatedly, we could have had a new roof on the rectory for a half of what was spent.'

'You mean that's this week's mag?' I said. 'They're not usually up to date. It's only the sixteenth today.'

'Shame on you, Mary Ruth. We buy new papers every week,' said Amy, 'and if you came more often you would know that.'

'I realized,' said Ina. 'I was trying to keep it away from you.'

'Give it back to me,' I said. 'It was kind of you to try and spare me, but I'm wanting to see if there's anything else.' I hadn't taken it in. I'd been distracted by the sapphires and hadn't noticed the date.

'I told you you'd be interested,' said Mrs Phimister smiling at herself complacently in her mirror and adjusting her towel turban.

'Well, I think it's a shame and a disgrace after all your work,' said Amy as she brushed Ina's hair. 'I thought she was supposed to be ill. Doesn't sound like much of an illness if she could eat all that.'

'I bet she was ill afterwards. Sounds disgusting to me,' said Mrs Phimister.

'And me,' said the loyal Ina, who loved her food.

'What is doubly insulting is that he told you a lie.' Mrs Phimister's voice came again. 'That woman is dressed to kill. She's an Italian contessa isn't she? Of course, they're two a penny over there. I suppose she thinks she's fit company for our royal family.'

I wondered if she expected us to stand. Ina let out a chuckle and hastily turned it into a cough as she received a sharp look from Mrs Phimister, who had more to say. 'What he saw in her I can't think. Everyone says she's not a patch on his first wife. Not that I knew her, but I can recognize a social climber when I see one. If you ask me, she was no more ill at Easter than I'm the Queen of Sheba.'

'And you're a long way off that,' said Ina slyly, adding in her careful, shopkeepery way, 'at least until Amy's finished with you.' Another sharp look, but dear, plump, cheery Ina smiled at her and the moment passed.

As Christabel dried my hair I read the whole article and looked at all the photographs. The raffle tickets had been a hundred pounds each and some of the food had been flown in in specially chartered planes. There had been three bands and a cabaret which included a choir of eight-year-old orphans who had sung *We Shall Overcome* in Welsh. The ball had ended with breakfast which included bacon, kidneys, eggs and chops, again as in Mrs Beeton. This was served at four a.m. and the whole evening was described by the Duchess of York as 'fab'. It made me feel sick.

I left the hairdresser's deep in thought. I would have some news for Kenneth on Thursday. Mrs Phimister's parting shot had been, 'Now you won't start thinking ill of me, will you Mrs Findlater?' She had given me a weaselly smile.

'Of course not,' I had replied truthfully. I had never thought much of Mrs Phimister to start with and I wasn't going to waste time on her now. Not now I really had something to think about.

Chapter 7

I was expecting Kenneth about noon. He was borrowing Allan's car to come up from Edinburgh. His visits are all too rare and I am always a little jealous of the time he spends visiting friends, but I never say anything. He's a big, cheerful, talkative man who loves company, just like his father.

I went to feed the hens, wondering whether to cope for the summer without a cockerel. I didn't want chickens, but hens alone can peck each other. Sometimes they all bully the same hen, though usually one becomes dominant. I once saw an old hen stretch her neck and issue a creditable crowing. It was a strange performance, but I have never seen any chickens hatched when there was no cockerel in the pen.

I must have spoken out loud because I heard Kenneth's voice right behind me. I spun round. He was pretending to be an old soul on a stick and was mumbling, 'Niver seen ony chickens wi'oot a cockerel i' the pen.'

Then, straightening up, he grabbed me. He is six foot four. He swung me round shouting, 'Ma, you're getting dottled. It's high time you retired. Talking to the hens indeed.' He started laughing, hugged me, plonked a big kiss on my forehead and announced, 'I'm starving. I've brought bacon and mushrooms. I knew you'd have eggs. I left at six and just had a coffee.'

'Well, come and cook your breakfast then. I'll join you for a treat.' We went into my kitchen and Kenneth started, as ever, to complain about my frying pan. I have told him to buy me a thin, high-grade French steel one, but I am still waiting. I did buy an Aga grill pan with ridges for the occasional steak, after much nagging, and I must admit it works better.

We sat down to eat with a big pot of tea. I had baked six loaves for his visit and how, I don't know, but he talked non-stop, drank three cups of tea, ate half a loaf and still finished before me.

'So you've been advising Catherine and Allan as well, have you?' I said as I finished my meal adding, 'I shan't want any lunch after that.' He smiled. 'Don't go running away with the idea that we're all past thinking for ourselves,' I said.

'I won't, but why is Allan hanging on for extra pension? Inflation will eat it up. I think he should settle into the Breton sailor's life and enjoy himself. I'm going to Inverness now to fetch Jamie,' he said next, and stood up. 'Ina told me he's flying up specially to see me. I thought we might offer to take him back to the airport on Saturday and go to see Alec.' I nodded as he asked, 'Do you want to come to the airport with me?'

'No, thanks; I have news for you, but it will keep. You and Jamie will have a better blether on the way home without my company. He's done very well,' I added. 'Most boys wouldn't train for nursing when you were leaving school.' I stood up to clear the table. 'What time do you want to eat? I'm making Mexican tacos.'

'What – no steak and kidney pie! Have you given up traditional food?'

'No, I haven't, but I thought we'd try tacos for a change.'

'Sounds good. May I invite Jamie and Malcolm?'

'Of course, I'd love to see them.'

'It'll be a treat for Malcolm. Eileen feeds them on fish fingers from what I've seen. I can't guarantee them, but I'll be back by five. Eat at seven-thirty?'

'Yes, take care.' He started to pile his dishes together. 'Go on, I'll do it. You can do tonight's pots,' I added, pleased he was trying to help and wondering when he'd last been in Malcolm's house. He's never liked Eileen.

'You're a very handsome woman for your age,' he said suddenly.

'Get out!' I picked up the egg-slice and waved it threateningly. 'You treat this house like a hotel, but don't patronize the cook. Go on with you!'

'Bye, Ma.'

'And don't call me Ma,' I said turning from the sink, but he had gone. Kenneth's visits are invigorating. He never stops talking and he ticks me off and teases me, but I like it. I took a long look in the mirror. I suppose I would have to retire one day. If Catherine and Allan were going to Brittany every summer, perhaps I could stay in their flat and go to Kenneth's for the winters. Until I was sixty-five, that is, when I'd be rich.

As I washed up the breakfast dishes I thought about when he was little. That time when he fell off his bike and split his chin open and that awful day when he sat and wept and didn't know why. It's hard to believe when I look at him now. I dried the dishes and put them away, found my bifocals and read the taco instructions, then I started to prepare the avocado and green peppers for the dip. There's always something new to learn, as Dad used to say.

Kenneth came back at five and lit my sitting room fire, saying, 'Sure as eggs we'll all sit round the table as usual.' He then hindered my progress by following me round the kitchen. Wherever I wanted to move to next, there he was. He stepped out of my way at once, but he was a nuisance. His father whom he had never known used to do the same. I found it moving, but I grumbled all the same.

'You know Mary Ruth,' he said, leaning against the draining board as I was washing Douggie's earthy early lettuces from the cold frame, 'I feel quite sentimental about this kitchen when I'm home. I shall miss it when you retire. It is lovely in here. It's warm. Everything's in its place, the cats' dishes, the dog's bowls and that heap of clutter on the fridge.'

'Those are important papers, not clutter,' I replied. It was a mistake. He moved over to the fridge and started listing what was there.

'Important paper number one, an envelope with "cat food, dish cloth, fetch cleaning", scribbled on it,' he announced, and then, waving a packet of seeds, added, 'Important paper number two, cress seeds, "best by end of 1989". Important papers my foot! Mother, admit it, you are untidy.'

'I don't criticize your filing system, Kenneth, so leave mine alone,' I said. 'Now, before the fellas come, I do have something to tell you.'

'Let's have a drink then and I'll listen quietly.'

'That'll be the day.'

He made us a gin and tonic, complaining about how my freezer compartment was organized as he rummaged for the ice. I wonder sometimes how I survive on my own. We went to sit by the little fire. I took a deep breath and said, 'I'm going to inherit a lot of money in five years. Granny had some jewels, from old Lord Fionn-glass.'

Kenneth said, 'Is this a joke?'

I said, 'No.' And before he could say any more I went on. 'Alec and I think it must have been because he was your father's father and she married Joe to give the child a name. They used to do that before single parents came into fashion.'

Kenneth looked blank and I hurried on. 'I checked the dates and I've seen the documents.'

'So Lord Fionn-glass and Granny? Granny was . . .?' He stopped.

'Old Mr Field said Joe never knew about the sapphires or about your father, you see . . .' I was stuck. 'I don't think there is any mistake,' I added gently. 'Why else would he have given them to her . . .?'

'These jewels, are they worth much? I mean he might have, she might have . . .' He stopped.

'Mr Field reckons they are worth ninety thousand pounds,' I said quietly. He looked across the hearth at me and opened his mouth, then he shut it again. I went on in a hurry, 'I don't want to tell anyone. What do you think? Granny was a dark horse,' I ventured, 'wasn't she?'

'Have you any proof that Joe was not my grandfather?'

'No, but neither Mr Field nor Alec could see any other reason.'

'So you've discussed it with Field and Alec?'

'Well, hardly discussed it, but Mr Field told me and then I asked Alec what he thought. I am as amazed as you are, Kenneth.'

'But it's not your grandfather who has changed,' he said. He went on slowly: 'So I might have been Lord Fionn-glass. I wonder what Donald would think of that?' He paused and went on, 'He wouldn't have been able to treat you so badly.'

'He hasn't treated me badly, Kenneth. What do you mean?'

'You've worked like a skivvy to prepare for this Easter visit. You've been writing to me all winter about it. Then, bingo! It's all off.'

'I think it was his wife's doing. I saw pictures of her wearing the matching tiara at a society ball. I was upset for the others, Kenneth. They had worked so hard and were so excited about the visit . . .'

'Well, that's history now,' he interrupted me gently. 'It's your future that matters. You'll be able to retire in August and let Donald find himself some other underpaid caretaker for his ill-gotten gains.'

'Family heirlooms aren't ill-gotten gains.'

'Aren't they? What has he done to earn all the stuff in this house? It was bought with the money made by the potters of Stoke. Anyway that's not the point. You'll soon be free and independent. Ninety thousand. I can't take it in. I haven't had such a surprise since Marie-Claire told me you had a lover. Who is he?'

'How does she know?'

'So it is true! All the family skeletons are coming out tonight.'

I ignored this and went on, 'I don't think we should tell anyone about the sapphires. Do you? I mean round here. I told Catherine and Allan.'

'They didn't clype, even when I gave them quite a chat on your finances.' He thought for a minute and added, 'I don't think we should mention it since Granny didn't. I'll tell Marie-Claire, if I may?'

'Of course. Family's different.'

'If it's legitimate. Well, what a business!' He was quiet for a minute. I waited until he said slowly, 'I think you're right. Nothing's for nothing.'

'I'm sorry to have sprung it on you, Kenneth, but I didn't want to write. We really don't know the truth, but I can't see any other reason . . .'

'It's all right, Mum. It must have been a shock to you too. So,' he said putting the last of the beech logs on the fire, 'Dad was born on the wrong side of the blanket. Do you think he knew?'

'No, I don't.'

'I don't think Donald can know either. Do you?'

'No.'

'Let's have a shufti at the sapphires. Are they under your mattress?'

'Don't be ridiculous. They're at the solicitors. They're not mine until I'm sixty-five anyway.'

'Will I have to be nice to you now, like everyone at church is to Miss Roland? Or has she been gathered?'

'No, she hasn't and if you don't go and set the table and let me go and tidy myself before dinner, I shall give my all to the Cats and Kittens too.'

He poked at the fire. 'Where's your peat?' he demanded.

'In its box, but the fire's not hot enough yet. Will you feed Napper?'

When I came back Jamie had arrived. He handed me a cactus covered with pink blooms. 'I don't know whether it's an Easter cactus late or a Christmas one early, Mary Ruth, but I thought you'd like it. How are you?' He kissed me soundly on both cheeks. 'It is good of you to have us at such short notice.'

'I'm very happy to see you, Jamie, and thank you for the plant. I hear you have been promoted, congratulations.'

'Thanks. It's not the biggest hospital in Scotland, but I am the youngest manager.'

Malcolm walked in then, beaming and carrying a bottle of wine. 'I brought a bottle to add to the festivities, Mary Ruth. Eileen doesn't drink nowadays and I do like a glass of wine from time to time.' He bent down and kissed me too. I remember them coming in breathless from biking up the drive to play with Kenneth as they gulped down glasses of water before they all rushed off outside, chattering and plotting the day's activities and now . . .

My tacos were well-received. As we sat drinking our coffee, Malcolm told us about the number of bandsmen he'd met at shows who had a frozen shoulder. 'We pipers are beggars for punishment,' he said.

'Do you mind being a country bobby again after your time in Edinburgh?' Jamie asked him.

'I didn't think I'd like it at first, but now I find it a steady life and Eileen is not able for the city. We have a fine house and her mother and father are nearby. I'm well-paid. I suppose you two think it's dull, but country life has it compensations. Doesn't it, Mary Ruth?'

'We'll never persuade these two high-flyers of that, Malcolm.'

At half past nine we did the fastest wash-up of dishes ever. Then we all crammed into my car and went to the pub, singing silly choruses all the way. When we reached home, I went to bed and I have no idea how late the others stayed, but Kenneth was up early and looked at the paintings in the little sitting room before breakfast.

'I've never had much opinion of the pictures in this house,' he said as we started our porridge. 'All those dead birds and faithful dogs on misty river banks do nothing for me. However, those are fine pictures. Someone had taste. Two of those still lifes are early Hunters and the loaf is certainly Miller, it's signed quite clearly. The girl on the swing is a Gavin. Worth ten thousand now. The children in the waves look like McTaggart, it'll be worth anything up to thirty thousand, but I like the MacNee farm horse the best. They could be worth seventy thousand altogether.'

'For a painter you make a good art dealer. How do you know so much about the value of them?'

'I follow the market,' he said and reached for the marmalade. 'Everything about painting fascinates me. Even prices.' He grinned at me. 'Especially prices. I'll never get over the fact that earth and eggs and oil mixed together and smeared on a piece of canvas can create a forest in snow, or Cairo in the heat, or a baby's face. It's magic!'

I smiled as I remembered Aunt Connie's remark when I told her that Kenneth was going to art school. She had said, 'There's no money in art.' I wondered if the mothers of the painters in the small sitting room had heard the same words.

'Now, I'm going fishing with Malcolm and Jamie and we're expecting you at The Pitbee for lunch at one-thirty. Did I mention this, by the way?'

'No.'

'Oh, sorry. Well that's what we decided, last night. You haven't made any other arrangements, have you?'

'No. I have some salad and fillet steak for us, but they'll keep. Who's ringing Alec about tomorrow?'

'I'll do it.'

We reached home at five. The Pitbee is a small hotel on a good salmon reach run by a witty Welshman and his English wife. They've been here for thirty years and have an encyclopaedic knowledge of the area and know every artist who has ever painted here. The disquisition on the arts which accompanied every course had given me a sore head and I went to lie down. Kenneth answered the phone which, as ever, I heard ringing just as I closed my eyes.

I slept for an hour and at seven found him preparing a salad. The fillet steaks were lying on a plate, covered with black peppercorns.

'Head better?' he asked.

'Yes, thank you.'

'I'm making supper as you can see. I thought you'd be hungry again after having such a big lunch. I know I always am.'

'I am,' I said, rather surprised. 'Who was on the phone?'

'You'll never guess.'

'No, I won't. Tell me.'

'Sounded a bit sheepish and I'm not surprised. He thinks Dorinda is selfish and rude and doesn't think much better of his father. She has him by the ears, he said.'

'Who said?'

'Julian. He's coming to see you. He's bringing his fiancée, Ffiona Crutchley-Gore, and her friend Miriam Simon. They'll arrive on Sunday, eat out, stay until Wednesday and would like the kennel-run ready for Miriam's wolfhounds. I'm meeting them for lunch in Perth. They've been visiting the Aunt Who has the Money.'

He was busy chopping an apple with my sharp knife. I was afraid he'd cut himself. He went on, 'It's high time he married, he needs an heir and one to spare. I met her last year, in France. Bit long in the tooth, but good child-bearing hips and she's the aunt's heir. Haven't met Miriam, she's Lord Simonson, the financier's daughter. Calls herself Simon professionally. Photographer. Landscape. She's good. Her mother was the famous "Pud", who looked like a pudding whatever it said in the obituaries.'

He started to make a dressing for the salad, sniffing at my olive oil in a censorious manner. It passed the test and he went on. 'It amazes me the kind of rich women rich men are prepared to marry. Fancy randy old Julian settling down with a plain, virtuous thirty-year-old, to breed.'

'I don't think that's a very pretty expression, Kenneth.'

'Wait until you meet her.'

'Kenneth!'

We ate and I assumed Kenneth was going to the pub, but he fetched the whisky and said, as he presented me with a glass, 'Now, tell me about your love life. I want to know who keeps the twinkle in your eye.'

'Isn't it enough to know that I am happy and shall continue to be so, even if I move?'

'So he doesn't live round here?'

'Kenneth, this is embarrassing me and it is none of your business.'

'Who is he? Do I know him?' he persisted. 'Did Granny know? I never thought you had a lover, but Marie-Claire was certain.'

'Well, I don't know how. I've never talked about him with her.'

'I know, but she says someone must care for you or you'd ruin the little ones. French logic, I suppose. Come on, tell, if only how you manage to keep it a secret round here.'

I maintained a stony silence.

'If I guess will you tell me?'

I am not a sensible woman. I said, 'Yes.' I hoped he'd never guess. I should have known better.

He sat for a little while and then said, 'It's Tom, isn't it?'

'Yes,' I said.

Tom had been a gauche young man and fonder of me than I was of him. When I was sixteen he asked me out every Sunday afternoon, much to my family's amusement, and we walked to Cramond or up Arthur's Seat while he talked about social injustice. I listened to him in the way I subsequently listened to my husband and I now listen to Kenneth.

He was studying engineering and Aunt Connie, who came for lunch every Sunday, used to ask with a little snigger if I had any admirers who were not 'rude mechanicals'. She wouldn't disapprove of him now. He is rich. Furthermore, postgraduate students of economics and management come from all over the world to study his company. He lives in Poole now and in Paris, where I see him on my annual trip to France.

When Kenneth was twelve and going away to school, Tom was newly divorced and he wanted me to marry him and go out to Hong Kong. It was there he met his second wife. She has developed multiple sclerosis. We shall never marry now.

'Silence gives consent,' Kenneth was saying.

'I can't think how you knew, but you are right.'

'Well, it didn't seem likely to be anyone round here, and the men who like you are always lively and energetic. When do you see him?'

'In Paris before I visit you. So now you know. Are you satisfied?'

'I am. It just goes to show, doesn't it? Give him my regards.'

'I will. Now I'm going to bed. What time is Jamie's flight?'

'We must leave at eight-thirty. I told Alec we'd make our way to him for about eleven-thirty. This has been some visit. I'm a wiser man than I was.'

'Well, you know more,' I agreed, and kissed him goodnight.

Alec and Kenneth were delighted to see each other. We walked on the west beach at Lossie in the afternoon. They'd spent my inheritance twenty ways before we set off for home.

After mushroom omelettes for supper Kenneth said, 'Life's not been kind to you, has it Mary Ruth? If Dad had been legitimate this house would have been yours and you could have glided down the stairs wearing your sapphires and your evening gown to welcome your guests.'

'Dinner parties with Colonel Fraser-Gordon and old Lord Daldrum before the gout got to him and Maisie his silent wife would have palled, Kenneth. I'd rather have lived with your father in married quarters anywhere in the world and had you to raise than that. I have a lot of good friends here, you know. I enjoy my life. I thought you realized that.'

'I do,' he said and then chuckled. 'I'm sorry I shall miss Julian showing off the house to Ffiona.'

'It's just as well. You might say something. You do go on.'

'Who, me? Well, perhaps I do. Onywye, I shall look at him with interest at lunch tomorrow. He is my first cousin, after all.'

'Once removed.'

'Once removed,' he acknowledged. 'Well, before I remove myself, tell me what you have decided to do.'

'What about?'

'The way you've been treated.' He sounded surprised. 'Give in your notice and come and live near us, Mum. Surely you don't intend to weather five more winters here?'

I must say this struck home. I was getting tired of winter.

'There's a flat of my father-in-law's free and the family love it when you come,' he said. 'All of them. Will you think about it?'

'Yes, I will,' I said, but I didn't like the hint of charity.

He left early on the Sunday and after church I read *Scotland on Sunday* while I waited for Julian, his girlfriends and the dogs to arrive. Frankly I could have done without them, though I have a soft spot for Julian. Aunt Connie went to concerts with a friend called Miss Crutchley-Gore, I remembered. She owned a swathe of the south side of Edinburgh and had a small moustache. I was looking forward to meeting Ffiona.

Chapter 8

After I had fed the dog at five, I went to mend the little sitting-room fire. The western sky was brilliant with colour. I hoped they'd arrive before it grew dark. It's only three hours from Perth. I took some bread and milk to their kitchen and a tray with a selection of drinks to the little sitting room. The sun was sinking and so reluctantly I closed the shutters, drew the curtains and went to light the hall lamps. I unlocked the front door, turned on the outside light and went up to close the bedroom shutters.

Then I went to my own kitchen, made myself scrambled eggs and settled down to watch *Songs of Praise* on the television. I must have fallen asleep because the next thing I knew was that Napper was alert at my feet and a very loud, very English voice was saying, 'God, we have decayed nannies festering in the back regions at my mother's old country house. Always a damn sight warmer than we are and they get their food hot at the table too. Where do you think she is?'

'Are we eating in here?' said a petulant female voice. 'I thought you said we were eating out, Julian. I'm in no mood for haggis pie or some such local dish. What a hellish place to get to. Mummy warned me. What do people do here?'

Before Julian could field that one, the other voice came in powerfully. 'We'll have to find the old dear. I want a tin-opener.

I've got masses of food for the hounds, but no tin-opener. Will she have one?'

'Of course she will, Miriam,' came Julian's strong voice, 'but this is Mary Ruth's kitchen. Don't go poking about in those drawers. We use the big kitchen by the yard. She'll be in her sitting room just through here. Hello! Are you in? Mary Ruth.'

As he stepped across the passage and knocked on my door I heard, 'Christ I am cold,' from the sullen voice.

This was followed by Miriam's lusty 'I thought you had good Scots' blood in your veins, Fee?'

'Only on my father's side. And Mummy always says—' Her mother's observation was lost in Julian's booming voice as he put his head round my door.

'Ah, there you are. At last. Good to see you.' He shook my hand and then kissed my cheek. Raising his voice he called, 'Come through, girls, I've found her.' Then turning to me he said, 'I'm sorry we are rather late. Thanks for the lights and the sitting-room fire. We had a longer lunch with Kenneth than we meant. We didn't leave Perth until nearly five.'

Julian is six feet two, fair and well-built, very like Kenneth. He is not so ebullient nor so talkative, but he is friendly. He bent to pat Napper as the two women came into the room, both smiling broadly. Julian introduced them. Ffiona was about thirty-two, five feet five, well-built but not fat. She had a long, plain, pale face and well-cut hair held up on both sides with Paisley-patterned hair-slides. She was muffled in a sheepskin jacket. She shook my hand and said politely, 'How do you do, Mrs Findlater? I've heard such a lot about you from Julian and his mother. I am sorry we are so late in arriving. I do hope we haven't kept you up.' I took a quick look at the wall clock. It said twenty past eight.

'And this is Miriam Simon.'

Miriam smiled, showing magnificent teeth, and shook my hand warmly. She was a surprise. She was tall, dark, sleek: beautifully groomed is the expression I believe. Her sheepskin coat was draped elegantly over her shoulders. She had a low, well-modulated voice for the old family servant. The friendly bellow she used to her intimates was gone. She was all grace and charm. She reminded me of Miss Wauchop.

'Hello!' she murmured. 'Super to meet you. I've heard so much about this house and the country round here. I'm simply dying to see it in daylight.' She paused and added, 'Could you be a real sweetie and open some tins for me? They're in the car. I've got these blessed wolfhounds with me as always. There are kennels here, Julian?' she said turning to him.

He nodded.

'Perhaps Mary here could help with Cain and Abel. These boots are no use for kennels, I'm afraid.' She laughed and held out a cream suede boot with a three-inch heel. 'I do have my proper boots with me, but there isn't time to unpack now. Julian's booked a table for us at the hotel.'

She is going to make history at The Commercial, I thought.

Ffiona spoke. 'I don't know about the dogs' dinner, but I'm starving. It's half past eight. Didn't you say nine to the hotel johnny, Julian?'

'I've booked us in for dinner at The Pitbee, Mary Ruth. How long do you reckon to get there?'

'About half an hour. You'd better go. I'll just put my boots and jacket on,' I said moving towards the door. 'The kennels are ready, Miss Simonson, Kenneth and I cleared them out for you. Where are the dogs?'

'They're Irish wolfhounds actually,' she corrected me, wrinkling her nose and giving a little smile.

'Where are they?' I asked, trying to sound interested in the things.

'They're outside somewhere. They won't be far away. You are kind.'

I shut Napper in and we all went out of my back door and Miriam called for the hounds. They came bounding round the house and I took them by their collars and set off towards the kennels.

'I'll bring the car round,' called Julian, going off into the dark the other way. 'Save carrying the tins. Wait there, girls. Only be a sec.'

'Dear God!' I heard Ffiona say as I walked away. 'Who on earth would want to live here? Mummy always says . . .'

The animals went quietly into the run, but as soon as I had given them two huge bowls of meal and meat as instructed they began to howl. They howled until eleven-thirty when the diners returned. I was in bed. They stopped howling abruptly and the next day I found they had been moved to Miriam's bedroom. One on each bed.

It was beautiful the next morning and Julian popped his head round my kitchen door and said that they were going to visit friends near Inverness for the day. I cleared the ash and reset the fire in the little sitting room for them, then I went upstairs, made their beds and cleaned their bathrooms. I didn't see them again as they came back very late.

On the Tuesday, which was wet and cold, Julian came into my kitchen at ten and said they'd be leaving at lunch-time instead of staying another night. He thanked me for my preparations and then he said, 'Mum sends her love, she's enjoying her granddaughters, and I wanted, er, that is—' he hesitated, but went on suddenly, 'I wanted to say how, er, how glad I was to see Kenneth on Sunday. What fun we had here when we were boys.'

'They were happy days,' I said. I was beginning to feel uncomfortable. What was the matter with him?

'Long time ago,' Julian blurted. 'I'm sorry Dad and Dorinda didn't make it at Easter,' he went on in a rush, 'fact is—' He stopped and then went on again, 'I can see how much work you did. Won't you come and have your coffee with us? The girls are cooking breakfast. We have hardly seen you. In about twenty minutes.'

I went and they were all charming, even going so far as to say that they had not been cold in the night. Ffiona said she liked the Kangxi pot in the dining room and Miriam promised to come again to take photographs. Julian said how sorry he was about Mrs Joe and we established that my aunt Connie's friend, Miss Edith Crutchley-Gore, was indeed Ffiona's aunt, now aged ninety-four and still living on her own in Morningside.

I heard Douggie calling and excused myself. I was not sorry to leave them, pleasant as they were, for I am not good at small talk. Douggie had come to fetch in more wood for me in case it was needed. Considering the amount we had in the house I suspected he really wanted a keek at the visitors. I went back to check with Julian if they wanted me to light the little sitting room fire for them. As I reached the door Ffiona was saying, 'Well, Dorinda's absolutely right. That's what I would do and soonest. What about Mrs Whatsit?'

I didn't wait for Julian's answer, but went back and told Douggie not to bother with any more wood. He nodded and went to the potting shed. Mrs Whatsit, am I, I thought.

They left at a quarter to one with more protestations of thanks and promises to come again in the autumn. I stood in the porch and watched them drive off through the increasingly heavy rain and then I locked the front door. I went upstairs, turned off their bedroom fires and stripped the beds. In the big kitchen I turned off the Aga, emptied the fridge, washed up the breakfast dishes left in the sink and then took the spare milk and butter to my kitchen.

Douggie was sitting by the Aga with Napper at his feet. 'Are you coming to the whist drive tomorrow, it's for Kirk funds? Are they away?'

'I am. They are. I'm sorry it rained today.'

'Not your fault. It was lovely yesterday.' He stroked the dog's head. 'It was good to see Kenneth.'

'Yes, he was in fine fettle.'

'I'd not say no to a cup of coffee,' Douggie went on. 'It's as cold as the grave in that potting shed.'

'You can't be growing anything in there. What have you been doing all morning?'

'Tidying up and overhauling the mower. It'll be summer soon.'

'Thank God! Would you like a slice of Helen's cake?'

We sat and chatted about politics which neither of us knows much about. We were in agreement for once which made us smile. Douggie maintaining that despite all the ballyhoo attendant on American elections they did at least work for their country's interest after being elected, rather than against each other as we think our politicians do. I accepted the further offer to go and have my tea before the whist drive. After he had gone I did my ironing and listened to the end of *Woman's Hour*.

At seven that evening, Lord Donald telephoned. 'Mary Ruth,' he said. He sounded surprised I'd answered my own phone. 'How are you? How are you? Donald here. I have someone coming to look at the house on Friday. He's an agent for a possible tenant I think I've found, for next winter. He's up in the area this week and said he would come on Friday morning, if that would suit you?'

'That's fine. That's the twenty-sixth. I'll make a note. What name?'

'Mortimer-Desmond. Hyphenated.'

'Anything else, Lord Donald?'

'Nothing urgent. Everything all right that end?'

'Yes, and I've nearly finished the household accounts for last year. There's been hefty expenditure, but there's a good deal in the cellar for when you do come.'

'No hurry for the accounts – I'm sure they will be as competent as ever. I'm sorry we couldn't make it at Easter, no harm done I hope. Is Julian about? I'd rather like a word if he is.'

'They left at lunch-time I'm afraid. I'm not sure where they are staying tonight.'

'Funny, he said they were with you till Wednesday. Nothing wrong, is there? He didn't say anything to upset you?'

'Nothing at all.' Why ever should Julian upset me, I thought. 'It's been very wet today, perhaps that decided them,' I added.

'Ah, well! We're off to the States on Saturday. Back at the end of August. Kenneth well?'

'Yes, fine, thanks. He's just been to see me. He met up with Julian and his guests in Perth on Sunday.'

'Splendid. Well, I'll say cheerio, Mary Ruth.'

'Goodbye,' I said. As soon as I had hung up I remembered that I'd meant to ask him if he wanted an inventory made, but if he was renting the house out surely he would think of it himself.

I enjoyed my meal with Stella and Douggie. I don't think Ffiona would have cared for it. 'It's only mince and tatties, Mary Ruth,' said Stella, 'and skirlie. Not much fun to make for one, so I thought you'd like it for a change.' I was delighted, especially with her skirlie. Fried oatmeal and onion tastes much better than it sounds.

The Kirk whist drive was fun and a number of my neighbours thanked me for my support and many commiserated with me over the failed family visit. I am not sure whether they were sympathizing with me or priming me to grumble about the disappointment I felt. I didn't take them up anyway, so I suppose I disappointed them.

Suddenly it was summer. Thursday started bright and sunny, there was no wind and by mid-afternoon the sun was hot. My mother-in-law used to say we never had any spring this far north. It was certainly true this year.

By Friday morning it was up in the seventies, or twenty-two as the weatherman says. My hens had laid six eggs, the cats had deserted their winter posts and gone prowling and Napper was basking in the sun. I was thinking of searching out my cotton skirt and sandals as I swept the veranda clear of bark and twigs to impress Mr Mortimer-Desmond.

It is hard to imagine who would want a winter rent of a house this size with no central heating, but I felt proud of it. It was clean and tidy inside, the windows were shining and thanks to Douggie, the gravel sweep and the paths were raked and free of weeds.

I thought I heard a motor, so I walked round to my back door. A blue Mercedes was parked next to my car. I looked round for the driver, Mr M.-D. I assumed. My door was open and I went in and called. No answer. I started round to the yard and a voice behind me called from the stableyard, 'Mrs Finlayson', at least I presumed it was calling to me. I turned and saw an elegant man coming through the big archway. He was wearing a double-breasted dark blue pinstripe suit and had a mane of golden hair. He was about thirty-five.

'Good morning,' I said. 'Mr Mortimer-Desmond? I'm Mrs Findlater, Lord Fionn-glass's housekeeper.'

'Ah yes, Mrs Findlater, I do beg your pardon. How d'ye do. Mortimer-Desmond. I believe Lord Fionn-glass told you that I was coming this morning.' He held out his hand and smiled. 'Lovely day. I was just casting an eye at these fine buildings. There's a walled garden too, I hear, and a garden cottage as well as these stables.'

'Yes. Do you want to look at them? I can fetch the keys.'

'That would be most obliging. I'd like to look at all the property while I am here.'

I fetched the keys and showed him round. He seemed very interested in the walled garden with its single plum tree, and the stables. I couldn't see how a winter tenant would be interested in any of this, myself. He kept noting which way the buildings faced and it was half an hour before he was satisfied and was ready to come into the house. I took him through my back door, but went straight to the front hall to show him the main part of the house.

'Here is the drawing room,' I said, opening the first pair of double doors. 'It faces south.'

'Very nice,' he said, walked to the window and asked, 'Is there any access to the terrace from the main reception rooms?'

'No, but in the winter it's just as well,' I replied. He didn't ask why.

He went out of the pair of doors into the big hall. I showed him the dining room, the little sitting room, the billiards room and the conservatory which he said would make a lovely palm court.

For a winter tenant, I thought. He had no more comments to make. It seemed odd to me, if he were looking for a house for someone to live in. However, as they say in the army, you're not paid to think.

We went upstairs and he looked quickly into the first two

bedrooms and one dressing room. He said, 'This is big enough to be a bedroom in a modern house, isn't it? How many bathrooms are there?'

'Two, on this landing,' I told him.

'Just two? Mmmm!' he muttered after glancing into the first one. 'Needs a lot of work doing. May I see the attics? Were they used as nurseries?'

'No, I live in the back wing and use what was the nursery bathroom. We use the attics just for storage.' We climbed the steep stairs together. I felt puffed, but he chattered on. Glad to reach the top of the stairs I told him, 'The furniture up here has been here since the Second World War.'

He was certainly thorough in the attics. He went through them all, shifting boxes and screens and chairs to open doors. He looked in every space. He scraped at the woodwork with his penknife, checking for rot I supposed, and leaned out of all the skylights to survey the roof. As we came downstairs he asked to see the back wing, and so we traipsed up to the top floor to see the nurseries and I showed him my bathroom and the old day-nursery on the way down and my little sitting room, before we went through into my kitchen.

'This was always the housekeeper's room,' I said. He nodded. 'If we go through here,' I went on, beginning to feel like a National Trust guide, 'we come to the galleried hall again and here, beside the cloakroom, is the passage that leads to the main kitchen, the pantries, the stores, the gunroom and the yard door by the kennels.'

He followed me and cast a cursory glance into the only heatable room in the whole house, the clean and tidy big kitchen. He didn't ask about the heating arrangements at all, even when I showed him the old boiler room, notable for its absent boiler. When we had seen everything I offered him a coffee, but he said he was in 'somewhat of a hurry' and would rather have a little more time to look outside. I was glad to show him out of the yard door and go about my business.

I was in my kitchen when he came to his car. He looked up at my window and I opened it wider and leaned out. 'Anything else?' I called. 'You do know there is a lodge at the end of the north drive? If you wait a minute I'll come and show you the way.'

However, by the time I had gone round he had turned his car and was facing the east drive which leads to the village. He was looking at his watch. 'I have an important call to make, Mrs Finlayson er . . . later. Thank you for your trouble. I know about the North Lodge. Good morning,' he called, then he drove off so fast that he sprayed my ankles with gravel.

I would have thought his was the kind of car to have had a phone in it. He wasn't dashing off to use the coin-box phone in the lobby of The Commercial in the village, surely. Curiouser and curiouser, I thought. As I turned to go in, Angus pulled up in his post van.

'Some folk haven't a moment to live,' he said, as he emerged holding my mail. 'Whoever was that, Mary Ruth?' He handed me my letters and waited for enlightenment. 'He was fairly going. He missed me on the top bend. I hope he misses Douggie on the lower one. He was coming along behind me, but he stopped to speak to Sandy in his van.'

'That was Mr Mortimer-Desmond, Angus. His Lordship sent him to look at the house for a prospective tenant for next winter. He didn't seem interested in how said tenant was going to keep warm and he didn't think much of the bathroom he saw. Apart from that I can tell you nothing.'

'That'd be fine company for you, a tenant. Was he interested?'

'He was more interested in the stables and the walled garden than in the house, as far as I could judge. It was odd altogether, Angus. I don't know what is going on.'

'Weel dinna fash yersel', Mary Ruth. It's a braw day. Enjoy it.' And with this homely advice he lowered himself into his seat and drove off.

It was all very well to tell me not to worry, but Mortimer-Desmond hadn't looked like a family solicitor looking for a winter let, to me. He was my idea of a slick operator from the City, not that

I've ever seen one. I must have been watching too much telly in the winter, I decided as I stood enjoying the sun on my back and opened my letters.

One was an appeal for orphans, victims of the Gulf War, including harrowing pictures. One was a receipt. The other one was from Carter's, but before I could open it Douggie pulled up and parked next to my car.

'Jings!' he exclaimed as he came towards me, 'I had a near miss with thon Mercedes. Some folk lack the sense God gave them. He was bang in the middle of the drive. We met head on at the first bend. It's well I only surge along steadily and my brakes work. We had a rare shuntin' to and fro to get past. A toonser I doubt. English registration. Who was he?'

'Mr Mortimer-Desmond, hyphenated. He narrowly missed Angus too, on the top bend. Lord Donald sent him to look at the house, but he spent most of his time outside. Casing the joint, I reckon. Part of an international gang. He was charming, but he would need to be, I suppose.'

Ignoring my flight of fancy completely Douggie said slowly, 'I saw thon fellow in the lounge at The Commercial last night, after the bowling. Mackie reckoned he was a scout for thon Dutch time-share consortium, or whatever they call themselves. The ones thinking of turning Daldrum Castle into a holiday complex!' The scorn in his voice was juicy. 'Complex is the word. That road is closed more often nor Cockbridge–Tomintoul. And it rains there all summer. And the midges!' Words failed him. 'What did you say he wanted?'

'To look at the house for a prospective tenant for next winter. Lord Donald rang. He's called Mr Mortimer-Desmond.'

'I don't care what he's called,' he said. 'He's never after a winter let here.' He straightened up and looked me in the eye. 'Winter let!' He went on, 'Here? In the winter? No one in their right mind would want a winter let here. Did you tell him about the logs he'd need to fetch? The kindlers he'd need to chop? A winter let! Tcha! What kind of a tenant, a polar bear?'

'It's not as bad as all that, Douggie. I live here and I've only been snowed in five times in twenty years.'

'Mary Ruth Findlater, the big house is too cold to bide in unless there's a steady Scandinavian high in the summer. No one could get through a winter in it unless there was a new boiler and the whole heating system was overhauled. It's only been used for a few shooting parties since the war.' He paused and added, 'and they're outside and in the summer. Think how cold all you women were in March. No, there's something going on and I just hope you are not going to suffer as a result.'

'Well, I don't know Douggie. I'm only telling you what Lord Donald said. I was telling Angus that he was more interested in the stables than in the house. I might have said more, but he went rushing off to make a phone call.'

'Sounds very odd to me. What did he have to say?'

'Not a lot. I think it's odd too. I wouldn't like him to rent a house for me.' Douggie was looking disapproving. 'He looked at the roof out of the skylights,' I added, remembering. We both stared up at the roof. 'Damn, he's left one open. I'll have to go and shut it.'

'Aye, an' I'll be making tracks. I'm going to prune the roses. Should be free of frost now.'

We went our separate ways and I opened my letter from Carter's as I trudged up the stairs again. It was from Miss Wauchop, drumming up business with an appeal to me *to check your attics for forgotten treasures. I have helped a number of clients to sell even worn or damaged items for quite remarkable sums,* she had written, and promised me that she had my best interests at heart. I put the letter back in its envelope as I reached the attic door.

Irritating as I found Miss Wauchop's style, I looked around the attic with a fresh eye. There was a fire-screen with a broken foot and a row of chipped gilt picture frames near the door. There were boxes labelled Plates Meissen (incomplete), Dinner Service Wedgwood (some cracked) and a library globe and four mahogany flower stands and an Indonesian gong, in the first room. I went through into the next where the set of Hepplewhite chairs was.

There was a lady's walnut bureau, twin silk-embroidered sofas, two inlaid chests of drawers and, against the wall, four enormous Italian mirrors. I went on through the accumulated treasures until I found the open skylight.

As I shut it I heard Douggie speaking to Napper far below me, outside. What a good man he is, I thought, so straightforward and so honest. Suddenly I realized the full import of what he had been saying. If that Mortimer-Desmond man was working as a scout for the time-share people that was what he had been doing here. Anyone who knows Daldrum Castle, halfway up a north-facing slope, would know it was useless as a holiday place.

I've seen the time-share place in Deeside. It's beautiful, with mature, sheltered gardens. Daldrum is bleak, windswept and forbidding. No one would invest in it to tempt the 'good lifers'. Whereas at Fionn-glass, I thought, we have everything except a working central heating system. We have a stretch of good fishing water and enough land for a golf course. We're only an hour from the airport. There are acres of policies to build on and plenty of underemployed locals to provide staff.

What an innocent I was. A real Mrs Whatsit! Mr Mortimer-Desmond probably thought I was a dottled old retainer kept to let the tradesmen in. No wonder he had been impressed, especially on the sunniest and warmest day of the year. He had gone off to phone His Lordship quickly enough. Donald was leaving for the States tomorrow. He would want to set everything in motion. To sell a place like this with all its contents would take a long time. I had been standing in a trance, but I began to focus on a large solitary picture frame across the room from me.

I had a struggle to reach it. I pulled at the dust-sheet which was covering it and revealed a portrait of a woman of about twenty-five. She was wearing a sapphire and diamond tiara and my choker, earrings and bracelets.

Lady Katherine, Wife to the Right Honourable Viscount Fionn-glass of Fionn-dhruim, on the occasion of Her Majesty the Empress Queen's Diamond Jubilee, 1897 was inscribed at the bottom.

So this was my husband's grandmother. She was a handsome woman. I stood thinking about Kenneth's words. I would have been the dowager, or whatever redundant viscountesses are called if her son had acknowledged his. From what I have seen of the world, my husband, had he been legitimate, would never have met me, let alone married me. Short as our marriage was, we'd been happy and I still had Kenneth. I looked at the letter in my hand from Miss Wauchop. I thought about the almost inevitable sale of this house, my home for so long. I thought about Ffiona Crutchley-Gore, the cancelled visit, that disgusting HAC Ball and Donald's odd behaviour in Edinburgh.

'Miss Wauchop,' I said to the ghosts in the attic, 'I believe I do have some treasures for you.'

Before I could change my mind I set off downstairs as fast as I could go to telephone her. Bloody time-share indeed. Festering old nanny indeed. Old Mrs Whatsit indeed. I was inspired.

I rang Carter's and asked for Miss Wauchop.

'Whom shall I say is calling?' purred the seductive voice of the receptionist.

'Mrs Findlater from Fionn-glass House.'

I was still panting from my hectic descent of the stairs. I was ready to do battle. I was ready for the assured and condescending Miss Wauchop. What I was not ready for was what she said.

'My dear Mrs Findlater, I was just about to telephone to you. Lord Fionn-glass is just this very moment off the line. He told me about the sale of course, and the inventories he wants and naturally, as usual, said I was to liaise with you. How fortuitous that you have rung.'

'Sale? Inventories?' I said to myself. So Mortimer-Desmond had reported back. Donald was acting fast. I had Miss Wauchop's letter in my hand. To give myself a moment to think I laughed and said, 'Funny coincidence, isn't it? I've just opened your letter about forgotten attic treasures and was going to ask . . . and here's His Lordship . . .' I tailed off. She was given to elaboration. I judged she would break in and I would find out what was happening, at last.

'Too desperately sorry about the furniture. We do recommend clients have a sale at the house if at all possible. It does so help with the provenance as I'm sure you will realize, but there it is. We shall, of course, take meticulous care to value every piece accurately, before giving Lord Fionn-glass our estimate for the private sale he is promised. It is a temptation to sell to the new owner, I do appreciate.'

'I'm sure we can, as ever, have every confidence in you, Miss Wauchop,' I enunciated. This punctuated style of address is catching.

She let a mirthless little laugh escape and continued. 'Now, I don't believe you've met our Mr Charles, have you,' she paused, 'Mrs Findlater?'

'I don't believe I have,' I replied, 'Miss Wauchop.' I was beginning to get the hang of this.

'Well,' she waited a moment and then, 'as I look at his programme it seems to me, Mrs Findlater, that it will not, I'm afraid, be at all possible for our Mr Charles to come to see you this coming week. However, in the week commencing Monday the sixth of May, his programme is, let me see . . . Aha! I think I see a little chink of light.' I have never seen a little chink of light in a programme, but Miss Wauchop saw one and crowned her efforts with a little cry. 'Tuesday the seventh, just for a preliminary look-see and then I really think it's over to you. I know that Lord Fionn-glass wants us to get on soonest and that in your capable hands he has every confidence, Mrs Findlater.'

'Thank you, Miss Wauchop. Soonest is the word then. I am most grateful to you, as I know His Lordship's timetable is pressing.'

'Absolutely. I told him it might be diffy to manage the summer sales, but he said to try our best. All the Americans and Canadians are here then, as I'm sure you know.'

'Absolutely! I'm sure we can manage between us, Miss Wauchop. It's amazing what we can do if we really, really try, isn't it? Now, I shall expect your Mr Charles on Tuesday the seventh. At what hour, may I ask?'

'Shall we say ten o'clock, Mrs Findlater?'

'Why not indeed, Miss Wauchop?' I hung up after we had made more mutual protestations of undying trust, made the coffee and took the mugs outside.

Douggie was hoeing one of the big borders, with his own hoe. Mine only takes up weeds. His is a more comprehensive tool and slices through every low-growing plant. His theory is that these 'prunings', as he calls them, do no harm. I dare say he's right, if you only want powerful root systems; I prefer flowers myself. We sat on the garden seat and drank our coffee. I didn't trust myself to speak.

'I'll start cutting the grass tomorrow,' he said, 'before it's too long.'

'Or it starts raining,' I said.

'Whissht! We're doing fine well so far. Let's not tempt fate.'

'No indeed,' I agreed, but I meant it in more ways than one.

Chapter 9

On the Monday Angus brought me two letters. One was from Miss Wauchop. It was brisk and businesslike. It said:

> Dear Mrs Findlater,
> Further to our conversation this morning, this is to confirm that Mr Charles, our valuer, will call at Fionn-glass House on Tuesday 7th of May at 10 a.m. to make a preliminary survey of the furniture and contents of the house, and make what further arrangements are necessary for the completion of the two undermentioned at the request of Lord Fionn-glass.
>
> 1 An inventory and valuation of the furniture which Lord Fionn-glass has requested prior to his selling the same privately to the company which is purchasing the house, and
>
> 2 An inventory and valuation of all the other contents which we are to remove and sell for him as soon as possible. The arrangements for the sale to be made through you, as usual.
>
> Assuring you of our best attention at all times,
>
> Yours faithfully,
>
> Regina Wauchop

I could even read her signature. Little did she realize just how soon, 'as soon as possible' was. I had three and a half months until

Lord Donald was due back from the States. I could work fast, too. The second letter was from Lord Donald himself.

Dear Mary Ruth,
In haste. You will have heard from Carter's by now that I have found a buyer for the house. I met young Mortimer-Desmond recently in town and thought we might be in with a chance when he said he was going north to look at Daldrum Castle. No one in their right mind would spend any money on that place.

I've told Carter's to set everything up with you. I know you are sixty and retire on August 29th though we have never talked about it, but I'd like you to stay put for the insurance's sake until December 1st, which is the completion date.

Under the circumstances I'm going to let you have the North Lodge, rent free, for three months after November 30th. Gives you an extra three months to find a house. I've made it a condition of the sale that you remain in the North Lodge until the end of February, if you want.

They will be moving into the gardens with diggers and building materials for the lodges. The big house is to be the restaurant and hotel and the central heating johnnies will be starting in early, but no one wants that gloomy North Lodge.

Tried to phone on Friday, but didn't catch you. I know this will be a bit of a shock, but all good things come to an end and frankly there's no point keeping a house we never use. Anyway Dorinda has her heart set on a place in the Alps for winter skiing.

Cheerio old thing, see you at the end of August,

Yours aye,

Donald

'And thank you very much,' I said, 'I hope you have paid your insurance for you are going to need it.' I had decided to sell everything in the house myself. Between them both His Lordship and Miss Wauchop were, so far, as she would have punctuated it, making it easy for me.

I went to the attics and began carrying what I could downstairs. I knew Mr Charles would take less time to list and evaluate everything if the items for sale were laid out for inspection and I wanted to arrange the sales as soon as possible. On Wednesday I'd get Mrs Inglis at it too. By a week on Tuesday we would be ready for him.

I decided to tell Mrs Inglis only that an inventory and valuation were under way. I wouldn't tell her, Douggie, Alec or anyone else, Kenneth included, that the house and its contents were to be sold. They'd know soon enough. I wanted to oblige Miss Wauchop and be prepared, hence the attic-clearing. That was my story and I stuck to it.

Naturally, I didn't want the whole County watching me selling off the family heirlooms bit by bit. I knew Carter's would need about six weeks to prepare for the sale before removing the goods to the salerooms. I hadn't read their catalogues for nothing. I would time the uplifting of the contents to coincide with the trades holiday fortnight at the beginning of July when Mrs Inglis was going to Butlin's at Ayr and Douggie and Stella were going to Menorca. I didn't want to involve them in any way. By the time they came home the house would be empty.

I'd have to think of some way of explaining it to Mrs Inglis. I thought I'd tell her I'd only just heard before her holiday and hadn't wanted to spoil it for her. As it turned out I never needed to lie to her, but I anticipate, as it used to say in the shilling shockers.

As I pulled out box after box, carried them downstairs, unpacked them and spread their contents along the gallery and in the bedrooms, I began to estimate their value. There was another thirty-six-place Royal Doulton dinner service with matching blue goblets, flutes and tumblers. It had 'Potts' stamped on all the boxes. I don't think it had ever been used. I found a set of Spode fruit-plates too. Garish things, but valuable. The twenty Hepplewhite chairs and the two carvers had navy leather seats and were in perfect condition. I left them in the second attic lined up neatly with ten huge gilded picture frames. The inlaid work-tables and chests of drawers, the heavy flower stands and the upholstered sofas and chairs I also left. The men would have to carry them down. I reckoned, as I worked in the hot, dusty attic and clumped up and down its steep stairs, that the china alone must be worth forty thousand pounds.

When Mrs Inglis came she was pleased an inventory was to be done, and showed a considerable knowledge of antiques as she helped set the hoarded valuables out. She was especially taken with three pairs of Staffordshire 'Mansion House' dwarves, six inches high with red faces and big yellow hats. I wouldn't have given them houseroom. She said they were worth about six hundred pounds a pair. I suppose it is just as well we don't all like the same thing. They had the same effect on me as the garden gnomes at Super Store.

I prefer pictures to china ornaments. If Kenneth was right, and the pictures in the small sitting room were likely to fetch seventy thousand, then clearly there'd be at least as much again from the other pictures in the house. There were eighteen Thorburns hanging in the big hall for a start. As I toiled I was astounded by what I found. There were six Highland-cottage and farm-life scenes by Miles Birket Foster tucked away in a middle attic. In the corner of the least accessible room I found an old haybox with eight carefully wrapped pearlware miniature horses in it. Also in the haybox, still in their wedding presentation box, were two Enoch Wood Staffordshire animals. I wasn't sure whether they were pigs or elephants.

There was a boat-shaped swinging cradle and a pair of mahogany high chairs. In the bottom drawer of a serpentine chest I found a dressing case crammed with tiny lacquered Japanese seal boxes. There were parasols and patent dancing shoes, ice skates and military uniforms. There were fans, muffs and top hats in their own boxes and First World War helmets, packs and gas masks. In a small inner room, which I had missed at first, I found a full set of drums, two flutes, a clarinet, an oboe, a violin, five music stands and two canterburies of music. This was just in the attics.

In the house, apart from the furniture, there was Kangxi ware and Wemyss ware, Sèvres figures, Meissen plates, Delftware tiles, Staffordshire groups and Wedgwood black basalt vases. There were books and maps, samplers and scrapbooks, cases of birds' eggs and butterflies. There were twenty guns in the gunroom and antique and modern fishing-rods and golf clubs. There was the billiards table with all its equipment and in the conservatory there were busts and pillars and urns, all of marble.

Out in the back regions, in the pantries and cupboards we had so recently been cleaning was, presumably, sixty thousand pounds' worth of silver cutlery in the twenty-two canteens I had not sold. I couldn't begin to evaluate the silver which I was carrying through to the dining room table.

There were Georgian and Victorian teasets, coffee-pots, cream jugs, spirit kettles, candlesticks, bon-bon dishes, cake plates with fancy scrolled edges, gravy-boats and quaichs. I found christening mugs, sugar bowls, porringers, dirks with silver handles and sixty-nine silver photograph frames. In some boxes pushed well out of sight were forty-two serving dishes and half a dozen wine buckets, covers of all sizes and twelve pairs of solid silver serving dishes with lids. I had seen a similar pair pictured in an old *Country Life* at the dentist's. It had been sold for twenty-five thousand pounds.

Outside in the stables were twelve saddles, a box full of horse-brasses, a governess cart with all its harnessing and a grey Fergie tractor which was a museum piece. There were two full-size tricycles hanging from the rafters in the old coach-house and implements of all kinds.

One afternoon, in the nursery attic, I found nine perfect Persian and Turkish carpets and runners all rolled up and reeking of mothballs. I was sure one silk and wool carpet would make at least ten thousand pounds. I knew less about the prices to expect for the furniture, but if the right sale could be found and more important still, the right buyer, I reckoned that there was the best part of a million and a half pounds in my hands.

I spent my evenings rereading old catalogues and making my own valuations. I didn't want cheating. I'd have to arrange for the other firm of auctioneers, Agostino's, to come and value the furniture after Carter's had been. It wouldn't do for the rival valuers to meet. I wanted as little gossip as possible.

I thought a lot about Miss Wauchop. After 'Our Mr Charles' had been and the sales were completed I'd ask her to send me the cheques made out to House Sales, not Household Account. I did not anticipate any difficulties. She had interrupted me so much when I had spoken to her on the phone I was sure I'd be able to hint that His Lordship had decided this was how to make the payments. I'd write to confirm it in careful terms. *Further to my call, would you please make the cheques payable to Mrs Findlater – House Sales.* Any sudden phone calls from her to His Lordship in the States to verify this seemed unlikely.

I practised the telephone conversation I would have with Miss Wauchop as I fetched and carried and set out the goods for the inspection of 'Our Mr Charles'. It worked perfectly. My willingness to work extra hard to expedite the sales was appreciated and she agreed that a special account for payment made sense. Lord Donald hadn't mentioned what he wanted to do with the money from the sales, she said. I smiled, for he hadn't authorized the sales either. I parted from her saying, 'It's such a pleasure to do business with you, Miss Wauchop. You really do know what you are doing.' She thanked me most graciously.

I wondered as I laboured how she would explain to her superiors that she had let me sell over half a million pounds' worth of His Lordship's possessions and put the money in an account he'd never heard of. On reflection I think I was beginning to understand how to launder money.

I had thought hard about this. I'd need help. I'd go to Millichop and Millichop in Moray Place in Edinburgh and tell them that I wanted my endorsed cheques banked by them. They had been Aunt Connie's 'men of business'. She has been dead for twenty years, but I was sure they would remember her. What would be more natural than for me to say that they were the only firm of solicitors I knew in Edinburgh? With a little sigh and a touch of the hanky to the eyes I could murmur, 'After all, family business is a great responsibility.'

I would need to imply that I was a wealthy woman, but as rich women in the country are usually unpainted, have untidy hair and wear classic suits when they go to town, I thought I'd manage. With luck I would persuade the solicitor, who would be licking his lips in anticipation of handling such a large sum of money, that the cheques which would be arriving were the proceeds of a family sale. Well, they would be.

On Tuesday the seventh of May I was up early; I fed the hens, gathered the eggs and by ten to ten was hanging out the washing in the sun and listening for the postie. I didn't want him to see Mr Charles, so I didn't walk round to greet him. When I collected my post it was an appeal from Camfam for a special fund opened for the Women and Children of Ethiopia, to make sure they were not forgotten because of the Gulf War. As Angus disappeared down the west drive Mr Charles arrived from the east.

He was in his fifties, tall and pale-faced and was wearing a grey suit. He was quietly spoken and shook hands with me with a little nod of the head. We went into the house and as we reached the big hall the long-case clock struck ten. It was always two minutes slow.

'A fine piece,' he said, taking out his own watch which was on a chain. He checked it and said, 'Your clock is slow, Mrs Findlater, but that is no concern of mine.' He looked at the mahogany and glass telephone box with interest. 'Ah,' he said, 'one of Archibald's showcases, turn of the century. What a good use to have made of it.' He then took his glasses from his top pocket, placed them on his nose with care, gave another little nod of his head and said: 'Shall we proceed?'

Mr Charles was efficient and shrewd. We started in the attics and he thanked me for the work I had done. He unbent sufficiently to say that not many people had the sense to realize that making a catalogue for a sale was a very different matter from an estimation. I left him on the gallery and went to make us a cup of coffee at eleven. We drank it in the drawing room, looking out of the window.

'A beautiful location, Mrs Findlater,' he said. 'Do you have much snow?'

'Some years, but not recently,' I replied. We chatted a little more about the weather, such a rich topic in these northern parts. He thanked me for his coffee and I left him to his work.

At a quarter to one he came through to my kitchen, knocking politely on the door and calling out to me as he did so. He said that he was going to the village for lunch, would be back at two, finished by four and would send his team the following Monday to start the inventories and the valuations for the sales.

'How long will it take?' I asked.

'Ten days, at the most. You appreciate, I'm sure, the importance of separating the items for the different sales. When my team has finished everything must be left in the labelled boxes. All being well we should have everything into the July sales in Edinburgh, Perth and Gleneagles. Storage is a problem as you will no doubt realize, so we shall not be uplifting the items until a week before the sales begin.'

'When will that be?' I asked, anxious to play my part. He was so well organized I had nothing much to say or to ask.

He flicked through his diary. 'The cataloguing should be finished by the twenty-fourth and that gives us one, two, three, four, five, yes – six weeks. Monday the first of July, subject to confirmation. I will pencil it in, so if you want to make a note, Mrs Findlater, I'll wish you good morning.'

'Of course. I'll make a note and will expect the removers on Monday the first of July,' I said as I wrote in my diary.

'Subject to confirmation.'

I smiled and repeated. 'Subject to confirmation.' I sincerely hoped there would be no delay. I only had until the end of August and I had to fit Agostino's in too.

Mr Charles was as good as his word. His team was very jolly and young. There were three of them and they worked hard. I saw very little of them, but every evening when I went on my rounds to see that all the doors were shut and all the lights were out, I could see what they had done.

Tea chests were piling up in the downstairs hall. The gallery and bedrooms were emptied and the dining-room table was cleared of all the silver, glass and china. If Mrs Inglis wondered why it was all being boxed she did not comment and I made no explanation. After she had scrubbed out the store cupboards in the kitchen area and they had dried, I locked them up. She may have thought they were full again.

I was both pleased and interested to see that the tea chests were colour-coded for the different sales and not labelled 'Silver', 'China', and so on. One of the young team told me it was a safety precaution advised by their transport manager to keep fine-art treasures in transit as anonymous as possible. 'Even our vans don't have Carter's all over them any more,' she had said. 'The name is there, but it is discreet and the men will have identity cards.' I was delighted to hear the vans were not going to advertise their origins boldly, but I didn't say so. I was keeping a low profile.

Meanwhile, Douggie continued to cut the grass; happily he only came in the evenings in May and June. Until the students were available in their long vacation, he ran the bar at The Pitbee hotel during the day. I missed his company, but he missed all the comings and goings too. Things were conspiring to help me.

Mrs Inglis spent two Wednesdays 'thoroughing' the attic, as she called it. It was like a showroom by the time she had finished. I went to Millichop and Millichop in Edinburgh and opened an account without any difficulty, and then I drove to Agostino's in Glasgow and arranged for their valuer to come on the thirty-first of May. When I mentioned Millichop and Millichop, the woman at Agostino's was impressed. There's no doubt, class counts.

Agostino's promised to uplift the furniture on the third and fourth of July. They were to send a Mr Esau to evaluate it. I gave them maps I had drawn of the area indicating the drive to come up. I had done the same with Carter's. Any of my neighbours who saw a van would only see it once, for I had worked out a different route for each van. This exercise took me a long time. I began to feel like Margaret Rutherford in *The Happiest Days Of Your Lives*, organizing the parents' day and keeping the two sets of parents apart.

The evening before Agostino's were coming to appraise the furniture I had a call from Julian. His first words sent a chill down my spine.

'How's it going?' he said. How was what going, I wondered.

'Not a good line,' I mumbled.

'The great move to the North Lodge. Isn't it all exciting?'

'Tremendously. There's lots to do.'

'Just thought I'd ring and see if it would be OK for Miriam to come and take some photos of the old pile and some inside shots, for old times' sake. Could you give her a bed next Tuesday? She's up in Sutherland at the moment, but she could come by on her way south.'

'Oh dear,' I said. 'The house is in turmoil, Julian. I am sorry. I have started sorting everything for Carter's. They are coming to value and catalogue for the sales your father asked for. If only you'd let me know sooner. I could make up a bed for her, of course, and the grounds are looking lovely, but inside is really in a mess. You see, he wants the sales as soon as he comes back.'

'Well, never mind, she's not really got time. It was just a thought. I'm off on Monday to Malaysia for six weeks. Business and pleasure, but I wanted to say hello and see how it was all going and I'm just about to ring Mim, so I just thought I'd mention it.'

'Kind of you,' I managed.

'I'll be coming in September to sort out some of the loot before the hammer falls. Ffiona has her eye on the Kangxi and the Meissen and I fancy the pictures in the little sitting room. Dad's coming to pick out a few bits and bobs for the girls when he comes home. I might have known things were under way. You always were a good organizer, Mary Ruth. Anyway, never mind. Have a good summer. My best to Kenneth.'

'Thank you, Julian. Love to your mother. I'll look forward to seeing you in September. I'm sorry about Miss Simon.'

'Don't think any more about it, Mary Ruth. You just press on and we'll see you in September. Cheerio for now.'

I was quite shaken as I put the phone down. A life of crime is a strain on an honest woman.

Chapter 10

The next morning I found one of my hens with a bald head. The others had started to peck her. I'd have to get a cockerel; there's no other way. I'd ask around tomorrow at the church fête, someone would have a spare. If the weather held we looked like having a good day. We hadn't had any bad snows for some years as I had told Mr Charles. We hadn't had any good summers either, but it had been dry for a week now and this morning it was gloriously sunny. I hoped it would last another day and give everyone a good day out.

Ours is the only Episcopal church for miles around. Our sister congregations from Drumloch and Daldrum come to support us, but they are few. The village turns out, of course, and clears the home-bake stall like a cloud of locusts. Dr McPherson, the parish minister, and the elders of St Modan's come and our Catholic neighbours whose church is in Knockglass. We in our turn go to their fairs.

This year our 'feet', as everyone except the rector calls it, was being held in Miss Roland's gardens. I was making shortbread as usual to add to my tablet for the baking stall when there was a 'Hulloo' from the yard. It was Mr Esau from Agostino's. He was a stocky red-bearded man with a bald, freckled head. He looked like a local farmer with a briefcase.

'Mistress Findlater,' he called from outside the open window,

'Harry Esau, Agostino's. Come to look at your furniture.'

I went to let him in. It was half past ten.

'Would you like a coffee, Mr Esau? I haven't had mine yet.'

'That'd be magic,' he said, 'I left home at six.'

'Well, in that case you might like a piece of shortbread too. There's plenty.' I pointed to the table.

'Yous feeding an army?' he asked. 'Or is this the famous country baking we're always hearing about?'

'No,' I said. 'It's for the church fête tomorrow and I wouldn't believe too much about country baking. Most people here eat Mr Kipling's jam tarts.'

'Another illusion shattered,' he laughed. 'Can you spare a wee bit shortbread? I haven't had any home-made for yonks.'

I could and he obviously enjoyed it. He was a cheery man with typical Glasgow patter and by the time we'd finished our coffee, I knew that his grandfather had left Wales to work as a collier in Ayrshire, that his father had been a removal man with Agostino's as he was too tall for the Ayrshire pit and that Mr Esau had joined the firm and risen to be an evaluator.

I had taken great care to dress myself as a rich eccentric and beneath my pinny I was wearing my only pure silk blouse with my tailored navy linen skirt. I had also found Aunt Connie's heavy gold bracelet and put on my good pearl earrings and my mother's gold chain and locket. It was as well Douggie wasn't likely to come wandering in, or Mrs Inglis. I looked oddly overdressed for baking.

I had fetched my good ginger jar from its place, stuffed it full of pencils and put it by the phone. I'd shoved half a dozen solid silver spoons and forks into the cutlery drainer by the sink and stuck some freesias untidily into a George V coronation mug on the table. I was quite tickled at these little touches.

I think it was wasted effort, as Harry Esau was a happy and uncomplicated man and all but calling me 'hen' by the time I had put the next pan of shortbread into the oven. He gave me two pounds for the church funds and it was obvious he accepted me for what I was supposed to be, the lady of the house, spending more time in the kitchen than the drawing room, reduced to selling up like so many others he had met.

When we had finished our coffee he produced a large book and a pencil from his briefcase. As soon as we went into the house he said, 'Ooh! I like your telephone box.' Then he looked closer. 'It's an Archibald showcase, isn't it? Made in Glasgow. And the Prince of Wales feathers too.' He looked up admiringly at the great carved plumes. 'Does it still work?'

'Yes,' I said, 'though I use the one in the kitchen,' then remembering my role added, 'nowadays.'

He went straight across the hall, opened the glass door and went inside. He picked up the receiver and grinned at me through the glass sides. 'I've never seen one of these used for a phone before. It's magic!' he said as he came out. 'Now, *jaickets aff*. First things first. Any pianos?'

'Three,' I said, 'there's the grand at the end of the hall, it's a Steinway, then there's an upright Bechstein in the drawing room and an old one I use in my little back sitting room.'

'Aha!' he said, scribbling away. 'How many long-face clocks?'

'Seven,' I told him. 'This hall one. Four in the dining room, a small one on the upper landing and an oak grandfather in the billiards room.'

'How many public rooms?'

I showed him and all the time he wrote busily.

'I'll be able to get on now,' he said. 'Don't let your shortbread burn. You've been busy,' he added, nodding at the packed boxes. 'I'll not disturb you any more. I'll need to come tomorrow. Is eight-thirty too soon?'

'No, I shall be up,' I said, adding, 'I'm always up early.' I hoped this would encourage the idea that I was one of the old school, and rose at six, summer and winter. When I think about it now, it seems ridiculous that I should have worried about being accepted for what I must have seemed.

* * *

Saturday was a beautiful day. Mr Esau arrived promptly and went to continue his work. I tried to catch the bald and bullied hen and succeeded only in making my thumb bleed when I caught it on some broken wire, and I let the hen escape from the pen. I meant to put her in the kennel-run so that I could collect her eggs, though I knew that if the heat kept up they'd all start moulting and go off laying. I was dishevelled and bloody and clutching seven eggs when I met Angus delivering my mail.

'My! My! Mary Ruth,' he said, 'what have you been doing?'

I told him.

'Losh,' he said, 'I'll bring a cock to you Monday. There's my Tam trying to find homes for the twa o' them. You'd better away and put a drop Dettol on that scratch. I'll see you at the feet,' he added. 'Take care.'

He drove away and I had a sudden vision of my future without him, without Douggie, without Mrs Inglis, without my home of twenty years. Napper was jumping up at me. My thumb was bleeding, the eggs were awkward to hold. 'Mary Ruth,' I said, 'one thing at a time. Church *feet* first and let the future take care of itself.'

The fête was splendid. Miss Roland's house has a long veranda along the south side where the trestle-tables from the hall, covered with sheets carefully drawing-pinned in place by Mrs Smart, were assembled. Stallholders coveted this area because it affords a degree of shelter if it's windy or wet. I've never understood the need for a veranda in this part of the world. They were intended to keep the sun out of houses, but there it is.

In other parts of the garden there were penny rolling, hoop-la and an old archery set which is our treasurer, Mr Phimister's, pride. Our local joiner Mac was helping him. This was cunning of Mr Phimister because Mac is an archery expert and if he isn't helping he wins all the prizes.

There was a tombola, ruled over by Colonel Fraser-Gordon, who boomed away all afternoon trying to persuade the kind and the holy to gamble. Church fêtes are funny things. There was a bran tub run by Connal's wife, Maureen, and pony rides for small children only on an old Shetland. For twenty pence they were led round the edge of the lawn, through the shrubbery, round the house and back to the drive by two busy little girls wearing jodhpurs and boots. For a pound you could have a tour of Connal's empire, the walled garden.

I put my tablet and shortbread next to the cakes, fruit loaves, buns and pancakes made by the bakers of the church. Everything was set out on little polystyrene trays, wrapped in cling film and priced. The first time I contributed my home-made tablet I had not priced it, a sin I never committed again. After greeting everyone and asking Mrs Smart to keep me a fruit loaf, if possible, I went to my station.

I always ran the plant stall which was by the greenhouse. Its isolation makes it an unpopular stall to work at, but it is well attended. When it pours I shelter in the greenhouse.

On an old kitchen table lay a number of awkward newspaper-wrapped bundles of herbaceous plants, some potted cacti, twelve geranium cuttings in tiny plastic pots and a few busy Lizzies in half-filled paper cups. Beside the table was a box of carnation cuttings and two big bunches of mint which had been ripped out of the ground as rank weeds, I suspected, rather than selected as offerings for the church fête. There were also some unwieldy lupins, uprooted by a thoughtless donor, which I was struggling to separate into portable sizes when I was greeted by a familiar voice.

'Ah! Mary Ruth. So this is where you are hiding, is it?' It was Martha Bold bearing a box of thyme cuttings, sensibly potted in small fibre pots. 'I've a little contribution for your stall. Note that some of these are golden thyme and charge more for them. They are all well rooted.'

She glared at the mint and the lupins and went on, 'You must get Connal to do that dividing. You are not making a job of it and furthermore you are getting yourself filthy. And what, may I ask, are you doing with that gold bracelet on? You'll only have yourself to blame if you lose it among all this earth. Shall I fetch Connal for you?'

'Yes please, Martha,' I said. She sniffed as she looked over my other offerings and then set off to find Connal.

My uncle arrived next and bought two of the geraniums. 'Martha has gone to find Connal for me,' I told him.

'I met her,' he said. 'She'll hunt him down. Arthur is trying to win the whisky on the tombola. Their boys are coming for a visit next month. He's so excited it's not true. They must be doing well to be able to leave their farm in August.'

'It is winter in Australia,' I said.

Alec tried to stand the mint up. 'Have you got a bucket of water? It'd look more appetizing if it wasn't so droopy.'

'It's a fine day. The Lord be thanked,' murmured Dennis, the rector, as he came round the corner of the greenhouse. 'Mr Phimister asked me to bring your float, Mary Ruth. Two pounds in ten pences. How good of you, as always, to look after this stall. It's very out of the way.'

'Oh, but it's well signed,' said Alec.

I said, 'I'll be busy enough, Dennis, and it's better than the stramash at the cake stall.'

He laughed, bought one of Martha's thyme plants and left.

It was also a good place to be because I didn't want to be caught up in local tittle-tattle which might lead to inquiries about the goings-on at Fionn-glass. All Mr Charles's team, and the voluble Mr Esau, would not have gone unnoticed in the village.

Alec and I struggled to separate the lupins and managed to price all the plants and cuttings before the first customers arrived. By the time Connal came we had sold most of our offerings.

'I'm sorry Mary Ruth,' he said. 'I've been in the walled garden. Mrs Bold said you needed me.'

'We managed thanks, Connal. How did your garden tours go?'

'Very well, but then they always do.'

He was glad to see my uncle and while I tried to sell a child with only five pence one of the fat little cactuses donated by Miss

Roland, five of which were unsold, they started in to talk and Connal lit his pipe.

'I'll take over the plants, Mary Ruth. You go and see who all's here,' said Alec. 'I'd like fine to have a news with Connal.'

I could hardly refuse so I set off warily.

As I rounded the house I met Angus and Bella accompanied as ever by his uncle Angus. Bella is a second cousin of Mrs Inglis and was all questions. 'Have you had the inventory? Are you clearing out the attic? Is it going to the sales? Uncle helped carry that lot up there at the beginning of the war. Didn't you, Angus?'

The old gardener laughed, showing all three of his top teeth.

'Mighty hard work it wis too. Mirrors and sideboards and boxes and boxes of breakables. Well, that's whit we wis tellt. I wis called up a month later. Life wis easier in the army!' This was obviously an old family joke and he roared again.

'They're saying in the village there's more than the attic being sold,' Bella went on.

'They'll say onything in the village,' cackled the old man, thoroughly enjoying himself. 'They've been saying Daldrum Castle is to be a holiday camp.' He laughed so hard at this he began to cough and Bella was distracted and beat him on the back.

'More like an army camp, Uncle Angus,' I said, 'which is what it was once.' He started to bellow with laughter again as I left them with a mumbled remark about my fruit loaf.

As I rounded the corner I could hear great raucous coughs coming from him and Bella, no doubt preparing to beat him again saying, 'Steady, now, Angus.'

I met Mr Rennie the head teacher and Dr McPherson the minister, who both asked after Kenneth. As we were speaking Arthur Bold came over to us and Mrs Gordon and her mother went by waving a greeting. I could see Martha over by the veranda talking to Douggie and Stella.

The sun was shining and everywhere I looked I could see people I knew. Donald Molloch, watched by Fred and Helen, was aiming at the bull's-eye on the archery pitch. Miss Roland was making a stately progress greeting everyone. She was accompanied by the rector. Colonel Fraser-Gordon was still selling tombola tickets with undiminished volume.

'Did you win the whisky then, Arthur?' I asked, turning to him.

'Na,' he grunted. 'Jist this auld wifie's graip.' He held out a lady's half-sized garden fork to show us.

Dr McPherson laughed and said, 'Well, Arthur, you know what they say about working hard and living sober. You'll be able to do both now.'

We all laughed and then Mackie from the pub, who had just won a half-bottle of brandy on the tombola, joined us saying, 'I can't get away from the stuff.' Mr Rennie congratulated him and then he and the minister moved away. Mackie said, 'Well, is it to be Daldrum Castle or Fionn-glass House for the time-share development, Mary Ruth?'

'Oh, don't ask me,' I said. 'Time will tell.'

'No one would want to go to Daldrum, surely?' said Arthur.

'What's wrong with it?' asked Mrs Phimister, as she joined us. 'My cousin Agnes has been housekeeper there for thirty years. It's a fine dry building.'

'It may well be,' said Arthur, 'but would you want to go there for your holidays every year?'

'I spent all my holidays there as a child. My aunt was housekeeper there before Agnes.'

'There's no answer to that, Arthur,' chuckled Mackie.

'No answer to what?' asked Martha as she approached.

'Whether we think Daldrum would make a good place for holiday homes, you know, a time-share set-up,' said Mackie.

'Daldrum!' said Martha. 'Daldrum! For time-share? You're joking. No one would want a share of that place. There are hundreds of better places for a holiday.' She paused, and as we stood silently digesting this she added firmly, 'You'd never get me there for one.' Thus, having made herself clear, she turned to Arthur. 'We'd better get weaving, Arthur, if you want to catch Donald Molloch. I see he's finished disporting himself with the bow and arrow and you'll not rest, I know, if you don't speak to him.'

To me she said, 'Alec has sold your plants for you, Mary Ruth, and—' lowering her voice significantly she mouthed at me, '—disposed of the unwanted you-know-what!' I must have looked surprised, because she leaned towards me next and hissed, 'Cactuses,' then resuming her usual powerful tones she went on, '. . . and he wants to be off soon. Daldrum Castle, indeed!' She added witheringly as she turned to Mackie. 'You'd have more chance persuading folk to holiday in the prisons at Peterhead.'

Accompanied by Arthur, she left us. I was anxious to escape any more inquiries from Mackie about time-share development in the area, so murmuring 'fruit loaf' I made for the now empty baking stall.

Here I found Mrs Smart, frugal, patient and hard-working as ever, picking the drawing pins out of the sheet over the stall with a knife. I think she has used the same drawing pins for the last forty years. She has a little tobacco tin to keep them in. She had saved me a fruit loaf for which I thanked her and paid her. She took the opportunity to sell me a strip of raffle tickets.

'Twenty-five pence each, or a pound a strip,' she said brightly, and without asking me how many I wanted, tore a strip off and held out her hand for my money.

'That's the way,' boomed Miss Roland from behind me. 'You may just be the lucky one, Mrs Findlater. I'm about to draw the raffle.'

'I've never won a raffle in my life,' I protested.

'Well, maybe your luck has changed. I'm ready when you are, Rector,' she said to Dennis, and nodded regally to him.

'I'll just ask the colonel how much longer he'll be, if you'll excuse me,' he said softly and walked across to him.

'Not many of the old school left,' Miss Roland said. I wasn't sure whether she meant our polite rector or the hectoring colonel. I didn't need to wait long. 'Lord Donald should be here today, and his wife. There's no way to keep up standards if the County don't bother. I heard he was coming for Easter, but then cried off at the last minute. Silly time of the year to be coming here anyway.'

She paused. I smiled weakly. I couldn't think what to say. 'June's the month!' she announced loudly. 'Nowhere better in the world in June. You can keep your Monte Carlos and your Egypts,' she added fiercely to me, though I still had not spoken. 'Scotland's the place to be in June and he knows it. Not your fault, of course, Mrs Findlater,' she conceded with a nod, 'you just have to do as you are told, but you will notice what a fine example the colonel sets.' She turned to where the colonel was still impersonating a showground barker. 'Fine man. Fine example.'

Drawn at last from the tombola, the colonel clapped his hands and drew the attention of the company to the raffle with one more sterling cry. Escorted by the rector, Miss Roland moved into the centre of the circle of people who were searching for their tickets in their pockets and bags.

The raffle was drawn with much applause for the winners. The first small prizes went quickly and then the big ones were heralded and shown off to the crowd. The big basket of fruit went to Mrs Phimister who smirked as she collected it from Miss Roland. The chocolates were presented to Eileen Malcolmson, the policeman's wife, and the sherry went to Donald Molloch who looked disappointed. Finally the whisky, a bottle of Grouse, was drawn for, and to my surprise I had won it. With Mrs Smart chivvying me and clutching my bag and my fruit loaf I went into the middle of the circle of the clapping folk to collect it.

'Lucky for some!' snorted Miss Roland.

'Well done,' barked the colonel. I thanked them and retreated.

'We'll know where to come now,' said Arthur with a little smile, and I was about to invite them to come for a dram when he was called to heel by Martha and they set off to find my uncle to go home.

'That's a fine win,' said Fred, grinning at me.

Helen added, 'He won some bath salts at the Scout Fair once, they turned me green.'

'Didn't improve the old bath either,' chuckled Fred.

'Oh! Get on with you,' Helen laughed adding, 'I've to get on myself, Mary Ruth, I start at five, but I want a word with you about Jean.'

She sounded worried. 'There's nothing wrong is there?' I asked.

'Lovesick, the poor lass,' said Fred and earned another rebuke.

Ina, who had popped out of the shop, came over to us.

'I'm just telling Mary Ruth about Jean. They're to be married in September,' said her aunt, 'and she cannot find a house for love nor money. I was wondering if the North Lodge might be a possibility and how I would set about finding out.'

'It's not Mary Ruth you want, it's the estate factor,' put in Fred.

'I know that, Fred,' said Helen. 'Away and talk to someone and don't hinder me.'

'We don't have a factor any more; Lord Donald rents the fishing to Colonel Fraser-Gordon and really I'm the only one to ask.'

'I know. Fred is living in the past. Well, what do you think?'

'It's not in very good condition.'

'That's what Douggie says, but it is a house. Do you think Lord Donald would rent it?'

'I doubt it,' I said truthfully. 'It would need a lot spending on it, but I could ask him for you. I'm afraid he won't be home until the end of August,' I added. She looked downhearted.

'That North Lodge is no place for a young couple to start life in,' said Ina firmly. 'It should have been pulled down years ago. Wouldn't you agree, Angus?' she added as the old man came by. 'Jean could do better than the North Lodge for a home.'

'Fairly aye, it wis niver much good when it wis lived in. Dark and crampit,' he agreed. 'She'd do better to try for one of thon mobile homes, over at Tillyknock. They've heaters and showers and everything. They're not cheap, but they're a damned sight better nor thon lodge.'

Bella and Angus had joined us. 'What lodge is that, Angus?'

'Thon North Lodge of Fionn-glass. Unfit for humans. Should be knockit doon,' the old man went on, adding, 'if His Highness hud haed to pay rates on it efter poor old Ellen moved oot, he'd hae knockit it doon then.'

What they would have said if I'd told them it was my future home I couldn't imagine, but I knew poor Jean and her young husband would have to double up with in-laws or go into a caravan like the rest of the newly-married couples round here.

Alec came to say farewell and Miss Roland offered the stallholders a cup of tea, prepared by Maureen, in the big kitchen. We were joined by Mr Phimister and the rector who proudly announced the takings.

'Up on last year,' he said, 'most gratifying.' He then thanked us all for our time and effort. The treasurer was much less pleased and cast a gloom over the proceedings, telling anyone who would listen how much the estimates were for the rectory roof repairs.

'You would think,' said Mrs Smart to me as we left, 'to listen to Mr Phimister, that he owned the church.'

'It's all his years of shopkeeping,' I said. 'He's never happy unless he can see a profit.' She looked at me coldly. I had obviously offended her, but I didn't know how.

Chapter 11

The rest of June did not fulfil its early promise, nor Miss Roland's staunch view of it as *the* month to spend in Scotland. I usually spend June working in the garden and as there was little point in gardening this year I had hoped to do some sunbathing and reading. However, chilly days were interspersed with wet ones and I spent my time packing up the pots and pans from the big kitchen and all the bedding and towels. I had arranged for them to go, with the other household goods of no interest to Carter's or Agostino's, to the sales in Esson in mid-July.

I took Napper for a couple of walks down to the North Lodge. It wasn't bad. It smelled dampish, but the weather was damp. The kitchen chimney had a good draught. The paper I lit in the grate burned up fiercely. There was a light in each room and a round-pin fifteen-amp socket in the kitchen and another one in the sitting room. There were no sockets upstairs.

It was dusty, but if I had really been going to live in it I thought I could have managed. Of course I went on the few dry days we had in June. To be honest, I wouldn't have cared to be there in the dark days of winter. It didn't get much sun even in midsummer and its plumbing was confined to a huge, stained, crazed china toilet bowl with a cracked wooden seat, crammed under the stairs. The only running water in the house was from a cold tap at the kitchen sink.

I spent the rest of my time sorting my papers, photographs and clothes and reading. Kenneth rang full of news. His exhibition was to be in Edinburgh in August and he was going to stay in Catherine and Allan's flat. Luckily, he was not coming up north to visit me. I promised to go to his exhibition, but when I would manage I wasn't sure, so much depended upon Agostino's.

My sister rang one evening towards the end of June and asked if she could come for the first few days of July. She was off to Brittany for the school holidays and thought I might like a quick visit. I told her I was going to Lerwick to see an old friend whose husband was working there. She said she was sorry to miss me and we parted amicably. I felt ashamed after I had hung up, not just of lying to her, but of the ease with which I had lied.

I received a letter from Carter's telling me the names of the men who would be coming to uplift the boxes. There was a stern warning to check their identity cards and an order to telephone if I had any doubts. All this care of the goods I was hoping to steal amused me no end.

Mrs Inglis's last Wednesday was beautifully sunny and we spent it turning out my kitchen and scrubbing the big sisal mat on the drying-green. We had our coffee outside and she told me about her coming holiday. She had plans to learn to swim to please her grandson.

'If it stays like this,' I said, 'you'll be able to swim every day.'

'I don't know whether I'll be able, however many days I try.'

'It's surprising what you can do if you are determined,' I said, thinking of my secret activities.

'That's what my husband says,' she replied. 'I've never tried to learn properly. It's not that I'm afraid.'

Oddly enough, looking back, I realize that I wasn't afraid either.

On the thirtieth of June, buying my paper after church, I met Douggie and Stella. They'd been to see her mother before going to Menorca. Douggie said, 'I'll be up this afternoon to give the grass a last cut.'

'It'll keep for two weeks,' I said. 'You'll have packing to do.'

'That'll be the day,' said Stella. 'Douggie packing his own bag! I hope I'm spared to see it, Mary Ruth. It'll be a great help to me if you'll keep him on the mower until supper-time.'

'That's us tellt,' said Douggie. He came at three, mowed until nearly six and his parting shot was, 'Isn't it just like a woman to arrange a holiday as soon as the weather improves?'

I was awake at four on Monday July the first. I lay for ten minutes and then I got up and took the dog for a walk. It was quite light and was going to be a scorching day. I made some fresh pancakes for the men. I had been told to expect them at eight. Sure enough, two big dark green vans drew up on the gravel sweep at the front steps at five to eight. There were four men and they presented me with their identity cards with much teasing about their companions' photographs.

'Would you buy a second-hand car from him?' was the first remark, and the general level of humour continued like this. I was so excited by their arrival and trying so hard to behave like a respectable careworn housekeeper that I thought they were first-class wits. I showed them the boxes in the hall and then the senior man after checking his lists asked for the attic.

'It's upstairs,' I said, and I thought that was witty too.

They accepted cups of coffee and my buttered pancakes and by ten they had emptied the hall. By twelve one van was ready to go. They all had lunch-packs and I made them some tea. Half an hour later I directed the first van down the north drive as the remaining men were loading the chairs from the attic. They had finished by three, and I sent them off by the west drive. I locked the door and went up to the attic. There was just one thing to attend to.

In the most inaccessible part of the attic, where the head tanks were, I had locked up the portrait of Lady Katherine in her sapphires and diamonds. I thought Miss Wauchop might find it strange that a family portrait was to be sold along with the forgotten treasures, the china and the silver. Old Lord Fionn-glass had taken the other family portraits and the crested silver to London after the war.

'Well, that's Carter's away,' I said to the portrait after I had unlocked the door. 'You're on your own now!' It was baking hot in the attic although the men had opened most of the skylights. I checked that everything had gone. It had. I closed the skylights and the doors and went downstairs.

On Wednesday Agostino's sent three pantechnicons. Two left on Wednesday night, four more came on Thursday morning and two more on Thursday afternoon. How those men worked! It was nearly six on Thursday before I signed the last ticket and directed the last van.

I went to close the doors of the bare and echoing rooms. There was nothing left to dust. The chandeliers had gone: the marble busts, the mirrors, the clocks, the pianos, the glass telephone box which fascinated everyone, had gone. The carved chairs, sofas, cabinets and tables had gone. There were no beds, no wardrobes, no dressing tables and not a single stool, bedside lamp or towel-rail left upstairs. No pictures hung on the walls: no curtains hung at the windows. No carpets, no rugs, no runners, not even a doormat was left. All I had to do now was wait for the money to roll in.

On Friday I sat in the garden all day reading in the sun. Napper lay at my feet and the cats came to inspect me as they went about their summer business. The hens were out and they took dust-baths in the mole heaps, foraged under the bushes and paraded after their new cockerel.

On Saturday I received a catalogue for Carter's china sale which was on the following Tuesday, and one for the silver sale in Perth on the Wednesday. At eleven I had a call from my uncle asking if I'd like to come out for lunch and go to his church garden party in Elgin. I went happily.

During the next four weeks I received fourteen sale catalogues from Carter's and Agostino's and read three novels which amused me at the time, though I can't remember what they were about. I drove to an evening barbecue at St Mary's at Knockglass, spent a day at the local agricultural show and endorsed eight cheques from Carter's for a total of £872,875 and sent them to the Edinburgh solicitors, Millichop and Millichop, for banking.

Sadly for her, though not for me, Mrs Inglis's daughter-in-law was stung by a rogue jellyfish at the end of their holiday and had such a violent reaction to the antidote that she was rushed into hospital. Mrs Inglis rang me to explain that she was staying at her son's house in Falkirk to look after the children and would let me know when she could come back to work.

In late July after the trades' fortnight holidays, the men came from Esson to collect all the household goods for their sale. They took the cart, the tractor, the tools and the big tricycles. Mrs Inglis rang again to say she would not be home until the end of August, for though her daughter-in-law was home she was still weak and needing help.

Douggie was back. He had little to say about Menorca except that the ground was stony. He spent his time edging the lawns, mowing, creating a new compost heap and hoeing the weeds on the gravel. A few vegetables began appearing on my draining board. We had tried beetroot this year. The total crop went in one pan and we ate them with our coffee.

'Pity they're so small,' he said, 'but they're fine and sweet.'

'They're lovely,' I agreed as we finished them.

'We might find a better place for them next year.'

'Yes,' I replied. I found remarks like this very trying. I still do not know whether Douggie knew that on the other side of the green baize door the house was empty. He never mentioned anything about the vans which had been noticed. 'Clearing the attics' had been the explanation in the village, Ina had told me in the shop.

Nor did Angus make any comment on the number of letters I received from Edinburgh and Glasgow from the auctioneers. Whatever they may have thought and whatever talk there was in the village, not one of my neighbours made reference to the coming sale of the house.

They must have known because I learned recently that some local tradesmen were being recruited by the new owner's contractors from Perth. Perhaps they thought I didn't know. More likely in their courteous way they were waiting for me to speak first. In the ordinary way we all commented on the government and the economy, aired our views on international questions and talked philosophically about crime and public morality, but a really serious matter like losing your home was obviously not considered a fit subject for gossip.

One day as we sat having coffee Douggie said, 'Would it not be wise to have a look at the North Lodge one day? I'm intending cutting the honeysuckle back and who knows, someone may be needing in.'

'Helen wanted me to ask His Lordship if he would consider renting it to Jean when she marries in September,' I said.

He picked this up at once and went on, 'It'll need rewiring and the lums will need sweeping. I'd be willing to look.' So we went together the next day.

'Tsch! Tsch!' Douggie hissed as we went in through the only door into the kitchen. 'Angus is right I doubt. It's not fit. Look there.' He pointed. In the corner were the remains of a woodpigeon. Investigating, we found an upper window open a crack.

'It never came through there,' I said in surprise.

Douggie sighed deeply and shook his head at me. 'It'll have come down a lum,' he said knowingly, but I noticed he hadn't mentioned the chimneys when we were in the kitchen. 'I was having a news with old Angus the other night,' he confided as we went downstairs. 'He says the roof leaks, but I dinna see ony signs myself. It seems dry enough up there.'

'It smelled very damp when I was here in June, when it was wet.'

'Bound to be, lying empty all these years.'

He looked under the stairs at the plumbing. He made no comment. He turned on the tap at the sink and when nothing happened bent down to find the stopcock. With a splutter, brown water dribbled into the flat stone sink.

'There'd be no using a washing-machine here,' he said. 'No

pressure at all.' Then he turned the tap off and bent to turn off the cock. 'There's one good thing, you'd surely go to the top of the council waiting list if you had to bide here.'

I thought for a minute he meant me, by 'you', but he didn't say any more. We walked around the outside and he shook his head at the state of the woodwork round the windows.

'It's better than nothing I suppose,' I said.

'It wants pulling down,' he said. 'Angus is right. D'you mind when Ellen bided here?' He shook his head and went on, 'Poor auld creature, lost her man in the Great War, put out here when they requisitioned the big house in the last one and if it hadn't been for Lady Mary, she'd have died here.' He didn't say anything else and I left him cutting back the honeysuckle which was hanging over the path. We never talked about the North Lodge again.

I went to Edinburgh for the opening of Kenneth's exhibition. It was well received by the critics, but more importantly he sold twenty pictures. We had two lovely days together and my high spirits went unnoticed by Kenneth because he was in such a state of excitement himself. He was busy for the three weeks of the Festival and yet anxious to go home to Marie-Claire whose baby was due at the beginning of September. I assured him that I would not be offended if he didn't manage to visit me, and was delighted when I reached Fionn-glass to find a letter from Agostino's.

All the furniture sales were complete and they were pleased to inform me that they had forwarded the sum of £881,652 to Millichop and Millichop. I was pleased too.

I was baking bread on the day before my sixtieth birthday when Mrs Inglis came into my kitchen. 'I'm back,' she said, 'though not to work today. The state my house is in it'll take me till next Wednesday to sort it. I've brought you a cake for your birthday and a card. How are you?'

'I'm very well, and thank you for the cake. Is all well now?'

'All's well in Falkirk. The children went back to the school Monday and Marjory is much better, but I don't think that man of mine has done a hand's turn since he came home.'

'Well never mind, there's nothing to do here. Will you have a cup of tea and a piece of fresh bread? The first batch is ready. I'm making extra to take to Alec tomorrow. He's invited me out for my birthday.'

We ate far more new bread than was sensible.

'My mother always called new bread "instant indigestion" but it's worth it,' she said. 'I think.'

'Did you learn to swim?' I asked, remembering.

'No. I can't say I learned, but I was getting the hang of it.'

'Well, there's always next year.'

'I'm not sure we shall be going to the seaside for a while,' she said, giving me an odd look. 'Poor Marjory's been desperately ill.' I felt embarrassed but decided to keep quiet, for fear of making things worse.

She went home at last, without going through to the house. I was exhausted. I knew all the money was at the solicitors, but I was waiting every day for the news that it was safely bestowed.

I knew His Lordship was due home any time. If he was quick he might be able to have it arrested. I couldn't expect Mrs Inglis to keep quiet once she saw that everything had gone. She wasn't stupid and it'd sound a weak story that I'd forgotten to tell her that everything was to be sold.

My birthday morning was sunny and warm. Angus arrived early at nine-thirty and gave me a bundle of mail. He wished me many happy returns.

'How did you know?' I asked.

'There's not much goes on hereabouts I don't know,' he said. 'I wish you well, Mary Ruth,' he added. 'Never you forget you've a lot of good friends in Balessie.'

'I won't, Angus.' He smiled and ambled back to his Ford. There was a letter from Millichop and Millichop. I opened it at once.

> I am happy to tell you that we have transferred the monies entrusted to us according to your instructions and have closed the account.

Their work was done, all I had to do was keep my mouth shut and my fingers crossed. Of course everyone knows now what I did with the money, but I was still afraid then that Lord Donald might be able to get it back. I hadn't liked to ask anyone legal, in case I raised suspicions. Anyway, this was a birthday present to remember.

I had cards from Uncle Alec, my cousin Verity who never forgets my birthday, my sister who was back at school after their summer in Brittany and a note from Kenneth enclosing a drawing from my four-year-old granddaughter, Sophie, of a tree with smiling faces painted on every leaf. I put them all on the mantelpiece in the kitchen next to Mrs Inglis's card, and went out for lunch.

Chapter 12

I reached home after my birthday lunch at half past four. Alec had taken me to a new vegetarian restaurant and his friends from Deeside were there too. They all made a great fuss of me. Martin was a fund of funny stories as always and we laughed all through lunch. I hadn't laughed so much for years or had such a lovely birthday party. I was nursing my crime and enjoying it. It would be a public scandal soon enough.

I let Napper out at the bottom of the west drive. He raced off ahead of me, making cursory stops and giving a quick glance at the car before bounding off again. I timed him once, and he can run at twenty-five miles an hour for about two hundred yards. If only I could have trained him to run straight I could have entered him in dog races. He doesn't even chase rabbits if he's in a running mood, but it is his acceleration which is most impressive. 'With one bound Jack was free' had taken on a new meaning for me since I'd watched Napper racing home.

Alec had given me an oil-painting which he had done of the harbour at Portsoy. I was looking forward to finding a place for it. I came round the last bend and there, in the yard outside my window, was a big silver Jaguar and a police car. I stopped next to it as Napper arrived at my feet.

'Well done,' I said to him and walked towards the door.

'Here she is, Malcolm; Mary Ruth, Mary Ruth!' It was Lord

Donald shouting first into the kitchen and then out of the window. 'We've been robbed,' he added as I passed the window, 'we've been robbed!'

As I walked through the back door he came out of my kitchen and pulled me by the arm along the passage into the main part of the house. Malcolm followed us saying, 'Hello, Mary Ruth. Happy birthday.'

'Hello?' snapped Lord Donald. 'Happy birthday? This isn't a social call, Malcolmson. We've been robbed, cleared out.'

We reached the hall. He threw out his arm dramatically and pointed to the great empty space. All the doors to the rooms stood open and the lowering sun lit up columns of dancing dust motes. It looked like a ballet set.

'Look! Look, Mary Ruth! It's all gone. Upstairs too. And the attics. And the stables. Every mortal fucking thing has gone. We've been done.' Then a new idea assailed him. 'When did you go out? Where have you been? How much of a start have they got? Roadblocks! Set up roadblocks! Don't just stand there like a stuffed dummy!' This last addressed to Malcolm.

Considering it had taken me over three months to empty the house, I couldn't help but smile at his suggestion that the whole place had been cleared since I had set off for lunch at half past ten. Malcolm cleared his throat and opened his mouth. 'I think roadblocks—' he began. He was interrupted by Lord Donald.

'You are not paid to think, Constable. Have I or have I not been robbed?'

'I don't know, sir. Perhaps Mrs Findlater knows something.'

This sensible remark set His Lordship off again. Only this time it was me he attacked. 'Well, since you are supposed to be my housekeeper, where is my furniture and for that matter my silver and my china and my pictures?' He paused for a moment and then flung his arm out towards the staircase and added, 'and where are my bloody stair-rods?'

'I've sold them, Lord Donald,' I said.

'Sold them! Sold them? Who to? Who told you to sell them? I

told you to get an inventory made. I didn't tell you to sell anything. Who's sold it all?'

'Well, Carter's—' I began.

'What!' Lord Donald glared at me, then he gave a little laugh. 'I thought for a minute you meant you had sold it all yourself.' He shook his head and then went on, 'I told them to value everything and prepare catalogues for the sales. But the furniture! They're supposed to be one of the top fine-art auctioneers in the world.' He snorted. 'Damn fools! I told them to leave the furniture. Well, they'll just have to bring it all back.'

He paused, lit a cigarette and said, 'My God, Mary Ruth, what a mix-up! I didn't mean you to let them take the stuff away at all until I had been through it.' He paced across the hall and then turned round to face us. 'Well, clever Carter's will have to bear the cost of bringing it all back. I'm selling the furniture with the house. I told them to get on as soon as poss, but I didn't expect this. I'll go and ring them now before they make any more mistakes.'

'They haven't made any mistakes, Lord Donald.'

'What do you mean?'

'I'm trying to tell you. I have sold everything.'

'You mean you have sent everything to Carter's salerooms.' He shook his head again. 'I suppose they'll expect me to pay for the storage,' he went on with a heavy sigh, then he looked at me and asked, 'Whatever possessed you, Mary Ruth? I spoke to some woman, and told her to cooperate with you to make an inventory of the stuff in the house.'

'I know and I told her to fetch the stuff and sell it.' Surely he would understand that.

'When was this?'

'April? May? Just when you went to the States.'

'You told Carter's to sell the stuff! By whose authority?'

'Well, mine.'

'Yours! What authority had you?'

'Your written authority to them.'

'Perhaps you should ring them up, sir,' put in Malcolm.

'When I want your advice, young man, I'll ask for it.'

I peeped at my watch. They'd be shut soon. I wanted to steer him off ringing them. The longer it took Lord Donald to unravel this the better.

He stood for a moment, thinking. Then he said, 'I can't follow this. You say you have sold everything through Carter's and that I gave you permission. In May? Have they sold it or is it in their stores?'

'No, it's sold.'

'Well, where's the money then?'

I didn't speak.

'Is it in the Household Account?' He sounded eager.

'No!' I said quietly.

'Let's go and sit down, shall we?' said Malcolm gently. 'Come along, Your Lordship. Perhaps I can get to the bottom of this.' He took out his notebook and then opened the door to my quarters.

We all went soberly down the passage and into my kitchen. We sat down round the table and looked at each other.

'When was the furniture uplifted, Mary Ruth?' asked Malcolm.

'In July.'

'When in July?' snapped Lord Donald.

'The first.' If he thought everything had been taken in one day I'd give him a day.

'Please, Lord Donald,' said Malcolm, 'let me try to find out what has happened. Was everything taken that day?' he continued.

'No!' I said.

'What other days did vans come?' he went on making a note.

'You ought to know that,' said Donald. 'You are the representative of the law round here, aren't you? You are supposed to keep an eye on property, aren't you? Even you can hardly have missed fifty huge removal vans.'

'Please sir,' said Malcolm, demoting His Lordship again as he reverted to his official language, 'may I suggest that as this is a very serious matter you allow me to proceed with my questions. I would recommend a cup of tea in these circumstances. Perhaps

Mrs Findlater would make us one.'

'Tea! TEA?' shouted Lord Donald at Malcolm. 'Is that all you coppers can think about? That and driving about the countryside in your panda cars? I suppose you were drinking bloody tea when the vans were driving away with my furniture. Well it's not good enough.'

Turning to me he went on, 'Where's my stuff gone? What have you done with the money? Answer me, woman, answer me! Don't sit there as if butter wouldn't melt in your mouth. What have you done with my furniture?'

Malcolm stood up and said, 'I'm sorry, Lord Donald. I cannot permit you to shout at Mrs Findlater like this. If you don't want to sit quietly and have a cup of tea and let me question her properly I must ask you both to accompany me to the station.'

'You won't permit me to ask my own housekeeper in my own house – or have you sold that too?' he snapped at me. 'Just who do you think you are, Constable – "Happy-Birthday-Mary-Ruth" – Malcolmson? Tell me that?'

'I am an officer of the Northern Constabulary ordered by my superior officer to accompany you, at your request, to investigate a possible theft of furnishings from your premises.'

'Don't come that talk with me, you jackanapes! Possible theft! The place is empty! I've been robbed. She has admitted that she's sold it. What more do you want? I insist that you arrest the woman.'

'I can't do that, sir, without—' Malcolm began.

'Can't? Can't? There is no such word as *can't*. Either you arrest her or I'll do it myself. I'll make a citizen's arrest. And,' he added viciously, 'I shall report you to the Chief Constable.'

'I cannot arrest Mrs Findlater, Your Lordship, without cautioning her and charging her.'

'Well, you know how to do that, I take it? Or are you just employed to play the pipes in the police band?'

Long after this I heard that when Malcolm had been asked by his sergeant if there had been any difficulty with His Lordship, he had answered, 'His Lordship was a little ruffled'.

Malcolm made one more attempt to explain. 'Lord Donald, so far I have only one statement from Mrs Findlater,' he raised his notebook and gave it a little shake. 'That statement amounts to "not all the furniture was uplifted on the first of July". No one who has seen this house would need to be told that. There is a lot more I need to ask her.' He looked sternly at him and said emphatically, 'Once Mrs Findlater is cautioned and charged she has the right to remain silent,' then for good measure he added, 'and she can then refuse to answer any more questions.'

I suppose I knew this, but after Malcolm had said it I hoped Donald would press him to arrest me. After all the trouble I had taken to sell the contents of the house I didn't want to see Donald getting his hands on the money. Sequestration I think it's called. Silence was my best safeguard. Bless you Malcolm, I thought. You are a good man.

This was not the view of Lord Fionn-glass.

'Officer!' he spat. 'I insist that you arrest this woman. She has admitted selling my furniture. I shall soon find out where she's hidden the money. I am not without influence. I'll find out where she's hidden it if I have to tear this place apart with my bare hands. We're not talking peanuts, you know, the contents of this house are insured for a quarter of a million pounds. Do you understand me? And by God, I'll sue those fools at Carter's for every penny they've got.'

Right behind him on the mantelpiece I could see the edge of the letter from Millichop and Millichop which had come that morning. I had nothing else in the house which would connect me with them. I had destroyed all the other correspondence I'd had from them and from Carter's, Agostino's and the firm in Esson.

Malcolm said, 'It's my duty to make it clear that it would be best for me to question Mrs Findlater at the station, before cautioning her and charging her.'

'It's your duty to protect my property for that matter and what you think best is of no interest to me. I can look after myself. I insist upon my rights. Arrest this woman.'

Malcolm turned towards me and said, 'Mary Ruth Findlater, I must caution you that you do not need to say anything, but anything that you do say will be taken down and may be used in evidence against you. I charge you with the theft of the contents of Fionn-glass House, the property of Lord Fionn-glass.' He smiled apologetically at me and asked, 'Do you understand?'

Before I could speak, Lord Donald said, 'Oh! don't worry about that, she's smart enough.' He groaned and clutched his head. Then he looked at me and said, 'I'm amazed at you, Mary Ruth. Amazed! After all these years when I've trusted you, depended on you, admired you.'

I had a sudden vision of the lavatory bowl in the North Lodge.

'You're a disappointment to me. I suppose it's your hormones,' he added. Then as he stood up he said to Malcolm, 'Take her away. I'm going to start the wheels turning.' He lit another cigarette and added nastily, 'I presume, Malcolmson, that you are capable of getting her to the police station and locking the door behind you. I'm going straight to the Chief Constable.' He swung round and left.

Malcolm sat down, opened his notebook and started to write. When he had finished he looked up at me and said, 'I don't know what to say, Mary Ruth.'

'It's a fair cop, Malcolm,' I said. 'I'll come quietly. You won't need the cuffs.'

'For the love of God, Mary Ruth, don't say things like that,' he blurted out.

'But it's true Malcolm. I did it.'

'I'm not wanting to hear another word and *please* don't pop up in court and say,' – he affected a girlish voice – 'the first thing I said after I was charged was, "It's a fair cop, Malcolm".' He sighed and shook his head. 'I'm going to be in the clart with the sarge as it is. I couldn't refuse to arrest you when Lord Donald insisted, but the fact that I didn't question you properly will be laid at my door. I promise you, Mary Ruth, there'll be real trouble for me if you ever say that again.'

'I was joking, Malcolm. But it's true. I did do it.'

'Mary Ruth,' he leaned over the table and took my hand, 'I won't stop being your friend whatever you have done, but I have just written in my note book *When charged, the accused said nothing*. If you start joking in court I may lose my job. Someone's head will have to roll. My superiors will be out for blood, especially with the Chief Constable breathing down their necks. Lord Fionn-glass does have friends in high places.'

He looked at his notes, shook his head and said, 'The first question every lawyer asks is, "When charged, what did the accused say?" I've written down *Nothing*. I can't alter it or rub it out. They rewrite police notebooks in some places, as I'm sure you know, but not here. Please try to understand.'

He looked so serious and worried that I said, 'I'm sorry Malcolm, I'll not say it again. And anyway I didn't say that after you had charged me. I couldn't get a word in for Donald Duck.'

He smiled. 'I wouldn't say that again either, but thanks. Now we must get organized. What's the time? Ten past five. You'll need a lawyer to go to court with you tomorrow morning in Elgin. They'll keep you in the police cells overnight.'

'My case is packed. It's over there.'

He smiled. 'There's efficiency. Do you have a lawyer?'

'Well, not really, but I know Mr Field in Elgin.'

'Well, if I were you I'd ring him now. I don't know what time the office closes, but you might just catch him.'

'Oh! But he's retired, the one I know.'

'There'll be someone there. Now get on. You will have to ask him to come to the police cells in Elgin to see you.'

I didn't argue any more, but I couldn't see why I needed a solicitor at all. I knew I had committed a crime. I had admitted it. What more did they want? What a lot I had to learn.

They answered promptly at Youngson, Dean and Field and I started to explain who I was. I was put through to 'young' Mr Field, and told him I had been arrested for the theft of Lord Fionn-glass's furniture. He wanted to know what time we'd be there. I turned to ask Malcolm.

'Shall I speak to him?' I nodded. He came to the phone. 'Police Constable Malcolmson, one-three-two, Glass Division, here, sir. I hope to have Mrs Findlater at the station by seven.' There was a pause and then he said, 'She made no reply, sir.' Then after another pause, 'She's an uncle stays in Elgin. Yes, that's him. I think so too. Thank you, sir.'

He hung up and said to me, 'Mr Field's first question, for no prizes: "When charged, what did she say?" Now do you believe me?'

'Yes, Malcolm. What was all that about my uncle?'

'He asked if you had any family nearby. You'll almost certainly be held for two weeks. Will your uncle take Napper?'

'I'd rather ask Douggie. It's safer there. He's well off the main road. I must turn off the Aga too, and then I'll get the dog's lead and food bowls and basket. I'll have to leave cat food outside for the cats, Malcolm. I'm sure Douggie will feed them when he comes, but they know how to live off the land.'

'Right, Mary Ruth, I'll put the basket and your case in my car.'

While he was gone I organized some cat food and put all the milk in the fridge into a bowl. I was rinsing the milk bottle as he returned. I hadn't thought about the letter from Millichop and Millichop, which would be such a help to the police, because I was concentrating on familiar domestic duties. There it sat, tucked among my cards on the other side of the kitchen. I handed Malcolm the bowl of milk and I carried the dishes of cat food. At the back door we placed the bowls in a row on top of the peat-bunker.

'Better close the window,' he said. 'Someone might break in.'

We both burst out laughing.

'Come on, Mary Ruth,' said our local representative of the law as he put his arm round me and ushered me into the house. In the kitchen he locked the window and I collected my handbag. 'Anything else?' he asked. 'Honestly, Mary Ruth, I can't believe this is happening.'

'Is the front door locked?' I asked.

'Yes, we came in through your door. The Aga off?'

'Yes, I've done it. Well, that's it then,' I said. He started moving towards the door. 'Malcolm,' I said hesitantly, 'will you take the cake Mrs Inglis brought me and give it to Eileen and the boys? It's a pity to let it go to waste. And may I take my birthday cards?'

'Yes to both,' he said, picking up the cake tin from the sideboard as I pointed it out. He opened the lid and peeped in.

'Thank you,' I said and gathered up my cards and the letter and put them in my bag.

I sat in the front seat of the police car and Napper jumped into the back and sat in his basket. Malcolm locked my back door and as he sank into his seat he said, 'Do you mind if I have a smoke? I'm fair scunnert with all this.'

'Of course not,' I said. I was wondering if they'd search my bag at the police station and what I could do with the letter in it. It hardly seemed sensible to shove it down the seat of the police car.

Malcolm offered me his packet of cigarettes and his lighter. 'Would you like one too?' he asked me.

'No, thanks,' I said. 'I stopped seven years ago.'

'Seven years, three months, two weeks and a day?' He laughed as he told the old smoker's joke. He started to put the packet and lighter into his top pocket.

'And half an hour,' I said, suddenly thinking how useful his lighter would be. 'I will have one, Malcolm,' I said quickly, 'I need something.' He fished them out and handed them to me. I lit one slowly. Douggie's house is on a corner. Parked just round that corner I would be out of sight. 'Do you mind taking Napper into Douggie's for me?' I asked Malcolm. 'I don't really feel up to explaining that I'm under arrest. I don't want to speak to anyone just at present.'

'Nae bother,' said Malcolm, adding, 'I'll park just round behind the hedge and I'll not tell them you're there. Don't worry.'

I knew they'd be in, so as soon as Malcolm had taken Napper on his lead with his basket and food, I pressed the button to open the car window. As the engine was off the button wouldn't work. For a moment I panicked, then I opened the door and lit the letter from Millichop and Millichop with Malcolm's lighter. It burned well and I lit the envelope from it as I listened for Douggie's door. It was well alight when I heard Malcolm saying: 'Of course I will, Douggie, thanks.'

I undid my safety belt and was stamping out the flames with my left foot as Malcolm came crunching down the path. I shut the door smartly, refastened my belt and was lighting my second cigarette in seven years as he climbed back into the car.

'That's all right, Mary Ruth – and I remembered to ask him to feed the cats.' He sniffed absently as he fastened his seat belt. My little fire was out, I hoped. I daren't look. 'He's a real gentleman is Douggie,' he went on as he turned on the ignition. 'Not like some we could mention. He didn't even ask me why I had brought Napper. He just said, "Tell Mary Ruth that guid folk are scarce."'

'He's probably the best friend I have, Malcolm.'

He grinned and said, 'I hope Kenneth will still be mine when I tell him my part in this astonishing business. Ready then? Next stop the cop shop!'

Chapter 13

My bag was examined closely at the police station. I was signed in, allowed to use the toilet and then locked up in a cell which was too hot. After half an hour I was given a bacon sandwich and a mug of tea. At ten to eight I was collected and taken to a basement interview room.

Here, looking worried and old, I saw my uncle Alec. 'Oh! Mary Ruth,' he said holding out his arms to me, 'whatever is going on?' I hugged him and found I was weeping.

'How good of you to come, Alec.'

'There, there,' he said, 'don't greet. Let me look at you. Here, use my hanky. Dry your eyes. This is Mr Field, he came to tell me what he knew and that's precious little.'

I shook hands with Mr Field. He was sturdier than his father and not so tall, but he had his long slender fingers. 'Shall we sit, Mrs Findlater?' he asked, and we sat down at the table. 'I am Henry Field,' he went on. 'I don't think we have met before, but I believe that you know my father. I asked your uncle to come this evening as there may be matters at home that will need dealing with. I'm sure you will understand that I am only here to deal with legal matters on your behalf.'

I nodded.

'We are alone, as you can see. Anything we talk about will be confidential.'

'Thank you for coming.'

'Mrs Findlater, I understand that you have been charged with the theft of the contents of Fionn-glass House, Fionn-dhruim, by Balessie, the property of Lord Fionn-glass.'

'That's right, I did steal them and I've sold them.'

'What have you done with the money?'

'Oh, I'm not telling, but I am guilty.'

'Not quite so fast, Mrs Findlater. It is not up to you to confess at this stage. Tomorrow I shall enter "No plea or declaration" on your behalf before the Sheriff and ask for bail, which you may not get. We shall be called about ten thirty I expect, and I think you will be remanded in custody for two weeks. You will not be held here, but in the women's section in the prison at Inverness. After that, depending on the police evidence placed before the Fiscal, you may be released on bail until the case comes to court. This could take a few months and the case may go to the High Court. If it does you will need a barrister, but we can deal with that later. Do you understand?'

'No. I have already admitted to His Lordship that I have sold the contents. I am guilty. Why can't I plead guilty tomorrow?'

'That is simply not how it is done. There has to be time to allow the evidence to be presented to the Fiscal and then time for him to decide whether to prosecute.'

'Well, it's a waste of time and money. I'm prepared to admit I did it. I realize I'll be put in prison, but I'm resigned to that.'

Mr Field sighed and looked at me. 'Mrs Findlater, this is a very serious charge. You may be sent to prison for a long time. You would not like it in prison. No one does. You must allow me to guide you. As your lawyer I have a duty to advise you. You rang and asked me to come here tonight and I have come. Now please let me try to explain again.' He leaned forward across the table, placing his hands in front of him, and looked into my face.

'Tomorrow morning we shall go before the Sheriff. He will ask me after the charge has been read to speak on your behalf. I shall make no plea – that is, I shall neither say that you plead guilty nor shall I say that you plead not guilty. This is a mere formality. They cannot try you without evidence. The police need time to collect it. The Fiscal needs time to decide whether you have broken the law at all and if you have, which court is most appropriate for your trial. Are you following me?'

'I suppose so.'

'I shall make no declaration, that is I shall make no statement nor any observation whatsoever.'

'Why can't I plead guilty and get it over with?'

'You can plead guilty if you wish, if and when we go to trial. You cannot, however, be tried on your own confession alone. They will need, for example, to know where the money is.'

'But I'm not prepared to say.' He looked down at his notes.

'Mary Ruth,' said Alec gently. 'You are in custody. You are not able to call the tune. Mr Field is trying to help you. You surely don't think the Sheriff would sentence you tomorrow just because you upped and said, "I done it, it's a fair cop, guv"?' He shuddered.

'That's funny, Alec, I said that to Malcolm. He nearly had a fit.'

'Who is Malcolm?' asked Mr Field quietly.

'The arresting officer, PC Malcolmson,' Alec said. 'He was at school with Mary Ruth's son.'

Now it was Mr Field's turn to shudder. 'Was that the officer to whom I spoke on the telephone?'

'Yes,' I said. 'He told me the first thing you'd asked him was what I had said when charged.'

'And am I to understand, Mrs Findlater, that you said when you were charged, "It's a fair cop, guv"?'

'No, I said, "It's a fair cop, Malcolm," I know him, you see.'

He put his head in his hands. Then he looked up at me and said, 'Tell me the worst. The officer told me that you had said nothing.'

'That's right, I didn't have time. Lord Donald started shouting again and telling Malcolm to take me away and to lock the back door.'

'And then you said "It's a fair cop"?'

'Oh no, I didn't say anything, even when Lord Donald said it was my hormones.' They both looked at me in silence. On reflection I think I was in a state of shock and cannot have sounded coherent.

'Did Lord Donald hear you say it?' said Mr Field, looking down at his notes again.

'Oh! No. He'd gone by then. I didn't say anything until Malcolm had finished writing in his notebook. I was only joking, but he gave me quite a lecture about not using expressions like that. He said he couldn't alter his book and his superiors would have the Chief Constable breathing down their necks . . .'

Field didn't look happy, but he looked up. 'How does the Chief Constable come into it?'

'Lord Donald had gone storming off to see him.'

'You mean the first time you spoke was after Lord Donald had spoken and left the room and the officer had written in his notebook?'

'Yes, and Malcolm had spoken too. He said something like, "Oh, Mary Ruth", and I said, "It's a fair—"'

'Yes, yes, I think I understand now,' said Mr Field, rather peevishly, I thought. 'I must ask you to be circumspect in what you say. On no account are you to repeat that remark.'

'No, I won't. That's what Malcolm said.'

'Well, you didn't listen to him, Mary Ruth,' said Alec mildly. We all sat in silence for a moment. 'I think this is probably enough for tonight,' Alec said with a sigh, 'I know I'm tired and I'm sure Mr Field is too. Is there anything else, Mr Field?'

'I don't think so. I do have your undertaking, Mrs Findlater, I hope,' he went on, 'that in the morning in court you will not say anything.'

'Very well, but I am guilty and I shall plead guilty to the charge. I am not ashamed of what I have done.'

'Well, we shall see,' said Mr Field.

His smugness irritated me and I asked, 'What do you mean?'

He looked directly at me and said firmly, 'When you next come to court and the petition is read out, there may be mention of goods which you are accused of stealing which you did not steal. Surely you are not going to plead guilty to their theft?'

'How could that happen?'

'When valuable goods are stolen, Mrs Findlater, and I gather from the constable's report that His Lordship talked of a quarter of a million pounds worth of insurance—' I interrupted him.

'I got much more than that for them,' I said cheerfully.

They looked at each other.

'It has been known,' continued Mr Field, 'for the aggrieved person, that is the person from whom goods have been stolen, to' – he paused for a moment and drew a disapproving breath – 'to add to the list of stolen goods in order to obtain the maximum insurance.'

'But that's dishonest,' I said at once.

Mr Field gave a wry smile and Alec laughed and said, 'You are honest, Mary Ruth, that is why I believe you when you say you have stolen the contents of the house. Why you did it and what you have done with the money I can't imagine, but I know you are truthful as I have known you all your life. You must remember that Mr Field has only just met you and you don't know him either. He will have much experience of dishonesty and I'm sure what he says is a possibility.

'Donald will be furious and his wife won't be best pleased, especially if it turns out that he was grossly under-insured. He will employ good lawyers who may well dig a pit for you. You are intelligent enough to have hidden the money cleverly, I am sure, but they will search for it, just as the police will.'

He paused, and he and Mr Field exchanged glances. 'However clever you have been though,' went on my uncle in his soft voice, 'you know nothing about the process of the law and I strongly recommend that you let Mr Field advise you. There is no point in having a dog and barking yourself.'

'I have often heard that expression,' said Mr Field, smiling for the first time, 'and believe me, if people would leave matters they do not understand to the professionals, life would be easier all round.'

I thought about poor Malcolm trying to question me as Lord Donald interrupted and shouted so rudely. He had been very patient and polite and I knew from seeing detective stories on the telly that the answers to early questions were the springboard of the investigation. What had I told him? That I had instructed Carter's to sell the goods and not all of them were taken away on July the first. It wasn't much. Miss Wauchop would soon tell the police that they hadn't handled the furniture. I hadn't thought what would happen after the crime. I had half expected to be sent to prison at once. Alec was right, I didn't know anything about the law, though I seemed to have created months of work for the various officers of the law. I must make my apology to Mr Field. In my own way I had been as obstructive and as rude to him as Lord Donald had been to poor Malcolm.

'Mr Field,' I said, 'I am sorry if I have seemed ungrateful or rude in any way. The truth is, as my uncle has just said, that I know nothing about the workings of the law. I am beginning to realize that. I can see too that my activities were only the first part of the story. I will pay attention to you properly and I will be quiet in court tomorrow.'

'This has been a trying time for you, I realize. I accept your apology.' He spoke graciously. 'Thank you. Believe me, clients have been much ruder to me on occasion. It is small comfort to know that nearly everyone seems to be rude to policemen when they are performing the less pleasant duties that fall to them. I gather, even from the little you have said, that Lord Fionn-glass was none too polite to Constable Malcolmson.'

'He was downright rude.'

'Now,' said Mr Field, 'although it is late, I think there are one or two things you should know. You will have time to digest them during the next few days. After court tomorrow I shall not have time to talk to you if you don't get bail. I will come to Inverness next week, but hear me out and it may help to set your mind at rest.'

He settled back in his chair, and I sat up and paid attention. The atmosphere between us now was much better and I could see Alec relaxing and looking less worried.

'Until we see the charges brought against you, we do not know what the best plea will be,' Mr Field said. He leaned forward and added very gently, 'Even if you do decide to plead guilty I can prepare a plea in mitigation for you.'

'By implying I'm potty,' I put in.

'That is not the term I would use myself, but I would remind you that it is a lot more pleasant to attend a weekly clinic and talk to a doctor than it is to go to prison, Mrs Findlater. Remember too that the law deals less harshly with a first offender. Lastly, I'm afraid the law is complicated.' He leaned back and said to both of us, 'About all lawyers can do is to keep their clients from making things worse for themselves.'

'Sobering, isn't it?' I said.

'Very well put, if I may say so,' said Alec to Mr Field. 'You are lucky Mary Ruth, to have Mr Field to act for you. I'm very grateful to him for letting me be a fly on the wall. He asked me to come tonight so that I could deal with matters at home. Where is Napper?'

'He's at Douggie's and he's going to feed the cats, but I never mentioned the hens to him.'

'I'll see to that, and I'll get Mrs Inglis to collect a change of clothes for you. By the sound of this you may be remanded again in two weeks. Tell me just one thing before we go: did you really sell everything in that house?'

'I sold everything,' I said.

'Is that great house completely empty?' Alec marvelled. 'Do you know Fionn-glass House, Mr Field? It's enormous. Every single thing gone. I can hardly credit it.'

'There's the portrait in the attic. I left that. It was of Lord Donald's grandmother. Oh! Alec, she was wearing my jewels,' I sobbed suddenly. 'The whole set. The tiara and my choker, earrings and bracelets. I don't know why I didn't burn it. What will happen when he finds it? They are mine, aren't they?'

Before Alec could speak, poor Mr Field raised a puzzled face to me. 'What jewels are these, Mrs Findlater?'

Alec and I explained about the sapphires given to my mother-in-law by Lord Donald's uncle. We told him that she had kept them a secret from her husband and that she had left them to me. Finally Alec said, 'Mary Ruth won't have them until she's sixty-five.'

'Why did the previous Lord Fionn-glass give these jewels to your mother-in-law?' asked Mr Field.

'Well,' said Alec, 'we can only assume because he was the father of her son, Mary Ruth's husband. The present Lord Fionn-glass is his nephew, the old boy never married.'

'What are these jewels worth?' Mr Field asked me.

'Your father said they'd be worth ninety thousand pounds, in five years.'

'What happens if you die before you are sixty-five?'

'They go to Kenneth.'

'Who is Kenneth?'

'My son.'

'Where are the jewels now?'

'In your father's safe.' He blenched and shook his head slowly from side to side.

'I'll speak to him about this.' He paused for a few moments and I thought he was finished at last, but then he said, 'Did you act entirely on your own, Mrs Findlater?'

'Of course I did.' I was annoyed. 'I know what I'm doing.'

'Well since I don't know what you're doing and you have refused to say what you have done with the money, I was thinking that perhaps your son might have been involved. Maybe he sees himself as the true heir,' Mr Field said briskly.

'I find that suggestion offensive,' I said, 'and insulting. If my son had suggested stealing the contents of Fionn-glass House, I'd have 'shopped' him. I brought him up to be honest and he is, as far as I know. Good God! You'll be suggesting Uncle Alec here was in it next. The most unlikely thief in the world.'

I can't remember when I'd felt so angry. I'd had enough of the law for one day. I just hoped I could hold my tongue about the money.

Alec, who must have felt appalled at my behaviour when I think about it, suddenly said, 'The most unlikely thief in the world is surely Lord Donald himself?'

Mr Field looked at him and said thoughtfully, 'Now that is a possibility and not without precedent.' He sat silently for a while and then turning to me he asked sharply, 'He didn't persuade you to do it for a nice little pension abroad, did he?'

'Whatever next? Why on earth would he have done that?'

'I can think of lots of reasons,' said Mr Field.

I was beginning to dislike this man and be sorry I had asked him for help. I was guilty, I was prepared to pay the penalty. I was sickened by the implied suggestion that I was wicked enough to have involved my son in the robbery, and irritated that I was not considered capable of committing a crime without help.

He began to explain and by the time he had finished, I realized his arguments were sound and that made me even madder. He said that Lord Fionn-glass could have wanted to collect the insurance and have used me as the cat's-paw. He suggested that he might not have wanted his wife or his heirs to know how much money he was getting for the contents of the house. I was angry and upset enough when Alec joined in.

His suggestion was that I had might have colluded with the former Lady Fionn-glass, or with Julian. I listened to him with growing amazement. Why couldn't they just believe me? I had had enough.

'Stop!' I shouted and leaped to my feet. 'I have about twelve hundred pounds in the building society. Go and look. I have not got the money and I refuse to tell you where it is. Leave me alone.'

'Fair enough,' said Mr Field, 'but I may as well warn you now that if you are found guilty, the court will almost certainly take what money you do have, as compensation for His Lordship.'

'That's not fair!' I snapped.

'There's no justice in this life, Mary Ruth,' said Alec, laughing despite himself. 'Haven't I always told you? It's no good adopting that injured tone.'

Right then I disliked him too.

'May I tell you a little story?' said Mr Field. 'We mustn't part on this acrimonious note. It's been a hard day for us all.'

'It's my birthday,' I said, remembering. 'Thanks for my card, Alec.'

'May I wish you many happy returns,' said Mr Field, rising and holding out his hand. I shook it and we sat down, but I didn't smile. In his quiet voice he went on: 'Let me offer you this little story as a birthday present. It was told to our class by our criminal law tutor in our final term. We thought, young and green as we were, that he was being witty and seeking to amuse. He said, "Gentlemen, always make it clear to your clients what the law is about. The law is about statutes. It is about procedure. It is about evidence. What it most definitively is not about is justice. Get your clients to understand that and you will have happy clients, whatever the outcome of their cases."'

Alec roared with laughter and Mr Field beamed. I can't say it made me laugh, but it did make me think. They left me then, and I spent my first night in custody and I slept beautifully.

PART TWO

And Then . . .

Chapter 14

'Of course, no good ever comes of marrying out of your class,' said Colonel Fraser-Gordon to Lord Donald Fionn-glass as he sucked the last fragment of meat off the pheasant leg he was holding. He laid the bone down on his large turquoise and gold dinner plate, picked up his napkin and wiped his mouth and moustache with care. 'And it makes no odds whether it's marrying above you or beneath you. In any case, Mary Ruth comes from a good class of people. What on earth did she bury herself here for, for all these years? Marrying the gardener's son indeed, albeit an army man, and finishing up as a housekeeper. I'm surprised at that uncle of hers, the schoolteacher. He's a varsity man. He should have advised her.'

He paused and looked under the silver serving dish lid. There were two potatoes left. He gestured to Donald who shook his head. He replaced the lid thinking, I'll fry them up for breakfast. He waited politely until Donald had finished eating, saying, 'I know the world is changing. Down in London they don't seem to be bothering to marry at all any more, but up here we stick to the old standards.' He looked with pleasure down the long, highly polished table, nodding appreciatively at the gleaming silver and the shining tantalus on the walnut side-dresser. 'Nothing wrong with spit and polish and knowing your place.'

Donald Fionn-glass swallowed the last of his wine and placed the heavy goblet down on the lace-edged mat provided, to save any drips from spoiling the high polish of the Knockspindie dining table. He had come to his neighbour after leaving his bereft house, and willingly accepted the offer of dinner, a bed and the use of the telephone.

He had rung home first, to hear from Cook that his wife had gone shopping. She lives in the bloody shops, he had thought as he hung up. Then he had rung his lawyer. Fat comfort he had been. 'Don't forget the settlement date is the tenth of October. Even if the police can trace the money, it will take a long time for you to receive it.' Even if? Christ! Some help *that* kind of talk. 'And,' he had gone on, 'if it's a matter of insurance, it may take years.' Years! He hadn't got years. He had had three years to find the money for the settlement. He had been so pleased to find a purchaser for Fionn-glass House – and now this.

Looking at his guest with sympathy, though his brusque voice disguised his feelings, Colonel Fraser-Gordon repeated, 'Cheese. Cheese. Don't bother with dessert when I'm on my own. Will you have some cheese?'

'I'm sorry, F-G,' said Donald. 'Beg pardon. Bit preoccupied. Cheese would be grand.'

The colonel grunted as he took their plates to the serving trolley. 'Never seen the inside of the dishwasher. That's why they've kept their colour. Present to my parents on their marriage.' Donald's blank look as he turned back to collect the serving dishes alerted him. 'Sorry, tactless of me, mentioning heirlooms. Under the circumstances. Er, I'll fetch the cheese. In the pantry.'

As he left the dining room Donald thought to himself, Poor old fellow. He's not what he was. Be talking to himself next. Must be lonely here on his own since he retired.

'Never a dull moment here,' said the colonel returning with a large cheese-dish. 'What with meals on wheels, reading the lesson twice a month, sitting on the bench, the National Trust, the community council, not to mention the estate, though I'm lucky in my factor. Still going strong.' He removed the cover from the cheese-dish with a flourish and presented it to Donald. 'Bit of Stilton still good. Camembert's leaking all over the shop. Not my choice. Daughter-in-law here last week. Brings me the stuff. Misplaced kindness. Thinks I can't get decent cheese here. No problem at all. Have an order from Allison's in Elgin. First-class grocers.'

'I remember Mary used to say that. Years ago.' Donald stopped, overcome with pity for himself and for his former wife. He must have been mad. Dorinda was beautiful, but definitely a bimbo – a word whose real meaning he had only learned after finding himself married to one.

'How is Mary keeping?' asked the colonel gruffly, as he pushed the plate of oatcakes and the butter-dish towards his guest.

'Well, thanks,' replied Donald, spearing a slice of Stilton and putting it on his plate. But not as well as she will be when I've paid her a million pounds on the tenth of October, *when I have raised it*, he thought sourly. He buttered an oatcake, placed a piece of Stilton on it and raised it to his mouth.

'And, er, Lady Fionn-glass. She well too?' The colonel had only met Dorinda once. 'A fashion plate,' had been how he described her to his daughter-in-law.

'Fine thanks,' mumbled Donald through his cheese and oatcake. She hadn't sounded fine when he had managed to speak to her on the phone an hour before. 'Donald, I can't speak to you now,' she had complained, 'I'm fixing a false nail before I go to Miriam's exhibition drinkies at the Barbican. I caught my nail in Harrods and my cab is waiting.' Then, acknowledging his problem, she had added, 'I don't know what you are making such a fuss about. Surely the insurance will pay up?'

'Have a nice evening,' he had said. What else was there to say?

Folding his napkin neatly, the colonel inserted it into his monogrammed silver ring and said, 'If you'd like to go through to the drawing room, Donald, and put a match to the fire, I'll see about coffee. I expect Bill will be here in about half an hour. He was going to Elgin first to see the arresting officer.'

'Righto!' Donald replied. When he had arrived at Knockspindie at five o'clock to find the colonel feeding his dogs he had poured out his troubles. The colonel had rung the Chief Constable at once.

'Had lunch with him today in Inverness, as it happens,' he had said. 'Fine man is Donaldson, big Highlander with a soft voice. You know the type. Lot of them in the regiment. Stout chap. He'll see you right, will Bill.'

As he knelt in the drawing room and put a match to the fire Lord Donald felt renewed anger seeping through him. Life in Scotland used to be civilized, just as in this beautifully run house where everything was orderly and gracious. It was in London that you had to lock your doors and your windows, even upstairs.

His mind went back to his holidays during the war, when he and Kenny from the garden cottage had fished all night in the pools where old Joe had seen the big fish lying sunning themselves. He remembered how happy they had been as boys and how devastated he still felt that Kenny was gone, whenever he came to Fionn-glass.

He put a small log on the fire and stood up. How proud Kenny had been when he'd first brought Mary Ruth home. Whatever old F-G said, she had had a good life at Fionn-glass. Whatever had possessed her to steal everything? He sat next to the fire, thinking. A lot of what I had in the house I never looked at, to be sure, but to strip it, even taking the carpet-rods and clips from the staircase . . . He began to seethe again with righteous indignation.

'That's the way,' said the colonel's voice. 'Now the evenings are drawing in I like a fire. 'Course in winter I move into the little morning room. Cosy in there and gets what sun there is. Now: coffee.' He poured the coffee, offering cream and sugar and promising brandy when Bill arrived. 'Matter of fact I'm looking for an excuse to open a rather special bottle. Last of my father's Napoleon. Not sure it won't be wasted on Bill Donaldson, fine man that he is, but you will appreciate it, Donald.' He sat down opposite Donald at the fire and sipped his coffee.

Comfortable and warm and quietly digesting his dinner, Donald began to relax. He picked up a worn poetry book lying on the side table and opened it. On the first page it said:

> When you are old and grey and full of sleep,
> And nodding by the fire, take down this book,
> And slowly read . . .
>
> W.B. Yeats

'Good collection that,' said the colonel. 'Need something to read at the end of the day. Even if you are a soldier.'

'I don't know any poems any more,' said Donald. 'I learned some at school, but I can't remember them.'

'Well, other matters to deal with at present. Plenty of time.' The doorbell rang in the distance. 'Nobody living in nowadays,' said the colonel. 'Have to do every damned thing myself.' He set off cheerfully saying, 'This'll be Bill. Now we'll see some action.'

Donald put the poetry book down and stood up as Colonel Fraser-Gordon ushered in the Chief Constable. They were so different in height Donald was reminded of a terrier rounding up a stirk.

'How do you do?' said Donald, shaking hands with the big man whose uniform was immaculate. No wonder F-G admires him so much, he's a first-class example of spit and polish, he thought as he sat down again next to the fire. Bill Donaldson sat on the sofa opposite to him and stretched his long legs out across the hearth.

The colonel said, 'You'll have a brandy, Bill?' The big man smiled briefly and the colonel added, 'Or would you rather have a malt?'

The Chief Constable smiled broadly and said, 'If it's all the same to you, Colonel, I do prefer the grain to the grape.'

The colonel laughed, and said, 'What did I tell you Donald?' and left the room.

'You've had a shock, I hear,' said Bill Donaldson.

'I'm devastated,' replied Donald. 'Mary Ruth has been my housekeeper for over twenty years. Her son and mine spent every summer together when they were boys. There was no distinction made, I can assure you. They were friends. Played together like cousins. Kenneth's father Kenny and I were the same when we were boys. I know people go on about class distinction, but not here. At Fionn-glass I like to think we were all one big happy family.

'It never made any difference to me that Kenny was the gardener's son. I loved him like a brother and when he was killed in Malaya my wife – my first wife that is – and I still came and spent our holidays here and we were as friendly to Mary Ruth and Kenny's parents as ever.

'Mary Ruth and my Mary still keep in touch. Mary came up for her mother-in-law's funeral in December. We were friends. I can't understand her at all.' He sighed and lit a cigarette. 'The place is empty. Looks like a stage-set for some opera. Doors open on all sides, the stairs bare, not even a clip or a carpet-rod left. Only needed an orchestra to start. Could have been a theatre. Incredible.'

'Must have been a great shock,' said Bill Donaldson, wondering if the gardener and the housekeeper thought of Lord Donald as a friend, and noting the fact that the first Lady Fionn-glass was still a friend of the housekeeper. Funny business altogether. The constable had said she was eager to admit the theft. Too eager, perhaps? And why was the big portrait left behind? Was there something there? Sentiment for the past, or something more? As he listened to Lord Donald's description of his desperate rushing from empty room to empty room with Constable Malcolmson the colonel came back and handed him a Morangie. He gave Donald a balloon glass and sat down with his own next to the Chief Constable.

'Cheers!' said the colonel.

'Cheers!' replied Lord Donald.

'Slainte!' said the Chief Constable, thinking suddenly of Cluedo. It was the Housekeeper in the Kitchen. Or was it, he wondered. He sipped his malt and turned over in his mind all he could remember about country-house frauds. It was usually an insurance claim for valuables long since sold on the quiet. It was a pity they couldn't question the housekeeper. The constable should have taken her to

the station and conducted his inquiries there and not let Fionn-glass force him into a caution and charge.

The colonel was speaking to him: 'I told Donald you'd see what could be done. Disgraceful business. You'll be taking charge of the inquiry yourself, Bill?'

Donaldson turned to his host politely and said quietly, 'No, Colonel, I've put Detective Inspector Sim in charge of the case. He's a very hard-working officer. Thorough, and—'

Lord Donald broke in. 'This is no job for a bumpkin, Chief Constable. There's a lot of money involved. I'm not even sure that the sale of the house will go through without the furniture. "Added to the ambience", they said. Though who the devil wants ambience in a country-house hotel I don't know.' He laughed heartily. 'All you need in a hotel is hot water, good food and a well-stocked bar.' He grinned across at the colonel.

Donaldson went on after a little smile at the definition. 'You will understand, Lord Fionn-glass, that Inspector Sim will be the one to ask you about the furniture and the other contents of your house, your insurance policy and the name of your insurers. Believe me, he is most efficient. He is meeting,' he glanced at his notebook, 'PC Malcolmson tomorrow at eight forty-five a.m. at Fionn-glass House.'

He glanced at his watch. He was at the end of a long day and he didn't enjoy hearing his staff called names. From long experience he knew it was better to say nothing. He put Lord Fionn-glass's rudeness down to shock. He leaned forward and said politely, 'Detective Inspector Sim will want to see you after he has inspected the house and been through Mrs Findlater's accommodation to see what evidence there is of her part in this matter. Will you see him here?' He turned to the colonel: 'If that is all right with you, sir.'

'Certainly. Glad to help. What time will we expect him?'

Lord Donald interrupted before Donaldson could speak. 'There's bugger all to see. He'll be here by nine o'clock.'

'Not so,' said the Chief Constable, placing his glass reverentially on the table at his side and preparing to rise. 'You will appreciate, sir,' he said to the colonel, beginning to think that Fionn-glass, like his housekeeper, was too quick to speak up, 'that there will be a great deal to do. Sim is going in daylight so that he and the constable can make a routine check of the windows and doors.'

Before he could continue Lord Donald banged his brandy glass down on his side table, leaned forward and shook his finger at the Chief Constable, whose immediate thought was that PC Malcolmson had been understating His Lordship's mood when he had described him as 'ruffled'. The man was raging.

'Now look here, Donaldson,' snapped Lord Donald, 'I appreciate your coming over and I know the colonel has a high regard for you, but I am not without influence and I am telling you that Mary Ruth has sold everything in my house, through Carter's the fine-art auctioneers and valuers in Edinburgh.' He paused and added spitefully, 'You've heard of them, I presume.' The Chief Constable remained impassive. 'I really must insist that you get on to them immediately and that this man – Simpson, is it?' He waved his hand impatiently as Donaldson made to answer, '– this detective of yours, gets on to Mary Ruth's bank and we get to the bottom of this.' He turned to the colonel who nodded gravely.

'Good God!' Donald went on. 'The stuff's been gone since the first of July. She said so when that *booby* Malcolmson was interviewing her. Well, I soon put paid to his antics.' He grinned at the memory and went on, 'He even asked her,' he sat back and assumed a silly voice like a comic policeman, '"Tell me Mrs Findlater, was everything removed on the first of July?"' Then, resuming his normal voice, he went on, 'Just as bloody if. You know the size of Fionn-glass House, F-G. Is it possible that it could all have gone in one day?'

'That was what my officer was trying to ascertain, Lord Fionn-glass,' said the Chief Constable, becoming more sympathetic to PC Malcolmson, 'when, as I understand it, you insisted that he arrest her.'

Now it was the colonel's turn to interrupt. 'D'you mean she's under arrest? I thought she was helping the police with their enquiries. You didn't tell me she was under arrest, Donald.'

'What difference does it make? She's confessed. Voluntarily. She has stolen every single thing in the house.'

'Not everything,' said Bill Donaldson. 'I understand there was a portrait in the attic.'

'Probably worth a hundred pounds,' said Lord Donald, dismissing it with a flick of his hand. 'I don't seem to be able to get you to understand, Chief Constable. She's cleared my house and she has the money. When will your inspector be questioning Mary Ruth? She's a sensible and responsible woman. I think she'll come clean as long as he's a bit smarter than Malcolm Malcolmson. "Happy birthday, Mary Ruth", that's what he said to her, F-G, would you credit it? All I want is for someone to question her and find out what she has done with my money.' He stopped abruptly and put his head in his hands.

Donaldson said, 'Lord Fionn-glass, as soon as Mrs Findlater was cautioned and charged she had the right not to say anything at all.'

Donald looked up, but it was the colonel who spoke. 'No business arresting the woman in such a hurry. Should have taken her to the station. Made a proper investigation.'

'Good God,' said Donald, 'these are mere technicalities. She knows where the money is. She must be questioned.'

Rising to his feet, the Chief Constable said, 'I am sorry, sir, I don't make the laws, I just have to see that they are carried out correctly. I can assure you that Inspector Sim will do everything he can, and I would anticipate his arrival here tomorrow at about noon. Now, if you will excuse me, I'll be getting along. Thank you for your hospitality, Colonel.'

He held out his hand to Donald. Red-faced, he stood up and shook hands. 'Thank you for coming.'

'I'll show you out,' said the colonel.

Henry Field was let into his parents' house by his father.

'Where's Mum?' he asked.

'Next door. Blind Dogs' committee meeting. Come in. I was just watching the news.'

They went into the comfortable sitting room and sat down. The old man turned off the television as the weather report appeared, 'Don't want to hear more bad news,' he said. 'How are you, Henry?'

'I've had a dreadful evening. I've been talking to Mary Ruth Findlater.'

'Ah, the dear soul. How is she?' asked his father, who was becoming deaf and only caught the ends of sentences.

'You'd better ask *where* is she.'

'Well, where is she?' asked the old man, smiling across the hearth.

'In the police cells, here in Elgin. Charged with stealing the contents of Fionn-glass House.'

'I can't believe it,' said his father, looking at him sharply. He'd heard that all right.

'She has just spent the last hour telling me she wants to admit it in court tomorrow morning.'

'You told her that was not how it is done?'

'I did, but she seems to think the truth is all that is required and she says she is telling the truth.'

'She will be. She's an honest woman. She admits it, then.'

'Not to the police.' Henry Field felt tired and leaned back in his chair.

His father asked, 'What did she say when charged?'

'Something about the goods not all being uplifted on July the first.'

The old man laughed. 'I can believe that. The place is huge, it must have taken weeks to move it all.'

'I dare say it did, Dad.' Henry sat up again. He was irritable. His father didn't seem to realize the seriousness of the case. 'It's going to take a long time to prove. She didn't admit the theft after she was charged. There's nothing down in writing.'

His father looked surprised. 'You mean she was charged before a proper police inquiry was held?'

'Yes. Lord Fionn-glass insisted on the police officer cautioning and charging her. Silly bugger.'

'Mary Ruth is an honest woman.'

'She may be, but she has no idea about the law.' Henry was beginning to wonder if his father's affection for Mary Ruth wasn't blinding him to the situation. 'She wanted to plead guilty tomorrow morning and expected to go to jail tomorrow afternoon.'

At this his father's eyebrows went up. 'She's an innocent, of course. You persuaded her to be quiet and let you speak in the morning?'

'With difficulty.'

'She will have done it, if she says so. I can't understand why she did it, she's never been greedy, but she is truthful. Well, I am astonished. Lord Donald was precipitate.'

'He was stupid. After all, even under English law a confession has to be after the charge. The Procurator Fiscal will need a lot of proof before him before he'll proceed.'

'Was anyone helping her?' asked his father.

'Not according to her, but that's not all, Dad. She says she has some jewels, which are in our safe. She *says* they were a gift from her mother-in-law. Sounds odd to me – not a sweetener for services rendered, are they?'

'Well, not services rendered by Mary Ruth,' laughed his father. 'The sapphires were given to her mother-in-law by the old Lord, in my father's presence. They are hers all right, as I told her in January. She had no idea that her mother-in-law had them. The likelihood is that the old Lord was Mary Ruth's husband's father. She's to have the jewels anyway.' The old man laughed and shook his head.

'Well, if she's to have them, why did she steal all Lord Donald's stuff? She won't say what she's done with the money.' Henry was developing a headache. His father's amusement grated on him.

'Well, I have no idea why she stole it,' said his father. 'Tell Mary Ruth I was asking for her,' he added. 'She's a good woman. The trouble is she won't realize that there needs to be proof before she can be taken to court.' Seeing Henry was rising to his feet he went on, 'You'll stay until your mother comes in? She won't be long. Will you have a drink?'

'No thanks, Dad. I must go. It's nearly ten and I'm in court tomorrow. Give my love to Mum. I just popped in to tell you the news.'

'I'm glad you did, I'm glad you did,' said his father who was saddened by the news when he had digested it. He was standing in the hall puzzling over Mary Ruth's motive after he had let Henry out, when his wife came home.

'Wasn't that Henry's car?' she asked him. 'What did he want?'

As he listened to Kenneth's repeated questions, Alec leaned his forehead against the window-pane to cool it. 'I've no idea what she has done with the money, she wouldn't say,' he said. He had a sore head and felt ready to drop. He had thought of writing to Kenneth and then decided that that just would not do. It's not every day your mother is arrested. It was clearly his avuncular duty to tell her only son. It was up to Kenneth to decide whether to come from France at once, or wait to see what happened – but Alec was beginning to wish he'd written instead of phoning.

'Of course, she'll understand. Marie-Claire! Absolutely. Ten-thirty tomorrow. No, Inverness . . . a woman's unit . . . Two weeks. Exactly. Hardly in chains. No, Kenneth, she is as sane as you or I. Right, yes, I'll do that. Tomorrow evening. Napper? No. Douggie.' He's not going to ask about the hens by name I hope, thought Alec. He paid attention again.

'I'll ask Mrs Inglis. Yes. Right. Of course. Yes. Love to everyone. Right. Yes. Bye.' He put the phone back on its hook and sighed. Then he reached for the telephone directory, 'Ing . . .' he muttered, fluttering through the pages. He unfolded his reading glasses with one hand and began running his finger down the page. 'Ing . . . Ah! Here we are: Inglis J. A.'

* * *

Malcolm Malcolmson acknowledged the Chief Constable's flash of his lights as he drove along the straight piece of road before Balessie. I wonder how he got on with Lord Donald, he thought. He could see the bathroom light was on. Nearly half past nine. He wished Eileen would put the boys to bed earlier. They shouldn't be up so late at their age. He had mentioned this to her once, but she had snarled at him, 'I'm stuck out here on my own all day and half the night, they're some company at least.'

He knew their social life was poor. It was all part of the job. Still, we're going out tomorrow. That'll cheer her up, he thought as he opened the door. Mounting the stairs two at a time he called out, 'Hello there!' and put his head into the bathroom. The boys were sitting in the bath playing. Eileen was sitting on the toilet seat, reading a magazine.

'Hello, Dumplings,' he said.

'Daddy!' they shrieked in delight, and aimed their water pistols.

'We're fighting the baddies,' they laughed and giggled, racing each other to refill their water pistols.

Eileen said, 'You're late. Your tea's on the cooker.'

'Thanks,' he said, and then turning to the boys, 'I'm not a Baddy, I'm your Daddy.' As they lifted up their pistols and aimed at him, he said, 'Mind my uniform.' They fired the pistols as he retreated.

Eileen said, 'Now look what you've started. Go away.' He went, and the excited children could be heard shouting,

'No, don't let the water out, Mummy! We're not finished yet.'

Down in the kitchen, Malcolm took off his jacket and hung it behind the door. He lifted the lid off the plate which was balanced on a pan of water on the cooker. A piece of gammon, curled at the edges, some dried-up potatoes and crusted baked beans lay on the plate. He turned off the ring and picked up the oven glove. He put the plate on the little Formica table and lifted the boys' plates to make more room. He put them by the sink full of soaking dishes and took a knife and fork out of the drawer.

He had eaten a quick crispy bacon and egg roll in the canteen, but he was still hungry and if he didn't eat his tea Eileen would be cross. He turned the kettle on and wiped up the tomato sauce the boys had spilled on the table. Then he took the HP sauce down from the cluttered cupboard next to the cooker and sat down to eat.

Eileen came in and made a pot of tea without speaking. Then she sat opposite him, lit a cigarette and said, 'Well, what kept you this time?'

Chewing the overcooked food, he told her.

Chapter 15

'Will that be all, Mrs Inglis?' said Ina to her second customer of the day, smiling cheerfully.

'Yes, thank you.' Mrs Inglis replied, after a quick check of her list. 'What do I owe you?'

'Six pounds thirty-three,' said Ina, wondering if she knew.

As Mrs Inglis found the money, Ina decided to ask her. 'Have you heard about Mary Ruth?' she asked. 'Eileen Malcolmson was in on her way to have her hair done. She says Mary Ruth is in the prison in Elgin.'

'There is no prison in Elgin. I would have thought you knew that. Do you have change of a ten-pound note?'

'All that shifting that was going on all summer when you were away. I don't suppose you know about that. Well, it seems she was selling everything. We just thought it was the stuff in the attic.' She rang the sum up on the till and handed Mrs Inglis sixty-seven pence and then three pounds coins. 'She's up before the Sheriff at half past ten.'

'I know,' said Mrs Inglis who had hardly been able to believe what Mrs Findlater's uncle, Mr Macleod, had told her the night before. She certainly had no time for gossiping. 'I'm going to collect a change of clothes for Mrs Findlater on my way to my work, and feed her cats.' She picked up her shopping and then, remembering how fond of Mary Ruth Ina was, she looked her in the face and said, 'There must be some mistake, Ina. Mary Ruth is a good woman. I must go, but don't worry.'

As she went out of the door, Ina heard Sandy coming in behind the shop. He did the school bus run every morning. She went through to the back saying, 'You'll never believe what's happened.'

'About Mary Ruth? I met Malcolm going off to Fionn-glass House to meet the detective. Funny business, isn't it?'

'Funny?' said Ina, annoyed to hear that he'd heard the news. 'It's unbelievable. I think it'll all turn out to be a mistake, so does Mrs Inglis. She knew all about it. She's going to collect some clothes for Mary Ruth.'

'She won't be allowed to take anything,' said Sandy. 'Not without police permission. She's under arrest. A quarter of a million, Malcolm said.'

Irritated by Sandy's complacent tone and superior information, she put her jacket on and said, 'Well, I'm off.'

'Where are you going?'

'To have my hair done. You never listen to a word I say. I told you this morning.' She would at least be able to ask Eileen about it in the sanctum of the hairdresser's.

As Ina opened the door of The Hair Shop, Amy looked up with a smile to greet her. She was teasing a strand of sandy hair through the stained, flesh-coloured rubber cap peppered with holes which was clamped over Maureen's head. Maureen said, 'Isn't it awfu', Ina? I canny believe i'. No' Mary Ruth. She's a lady. Will she go tae the jile?'

'Is it true?' asked Amy, neatly hooking another strand of hair.

'Well,' said Ina, back in her accustomed place as the dispenser of information to the village, 'what Eileen told me and what Malcolm told Sandy this morning seems clear enough. The house is empty. She was arrested at Lord Donald's insistence and she's up before the Sheriff at half past ten. I can't believe it. Mrs Inglis was in, she was off to fetch some of Mary Ruth's things for her, though Sandy says the police won't let her have them.'

'Why no?' asked Maureen.

Ida had no idea, so she compromised with, 'That's what Sandy said anyhow.'

The three women were silent for a moment. Eileen, raising her voice over the drier's roar, shouted at them, 'Malcolm said she had a case packed and everything.'

They all stared into her mirror. Ina leaned round the drier hood and bawled in to Eileen, 'You mean she knew she would be arrested?'

'I suppose so,' she said.

Maureen announced, 'Bound to be, sooner or la'er. There was an awfu' lot o' valuable stuff in tha' hoose, an' she was responsible for i'.'

'Well,' said Ina, taking off her jacket and hanging it up on the hooks provided near the door, 'all I hope is that she's got a good lawyer.'

Amy put on her rubber gloves and started to dab the bleaching lotion on to Maureen's hair. 'Sit at the basin, Ina. Christabel will wash you in a minute.'

'And,' roared Eileen over the drier, 'Douggie's got Napper.'

'What did Douggie say?' Amy mouthed into Eileen's mirror as she moved round Maureen's head, basting it.

'Nothing, or so Malcolm said. Oh yes,' she said remembering. 'He said to tell her "guid folk are scarce"!' She wriggled out from under the drier and addressed them all in her normal voice. 'If you ask me, there's much more to this than we ken. Lord Donald kept interrupting Malcolm when he was trying to interview her. He insisted Malcolm arrest her.' She paused and added dramatically: 'I shouldn't be surprised if he wasn't involved in some way. Perhaps for the insurance.' Then she dodged back under the drier.

Settling back with her neck swathed in a towel by Christabel, who was waiting for the water spray to reach the right temperature, Ina spoke up: 'They can't have been in it together to defraud the insurance. Mary Ruth is a good woman. She'd never in a million years do anything wrong.'

Amy pulled off her rubber gloves and dropped them in the

spare basin. 'I think that too, but whatever has she done it for?'

'The money?' asked Maureen as she sat stinking of chemicals waiting for her hair to turn golden; but even she was puzzled. She and Connal had worked for Miss Roland for over forty years, ever since Connal had left the army to be chauffeur, gardener and general servant at The Laurels. Miss Roland hardly ever spoke to Maureen. Her instructions were delivered by Connal. They would no more collude with her to defraud the insurance than fly. She couldn't believe it of Mary Ruth either. 'Well, it'll be in the papers the night,' she said comfortably, pushing the cotton wool up her right temple to mop up a drip. 'So we'll ken aw about i' then.'

'I need to know now,' said Inspector Sim to Mrs Inglis as they sat on either side of Mary Ruth's table. 'The early stages of an inquiry such as this have to be conducted quickly, before all the village gossips begin to embroider what happened and vital details are forgotten.'

Furious at being classified as a village gossip, Mrs Inglis sat tight-lipped and flushed. She hated to let anyone down and here it was, half past ten, and she had had to ring up and tell Mrs McPherson, the minister's wife, that not only would she be very late to work this morning but that she was helping the police with their inquiries. She knew she was going to weep if the interrogation went on much longer. A subdued PC Malcolmson was sitting with his notebook at the other side of the table next to Inspector Sim. He hadn't looked at her once.

'I have told you,' she said. 'I was away from the end of June. I didn't go into the house on Wednesday. I brought Mary Ruth a birthday cake and then I went home.'

'Well, where is the cake?' said Detective Inspector Sim pleasantly. This was a new bit of information. 'Can you see it anywhere?'

Mrs Inglis looked round. 'It was in a blue tin. I can't see it.'

The tin, remembered Malcolm with horror, was on the back seat of his car. He had forgotten to give it to Eileen and the boys. It was hardly material to the business and he didn't fancy mentioning it.

Not after what Sim had said to Mrs Inglis, who was packing a selection of clothing when they had found her in Mary Ruth's bedroom. It was Sim who had seen her car through the window as they came down from the attic where they had been puzzling over the portrait.

'It is difficult for me to believe that you knew nothing of what was going on, Mrs Inglis. I understand you worked here once a week,' Sim went on, wondering where the cake had gone. It wasn't in Mrs Findlater's list of possessions. 'It must have taken a long time to pack up everything in the house,' he said to the silent Mrs Inglis.

'I have told you, Lord Donald wanted an inventory made. I helped bring the stuff down from the attic. It was all packed up later by the people from Carter's,' repeated the poor woman, beginning to sniff and wipe her nose. 'I don't know where the cake tin is, I never saw any vans, I didn't know the house was empty. I only came to collect some clothes when Mrs Findlater's uncle asked me to.'

'Is that all you collected?' said Sim sternly. 'You didn't take any letters or a briefcase, for instance? There are no papers of any description so far as we can see. That is unusual, Mrs Inglis. Please don't upset yourself. This is a very serious matter. I certainly was not informed that you had a key. Were you in here last night, perhaps putting a match to some old papers for Mrs Findlater? Something she said she didn't want us to see? Love letters, that kind of thing?'

'No, I was not.' She was very indignant. 'You can ask my husband. He'll support me.'

He would, wouldn't he, thought Sim.

'I was at home all evening,' went on the distressed woman, 'and it was nearly ten o'clock when I had the call from Mr Macleod. I was very upset. I've known Mrs Findlater for over thirty years. She is a lady.' She burst into tears.

Malcolm remembered suddenly that Mary Ruth had asked him for her birthday cards. He tried to recall how the mantelpiece had looked. Surely there had been a letter there too. Without being obvious he twisted his head round a little and looked at the mantelpiece.

'Could you try not to fidget, Constable,' snapped Detective Inspector Sim, who did not like to see women crying and didn't think Mrs Inglis had taken any papers away. She would have been a fool to come in again, if she had been here last night, when there was a police car in the yard this morning and she was no fool, he could see that. She obviously had no idea that she should have rung the bell and asked for permission to collect clothes under supervision. The fact that he had not bolted the back door when they had entered the premises at eight forty-five annoyed him further. He made a mental note to ask Malcolmson why he hadn't bolted the door yesterday and left through the front door.

As Mrs Inglis wept and Constable Malcolmson burned with embarrassment, worry and guilt, Detective Inspector Sim made up his mind. It was nearly eleven. There was nothing else to do in the house. He would get his sergeant to organize a thorough check and call a policewoman on the car phone to come and search Mrs Inglis. He'd ring his sergeant and find out what he had learned from Carter's and Mrs Findlater's bank. He might know something useful by now.

Angus came into the shop. 'It was no use taking Mary Ruth's mail up to the house, from what I've heard, so I've brought it to you, Sandy,' he said. 'You had better hold on to it for the inspector.' He waited.

Sandy said, 'Right, I'm afraid she'll be in Inverness by tonight.'

'So it is true,' said Angus. 'Oh! me.'

Before Sandy could speak again the door opened and Mrs Phimister came in. She had made friendly overtures towards Sandy since she and Mr Phimister had retired successfully from their furnishing and haberdashery business in Inverness and moved into the village. She knew from long experience what a trying job shopkeeping was and felt some sympathy with him, though he was never very friendly.

She devoted herself to working for the the Lifeboat Committee. She considered most of the villagers to be socially beneath her so she didn't go to the bowling, and apart from the colonel's one party a year for the church members she didn't mix with the County. Ignoring the postie, she plonked her basket down on the counter and asked, 'Is Mary Ruth in the jail or is she not?'

Sandy smiled nervously and Angus said, 'Just what I was asking, Mrs P.'

'I ask,' she said, ignoring the abbreviation and the interruption, 'to let you understand, because I have just been to make an appointment at the hairdresser's and I could not get any sense out of them. Eileen Malcolmson, who should know better in her position than to be blethering all over the village, says Mrs Findlater is under arrest and that she has robbed Lord Fionn-glass. Well, true or false?' She tittered and tipped her head to one side. It was not an appealing gesture.

Sandy gulped. Mrs Phimister's attempts at coquettish camaraderie made him nervous. 'I'm afraid it is true,' he said soberly.

'True that she is arrested, I presume you mean,' Mrs Phimister said sharply. 'British justice demands proof. We are not living in a banana republic.' She simpered at her little joke and went on, 'She may be a misguided woman, all that ludicrous cleaning and polishing for people who never even bothered to come. I heard the curtain-cleaning bill alone was two hundred pounds. As my husband said at the time, more than once,' she added as though that made his pronouncements unchallengeable, 'we could have had a new roof on the rectory for the money that was spent, but . . .'

She had lost her thread but drew a deep breath, blew her nose on a neat hanky, wiped her pink-rimmed eyes and started off again. 'None the less she deserves a fair hearing, as I told that little minx Eileen Malcolmson.' She sniffed. Angus and Sandy stood silent.

'What a waste of money, all that work just for a weekend. Took them months. Scotland is mocked by the likes of the Fionn-glass family. It won't do. I'm no republican, but I do wish the landowners would behave responsibly. Now it appears the housekeeper has sold the lot. What is the world coming to? I thought you would be able to tell me, Sandy.' She leaned on her basket and waited.

'All I can tell you, Mrs Phimister, is that Constable Malcolmson took her to Elgin police station last night and that she's before the Sheriff this morning,' said Sandy, stung at her suggestion that he did not understand the difference between an arrest and a conviction. He had gathered quite a lot of information during the course of the morning, but he wasn't going to dish it up to Mrs Phimister, however much she ferreted.

'Well, I never thought it made sense for a woman of her calibre to be a servant. Furthermore, as I said, I totally disapprove of absentee landlords. Have you any bread flour, Sandy? I'm needing to make bread. I have the family coming on Sunday and they like my home-made.'

Mrs Inglis, shaking with emotion, allowed the young policewoman to search her, then the two women collected a selection of Mary Ruth's clothing. The policewoman made an inventory of them and after Mrs Inglis had packed them she drove off, sobbing, to the manse, over two hours late for her work.

Still sitting in Mary Ruth's kitchen, Detective Inspector Sim addressed PC Malcolmson. 'Take me through the events of yesterday after Lord Donald had gone.'

'Well, Mary Ruth—'

'Mrs Findlater,' corrected the inspector.

'Mrs Findlater turned off the oil supply to the Aga. We put cat food outside, for the cats.' Sim's nostrils quivered. Malcolmson went on quickly. 'She pointed out a small suitcase. I put it in the car. She was washing out a milk bottle when I returned.'

'You left her alone?'

Malcolm nodded then he took a deep breath. 'She then offered me the birthday cake in the blue cake tin for my children, so as not to waste it. Mrs Inglis had brought it.' He paused, but Sim remained silent. 'It is in my car. I forgot to give it to Eileen – er – my wife, sir. Then we put the cats' food outside and took the dog to Douggie's. Oh! and she asked if she could have her birthday cards. It was her birthday,' he added lamely, 'and I said yes.'

'You are not hoping for a long career in the police force I take it, Malcolmson?' said the inspector. 'Go and bolt all the doors. We shall leave through the front door, and I shall retain the key. That way we may prevent all and sundry walking in and out of the premises at will.'

As the two police officers reached their cars Sim said, 'You go first, show me where the dog is and wait.'

'Yessir,' said Malcolmson.

They pulled up one behind the other in front of Douggie's house.

'Is this where you parked?' asked the inspector.

'No sir, Mary Ruth didn't want to— er, I parked round at the side of the garden, there,' he pointed.

To Malcolmson's surprise, Detective Inspector Sim walked round the corner. Under the hedge there was a little patch of ashes with part of a charred envelope lying on top.

'Do you know anything about this?' said Sim, bending down and looking hard at the ash and the piece of envelope.

'No sir,' said Malcolmson, truthfully.

'But this is where you parked?'

'Yessir.'

'Mrs Findlater did not smoke. At least she had no cigarettes, no matches and no lighter among her possessions.'

Malcolm Malcolmson felt sick. He had given her his lighter. He had left her alone for five or six minutes in the car. Suddenly he recalled the smell of burning as he had got back into his seat after speaking to Douggie.

'What do you make of this, Constable?' When Malcolmson did not answer, Sim continued, 'In the boot of my car you will find a small brush and shovel, some polythene bags and some labels. Here is my key. Collect all this ash and paper and label it. Try not to scoop up half a pound of gravel with the ashes. I shall go to the house.'

There was no one in the house. When he returned, he told the constable to put the sample of ash in the boot and get into the car.

'Now, Malcolmson,' he said turning slightly towards him. 'I read your report last night, but I should like to see your notebook.' It was handed over at once. Despite himself, Sim was impressed. Times were recorded and the facts were as in the report, except for one thing. 'It says here, "Lord D. v. angry." Why have you said "ruffled" in your report?'

'I suppose because he was justifiably angry, sir. He's not a bad man. My father-in-law used to be his ghillie. He's a good laird, as they go.'

'I'm going to meet him at noon. Tell me exactly what was said when you charged Mrs Findlater, which I am sure you realize was a mistake.'

Malcolmson sighed. 'Yes sir. I was trying to question Mrs Findlater and he kept interrupting. Then he told me to arrest her. I told him I couldn't.' He paused and smiled a little.

'What did he say to that?' asked Sim.

'He said, "They don't just pay you to play in the police pipe band, do they?" I do play the pipes, sir. I took them up again when we moved back north. I was in the Lothian police for four years.'

'I know,' said Sim. 'Go on.'

'I said she wouldn't need to say any more if I charged her and that I had a lot more to ask her. He was very angry and insisted. I was very annoyed with myself because I know it's wrong to let the suspect know any more than necessary. I've known Mrs Findlater all my life, sir. She is a good woman. I was sure she'd tell me all about it. I should have taken her to the station. I'm sorry, sir.'

Sim nodded. 'Not easy.' He handed his notebook back to Malcolmson and said, 'I've got my sergeant on to Carter's and her bank. She may be a good woman, but she's hardly a master criminal. We'll find the money. You are quite certain you made it clear to Lord Fionn-glass that she could refuse to speak after being cautioned and charged?'

'One hundred per cent, sir,' said the constable.

'Well, off you go then and resume your duties. Keep your ears open. I need all the help I can get. It's a long time since the first of July.' He drove to the village shop, thinking hard.

Mrs Phimister gave the inspector a piercing look as she came out of the shop. This must be the great detective, she thought. Hmm! He caught the door before she let go of it and nodded to her. There was no one in the shop. Sandy came in from the back when Inspector Sim coughed.

'I didn't hear the bell,' he said. 'I'm sorry to have kept you.' Ina slithered in to see who it was. She was holding one of Mary Ruth's letters.

Inspector Sim took out his identification and told Sandy to reserve all Fionn-glass mail. Sandy said, 'Angus the postie left today's here . . .'

Ina butted in cheerfully. 'Do you want me to send it on to her?'

'No,' he said shortly. 'Mrs Findlater is under arrest. I need all her mail to help me with my inquiries. I will take what you have now and naturally I shall sign for it. As for the rest, please keep it until my sergeant comes.' Sandy picked up the mail from the pigeon-hole behind him and handed it over.

'What about this one?' asked Ina. 'It's from her cousin. I was going to send it to Inverness prison. That's where Eileen said she'd be.'

'I will take charge of that too, thank you,' said Sim, wondering where he had heard the name Eileen. 'I'm sure you will appreciate that I must have all Mrs Findlater's correspondence if I am to do justice to her case.' Psychology usually worked, he knew. It did this time.

'Oh! If there's anything we can do to help,' they said together.

'Well, I need to see the man who has Mrs Findlater's dog. He was out when I called and I need directions to Knockspindie

House,' said Sim, signing for the letters. 'Much obliged,' he added as he pushed the book back to Sandy, 'and who is Eileen?' he asked casually.

'Eileen? She's Malcolm's wife. She told us all about the robbery and Mary Ruth being arrested and the quarter of a million pounds and . . .' Ina tailed off as Sandy signalled to her with a heavy frown. Then she plucked up her courage and added, '. . . when she was in before she went to the hairdresser's, first thing.'

'Did she indeed!' said the inspector. Malcolmson's promotion prospects looked dimmer still.

'Well,' Ina went on after looking at Sandy and then at the clock, 'Douggie will be home for dinner at twelve, wherever he is, and the gates to Knockspindie are, what, a mile?' she looked to Sandy again who nodded, 'A mile west of the village. On the right-hand side. You can't miss them.' Something in the inspector's face made her laugh. 'I promise you, Inspector. There's a wood most of the way and then a gentle bend right and the lodge is easy to see; it's empty at present, but you can't miss it and the gates are there. You must have passed them as you came in this morning. In fact I know you did because Mackie was in earlier and he passed you.'

'Thank you. Who is Mackie?'

'He runs the pub next door,' said Sandy.

'Ah – just popping in there for a snack, so I'll meet him. Good morning.'

Finishing the excellent home-made broth, disappointingly served with two pieces of steamed white bread, Sim listened to Mackie agreeing in the public bar with an unseen drinker, that 'You can never tell.' He rang the bell, ordered a coffee and went to the Gents while it was being prepared. He caught sight of a big farmer on his own, leaning on the bar. As Sim went through to the lounge bar he heard Mackie say, 'Anything else, Tibby?' and then he brought through the coffee which was very good and made up for the bread. As Mackie handed him his change he said, 'You'll be the inspector in charge of the Fionn-glass case?'

'I am: Sim's the name.'

'How d'you do?' Mackie stretched out his hand. 'If there's anything I can do to help, let me know, I'm always here.'

'Thanks,' said Detective Inspector Sim, but he wondered just how much help he'd be given. He knew from experience how clannish villages could be.

Chapter 16

Henry Field held the Elgin Court House door open for Alec Macleod, who was in a mild state of shock. His sister Mary's daughter, Mary Ruth, was on her way to the jail in Inverness. He had hoped she would be released into his custody, but the Sheriff had thought otherwise.

After explaining to her that she could wear her own clothes and have up to five hundred pounds with her, Sheriff Kind had remanded her for two weeks. She looked as composed as ever, and thanked him before she was led away by a young policeman. She smiled at her uncle and Mr Field as she went out of the court.

'I'll be going to see her on Tuesday,' said Mr Field. 'Her remand is no surprise. She may be remanded again for another two weeks, but then I'm sure she'll be allowed out until the trial. After all, she's not a danger to the public. Try not to worry. You will be allowed to visit and so will the rest of her family. Now, I'll let you know what happens after I've seen her. Are you all right? Can I give you a lift home?'

'No thank you. I am shocked, but I think a walk will do me good.'

Alec set off along the High, counting his breaths in, holding them while still counting and then counting them out. He would have a glass of dry sherry when he reached home and put his feet up on the sofa.

As she left the optician's, Martha Bold saw Alec with a strained look on his face almost marching along the busy High. Friday was always a busy day. He didn't seem to see anyone and his breathing looked odd. There's something up with him, she thought and angled herself to intercept him. He nearly had a heart attack when she caught him by the collar of his jacket and boomed, 'What's up with you, Alec? You don't look yourself.'

'Diarrhoea!' spat Alec, forgetful of his immortal soul. Martha was too much to bear today. 'Can't stop, whichever way you take it.' He shook himself free and hopped into a cab at the rank. Before she had drawn breath he had gone.

'There's something far wrong with him,' she announced to the High, staring after him, 'and it's not diarrhoea!'

Alec's phone was ringing as he opened his door. He answered it without thinking. Mrs Inglis was upset. She had been given a coffee and a lot of sympathy and sent home by Mrs McPherson, the well-meaning minister's wife. At home she had nothing to do except consider the indignities she had suffered. She told Alec at length about them; he listened patiently while trying to reach the sherry bottle and a glass, maddeningly just out of reach. I'm getting too old for this, he thought gloomily. After twenty minutes Mrs Inglis was sounding calmer.

'Dreadful, dreadful,' murmured Alec. 'Make yourself a nice cup of tea. Or have something stronger, and don't imagine that you are under any suspicion. Mary Ruth has told Mr Field quite categorically that she arranged it all by herself. There is no reason why you should have been treated so if I hadn't asked you to collect a change of clothes for her. It's my blame and I do apologize.' This was a mistake.

'Oh! Mr Macleod, it's not your fault. I should have thought to ring the bell and ask the police permission. I just didn't think,' said Mrs Inglis, but before she could start again Alec told his second lie of the day.

'I'm sorry, Mrs Inglis but there is someone at the door. Please excuse me. I'll be at home this evening when your husband comes with Mary Ruth's things. Do forgive me, I must go.'

He hung up the phone slowly as she was saying, 'I'm so sorry to have bothered you.'

Martha Bold went in through her kitchen door, wiped her feet on the mat and put her shopping basket down. She picked Arthur's mended glasses out of it and went into the living room. 'Here you are,' she said. 'Mind you don't break the arm off again. He said it was very worn, but he did it for me this time.'

Arthur looked up from his chair, put his book down and said, 'I would have fetched them myself, Martha, but thank you all the same.'

'I was in the High,' she said, 'and just who do you suppose I saw? Marching along mumbling to himself and when I spoke to him leaped into a cab shouting that he had diarrhoea, if you please, at the top of his voice, in the middle of the High. I was worried about him. He looked ill and older somehow and, well, just not himself.' She took off her jacket and went into the front hall to hang it up. 'Well?' she said as she came back. 'Guess?' She stood in front of Arthur with a knowing smile. He'd never guess, not in a month of Sundays.

'Alec Macleod,' said Arthur. 'He'll have been coming from the Court House. Mary Ruth was up before the Sheriff this morning. It seems she has sold the contents of Fionn-glass House and no one knows what she has done with the money.'

'And how do you come to know so much about it,' asked Martha, 'if you don't mind my asking?'

'Mrs Wilson next door told me,' said Arthur. 'You know she goes to look out for the children for her daughter-in-law, on the evenings when she works in the police canteen. Well, last night at about seven Malcolm Malcolmson brought Mary Ruth in. He couldn't believe it either. First she was booked in and then she had a bacon roll and then Mr Field – junior, of course – and her uncle were in to see her. She'll have been committed to prison for two weeks in Inverness, pending inquiries.' It was not often that Arthur knew more about the goings-on in the world than Martha. He was a gentle soul, so he kept the note of triumph out of his voice. None the less she was indignant.

'I don't believe you!' she gasped and sat down opposite him. 'Mary Ruth? A thief!'

'Quite a spectacular one. The stuff was insured for a quarter of a million, but she got more than that for it.'

'That bodes ill,' said Martha. 'There'll be hell to pay if he was under-insured. I wonder if they know at Knockglass?' she said, perking up suddenly. 'It's twelve o'clock. Helen will be in preparing dinner for Fred and Donald Molloch. She's been very good to him since he's been alone. I'll just give her a ring before I make your dinner.'

She went into the front hall, glad to have redeemed something from the disaster. Arthur was happy to overhear her telling Helen all. He had to admit, she could tell a story. He picked up his book. Dinner might be a little late, but Martha was making the best of things, as she always did.

'It's twelve already,' said Lord Donald waspishly. 'These local coppers are not up to much, F-G.'

'They're good men,' replied Colonel Fraser-Gordon. 'I appreciate your impatience, but have faith.' Before Lord Donald could say anything more the telephone rang. Excusing himself, the colonel went into his study across the hall to answer it. Donald Fionn-glass paced down the drawing room and gazed unseeing out of the window.

'Good afternoon,' said the colonel accurately.

Miss Roland's stern voice came through loud and strong. 'Colonel Fraser-Gordon, Madge Roland here. I am sorry to bother you, but after due consideration I could think of no one better than you to ask for help.'

'Always glad to be of service,' said the colonel. 'How can I help you, Miss Roland?'

'I have just received the most peculiar piece of news from my man Connal. Admittedly his informant was his wife, but I trust *him* implicitly and I have no alternative, after questioning him closely, but to believe him. He tells me – by the way, I have not communicated with anyone else—' thus exempting herself from any suspicion of gossiping, she continued, 'he tells me that the village is "throbbing" with the news that Mrs Findlater, Mary Ruth Findlater, who sits in front of me in church, has stolen all the furniture and the fittings from Fionn-glass House, cleared the stables and the attics and even taken up the stair-rods and has sold the lot to Carter's in Edinburgh. All without permission, you understand, and,' her voice trembled with disbelief, 'has admitted it and was up before the Sheriff in Elgin this morning. So I thought I would ring you for enlightenment. I can hardly credit it. I used to sit on the Vestry with Mrs Findlater.'

'Sadly,' said the colonel, 'I have to tell you that what you have heard is correct. I have Lord Donald here waiting for the detective inspector in charge of the case to come and interview him.'

Miss Roland was silent for a moment, then she said, 'Has anyone informed the rector? Living over at Drumloch he may not know and he will have to go and see her. It is his duty. She must have proper counsel. I dare say she has been under stress. You will remember she hid herself away at the church garden fête, only emerging in time to win the whisky in the raffle. Poor creature. Shall I ring the rector or will you?'

As the colonel tried to think his way through this confusion, the doorbell rang. Muttering an apology he went to let Detective Inspector Sim in. He showed him to the drawing room door and returned to the redoubtable Miss Roland.

'Detective Inspector Sim,' said Sim, holding out his hand to Lord Fionn-glass, who was pleased to see a tall, spare man with shrewd eyes wearing a well-cut dark grey suit. This was no bumpkin.

They sat down. Sim opened his notebook, refused a cigarette and said, 'I have some news for you, Lord Fionn-glass. My sergeant has been in touch with—' he consulted briefly, '—a Miss Wauchop is it? At Carter's.' Encouraged by a nod he went on. 'She reports that she acted according to your instructions of Friday the twenty-sixth of April, received by her first over the telephone and then subsequently confirmed in a letter. She said you wished her to cooperate as per usual with Mrs Findlater. She said Mrs Findlater had often sold goods for you, and that you had authorized Carter's in writing to receive goods for sale from her on your behalf. Is this the case?'

'That was for the odd bit of silver to keep the place going. It wasn't permission to sell every last stick.'

'Miss Wauchop sent a cheque for two thousand three hundred and eleven pounds to Mrs Findlater on March the seventh.'

'That was for a canteen of cutlery, I know about that,' snapped Lord Donald. Was the man ever going to tell him something he didn't know?

Sim went on without acknowledging the interruption. 'Miss Wauchop authorized eight cheques for Mrs Findlater between the seventeenth and the twenty-ninth of July. She sent the cheques to the Mrs Findlater – House Sales account.'

'That woman is a gushing and incompetent fool. There is no such account. There is a Household Account in Mrs Findlater's name.'

'Well, certainly that is the account which received the money in March, according to the report from the bank mana—'

'I asked that woman at Carter's to arrange for two inventories to be made. That much she did get right. My wife tells me the inventories and valuations have arrived at my London home. I came straight here from the airport. We've been in the States all summer. I came to select what I wanted from the house before the sale and to earmark what my son wants for himself.'

He stubbed out his cigarette fiercely and stood up. Sim waited, and while Lord Donald strode down the room and back again, quietly read through his notes. 'The arrangements for access to the house were to be made with Mary Ruth,' Lord Donald said finally, sitting down again. 'I did not instruct the sale of the contents of the house and I most certainly did not tell this chop-chop creature to sell the furniture, which I wished to sell with the property.' He shook his fists with irritation. 'The silly woman must remember that. She had the nerve to tell me that it was a mistake to remove the contents as they'd get a better price sold at Fionn-glass. "Their provenance would be better", she had the cheek to say. As if my word weren't good enough. I refused. I didn't want half the bloody tinks in the county pawing through my stuff.'

'I quite understand,' said Sim. 'You say there is no account called House Sales?'

'I have just said so.'

Sim continued courteously: 'However there is a Mrs Findlater – Household Account, as the bank manager told my sergeant?'

'Yes, God dammit! It's been administered for over twenty years by my housekeeper, Mary Ruth Findlater. She pays wages and repair-bills, the TV licence, that kind of thing, household matters. How much was in that account?'

Sim had no intention of mentioning money to Lord Fionn-glass until he had to, especially not the amount paid out by Carter's. 'I don't have the figures here,' he said smoothly.

'What did she get for the stuff? You can surely tell me that.' Sim appreciated Lord Donald didn't believe him and that he could ring Carter's himself, but he hesitated to see what would come next. He was not disappointed. 'I suppose the wretched woman's got half a million out of me.'

'Was that what it was insured for?'

Lord Donald sat up and looked hard at the inspector. 'I'm not a fool, Inspector. Malcolmson must have told you what it was insured for. Am I right in assuming you have me under suspicion?' It was the first time Sim had heard Lord Donald speak in a normal voice and indeed appear to have thought before he spoke.

'In my experience of country-house thefts, Lord Donald, and I think you will find your insurance company will tell you the same, crimes of this magnitude are often an inside job. Being under-insured saves paying high premiums which are prohibitive for isolated houses, as I'm sure you know.'

Donald nodded in agreement and said drily, 'That's why I had a trusted housekeeper, living in.'

Sim acknowledged the sick joke with a little grimace and said, 'If some or all of the contents are sold and then insurance is claimed, a lot of money can be made fairly easily. Now, Lord Donald,' he went on, 'I was given the barest outline last night by the Chief Constable. However, I had a good report from Malcolmson of what you and Mrs Findlater said yesterday. I have seen the size of the house. I have heard endlessly what a good and kind woman Mrs Findlater is – even you told the Chief Constable that she was sensible. How can I be sure that you did not put her up to it?'

Donald sat thinking. After a while he said slowly, 'I was a fool to butt in and insist Malcolmson arrest Mary Ruth. I gathered that much from the colonel last night.' He looked hard at Sim as though for the first time. 'I can see that from your point of view it would be exactly the thing to do if I had instructed Mary Ruth, to stop her from being questioned.' He stood up and walked around the room again. 'I'm sorry, Inspector. I'm not in collusion with my housekeeper. I am the victim of a theft but I understand you. I could have used Mary Ruth and be going to pay her off later in France, say, where her son lives. That's a thought. Do you suppose her son was in it with her?'

'I shall be covering every aspect, Lord Donald, rest assured. For now there is one thing that puzzles me. Why did she leave the portrait behind?'

'I've been wondering about that myself.' Donald sat down again and lit another cigarette. 'It was of my grandmother. I can't even think why my uncle left it in the house when he finally settled in London. He took the other family portraits, some of them bigger than that.'

'I can't see the fact that the late Lord Fionn-glass left the portrait of his mother behind has any connection with Mrs Findlater leaving it. Can you?' asked Sim, much relieved that Lord Donald appeared rational at last.

'No; it's just that it is strange that it was left behind by my uncle. She's wearing the tiara which he kept in the House of Lords. I had it reset for my wife, my present wife. My first wife and I were separated when my uncle died. It was only last year that I decided to go to the Opening of Parliament and found the tiara with my coronet and robes.'

'How does that help us?'

'It doesn't, but there is some mystery there.'

'What about the necklace and the earrings, and aren't there some matching bracelets too?'

'That's a thought. Perhaps he didn't want my parents to see them. My uncle had no children. Mother acted as his hostess for many years, both before Dad died and after. My uncle was over ninety when he died.'

'So your mother and your uncle were on friendly terms?' asked Sim.

'Very much so.'

'So he would not have minded your mother wearing the family jewels as long as they were passed on to your wife?'

'Not at all; but she never wore the tiara.'

'And the rest of the jewellery?' Sim pressed.

'Never seen it. Is it important? He probably gambled it away or sold it to pay some racing debt. He was a rogue even in his seventies, and Dad always said he'd been a real sport when he was young. After all the girls, I gathered, though he never married.'

'So you said,' Sim reminded him.

'I didn't actually, I said he had no children. He never married either.' Lord Donald paused and looked hard at Sim. Then he went on slowly, 'Could it be the jewellery was given away and he didn't want anyone to know it even existed, and that is why he left the portrait behind? Given away perhaps to some girl he couldn't marry?'

'Why couldn't he have married her?' Sim asked.

'Married already?'

'Well, you don't give jewels to a woman you love for her to hide away from her husband and never wear,' said Sim.

'That's true,' said Donald with feeling. 'My wife would certainly want to wear them.' Indeed when she sees the portrait, he thought grimly, she will want to wear them.

'Well, what other reasons stop people marrying?' asked Sim.

'Religious differences? Well, not nowadays, but when my uncle was young?' went on Donald, answering his own question with another.

'It is a puzzle,' said Sim, 'without a doubt.'

He opened his notebook at a clean page and was about to ask for the name and address of Lord Donald's insurers when Donald said, 'Anyway it still doesn't help us decide why Mary Ruth Findlater, housekeeper, daughter-in-law to the head gardener of Fionn-glass House, should have sold everything in said house and left a portrait of my grandmother in the attic. Now, what else do you need to ask me?'

Sitting in his study, Colonel Fraser-Gordon hung up and stared at the phone. Miss Roland seldom rang him, but she always left him bemused. 'Am I the man who led the best regiment in the British army to its most glorious victory,' he said to the telephone, 'and if I am, why can't I understand women?' He sat puzzling to himself, glad he could not catch any sounds of rage coming from the drawing room where Lord Donald and the elegant Detective Inspector Sim were also puzzling. He looked at his watch: nearly time for lunch. He stood up.

There was no doubt about it – Mrs Findlater was a beautiful, kind and gracious thief, whereas Miss Roland was an opinionated old battleaxe who had never stolen anything in her life. As he heard Donald showing Sim out, he smiled to himself as he decided which of the two women he much preferred.

The Balessie Outdoor Bowling Club's annual dinner and dance

went with even more of a swing that night, as the speculation about Mary Ruth's Great House Robbery waxed in the packed hall. Eileen Malcolmson was in great demand and Douggie was plied with drink to an extravagant extent by those who frankly didn't believe his word.

'I'd no idea at all,' he said over and over again, adding: 'Well, just a small one then,' to the eager questioner. Angus the postie too was hard-pressed and was also considered to be holding back vital information.

The number of folk who had seen the vans and thought at the time that it was odd, was balanced by the number who had never noticed a thing. The expression: 'You could have knocked me down with a feather' was over-used. Meanwhile, as her neighbours and friends enjoyed their evening, Mary Ruth sat in her hot, dry, orange-painted brick cell in Inverness and composed a letter to her son. She made a few false starts before she managed to say what she wanted. Then, just as the speeches began in the Balessie Hall, her light went out and she lay down on the narrow, hard rubber mattress and waited for sleep.

Chapter 17

Detective Inspector Sim stood in the ante-room to the Chief Constable's office and looked through his report. Monday 9 September was typed neatly at the top. What a week it had been. Sim had interviewed all the principal witnesses and the villagers of Balessie himself, paying particular attention to the publican. If anyone in that God-forsaken village knew what went on, he reasoned, it was clever Mr Mackie, but he had met with a master. Miss Wauchop of Carter's had been a fount of information, Carter's bank, after a slow start, had told him plenty and Mr Esau of Agostino's had been forthcoming but Mackie, rather as Sim had expected, was not giving anything away.

Sim's sergeant had thoroughly searched Fionn-glass House for any evidence of Mary Ruth's transactions, interviewed the auctioneers at Esson and Mary Ruth's sister in Edinburgh, arranged for her brother to be questioned in England and for her son to be interviewed in France. The two men had been up until two-thirty writing the report. Sim was waiting patiently for the Chief to switch on the ENTER light over his door. Expensive gadget, he was thinking. Anyone can call out Come in, or open the door.

The door opened. 'Come in, Sim. Sorry if I've kept you. I've just had Lord Fionn-glass on the line, again. He is suggesting we try Agostino's now. He thinks they must have sold the furniture if Carter's didn't. I told him that I was sure you had it in hand.' The

Chief Constable waved Sim to a chair and took his report when it was offered.

'It's in my report, sir.'

Behind the Chief Constable there was a large window looking out over the rooftops of Inverness. Sim wondered if a marksman would be able to shoot the Chief Constable where he sat. This isn't Northern Ireland, he reminded himself, but he was glad that his office looked on to the car park and that his desk faced the window.

Donaldson read slowly and without comment, turning over the pages neatly. When he had finished he said, 'You have done well in so short a time, Sim. Have you been to Millichop and Millichop yet?'

'No, I'm due there tomorrow morning. The partners had left early on Friday when I was trying to contact them. It's a Monday holiday today in Edinburgh and Mr Millichop is sailing off the west coast.'

'What put you on to them?'

'Agostino's. Like Lord Fionn-glass, once I'd read the inventories, valuations and copies of the sales receipts from Carter's, I also saw the discrepancy and similarly I couldn't think of anyone else in Scotland other than Agostino's to sell a houseful of antique furniture.' He shook his head and went on. 'Their Mr Esau was severely shocked; he kept saying, "But she's a good wumman and her shortbread was graund." He also said he felt heart sorry for her reduced to living in the kitchen and that she was most helpful about those blessed stair-rods.' The Chief Constable looked up, Sim smiled at him and went on. 'It transpires it was Harry Esau of Agostino's who persuaded her to let his men unscrew the things. He said they had a client looking for Victorian stair-rods. She had agreed with him that modern hoteliers prefer to carpet stairs from side to side, and so on. He thought she was "magic". I shall look forward to seeing this woman.'

'So shall I. She's a whole lot cleverer than I had anticipated. I assumed the money would be in her bank and that she had someone local helping her. Someone we might be able to question.' The Chief Constable looked hopefully at Sim.

'No one, I'm afraid, will admit they saw anything. Unless they are all consummate liars, it looks as if she has done it all alone; well, anyway, not with the connivance or help of her friends or neighbours.' Sim, relieved his report was being well received, added, 'We'll get there, sir.'

The Chief Constable raised his eyebrows and said, 'I hope so, and before Friday when she's up before the Sheriff again. If we don't have the case ready for the Procurator Fiscal, she'll be remanded in custody for a further two weeks and there's some woman in Elgin already writing to the papers and stirring up the Women's Institutes claiming we are being unjust to Mrs Findlater by holding her in custody in a men's jail.' He sighed and looked back at the report. Then he said, 'Do you think she had any help from her family? It says here that her son was "astonished and astounded and declared with passion that she was a most good and virtuous woman and that surely there was some mistake." Sounds like *Private Eye*.'

'My sergeant's interpretation of the French police report they faxed us,' Sim smiled again. 'I think we'll find she has stashed the cash with Millichop and Millichop. Very bright of her. A neat bit of laundering. I suppose she told them it was her old auntie's house being sold up and as she came from Edinburgh she felt she could trust them. That sort of rot. I've made inquiries. It's a very old-fashioned firm. I dare say they have a lot of dowdy old ladies from the country as clients.'

'From what I heard from Colonel Fraser-Gordon, she isn't a dowdy old lady.'

'Well, a dashing woman of the world then. She's bamboozled them, anyway. They're probably all about a hundred themselves.'

Detective Inspector Sim was wrong.

Mike Millichop had a freckled face, a sunburned nose and bleached reddish-gold hair. He was thirty-four, but he looked about eighteen.

He was friendly and ordered coffee for Inspector Sim, which was brought in on a silver tray by an extremely fashionable young woman.

'She was a very handsome and cheerful woman,' he answered Sim. 'I remember her clearly. She came here because her aunt had been a client of ours, but whether she's the Mrs Findlater you're talking about, Inspector, I don't know. I mean after all there must be hundreds of Mary Findlaters in Scotland, especially up in your part of the country.'

Sim recalled Miss Wauchop saying that "everyone" at Carter's knew Mrs Findlater, had known her for thirty years, yet the letter Donald Fionn-glass had sent authorizing Mrs Mary Ruth Findlater to sell goods for him was sent only four years ago. The two Mrs Findlaters were friends and apparently interchangeable in the eyes of the staff at Carter's. Was it possible they were in this together? He took out a photograph of Mary Ruth which he had borrowed from Alec Macleod.

'Is this the woman who came to see you, Mr Millichop?'

He was not sure. Another photograph was proffered. This one showed Mary Ruth standing in her son's garden in France, holding her baby granddaughter.

'That's her. She's tall. Yes, that is Mrs Findlater.'

'You are sure?'

'Quite sure. She came to see me in the summer and asked me to open an account for her. I understood she was selling up in the north and that I would be receiving cheques regularly, and I did.' Mr Millichop smiled politely at Detective Inspector Sim. He had nothing more to say.

'Mrs Findlater is accused of selling the contents of Fionn-glass House, the property of Lord Donald Fionn-glass,' said Inspector Sim. He was pleased to note that the smart young lawyer sitting behind his elaborately carved desk with its collection of telephones and VDU screens and keyboards was staring at him, his mouth open in surprise.

'She is on remand in Inverness prison. She admits selling the fine arts and silver contents through Carter's whose bank confirms clearing their endorsed cheques and crediting your account, but last Friday I found she had also sold all the furniture through Agostino's who tell me the money was sent directly to you. I do appreciate you are bound by client confidentiality, but we are talking about a lot of money. Time is of the essence. I can obtain the power to see your bank statements, but I would like to ask what you did with the money. You can imagine how Lord Donald feels.' Much to his surprise Mike Millichop threw back his head and roared with laughter.

'What is so amusing, may I ask?' said Sim stiffly.

'Gone! Gone! All gone,' cackled Millichop. 'Confidentiality is not an issue. The bird has flown, Inspector. Flown to Ethiopia. I disposed of the money as she wished. It went to Camfam's Special Appeal for Ethiopia, which closed early thanks to Mrs Findlater's tremendous contribution. I think the shipment went on the first of September.'

He paused, ran practised fingers over the keyboard next to him, focused on the screen and said, 'Yes, here it is. I closed her account here on the twenty-first, sent the monies to Camfam as requested and on the twenty-seventh of August when I received their receipt, I wrote to tell her that I had carried out her instructions. Sent first class.'

Sim thought grimly of the letter ash and the partly burnt envelope outside Douggie Robertson's house. Forensic had said it was good-quality paper. 'May I trouble you for a sheet of your notepaper and an envelope similar to the one you sent to Mrs Findlater?' he said. 'And please will you let me know how much money you sent to Camfam.'

'One million, seven hundred and ninety-two thousand, four hundred and twenty-seven pounds!' Mike Millichop read off the screen and began to laugh again.

Well, that's one in the eye for you, Lord Donald, thought Detective Inspector Sim, bowing his head to hide his own thin smile from the laughing solicitor.

* * *

'This is no laughing matter,' Lord Donald snapped at his wife.

She continued talking as she stretched out across the bed, 'And now you are going to claim the insurance and get nearly two million pounds and we shan't have to have any more ugly old furniture in the flat and everything in the garden will be lovely. Do come to bed, Donald, Kitten's cold.'

Removing his dress-shirt cuff-links Donald ground his teeth. Kitten, he thought, some kitten. And if she was bloody well cold she should wear a proper nightdress. The cost of the nightclothes she bought was in inverse proportion to the warmth they provided. He went into his dressing room, undressed, pulled on a bathrobe and went back to the bedroom. Dorinda lay provocative and pouting. Donald looked at her with no feeling at all. She had driven him wild when he had met her. 'I threw away my wife and daughters for this,' he said to himself bitterly.

'Sit up,' he said sharply to Dorinda. 'Here, put on your dressing gown and listen. We are in difficulties. If I haven't explained properly before, I'm going to do it now.' With bad grace Dorinda sat up, put on her short frilly gown, tucked her feet under it and sat, a baby-doll figure in the middle of the bed, looking up at Donald through her eyelashes.

She's like a child, he thought. I mustn't be too hard on her. She's younger than my daughters. He remembered his sister's words. 'They don't like her, Donny, and they never will. She's displaced their mother, but what's worse, she's stolen their father from them.' He sat on the small pink velvet bedroom chair and looked at her.

'Dorinda, Mrs Findlater is a widow, not a funny old maid as you seem to think, and she's a very clever woman.'

Dorinda sighed and started to open her mouth.

'Hush my dear,' he said gently, 'and listen. When I divorced Mary to marry you I had to make a settlement for her. There is no way out of that. I have to give her a million pounds on the tenth of October.'

Dorinda said with a trace of a pout, 'Donald, I know all that. Do we have to go through it all again?'

Less gently, he went on, 'Please don't interrupt me. Let me finish. I have had three years to find the money and you know how happy I was in April when Mortimer-Desmond found me a buyer for Fionn-glass. The asking price was one million pounds, but they would only go to eight hundred thousand unless I would throw in the big furniture, which we don't need and you don't want. Right?' She nodded. 'Well, I'm not sure they will pay me even eight hundred thousand now as the furniture and fittings have all gone. That's my first worry.'

'Donald, you don't need to worry. I'll help you,' she cried taking up another of her poses. Baby Doll was gone. Virtuous Wife ready to 'Stand By Her Man' had taken over.

'Thank you,' he said, wondering what sacrifice she might be persuaded to make. The house in Gstaad. Her newly-ordered Porsche. Her account at her couturier, Yatsuki, shifty little Korean sod. 'Now, you keep talking about insurance—'

'I do not,' she snapped. 'You are the one who is always complaining about paying premiums and that safe I asked you for was a good idea. Carlo isn't a con man. The man who came from the insurance company to look at it said it was excellent.'

'Pity it wasn't bigger, was all I said. I did not say your mother's cousin was a con man. Anyway, let's not start on about all that again. I am trying to tell you what the situation is at present. I had the contents of Fionn-glass insured—'

'Exactly, that's what I keep on reminding you about. You said that policeman said she had made nearly two million. You'll get that from the insurance. Where's the problem?'

'The problem is that I was under-insured, I've just been checking. The most I can expect will be two hundred and fifty thousand.'

'A quarter of a million! That's not fair. You must sue her!'

'She hasn't any money, Dorinda, it would cost more in lawyer's fees than I'd get back.'

'Well, then, you must get it back from Camfam.' With the air of one who has solved a knotty problem, she patted the bed and went on in a little whispery voice, 'Kitten is happy again. Is Tiger going to come and play now?'

Filled with rage, Donald said through clenched teeth, 'Dorinda. The money cannot be "got back", just like that. Inspector Sim spoke to Camfam today and I have just spoken to Shackleton. They both tell me the same. The money was received in good faith and spent. It has been turned into food and medicine and Range Rovers. It is in Ethiopia. As far as we are concerned it is gone. Gone. Do you understand plain English?'

'There's no need to shout at me.' She wasn't pouting now. 'I didn't know it had gone to Ethiopia. How am I supposed to know a thing like that if you don't tell me, and being under-insured is stupid. My father told me that. I'm not so dumb as you like to think. All that jewellery you gave me is properly insured and kept in Carlo's safe.'

She flung herself off the bed and thrust her feet into her slippers. 'I'm going to make a cup of coffee. You'll have to sell something else to pay back bloody Mary. It's not my fault you were robbed.'

'A moment ago you thought it was funny!'

'That,' she said briskly, 'was before I knew you were under-insured.' She went towards the door, but spun round at Donald's next words.

'Well, since we are scoring little points, all that jewellery I "gave" to you is not yours. It's family jewellery and until I die it belongs to me and then it will belong to Julian. I told you and you had no need to insure it because I have it listed and I pay for it already. Furthermore, if I can't raise the money for Mary by the tenth, it will have to come out of Carlo's little safe and be sold.'

'I suppose you'll want my engagement ring, too?'

'Of course not, but you may have to cancel the Porsche.'

'Cancel the Porsche! But I've had it custom-built.'

'I know. That is why it's costing so much. They, wisely, have a cancellation fee. I can't raise a million pounds in a few days, Dorinda, without some sacrifice.' He softened his tone a little. He had to be careful. She could be wilful.

'You have stocks and shares.'

'I do, and they are pledged to Lloyd's. I am quite likely to lose most of them from what I hear.'

'What about the house in St John's Wood? You could sell that.'

'There are tenants there who have to be given proper notice and Julian has spent a lot on his flat. He won't want to give it up.'

'Oh! Tiger!' Dorinda rushed up to him and flung her arms round him. 'Ffiona will help us. She's going to inherit a fortune. That old aunt of hers is worth at least five million. Miriam told me. She'll be your daughter-in-law. She won't want to see the family jewels sold. I don't mean she'll give you the money, but she could lend it to you.'

Youth is a wonderful thing, thought Donald, folding his arms round her. It had been a mistake to try to explain his worries to her. Perhaps it would work out. Not, of course, by begging or borrowing from Ffiona, whose lawyers in Edinburgh and her vixen of a mother wouldn't let a penny piece come his way, but something might be arranged with Julian.

At the worst, he could sell the crested family silver, though he was loath to admit how much of it there was or how valuable it was. He hadn't exactly declared it when his estate was being valued for the divorce settlement. Well, how was he to know what was in his uncle's vaults at the bank? The stuff in his uncle's flat where Julian was now living was pretty impressive.

Holding Dorinda against him was proving much more agreeable than trying to explain about money to her. 'Does Kitten want a cup of coffee?' he murmured into her hair. God, she did smell gorgeous. She felt wonderful too. She didn't want coffee. Tiger bowed to the inevitable and climbed into bed with his delicious eager wife.

Arthur Bold lay pressed up against Martha's hot thighs. She was a comfort was Martha. Her last words before she turned on her side and went straight off to sleep had been, 'If they don't let her out on bail on Friday, Arthur, I'm going to write to the Secretary of State.'

She would too, he thought as he placed a cautious arm around her and composed himself for rest.

Alec Macleod turned over again, remembering snatches of his conversation with Kenneth. A son, born that morning, Jean-Marie Alexandre. In his honour. How much had he weighed? He'd have to tell Mary Ruth tomorrow. Three and a half kilos or four and a half? Which had he said? Three and a half would be seven pounds plus . . . As he struggled to work out what point-two of a pound was in ounces and multiply it in his head by three and a half, he dropped off.

Mary Ruth thought about the rector's visit that afternoon. She had been locked up for ten nights now. The heat was wearing and the night-time sanitary arrangements were primitive. A pale pink plastic, though lidded, 'chanty' was standing in the corner and the food was repetitive, but she'd had so much to think about she hadn't been bored for a moment. It was so restful just to do as she was told. Dennis had seemed like an alien. He always had been other-worldly, but as he sat and talked to her gently about the doings of Daldrum, Drumloch and Balessie she felt as if she had never known the places or the people. He had stayed for over an hour and assured her as he left that they would pray for her.

As she lay on her back relaxing every muscle in turn she wondered where he'd slip her in amongst 'all those who in this transitory life are in trouble, sorrow, need, sickness or any other adversity'.

She smiled at the thought of Mrs Smart, Miss Roland, Colonel Fraser-Gordon and Mr Phimister, the backbone of the congregation, praying for their erstwhile other regular. Would she be prayed for for ever, like Monica Witherspoon? She didn't seem to be in the good books of the Almighty. They had been praying for her for years. She hadn't died, nor had she got better. She just ate three meals a day and grumbled when anyone went to see her in the nursing home that she wasn't fed.

I would drop her from the list, thought Mary Ruth, if I were the rector. Old Monny's grim determination to remain grumbling at vast expense definitely gave the impression to the faithful few that prayer was ineffective. And it wasn't. Hadn't she prayed that Camfam would spend her contribution and see it went to help the Ethiopians before anyone could stop it? This very day a letter from Mr Field had informed her that Lord Donald couldn't get his money back from Camfam.

'If you are there, God,' Mary Ruth said in a good strong voice, 'Thank you!' The spyhole in her door flicked open.

The prowling night-guard will be telling them all the morrow that I'm a religious maniac . . . she thought and fell asleep.

Chapter 18

'Ooh! I am going to miss your silky skin,' said Miriam as she lay pressed against Julian's side in the bed in her studio in Paddington. 'I'll never forget these Thursday afternoons,' she added and slid her left hand down his right thigh.

Julian lay on his back, happy and relaxed. He closed his left arm around her and mumbled into her hair, 'What do you mean? I'm only getting married, I'm not emigrating.'

'So am I,' she said.

'So are you what?'

'Getting married, Julian. The party's over.'

'What? You didn't tell me.' He turned to face her and said sharply, 'Getting married? Who to?'

'Don't glare at me like that,' she said. 'To Harry, of course. You've known about it for yonks. Don't pretend you didn't.' Julian was silent, 'I'm not the only one with a desire to settle down,' she went on. 'You and Ffiona are tying the knot next month: it's not abnormal to want to marry.'

'Mim,' he said, 'are you telling me that our Thursdays are over?'

'Oh Julian, of course they are! I'm marrying Harry on the twenty-sixth and I'm going to be a good wife and I hope a good mother. You surely didn't think I was going to keep meeting you here every Thursday?'

He sat up at this and said, 'Well, yes, as a matter of fact that is exactly what I did think. Why not?'

'Julian,' she said as she sat up, 'you are not telling me that you seriously expect me to keep on having a weekly afternoon of sex with you after I'm married?'

'Why not?'

'Why not? I'll tell you why not – because I shall be a married woman and you will have Ffiona to wife. That's why not.'

Julian groaned and said, 'Mim, my darling Mim, we have a beautiful arrangement. Why spoil it? Ffiona has no idea how it is between us and I presume Harry doesn't know anything about us.'

Miriam pulled up the duvet to cover her breasts. 'You don't seem to have heard what I said,' she snapped. 'I'm getting married in two weeks' time. No one else has offered,' she looked hard at Julian, 'so I'm going to marry Harry and I'm not going to jeopardize everything by betraying him from the start.'

'Betraying him?' Julian was amazed. 'What about me? You and I are good music, Mim. We fit. We like each other and we please each other. Or so I always thought. Why throw all these years away?'

'Because we are both getting married, that's why.'

'Miriam, marriage is a convention, a duty. It's not the end of all fun and private joy. You and I love each other—'

She interrupted him. 'If you love me so much, why didn't you ask me to marry you?'

Julian was silent.

'I'll tell you why – you can't afford me. We've a huge amount to pay Lloyd's and your father has too, Daddy told me. Your housekeeper has robbed you and by the way, Dorinda is making a laughing-stock of your father with that cousin Carlo of hers.' She beat her hands on her knees. 'Oh! Julian, you're marrying Ffiona for her money, if the brutal truth be told. She's a friend of mine, remember. I introduced you and don't think I didn't notice how your attitude to her changed when you heard about the aunt who owns half of Edinburgh.'

She reached out for a cigarette and lit it. She didn't offer him one. She went on firmly, 'You have to admit that we are finished. Let's be adult about it. It all comes down to money. Ffiona's money will help you, perhaps, but not the rest of your lot. You know what her mother is like.'

'I think it's primitive to marry someone your father has chosen.'

'And I suppose it's civilized to stand up in St George's, Hanover Square and promise to be one flesh with Ffiona while continuing to fuck me on Thursday afternoons.'

'Don't be crude.'

'Well, don't be hypocritical then.' She reached out to the ashtray and said, 'Anyway, I've known Harry all my life. His mother and Daddy's first wife were sisters. It's not primitive to keep money in the family. It's common sense. Daddy and my half-brothers, all my mother's relatives in Berkshire and Harry's parents are happy about it.'

'You sound like rabbits!'

'Now who's being crude? You know I loved you, Julian. I would have been happy to marry you, even though you're not seriously rich, and earned my own living. We could have managed, but there it is. Now come on, don't sulk and spoil our last meeting. Come on. Please.' She paused and smiled at him. His heart turned over and he made a clumsy grab at her. 'No, don't. It's over, Julian. Aren't you going to wish me well?'

'I've never met this Harry. He's in South America, isn't he? Are you going to live there? Am I never even going to see you again?'

'Don't be silly, we're going to live in Lowndes Square. Harry's going to manage the Home and European portfolios. Daddy's retiring next year.'

'So it'll be roses, roses all the way and Daddy will be able to play with the little sprogs, when you get round to them. Won't that be nice? You'll be a real Yiddisher momma by the time you are forty, Mim. Fair, fat and forty.'

Miriam stubbed out her cigarette, stepped out of bed and went into the shower without another word. She dressed after that, brushed her hair and painted her lips. She put her pearl drop earrings in and stood looking at Julian lying in bed, sour-faced and cross.

'Your family has neglected its property and its investments,' she said quietly. 'You were mad to get me into bed, Julian, but money matters. It is influencing me and it's influencing you. You have dazzled Ffiona. She loves you. Just see to it that you don't hurt her – she's been hurt enough. Her mother wants putting down. I am going now. Please lock the door behind you and put your keys through the letter-box. You won't be needing them any more.' She turned, picked up her shoulder bag and, followed by Cain and Abel, her Irish wolfhounds, left the room.

As Donald Fionn-glass came into his flat he found Dorinda and Ffiona peeling the coverings off the portrait of his grandmother, which had been delivered that morning.

'I don't know where we can put her,' he said, 'or why she was left in Fionn-glass.' Then he added, 'The last of the Mohicans. All her lovely companions are faded and gone.'

'That's "The Last Rose of Summer",' said Ffiona unexpectedly. 'We used to sing it at school.' Donald looked at her in amazement. What on earth was she talking about? The Mohicans were North American Indians.

'That's my tiara,' cried Dorinda. 'Look! Oh! Donny, can I have my portrait painted wearing the tiara? I've heard about a marvellous little Czech who's painting absolutely *everybody* this year. We could hang them both in the dining room. Julian is going to take those horses I don't like.'

'Who said Julian could have them?' asked Donald sharply. 'They're by Stubbs. They're very valuable. He never asked me about them.'

'Oh, don't get in such a tizzy. We thought they'd fit well in the dining room at St John's Wood. Don't be so touchy, Donald. He is your son.' She took another look at the portrait. 'Where are the other jewels, Donny? Look, there's a necklace and earrings and two bracelets.'

'I've no idea, Dorinda. The picture's nearly a hundred years old. They could be anywhere.'

'Perhaps they're in your uncle's vaults. I could wear the whole set for the portrait.'

'We'll see,' said Donald and went towards his study door, undoing his tie.

'Don't forget we're taking Ffiona and her mother to the opera,' Dorinda called after him. 'It starts at eight. I've ordered a cab for seven-thirty. Julian should be in soon.'

Donald swung round trying not to look as if he'd forgotten. He noted Ffiona was wearing her black velvet and pearls, her neat, straight blonde hair fastened with a little black velvet bow. Pure 1950s, he thought.

'Mummy's giving up her bridge tonight,' said Ffiona smiling at him. 'Tonight was the only night we could get tickets for *Tristan and Isolde*.'

Donald smiled back. Sodding Wagner, he thought, and that skinny little whore Nina Crutchley-Gore. He might have known there'd be something laid on just when he wanted time to think. His lawyer had told him at ten that he had to find six hundred and fifty thousand for Lloyd's. He'd spent all day trying to work out how to raise the money without forfeiting the stocks and shares he had used as a guarantee.

Julian came in cheerfully saying, 'Hi Fee, Dorinda, Dad.' All the way from Paddington he had been thinking about Miriam. *I'll get her back.* It was natural enough to try and put old liaisons behind you a fortnight before your wedding. I'll wait a little while, he'd thought, and I'll give her a buzz while I'm changing and wish her well. No point making an enemy out of her. Ffiona might become suspicious. She's a tough cookie is Miriam. He dropped a kiss on Ffiona's head and said, 'I'll just get changed and then I'll make you a G and T that'll warm the cockles of your heart,' and sprinted up the stairs.

'And one for me,' called Dorinda following Donald into his study. Ffiona was surprised to be left alone in the hall, but applied herself to admiring the jewellery in the portrait. Where is it now, she wondered.

'And we're going to Boccaccio's for supper,' added Dorinda as she closed the study door. She realized Donald had forgotten about the opera. She knew he didn't like Wagner and the last time they had been to Boccaccio's he had said the prices were ruinous and he would never go there again, but she had a very good instinct for survival. Now was not the time to let Ffiona and especially her mother know that times were hard.

'I wish you'd tell me about these outings, Dorinda,' said Donald peevishly. 'I've had a hell of a day. I really don't feel up to big fat opera singers bawling in German and that greedy shrew Nina.'

'I did tell you, Donald, last Thursday and again this morning and it's in your diary, look.' She pointed it out.

'Well, give me half an hour and ask Julian to come in, please. I've got bad news I'm afraid. Is Nina coming here for a drink?'

'Yes. She's coming at half six. I've organized the champers.'

'Christ, she'll be able to swing a magnum if we're not leaving for an hour. Can we have something to eat, please?'

Dorinda pouted. 'What sort of something? It's Cook's night off.'

'Surely you can prepare some sandwiches, Dorinda? There must be something in the kitchen. God knows, the food bills are high enough. Get Ffiona to help you. She's not going to be doing much entertaining flanked by my Stubbs you're so busy giving her, if the family finances collapse. She'll need to learn to make sandwiches. Now hurry up, there's a good girl. And don't forget I want Julian. I'll be in the drawing room for a drink and a sandwich by half past, I promise. I'll be charming to Nina and changed too, by then. Now get a move on.'

He sat at the desk and picked up the phone. By the time Julian came in with a gin and tonic in his hand Donald was even more depressed as he listened to Shackleton. He waved to Julian to sit. 'What will they offer?' he asked. 'How much? Bloody ridiculous. We'll have to try again. Well, see if you can persuade them. Right.' He put the phone down and sighed.

'Bad news?' asked Julian.

'Bad news. First the storms of eighty-seven are to be paid for as I told you this morning. I have to pay your mother a million smackers on October tenth and the people who were going to buy the house are now offering six-fifty instead of eight hundred thousand which they offered last week rather than the original million, as the furniture is gone.'

He ran his hands through his hair and looked ruefully at Julian. 'I also have some unpleasant news from my insurance company. Shack tells me I'm not getting a quarter of a million from them as that was only one-fifth of the value of the goods insured; I'm getting fifty thousand for the contents of Fionn-glass instead. Something to do with "averaging". Frankly, I don't care what they call it, it's daylight bloody robbery.'

'What are you going to do, Dad?' Julian said, wondering who else besides Miriam and her father knew of the mess his father was in.

'Well, I toyed with the idea of shooting myself. I then wondered if your mother might be amenable to waiting for her share of the family pennies. I turned both these ideas down, I hope you'll be pleased to hear.'

He stood up and went over to the sideboard and poured himself a large whisky. 'I think if I sell all the silver my uncle had in the vaults, of which a tithe has to go to your mother, forget Gstaad, cancel the Porsche Dorinda has been designing and flog the Stubbs she doesn't like, I may manage. I'm not looking forward to seeing Nina tonight, I never am, but if she has a whiff of this she'll tie up Ffiona's inheritance tighter than a choirboy's bum. Anything useful to suggest?'

'Well, first of all you must let me buy our part of St John's Wood. I can easily get a mortgage and second, there's some very good stuff there. I've just had Steadman's in to value it for the insurance. The Queen Anne cabinet in the hall is down for twenty-five thousand and there's a pair of George I pier glasses at fifty thousand each for starters, and those are the valuations. Probably fetch far more at auction. They're family stuff, Dad, not mine, Ffiona won't mind. We'll raise the money somehow.'

Donald embarrassed him by weeping. His face crumpled and his shoulders shook. Then after a moment he pulled himself together and said, 'Thank you for your help, Julian. We'll talk about it in the office tomorrow.'

'You'd better get changed,' said Julian. 'It's nearly half past.'

'Aye,' said Donald finishing his whisky and then blowing his nose hard. 'What's that bit in Pagliacci? Ah! yes.' He threw out an arm, then roared unmusically, 'On with the motley, let joy be unconfined!'

The door opened and Dorinda put her head in. 'You haven't time for singing, Donald. I'm changed, you'd better hurry up. Nina will be here in five minutes. Ffiona's making the sandwiches. Go and help her, Julian.' Donald inclined his head and she closed the door.

'I must say, Julian, I'd have preferred a bit of Gilbert and Sullivan to Wagner myself. Not really in the mood for soul-searching.'

Julian laughed. 'It's not so much the opera as being seen. Dorinda and Nina wanted to go tonight because Crispin Topp is going to be there.'

'Crispin Topp! Who's he when he's at home?'

'Editor of *Topp Gals*! Read by all the top girls, don't you know. He's a distant relative of Nina's and she cultivates him so she can be where he is and get a mention in his mag.'

'Women!' Donald shook his head. 'Is Ffiona into all this high-society stuff?' he asked as he went to the door.

'No, thank God,' answered Julian. 'She spends all her time in the Victoria and Albert. She's seriously into paperweights. She's got a very good collection,' he added, but his father had gone. Julian leaned over for the phone. This time it was answered. Miriam sounded odd. He assumed Harry was there.

'Wanted a quick word,' he said.

'No, thanks,' she replied, 'I've ordered them already.'

'It's me, Mim.'

'It's very kind of you, but no thank you.'

'Meet me at Prospero's at six tomorrow,' he said quickly. He was sure she was about to hang up.

'Well, I'll pop in and have a look, but I don't think I need any more,' she said brightly and hung up.

Well now, was that a yes or no, thought Julian and went to see why Ffiona was making sandwiches.

'Flowers of London,' said Miriam to Harry as she put the receiver down. 'Touting for custom at this late stage, silly beggars.'

Harry laughed. Miriam was going to be a fine wife. She had the sense to know what she wanted and she knew how to handle opportunists. I am a lucky man, he thought.

Chapter 19

'Well, Friday the thirteenth is turning out lucky so far,' said Donald Fionn-glass as he and his son belted up. 'It's been very interesting,' he said as he turned the ignition key. 'I hadn't been to my uncle's vaults before. That silver is quite something, all those tureens and that Menteith.'

'If the valuer is right, Dad, that's two hundred thousand in the kitty,' said Julian, who was fretting to get back to his office.

'With the stuff from your flat and if the pictures in the office my uncle always bragged about really are worth eight thousand each, then I'm well on the way. I read this article,' he explained as he waited to get out of the side street, 'in this magazine at the dentist last week.'

Julian waited impatiently for the information, wishing he'd suggested his father had gone to the vaults alone. He had a lot of work to do before his wedding.

There was a gap in the traffic and the big Jaguar glided forward. 'It was about pictures bought at the Great Exhibition of 1872,' Donald went on. 'My uncle told me that his father hadn't paid above forty pounds for any of the Vollmars or Hoefers he'd bought and we've got forty of the buggers hanging about the offices. How's your mental arithmetic? I make it three hundred and twenty thousand minimum . . .'

'That's great,' said Julian, thinking that his father obviously hadn't any pressing business if he had time to be counting pictures.

'... so when I get back to the office and ring Who-ja's about your contribution, gratefully received I can tell you,' he added, giving Julian a little sheepish smile, 'I'm going to ask them to come and look at the pictures too.' He turned left into the lane behind their building and slid into the underground car park.

How he has the energy to do any work beats me, thought Julian. After six weeks at Baltic Mansions I'm worn out just watching him and Dorinda gadding about. Donald turned the ignition off and said, 'Well now, things are looking up. Thanks for coming, Julian.'

'My pleasure,' said Julian, still thinking about Dorinda. She was so extravagant. Why pay a cook and eat out nearly every night? I couldn't possibly live that kind of life—

His father said interrupting his thoughts, 'At least I've got your mother's money. She's very sensible, she'll manage her affairs properly.'

Which is more than Dorinda ever will, thought Julian. The bill last night at Boccaccio's was nearly seven hundred pounds and I was hungry again at bedtime. He grimaced as he recalled eating up the stale sandwiches.

As they got out of the car Donald said, 'I think I might be able to save the Porsche for Dorinda.' He sounded cheerful. Julian's chilly silence as they walked towards the lift made him apologetic. 'I'll still owe them a tidy sum even if I cancel.'

Julian entered the lift and pressed the button. 'No need to explain to me. It's your business, Dad,' he said, but privately he thought Dorinda needed a customized Porsche like a hole in the head. All she did was spend money. He had some sympathy for his father because Dorinda was bewitchingly attractive, but so stupid. 'The Malaysian business is coming together well,' he said as they left the lift. 'I'm sure we'll manage to save your portfolio – that's the main thing.'

'And maybe Shack will have squeezed some more out of the buyers,' said Donald as they reached his office door.

That'll be another huge bill, thought Julian. Nothing's for nothing. 'I'll get on, Dad,' he said.

'Just come in and see if there's a message from old F-G. He was going to let me know about Mary Ruth.'

'Right,' said Julian, 'then I must get on. The Algerian contract is coming up in ten days.'

'Any more trouble with our Arab friends?' asked Donald as they walked across his room.

'Well no, so far so good. I told you there are fundamentalist stirrings in all the Arab countries, but the last time I was there Yusif asked me if we had a London branch office. He seems to think Scottish Glen Holdings is up some quiet valley far away from the City.'

'That's our name for you,' said Donald proudly. 'My grandfather chose it instead of Potts and Findlater for that very reason, so I was told. Smacks of sheltered glens with contented sheep and sturdy, sensible farmers—'

'Is there a message from Colonel F-G?' asked Julian, wondering briefly what his great-grandfather would have said if his housekeeper had stolen so much as a silver teaspoon.

'Yes, here we are,' said Donald and read out: '"Mary Ruth Findlater was up before the Sheriff at ten and released into the custody of her uncle, pending trial."'

He sat behind his desk and smiled at Julian. 'Now that was good of F-G, wasn't it? They've obviously got the case against Mary Ruth organized, though she's got bail which surprises me.'

'She's hardly a danger to the public,' said Julian, suddenly remembering that he'd asked Kenneth and his wife to the wedding. Perhaps I could just forget to send an invitation. What a mess it all is, he thought. 'It costs the taxpayer a fortune to keep people in jail,' he said adding, 'I suppose she'll stay with Alec. Poor old man, he must be horrified.'

Donald looked up at him. 'Never mind Alec,' he said irritably, 'there are other things to worry about. I'm still puzzling over why she left the portrait, but more importantly, as Dorinda keeps pointing out, where are the other sapphires? They would be a very great help in present troubles.'

'Well, they weren't in the vaults,' said Julian, wincing at the inaccurate quote. 'It's odd altogether. Was anything else left behind? What did Sim say?'

'His sergeant had found about seven hundred quid's worth of booze in the cellar, unopened and with Allison's delivery note attached. It was the order for our Easter visit. I'm surprised she didn't send it back.'

'I'm surprised she didn't sell it,' said Julian as he went off to his own room. Thank God the builders are nearly finished and I'll be able to get back home soon, he thought as he reached his own desk. Even paying the mortgage won't hurt so much after two months of sharing a house with Dorinda. He started to open his mail.

Lord Donald was not over-cheerful, whatever impression he had given Julian. He had cancelled the house at Gstaad without telling Dorinda. She was going to ski there for a winter break after Julian's wedding. He was not looking forward to telling her that skiing was all she'd be doing. Showing her sister and her mother the site and the plans and choosing accessories for the new house was right out.

I don't want the word out that I'm in financial difficulties, he thought. The cancellation of the house isn't going to be easy to hide. Dorinda's been trumpeting its purchase all over town. He began to open his mail. I don't feel like work, he realized, and thought about Julian's offer of help. I'm not so sure Ffiona will be equally willing; I'd better ring the auctioneers and get the stuff moved pronto. He reached for the phone book. Perhaps she hasn't really looked at it yet. Must remember to tell them about the pictures here too.

As he waited for an answer he gave a little sigh. I am learning a lot, in particular that I was a much richer man than I knew in April and that now I can't really afford a Porsche. He thought about his wife. A temporary shortage of funds, I'll tell her. I'll blame the theft for the loss of the Gstaad house and sweeten the pill by reinstating the threatened Porsche, but it's not going to be easy. What madness possessed me to allow her to order it, he was thinking when Steadman's answered.

When he put the phone down he did a rough calculation. Then he rang his lawyer. 'I've had an idea, Shack. I'm going to ask Mary to let me sell one of the flats in St John's Wood. Then I'll be home and dry.'

'She won't do that. I know we were distancing your assets when we put them in her name, old son, a classic example of a good idea at the time,' Shackleton chuckled briefly and Donald flared his nostrils and tapped his fingers on his desk. Shackleton was altogether too flippant, he was thinking as the rich voice continued, 'but Mary sees those flats as a sacred trust for the girls.'

'Well, it's worth a try. I thought if I pay her bang on time it might help her to sympathize with my shortfall of half a million for Lloyd's.'

'I don't think so. She'll say you had the good times and now you must pay.' Shackleton sang the last four words. Donald was beginning to seethe when Shackleton asked, 'Can't you find another directorship?'

'Be sensible, Stephen. They want younger men now. I lost the Hornick Trust last year and no one's sniffing around as far as I know. Surely if I chat her up at Julian's wedding . . .?'

'Well, if you are serious all I can suggest is that you offer to make the attics into a studio flat, at your expense, put in a shower and a kitchenette—'

Donald interrupted. 'They're called galley kitchens now.' Dorinda had told him that.

'OK, a galley kitchen. What we have to do is show Mary that the girls will still have a *pied-à-terre* and one valuable flat producing a good income between them. I still don't think much of your chances, but try by all means. You don't want to lose your share portfolio.'

'Wouldn't be able to afford you then, would I?' Donald laughed, but he wasn't smiling. He hung up and sank into gloomy reflection as he thought about the big family house in St John's Wood where he had hoped to live with Dorinda. Another unnecessary expense, he thought sourly. Dorinda *had* to live in town, she had said, so instead of having the pick of the flats in the big house in Hamilton Terrace and letting Julian have second choice, a double flat in Kensington it was. And I'm still paying for it, he grumbled to himself. I must have been addled when I met Dorinda, he thought moodily. What did my mother say? 'There's no fool like an old fool.' God, I resented that remark, but that was three years ago.

He sat up and started to think positively. This is no good. I will talk Mary round and sell at least one of the first-floor flats. It'll fetch around four hundred and fifty thousand and with the cash from Julian and the German pictures sold . . . the Malaysian deal through . . . the Algerian business falling into place . . . Idly, he looked at his diary.

Christ! Sand and Cement International Directors' meeting in half an hour. He rang the bell and ordered his secretary to run out for a ham sandwich with mustard and make him a cup of coffee, while he found the file and had a skim through the agenda.

In his office Julian was eating a cheese sandwich, drinking a diet Coke and dictating between mouthfuls as he tried to catch up on the missed morning's work. At three he went to see his bank manager. An hour later, after arranging to use the flat as collateral, he had borrowed three hundred thousand pounds and promised to pay it back at seventeen per cent. I'm sorry I spoke, he thought as he settled down to sign his letters.

Ffiona rang him at ten past five. 'A friend of my mother's has heard you are selling some Queen Anne furniture. Will you please meet me at the flat at six and tell me what else you have decided to sell, without consulting me – if you don't mind, that is.'

He suddenly remembered his date with Miriam. Six at Prospero's. He'd have a job making that now, but he had to see her. 'Make it eight, Fee, I've an urgent appointment.'

'Drinks with the old gang I suppose. Honestly, Julian, grow up!'

Cursing under his breath he rushed out of the office nearly knocking his secretary flying and ran down the stairs hoping to catch a passing cab. Who the hell has been talking, he wondered, as he bobbed up and down with impatience, waving his arm and shouting 'Taxi!' And which of Nina's wrinkly cronies was it?

'Want a lift, Julie,' shouted Jumbo Massingham leaning across the passenger seat, 'or are you doing a war dance?'

'Yes please,' said Julian and clambered into the front seat.

'Where are you bound, sweetie? She must be hot stuff. You're positively puce with anticipation.'

'Prospero's. You magic man! Step on the gas!'

'Is one permitted to know whom one is going to meet? Or would it be indiscreet to ask?'

'The latter. I am very glad to see you. How's tricks?'

'Well, you know I've set up on my own, don't you? Dad was becoming quite impossible. Poor old Bimbo, I think he's ill to be frank, but he won't go and see a specialist. Remember when he fell down the stairs at Fionn-glass when we were shooting last year? Well, he's done it several times. Poor Freddie is at her wits' end. She even rang my revered mother to try and get her to work on him.'

Julian laughed. 'God, you think she'd know better than that, after all these years.'

'Exactly!' crowed Jumbo, landing a big hand on Julian's thigh. 'You understand Madre. Freddie must have been desperate to call her. Useless, of course, the sooner poor old Bimbo falls under a bus the better she'll be pleased. She's itching to get her feet under the table in Gloucestershire and play the dowager. Doubtless I shall have to take up residence and administer the estate. Ghastly thought. Buried alive, I'll be. Will I have to toddle along to the local and drink cider with the peasants? Or is that only in Somerset?'

'It's only in story-books, Jumbo. They're into designer beers now.'

Jumbo laughed and patted Julian's leg again. His habit of patting him and calling him silly names had developed at Eton. Julian didn't notice it any more and as Jumbo was so big, six feet seven and over twenty stone, no one else commented upon it either.

'To escape going bush I'll have to take my seat in the Lords. Not a nice thought. There's not a pretty botty amongst them.' The traffic was at a standstill. Jumbo always talked about himself so Julian didn't worry about having to answer any questions, but he was worrying about the time. He looked at his watch.

'Control your impatience, darling. I know a short cut through a block of flats. I'm doing the conveyancing and I had to look at them recently. Cuts out all the lights.' He steered into the inside lane and was silent for a hundred yards, then, patting Julian again he said, 'I wish with all my heart, Julie, that I had an uncomplicated life like yours and that I was not the eldest son of a dotty peer and that I had never gone against my own inclinations and married.

'We shall be at your nuptials by the way, spruced up and looking in our prime. It's a long time since I was considered a "best man",' he cackled as he swung into the block of flats and stopped at the chain barrier. 'Hop out Julia, there's a good girl, and unchain the chain.'

Julian did as he was told and waited until the big Bentley had passed. Then he re-hooked the chain wondering what he would say to the caretaker if he appeared. This was a typical Jumbo trick, but he always got away with things. Always had.

With Julian safely back in the car Jumbo continued his monologue. 'Nothing against Jane,' he said as he wound through the parked cars in the courtyard. 'She keeps well out of my way. She's running the Gloucester end for Bimbo, really. She's into horses and dogs and the kiddiwinkies keep her amused.' He giggled and said, 'Watch this! This is the cunning bit,' and swept into a tunnel at the end of which they came out into Church Street Lane about fifty yards from Prospero's. It was just six o'clock.

'Thanks Jumbo,' said Julian as he climbed out of the car.

'Always a pleasure to serve sir,' replied Jumbo and with a vile wink, drove off.

Prospero's was a dark, cosy restaurant and bar. It was ideal for assignations as the tables were set between high-backed hooded settles and the waiters, Georgiou and Mario, were discreet. Every evening at six the proprietor Dmitri Prospero came out of the kitchen where he had been preparing the evening meals, to sit draped in an enormous white linen napkin and eat his own meal at the table nearest the cash register. The bar was at the back and next to the Gents there was a fire door through which it was possible to slip away unseen.

Julian went down the dark room between the murmuring tables and peeped into the bar. He didn't expect Miriam would be there. There were only two men in the bar and he didn't know them. He went back towards the street door, said good evening to Prospero and sat at the table opposite his. He sat craning his neck round the settle, watching for Miriam. Georgiou nodded to him as he presented Prospero with his *moules marinière.* The door opened and Miriam came in.

'Georgiou,' she called, 'I've a cab waiting. Have you seen the pair to this?' She held out her pearl drop earring.

Georgiou looked at it and said, 'I'm sorry madam, but no.' She turned to Prospero and grimaced.

'If he turn up, I keep him for you,' he said gallantly and sucked noisily at a mussel.

She turned towards the door and Julian, terrified she hadn't seen him, leaped up banging his thigh painfully on the table and cried, 'Well, hello, Miriam. Fancy seeing you.'

She glanced at him briefly and said, 'Julian, I'm sorry, I have an appointment. I can't stop.'

'Mim,' he managed before she swung on her heel and headed for the door. He went after her and opened the door for her. She went out and he followed her. In the street she turned to him and smiled at him as though they were the best of friends. He felt more aroused by her than ever before. He felt dizzy with excitement. She was going to offer him a lift in her cab and take him away to bed. He began to listen to her. She was speaking very quietly and quickly.

At first he couldn't understand. She was smiling and tilting her head and gazing into his eyes and saying, 'So don't ring me at home again. Got it? Don't! I've had a hell of a time managing to get here, but I wanted to be sure you have the picture. No more calls. Got it? And if you ever call me Mim again in front of anyone, up to and including the waiters at Prospero's, I shall tell Ffiona about our Thursdays and for good measure, I'll introduce her to a particularly well-placed duke whose wife is shortly to be disposed of and who would be very happy to get his hands on her Edinburgh money. In case you haven't spoken to her today, she is now a very rich woman as her aunt died this afternoon. Do I make myself clear?'

'Perfectly,' said Julian. She stepped into her cab without another word, still smiling graciously at him. As the cab moved off he saw her putting her earring on. Then she took the other one out of her purse and put it in her other ear.

There seemed little point in going back into Prospero's and Julian set off homewards, baffled. So much for the sweet reconciliation, the agreement to wait a little before resuming what had been a lovely Thursday-afternoon habit. As he strode through the Kensington crowds he began to worry. I'd better honey up Ffiona. I've promised Dad she'll be at the flat on Tuesday at ten to let the men in to collect the furniture and I haven't asked her if she's free or if she minds selling it. She didn't sound very pleased on the phone.

He dodged round an entwined stationary couple, staring hungrily into each other's faces in the middle of the pavement. His mind was racing. It's my furniture. We've more than enough furniture. She's marrying me, not my furniture. Surely she isn't going to be sticky about it. Not now she's a multimillionaire in her own right. Unfortunately, he knew only too well, it was often the way. 'The more they have the more they want,' he said to the front door as he put his key in the lock. If the furniture means so much to Ffiona, he decided as he opened the door, I'll say it was all a mistake. I'll speak to Dad.

In the flat he looked into the study and the drawing room. No sign of Donald. Then he heard a violent crash from the main bedroom. Dorinda's voice rang out piercingly. 'A mistake! Is that what you call it?' Another crash. If Dorinda's throwing furniture about, I think I'll keep out of the way, thought Julian and went up to lie down before dinner.

It had been a mistake on Donald's part to laugh when Dorinda picked up the dressing-stool. Now it lay amongst the remnants of the cheval-glass. Her silver-backed hairbrush had just missed his face and hit his bedside lamp. She stood panting and clenching her fists. Then she hissed, 'I don't call it a mistake. I call it a deliberate attempt to make me look a fool in front of everybody.'

'Oh! Dorinda,' he said gently, 'why should I want to make you look a—, look foolish? It would reflect on me, you know. It was a mistake, my mistake, to order the Porsche and the house before I knew how much money there would be from the sale of Fionn-glass. I expected at least half a million over what I needed to pay the settlement. I am sorry. It was fun sitting beside the Pacific and planning the house in Gstaad. I was interested too, you know that. What I didn't know until last week was that Lloyd's would be wanting money too. I don't have a gold mine, you know.'

'I don't feel I want to go to Gstaad at all now,' Dorinda said pulling a face and beginning to cry. 'You've spoiled it. I'm going to cancel the skiing too,' she said firmly, wiping her eyes and thrusting her pretty chin up bravely. 'If I can't have my own house there, I'd rather not go.'

Donald was not convinced this idea would prevail, but at least she seemed to have calmed down for the moment. 'Dorinda, listen, I think with the silver we saw today and the money Julian is going to give me—'

Dorinda interrupted. 'I saw Poppy Gill today, Nina's friend, the one who is moving into the Queen Anne house and I told her about the Queen Anne stuff you said Julian was willing to sell. She was very interested. I thought it might be more discreet if it was sold privately so I told her to ring Ffiona.'

'Good thinking. I'm sure we can manage and I don't see why

you shouldn't have the Porsche if you've set your heart on it. I don't want you to be sad. I just have to go carefully at the moment.'

Dorinda sniffed and said, 'Would you like to see the dress I've bought for Julian's wedding?'

Mindful of the hundred dresses she had in her dressing room Donald sighed, but he disguised it and said, 'Yes: come on Kitten, try it on. You've got time before dinner.'

She skipped into the dressing room saying, 'Close your eyes then.' He sat down on the pink velvet chair and closed his eyes. I mustn't fall asleep, he thought, but oh, how tired I am.

'Now you can look.' Dorinda's voice sounded. He opened his eyes.

She was wearing a white Thai silk suit with a skirt which stopped a foot above her knees. It was simple and he knew from experience it would have cost at least three thousand. She'll upstage the bloody bride in it. What can I say, he thought desperately.

'Well, what do you think?' She pirouetted in front of him, certain of the effect. She looked ravishing. 'I wondered if white was really right for someone else's wedding,' she was prattling, 'but I am the bridegroom's father's wife and I thought I shouldn't look dowdy.'

'You certainly won't do that.' He tried to sound enthusiastic. Whatever will Mary think, he thought. Or Ffiona. Or the girls. I can't cope with this. 'It's lovely,' he said. 'Now hop out of it and let's go and have a drink before dinner. Julian should be in soon.'

Julian paid the cabbie and rang the bell of the St John's Wood flat. It was well-lit along Hamilton Terrace, but there were break-ins in the neighbourhood almost every day and he had made Ffiona promise to keep the chain on if she was in alone. 'Who is it?' came a little voice.

'It's me, Julian.' She opened the door and he was shocked to see her tear-streaked face. 'Are you all right?' He put his arms out and she pressed herself into his chest. He shook her gently. 'Ffiona, you're not hurt? No one's broken in?'

'Oh! Julian, I've been here since seven o'clock. I couldn't face Mummy tonight. Why didn't you tell me you were going to sell the little cabinet? I do like it and I am so fed up with all the nice little pieces of furniture in our flat disappearing.'

'Wait a minute,' he said. 'Wipe your eyes and blow your nose and tell me what has upset you so much.' He gave her his handkerchief.

She did as he said and they went into the flat. They sat on the sofa in the hall and she gulped and sniffed for a minute, then said, 'Well, first of all Dorinda told Poppy Gill, that shrill little show-off Mummy's so fond of – I can't think why – that she knew you wanted to sell some Queen Anne furniture and if she was interested she was to ring me. Well, that would have been bad enough, but I was out and Mummy answered and of course she didn't know anything about it. When I got in she asked me why I hadn't mentioned the sale and I had to admit I didn't know either.' Here she broke down again and cried into his handkerchief.

Julian was filled with remorse and pity. He could just imagine Nina grilling Ffiona. She had always been jealous that Ffiona was her aunt's heir and kept a very close watch on her. 'I'm so sorry, Ffiona. It's no excuse, but my father was blubbing last night and he is in a mess. I didn't think. I was trying to help him.'

Ffiona looked a little less anguished, but she went on in a burst, 'It was terrible, Julian. She said you obviously didn't confide in me and that it was a funny way to behave six weeks before our wedding and what else had you hidden from me. She went on and on, Julian, and although I know it is none of her business I had to agree that I didn't know. She's always tried to protect me because of my inheritance. I know she means well, but I'd never really had a boyfriend until you came along. I couldn't believe it when you rang me up the first time after Miriam had introduced us at Jumbo and Jane's party. I'm not glamorous like Miriam—'

Julian broke in and said softly, 'You've got beautiful blonde hair, Ffiona. Ffiona means the fair one, I looked it up. Fionn-glass is the fair place. One day you'll be the fair lady of the fair place.'

'Mummy says it'll go mousy. Hers did. She has it touched up now.'

Julian felt tears sting his eyelids. What need was there to say such a thing? His mother would never have been so cruel to Kathy and Lizzy. In fact it was his mother who had first remarked on the beauty of Ffiona's hair. She wasn't glamorous. She wasn't pretty and she certainly wasn't made for country life, but she was neat and peaceful to have around and she was willing in bed and she loved him. He knew that without Miriam needing to tell him.

'I can't tell you what it meant to me, Julian. I thought you were sweet on Miriam, though I knew she'd never marry you, of course. She was betrothed, that's the right word isn't it, to Harry.'

'I was taken with her for a while, but it was all over long ago. I knew about Harry too. Who didn't?' I for one, he thought. 'She's fun though, and I shall never forget her for introducing you to me.' Oddly enough he meant it, he realized. I could do much worse than have a loving wife, he thought. Ffiona and her paperweights will be easier to live with than Dorinda.

There had been another row brewing as he had left. She wanting to go to a nightclub to join a party of her mother's cousin Carlo, his father wanting bed. Sleep. Rest. Poor soul. How cousin Carlo could afford nightclubbing was a mystery to Julian. He sold safes to rich women. Funny way to earn a living.

'I wouldn't have minded so much if it hadn't been the Queen Anne cabinet. I had one very like it. It was in my sitting room. Mummy sold it without telling me,' Ffiona was saying.

'How come, if it was yours?' asked Julian, some native wit telling him not to speak ill of Nina whom he could happily have strangled.

'Well,' she said sitting up, 'Daddy left her a life interest in the flat and a pension. You know he was quite a lot older than Mummy.'

'Aha!'

'Yah, well, in his will the flat and the furniture is left to me. Mummy says inflation has eroded her income and every so often she sells some of the furniture. I wouldn't mind so much if she'd tell me, but she tends to forget. In May she sold the Queen Anne cabinet and I was so pleased about the one here. I'm so looking forward to having my own home to care for.'

'I'm not selling anything, Ffiona, unless you say so. What else do you especially like?'

'The pier glasses in the drawing room. They make the room so light, and I just love them.'

'How about the dining room? Anything there you like, or don't like?'

'You mean the table and the chairs.'

'What else is there?'

'That silver thing in the middle of the table.'

'You shock me, woman. You mean my grandfather's epergne!'

'Well, if you like all that big ornate silver, I'll—'

'Ffiona. Tomorrow we'll make a list of all the ugly, heavy, over-elaborate, rude, crude and unattractive objects in this flat and on Tuesday when the van comes they can take them away. Now will you come to bed?'

'Julian,' she murmured later, 'I didn't tell you, my aunt died this afternoon. Will it worry you having a rich wife?'

'Only if she keeps me awake talking nonsense,' he replied sleepily, and said a little prayer of thanks that he hadn't answered, 'I know.'

[illegible]

[illegible]

[illegible]

[illegible]

[illegible]

[illegible]

[illegible]

[illegible]

Chapter 20

'Come away in,' said Douggie Robertson. 'I'm fine pleased to see you. Come in Mr Macleod and welcome. Stella's away down to the shop, she'll be back directly. Be quiet, Napper,' he called into the house adding, 'he knows who all's here. Just listen to him.'

Mary Ruth stood awkwardly in the hall while Douggie closed the front door and the porch door behind Alec. When he opened the living room door Napper burst into the hall and leapt into Mary Ruth's arms. He began licking her face, his tail wagging all the time. She twisted her face to the side and held him out from her. He wriggled closer and started licking her ear and her neck. She found tears running down her cheek, not just because of the effusive welcome from Napper, but because Douggie was behaving as though nothing had happened. She put the dog down and felt for her hanky.

Douggie showed them into the clean and tidy living room and bent over slowly to turn the television off. 'I like to watch the racing,' he said. 'They say it's even better if you bet, but I never started the habit and now I don't want to.'

Alec smiled and sat in the big comfortable chair which Douggie indicated. Mary Ruth sat opposite him by the side of the fire. Douggie sat on the sofa and patted Napper who had moved to his side. Mary Ruth blew her nose and sniffed. The dog was looking round at her, his tail still thrashing.

'I see you,' Douggie said to the happy dog. 'Yes, yes, here's your mistress come to see you.'

'There's no doubting he's pleased to see you, Mary Ruth,' said Alec. The dog went to him at once. 'I see you,' said Alec and leaned forward to stroke the excited animal's head.

'We'll wait for Stella to have a cuppie,' Douggie said. 'Now, how are you? What's going to happen to you?' He looked at Mary Ruth. He had never used her name when he spoke to her, she realized suddenly.

'I'm all right thank you, Douggie. I've been released into Alec's care until December the twelfth when I've to appear at the High Court in Inverness. Mr Field, the solicitor, thinks I'll get five years.'

'I hope it's only five years,' said Douggie. 'Rich people don't like losing money any more than the rest of us. I wouldn't be too confident.'

'That's my feeling too,' said Alec. 'We'll have to wait and see, but Mr Field seemed to think she'll only get a five-year sentence because she's a first offender.'

'And he says that The Valley, the women's jail, is a lot better than Inverness jail,' added Mary Ruth.

'Jail's jail!' Douggie said. 'Like the army. How long will you get off for good behaviour?'

'About a third, Mr Field told me.'

'Well, watch your step then. People are bored in prison. They make trouble for newcomers. You're not a professional. It may not be as easy as you seem to think to keep yourself right.' Douggie sounded very gloomy.

To change the subject Mary Ruth said, 'Has Napper been good?'

At the sound of his name the dog came over and jumped up on to her knee and Douggie perked up and said, 'He's been first-class. Have you seen Mrs Inglis yet?'

'No, I haven't been anywhere else. One of the conditions of bail is that I don't interfere with any witnesses. It sounds dreadful, but I only want to ask you about Napper. If I'm for the jail I'll have to find him another home. I got out yesterday. I'm squeezed into

Alec's spare room among his painting gear. There isn't room for Napper. I'm enough trouble as it is.'

'You are welcome Mary Ruth,' said her uncle, 'and we'll make it tidier for you. I don't do much painting in the winter anyway. I like the warmth too much as I get older.' He smiled at Douggie. 'I can't say that coming to see you and Stella and Napper,' at the sound of his name the dog pricked his ears again and Alec smiled at him and continued, 'I can't say visiting you can really be considered interfering with witnesses. Mary Ruth is very nervous.'

'That's reasonable enough,' said Douggie. 'I've been interviewed. I hadn't anything to tell them. Are you warm enough?' he added, although the fire was burning brightly.

'Perfectly,' said Alec. 'There's nothing like an open fire. I miss mine. I wouldn't go back from my central heating now, but I am enjoying your fire, Douggie.'

'Aye, it's cheery and I think a good draught through the room is healthy. Some of thon new houses are like hot-presses. It's no wonder there's so mony colds and flus about,' Douggie said. 'Mind, Stella's aye telling me it'd be easier for me if we had central heating here. It wouldn't be easier on my pocket, that's for sure.'

'How is Mrs Inglis?' asked Mary Ruth. 'I wrote to her last week.'

'Aye and she was fine pleased,' said Douggie, 'but she'd dearly like it if you went in by. She's brought the cats home. It was easier than going all the way up yonder to feed them and it'll be winter soon. We put your hens down to Tibby. I hope we did right.'

'Oh Douggie, of course you did. I never realized what a lot of trouble I was making for everybody. I felt guilty about bringing Napper here when Mrs Inglis has always had him when I've been away for a night or two. I know she loves him.'

'Well, there's no need to worry about that. She knows he's easier managed here. We're well away from the main road, but she'll tell you herself.'

They heard the back door open and Stella came in. 'Oh! It's you, Mary Ruth. I saw the car. I couldn't think who it could be.' She came straight over to Mary Ruth who stood up to greet her. Stella put her arms round her and kissed her. 'Welcome home,' she said. 'We have been worried about you.' She pulled away and looked hard at her face. 'You look all right. Have they been feeding you properly? Martha has been up to high doh about locking you up, as you'll know, Alec.' She went across the hearth and gave him a kiss too. Then she looked at Douggie and said, 'Haven't you made them a cup of tea?'

'I can't do right, can I?' he said and laughed. 'I said we'd wait for you to come back because I thought I'd be sure to use the wrong teapot or the wrong cups and now I'm getting a row anyway.'

Stella shook her head and said to Mary Ruth, 'Martha didn't think Inverness prison was the place to send a woman. She was stirring everybody up. You know what she's like. Does she know you are out?'

'I should think so. It was in the paper last night. I haven't seen her.'

'Have you seen Mrs Inglis yet? She's hoping she's done right fetching your cats down here and putting the hens over to Tibby.'

'I've told her all that,' said Douggie. 'Here, sit down and have a news and I'll go and put the kettle on.'

Stella put a shovel of coal on the fire and said, 'Are you really all right, Mary Ruth?'

'I'm fine and Alec is looking after me. I came to thank you for having Napper. I don't know what to suggest about him.'

'He must stay here. He's nice company for Douggie now he's home so much. Lord Donald has said he doesn't want him to go to Fionn-glass any more. Mrs Inglis has lost her job there too, of course. Nothing left to clean. It's going to be a time-share place, but I suppose you know that.'

'I hope it'll bring some work into the village.'

'It'll do that all right. Jean's young man has been given the foreman's job. He's delighted – and that reminds me, Helen was asking for you and said she hoped both you and Alec would come to Jean's wedding. It's on a Friday, the twenty-seventh. Two weeks yesterday. She sent your invitation weeks ago she said, but she hadn't heard. I suppose you had things on your mind,' she added with unconscious humour.

'I did have an invitation, but I knew I probably wouldn't be able to come so I didn't like to accept,' said Mary Ruth, smiling a little despite herself. 'I sent her present though. I'm sure she'll understand.'

'Well, I'd like to go,' said Alec. 'I won't stay all the evening. I think my dancing days are over, but I'd like to go and I think you should come too. You can't sit about doing nothing until the middle of December.'

Douggie and Stella added their voices and by the time the tea, in the best cups, had been drunk and Stella's fruit cake had been relished, Mary Ruth had changed her mind and promised to go to Jean's wedding. Alec was delighted. On their way home they called on Mrs Inglis and reassured her that her cat and hen disposals were just the ticket.

Mary Ruth was exhausted by the time they reached the flat. The phone rang as they sat down to supper. It was Kenneth. He was arriving at the airport at six p.m. on Monday. They promised to meet him.

'Now,' said Alec at ten o'clock, 'go to bed.' She went.

On Tuesday morning, Kenneth and Alec were walking steadily by the river and talking about Mary Ruth. She'd found herself dreading chance meetings with people she knew and had refused to accompany them. Kenneth had kept her up talking until two in the morning and she was preparing lunch while they were out.

'She's under strain,' said Alec. 'I thought we'd jollied her into going to Jean's wedding next week, Helen's niece. Her mother stays in Edinburgh now, but the wedding's at Knockglass. I don't think she will go, though.'

Kenneth said, 'She told me. She is shocked. I don't think she had thought this thing out at all. She told me she thought she would just be sent to jail and that would be that. She's been too long on her own. I blame myself. I should have persuaded her to come and live with us. You know how it is with us. There'd be a welcome for you too, Alec, if you'd like to come. The extended family means just that in our part of France, though things are changing there too. She's not potty, she's just in a world of her own. She had never thought about Napper or the cats or the blessed hens for that matter, let alone the fact that Douggie and Mrs Inglis would be affected.'

Alec shook his head and said, 'She thinks the jewels will be hers too. She fancies retiring on them. Once Lord Donald hears about them, that will be the end of that pipedream.'

'How come? They were left to her.'

'He will want some reparation, Kenneth – wouldn't you? Jail may be Mary Ruth's punishment for the crime, but he'll sue her for every penny as compensation, surely? They are worth at least ninety thousand without the added spice of belonging to the illegitimate heir's widow, or whatever the tabloids will call her. I should think they'll be worth twice as much after the trial.'

'I hadn't thought of that, but you're right. I asked her if Donald knew about them and she said not, only you and I know. If we keep stumm—?'

Alec smiled. 'That's a thought. Didn't she tell Catherine and Allan?'

'Yes, and I told Marie-Claire, but we're all family. I'll speak to Catherine and Allan. Mum might as well salvage something out of all this.' Alec nodded and the two men walked along the river bank for a while in silence. 'I'm glad she gave it to Camfam,' Kenneth said suddenly.

'So am I, but we'd better ask Mr Field to spell it out to her about the jewels,' Alec said. 'If we try to tell her, she may come over all remorseful and own up. I wouldn't put anything past her. You should have heard her telling Field she was guilty and was going to confess to the Sheriff the first morning in court. It was a *tour de force* on his part to get her to see sense.'

'She managed to sell everything very sensibly,' said Kenneth, who had been amazed at the depths of his mother's cunning. 'She can't pretend to be stupid, Alec,' he said as they waited to cross the road.

'No, indeed,' Alec replied with a smile. 'She's far from stupid. That certainly is no defence. What can she plead in mitigation? She's not mad and she's not stupid . . .'

'Kind-hearted?' asked Kenneth and laughed. 'Not much of a defence. I'm just hoping that Field will keep her right,' adding, 'and you, of course. I have to go back tomorrow. I'll come back for the trial, but I am so busy at present. I got three commissions from the Festival exhibition. Little did I know what was going on at the time. I can't afford to turn any work away, especially now I'm going to have to keep travelling up here.'

'Yet another complication she didn't think of. It's a tangled web.'

Kenneth sighed. 'It is indeed. What is really terrible is that she isn't going to see Jean-Marie Alexandre as a baby. She would have been coming in just a couple of weeks.' He looked down on his uncle as they reached the street door, 'I can't bear the idea of her being in prison. It's the only time I have felt at one with Martha Bold. Will you look after her and keep in touch?'

'Need you ask?' asked Alec as they climbed the stairs.

At the airport, Kenneth put his arms around his mother and hugged her. 'Take care of yourself, I don't know what to say apart from that.'

'You've said plenty, but thank you for not telling me I did wrong.'

He pulled back from the embrace and looked down at her. 'I don't think you did, but that isn't what the court will think. I'm proud of you, but you'll have to pay for it. In more ways than you realize.'

'Oh, Kenneth! I'm paying now. I'm not going to see my grandson until he's five, if I'm lucky, for a start. When I arranged the great robbery it was like a game. I never thought of the consequences.'

'Well, when I said to take thought for your retirement, I didn't mean you were to do it at Her Majesty's pleasure, but please do what Mr Field advises. Alec told me about your initial meeting with him. You are in no position to judge what's best. Promise me you'll listen to him.'

'I promise,' she said and kissed him. 'Give my love to Marie-Claire and the girls and give the baby a big hug from his wicked granny.'

'You're not wicked, you're . . .' Kenneth struggled to find the right word and failed. 'What's worrying me,' he went on, 'is that they'll be confounded by your behaviour. Usually people have a chance to get stolen property back or at least the worth of it. They'll be mad with you.'

Alec and Mary Ruth drove home from the airport without saying much. They had three months to wait until the case came to court.

Three months during which Miriam Simonson married Harry Aronson in London and enjoyed her wedding reception at Claridge's, and Jean married her young man in Knockglass and danced until after midnight to 'The Stramash' in the village hall with her neighbours. These included Mary Ruth after all. She had been unable to resist Martha Bold who had offered to let Arthur drive them all to the wedding. Despite her earlier misgivings, Mary Ruth had enjoyed herself and Alec wrote to Kenneth and told him so. And Julian married Ffiona.

Kenneth and Marie-Claire did not receive an invitation to Julian and Ffiona's wedding, and Dorinda did not offer to put up Julian's sisters and their families. Donald had hinted that he would like to invite them, but Dorinda was sulking because the sapphires had not been found. She claimed that her white silk suit had been bought with them in mind and asked Donald repeatedly to tell the police to question Mary Ruth about them.

A couple of days before the wedding he mentioned this idea to Shackleton, who told him to leave the police to their business. 'Furthermore, Donald,' he said, 'I'm trying to claim from Carter's and Agostino's for you and it's not made any easier by your stream of telephone calls to them. They don't know who is in charge. You did give Carter's written permission for Mrs F. to sell things for you, there's no getting round that.'

Donald cut in, 'I've told you that was—'

'Listen, old son,' Shackleton carried on, ignoring his interruption, 'it is going to be difficult to get much joy out of Carter's; quite apart from anything else their Miss Wauchop appears to have accidentally wiped out all the names of the buyers on the computer and,' he paused, 'lost the disk, or so they tell me.'

'They told me they'd let me have a list of the buyers,' Donald said.

'Well, maybe the disk will turn up. Technically, you are entitled to the return of your goods and I'm still trying to get them back. I have some hopes of Agostino's, but don't queer the pitch for me. I can't for the life of me think why you didn't tell me you were selling up before you went to the States. I could have overseen all the negotiations and the valuations and so on. Trust me, old son, I'm doing me best.'

Donald was chastened when he put the phone down. I'd better go and collect Mary and the girls, he thought. He had offered to take them out for dinner. They were staying at Julian's flat for the wedding. Nina had told Ffiona that she was a fool and that they could perfectly well have afforded a hotel, but Ffiona ignored her and had made up their beds herself.

The day before the wedding she spent a happy afternoon with her future sisters-in-law trying dresses and head-dresses on Katherine's daughters who were to be flower girls. Lizzie's baby was there too and crawled about grabbing at her cousins' dresses and chewing everything she could lay her hands on. At five o'clock they all went to St George's for the rehearsal. Jumbo who was to be best man was late and he pretended to have lost the ring, which annoyed Donald who was preoccupied with where Dorinda would sit and with whom.

'She'll be with cousin Carlo I should think,' said Jumbo in a stage whisper to Julian. 'The word is that he's come into a lot of money.'

Lizzie kicked his ankle and Katherine promised that her husband would usher Dorinda into a good seat. 'He'll put her where she can see everything,' she said loudly to her father.

'She'll be wanting to be seen,' said Lizzie truthfully, though tactlessly. 'Dad said she's bought a whizz of an outfit,' she added to Ffiona, who was beginning to feel overwhelmed by it all. She had suggested a quiet wedding to her mother.

'If you have a quiet wedding,' Nina had replied, 'you might as well announce that you are preggers on the six o'clock news.'

Since this was Ffiona's dearest wish she couldn't see anything wrong with it, but she was not used to arguing with her mother and had given in.

The rehearsal was called to order by the vicar. The little girls, solemn and dutiful, behaved beautifully and Nina, not one for a bit part, confined herself to confiding in Lady Mary at the end that she had never thought Ffiona would marry, 'because,' she whispered, 'she takes after her father's side. All the women were horse-faced, and most of them had moustaches.' She then gave a little hiccup and took Ffiona home.

Lizzie and Katherine had only met Ffiona twice before, but they had warmed to her and told their brother so. The children were being fed by Katherine's nanny in the kitchen and the brother and sisters were in the basement living room drinking gin and eating nuts and crisps.

'She's a gentle soul, Julian,' said Katherine, who thought that Ffiona had been marvellous with her daughters.

Lizzie was more forthright and said, 'She's one hell of an improvement on Dorinda. She'll be the death of Dad. He looks terrible.'

'He has got money worries,' said Julian.

'It's not just money,' said Katherine. 'Poor Daddy, he's exhausted. Last night when he took us out for supper he fell asleep during dessert. Mum was amused, she said he'd been doing it for years.'

'I shouldn't think he's allowed to sleep at the dinner table when

Dorinda's there,' said Lizzie. 'We haven't seen her yet. How is she?'

'Much as usual,' said Julian. 'Elegant and busy all the time.'

'Busy doing what?' asked Katherine.

'Shopping and having fittings and arranging things. She sells nearly-new couturier clothes in the HAC shop one morning a week and goes to exhibitions and the opera, you know the kind of thing.'

'Huh!' said Lizzie. 'It's easy to see she hasn't a baby to care for.'

'You should get a nanny, Lizzie,' said Katherine. 'I know I could never manage two of them on my own. Lizzie,' she said turning to Julian, 'is into bonding.'

'Bonding?' asked Julian. 'What on earth is that?'

Katherine laughed and said, 'Really getting to know your baby by doing all the smelly bits. Ffiona knows all about it. You may not be allowed a nanny either.'

Julian groaned, but before he could say anything, Lizzie asked: 'Is Dorinda going to have a baby?'

'I've no idea,' said Julian. 'I don't think it's on Dad's agenda and she leads such a busy social life I don't think she's got time for a baby.'

'Oh! Julian,' his sisters said.

'What do you think nannies are for?' added Katherine.

'I'm beginning to think Dad's going to need one soon,' said Julian. The girls looked at him with interest. He went on. 'He's driving himself mad about some jewels he thinks Mary Ruth has stolen and sold. A portrait of his grandmother arrived at the flat. It had been left at Fionn-glass; it was all that was left. Anyway, his granny is wearing her tiara and the sapphires and diamonds to match and ever since it came Dad has been ringing up fine-arts auctioneers all over the country and pestering them for lists of jewellery sold in the last six months.'

'What makes him think Mary Ruth's sold it?'

'I don't know. He's doing little else in the office at present. He's even talking about getting a private detective. He's heard about one who did some work once for poor old Bimbo Massingham.

Charges three hundred a day, plus VAT. He even asked Agostino's for a list of the buyers of the furniture so he can contact them and arrange to inspect their purchases for secret drawers.'

'If Mary Ruth had found jewels, why would she have left them to be sold in a drawer, secret or otherwise?' asked Lizzie.

'Exactly!' said Julian.

'Poor Daddy, this isn't like him. This theft has unhinged him from the sound of it,' said Katherine.

'Well, I'll tell you this,' said Julian. 'He's going to be in charge of the office while we are away on honeymoon and I'm scared to leave him to look after the Malaysian deal. I've spent half the afternoon arranging for our general manager to keep in close touch with me. I don't want Dad to botch it while I'm away.'

'Is that what you were doing when you were in Malaysia in the summer?' asked Katherine. 'I'd love to have come. I've heard so much about the east coast. They say it's quite unspoiled.'

'Yes, it's lovely. We're trying to set up a cocoa plantation. There's an awful lot of money in chocolate. Easter eggs are big business nowadays. There's a lot of corruption in West Africa and the trees there have been terribly neglected. We've a trial plantation running in Malaysia; it's only seven hundred acres, but if it comes up trumps we're set to clear eighty thousand acres of equatorial forest and go for the market. It's taken me three years to get the Malaysian government to grant us the rights to clear fell and move all the people. There's a new factory near to us which will provide the pesticides and if all goes well, we'll be in the money.'

'What about the people?' asked Lizzie. 'The ones you are moving. Do they want to move?'

Julian said shortly, 'I don't suppose so, I haven't asked them. We'll be bringing employment to the area.'

'What kind of employment?' asked Katherine, prepared to take an interest as Lizzie was doing so.

'Well, after the felling, it's mostly spraying to keep the bugs down.'

'Sousing all the trees with chemicals, you mean?' asked Lizzie.

'Spraying pesticides, yes,' said Julian defensively, as Lizzie was sounding cross.

'Well, I shan't be buying any of your product. I don't want my daughter poisoned,' snapped his sister.

'Don't be ridiculous,' said Julian. 'It's not going to poison the trees and the crop. It's going to keep them healthy.'

'Oh Lizzie!' said Katherine. 'Let's not talk business. I'm worried about Daddy. What are we to do to help him?'

Upstairs in the elegant, redecorated drawing room, sitting on either side of the coal-effect electric fire, their mother said to their father, 'Well, I don't see how I can help, Donald. Things sound precarious.' She had been surprised at Donald's confessions of his money worries, but she had asked him a question and she wanted an answer. 'Are you sure she doesn't want one?' she asked again. A sudden thought struck her, 'You did tell her,' she persisted, leaning forward to emphasize the point, 'didn't you?'

'The last thing Dorinda wants is a baby,' said Donald. He was reluctant. He couldn't see that it mattered, certainly not to Mary. She'd got her money. There were so many things he wanted to talk over with her. Her judgement was good. He had realized at last that he had hurt her by leaving her for Dorinda, but he wanted her help. Why did she have to bring in such a matter when they had so little time? 'I know what Dorinda likes doing and it's not looking after a baby,' he said firmly and he hoped finally.

'Donald,' said Mary, who was determined, 'you haven't answered my question. Have you told Dorinda that you had a vasectomy?'

'Yes, yes, a long time ago.'

'Are you sure she understands what it means?'

'Oh, Mary, don't be ridiculous, she's a grown woman. Of course she understands. I am quite sure she doesn't want a baby.'

'Well, you must know her better than I do,' said his former wife. 'I'd have thought having a daughter to show off and marry off would have been just what Dorinda would enjoy,' she went on.

'Women change their minds you know, Donald, especially as they get older.'

'My God, don't I know it! Look at Mary Ruth. Whatever possessed her? We were always such good friends.'

'I was good friends with her, Donald. We spent many happy summers together with the children. You weren't there as often as you like to pretend when the children were small. You are thinking of your childhood summers with Kenny. Perhaps she was annoyed you didn't all go at Easter. Julian said—'

'She's my housekeeper, Mary, not my keeper,' Donald snapped. 'It's no business of hers what I do. She's been paid to live there all these years—'

'Yes,' said Mary sharply, 'and it saved you a lot of worry and expense having her there taking care of everything. I can't understand what triggered her off. She's put up with a lot over the years.' She paused and thought for a while. 'What did she say when you told her you were having to sell the house?'

Donald looked across the hearth at her. 'Want the other half?' he asked. She nodded, and he went to the sideboard and began to refill their glasses. Mary knew him too well, he thought. He couldn't hope to avoid telling her that he had never mentioned selling the house to Mary Ruth until after it was sold. 'Ice?' he turned to ask her.

'Please.'

'I didn't tell her,' he admitted, as he handed her her second drink, 'until I knew it was sold.'

She was not surprised. Donald was a law unto himself. Always had been. 'Well, perhaps that was the feather that tipped the scale. You and Dorinda arranged to go with a big party at Easter. She did a power of work according to Julian and then you cried off. Then you sold the house over her head.'

'I offered her the North Lodge, rent free.'

Lady Mary looked at her former husband and shook her head from side to side. 'Donald,' she said 'your judgement is terrible. That North Lodge was not fit for anyone to live in. I spent a whole summer, it must be thirty years ago now, arranging to get poor old Ellen out of it and into a council home. It was condemned then as being unfit. Whatever were you thinking about?'

Donald was annoyed. 'I was thinking about Mary Ruth,' he said. 'I've paid her stamps and she was sixty in August and though we had never discussed it I assumed she was going to draw her pension.'

'And live where?' asked Mary.

'Well, I hadn't really thought about that. I suppose she would have stayed on at Fionn-glass if I hadn't had to sell it to pay you.'

'Well, really Donald, that was hardly my fault and it certainly wasn't Mary Ruth's.'

'These things happen, Mary.'

'I realize that, but you can't leave your responsibilities behind, just because you put your old wife aside. Mary Ruth is one of your responsibilities.'

Donald suddenly remembered that he wanted Mary to sell at least one of the flats upstairs which were in her name. He smiled winningly at her and tried a different approach. 'I didn't treat you very well. I'm sorry, but I have paid you out.' He added cheerfully, 'No hard feelings I hope.'

'Not any more. I'm only sorry you had to sell Fionn-glass to pay me. I loved it. I went with Mary Ruth to have a look round in December, after we had been to Mrs Joe's funeral. Still, I'm glad it's going to be used and enjoyed by people again. We should have sold it years ago. Such a lot of upkeep and it would have saved all this trouble and given the girls a good start too.'

'Ah!' said Donald, taking up the cue. 'That reminds me. I was going to ask you if you would consider selling one of the flats upstairs.' Mary raised an eyebrow and he added hurriedly, 'I'd be quite happy to do up the attic as a studio flat for when the girls visit town, but I need rather a lot of cash for Lloyd's right now and I don't want to have to give up my portfolio to pay them. If it hadn't been for Mary Ruth taking leave of her senses I wouldn't have dreamed of asking you.'

Mary looked hard at him. 'Mary Ruth has nothing to do with it. One of your other responsibilities, Donald, is to our daughters.' She finished her drink and put her glass down.

She wished Donald would go. She had offered to bath her granddaughters so that Nanny could have an evening out in the West End. The girls were going to prepare supper. Her sons-in-law would be arriving soon. Donald's essentially childish hope that everyone would help him out of difficulties of his own making had not altered over the years. She had been shattered when he had left her for Dorinda and beneath her well-mannered exterior lurked a gleeful realization that he was not as happy as she was.

He sat quietly hoping she was going to tick him off and then agree to the sale. She had a soft heart, he knew. 'Donald,' she said, 'I may be soft-hearted, but I am not soft in the head. Whatever you or Dorinda may think, the girls are every bit as entitled to a flat in London as Julian is. The flats are in my name, but they are part of the girls' inheritance. As you have to pay Lloyd's you'll have to sell something of your own. I will never agree to selling the flats. I don't care if Julian is paying something towards this flat, which is far and away the best in the house: he earns good money. He told me he was sorry for you. I am not. Your lifestyle is expensive, but it is of your own making. When you were invited to join Lloyd's, you thought it was splendid. You never minded receiving money as a Name. You can't complain now.'

'I do have something to complain of,' said Donald hastily, as she made to rise. 'Do you remember seeing some sapphires? They matched the coronet which was in the House of Lords. There was a portrait of my grandmother wearing the whole set in the attic at Fionn-glass.'

'I remember the portrait. I could never understand why your uncle had left it in the attic. Perhaps it had strong Fionn-glass connections for him, but I never saw the jewels. Sold long ago, I'd say, to pay for some peccadillo. You know what a rascal he was.' She picked up her bag.

'Are you sure you never had them?' asked Donald, frantic by

now as she stood up and began to move to the door.

She stopped and looked down at him. 'I most certainly did not. Who would have given them to me? You didn't, and if your uncle had I would have told you.'

Donald knew this was true. Was he never to find the damned things, he thought. Mary was saying, 'Julian told me you were wasting office time trying to find them.'

'Oh, did he indeed? Cheeky devil! They have disappeared. They are valuable. Why shouldn't I look for them?'

'When did you last see them?' asked Mary.

'I've never seen them.'

'Well, how do you know they exist then?' she asked, still looking down at him.

'They were in the portrait,' he said crossly. 'I've just told you.'

'There is such a thing as wishful thinking, Donald. Many portraits embellish the truth. Beautiful wives and pretty children abound in portraits. A set of jewels is easily painted. What do they matter now, anyway? They can't be worth much, compared with what you have lost.'

Ignoring this neat remark Donald said, 'It's a matter of principle. I believe Mary Ruth has stolen them. All I want is to find them.'

'If Mary Ruth has stolen them,' said Mary going towards the door, 'they'll turn up in the list of stolen property. She's no thief. Well, no ordinary thief.' She turned at the door and looked at him slumped in his chair. 'I'll see you in church, Donald. Dorinda will be expecting you, surely? It's after seven. I hope tomorrow will go well, especially for Ffiona's sake. She seemed terribly nervous to me this afternoon. She's a nice girl, Julian is lucky. If he looks after her he'll have a good wife. Thank you for my drink.'

As she left the room Donald ground his teeth and cursed Mary Ruth.

Chapter 21

Mary Ruth came into the flat and took two Hallowe'en masks out of her shopping bag and showed them to Alec. 'I'm going to send them to France for the little girls. I hope they'll be there in time.'

'Should be, the post's usually good, isn't it?'

'Mmm! They're not going to be easy to wrap,' she muttered as she practised with a piece of newspaper. 'I don't want them crushed.'

'Put them in a padded envelope.'

'That's a good idea. I must be getting dottled. That's what Kenneth said when he caught me talking to my hens.'

Alec smiled. He was glad that she had relaxed and went out regularly now, but she had been a long time this morning. 'Have your coffee and tell me what kept you. It's half past eleven.'

Mary Ruth accepted the mug he was holding out and smiled at him as she sat saying, 'Oh, Alec, I'd forgotten what fun it is to walk to the shops and listen to people talking. I was so busy eavesdropping in the butcher's I forgot the bread and had to go all the way back to the baker's for it. That's why I'm so late.' They both laughed.

'I've done that too,' said Alec, 'but I have more excuse than you.' He drank his coffee and went on: 'You know Mary Ruth, although Fionn-glass is lovely, especially in the summer, you were living an unnatural life. Human beings are gregarious. I used to wonder how you managed, and I wasn't the only one, but you're not senile. You were lonely.' He fell silent and then pointed to an envelope on the table. 'That came for you.'

She picked it up. It was stamped *Crown Office, Edinburgh.*

'Oh, Alec,' she whispered.

'It'll be the indictment.'

It was, and though they read it twice before they rang Mr Field to make an appointment and ten times before they went to see him, it still awed them. It read:

> Mary Ruth Findlater, you are indicted at the instance of Fraser Hanratty, Her Majesty's Advocate, and the charge against you is that between 1 July and 29 August 1991 at Fionn-glass House, Balessie, owned by Lord Fionn-glass of Fionn-dhruim and occupied by you, you did steal furniture, glassware, silver, carpets, rugs, ornaments, paintings and other contents of the said house, to a value of £1,750,000, or thereby—

It went on to specify in meticulous detail every item which Mary Ruth had sold. There were thirty-seven pages.

'It sounds like the Great Train Robbery,' Mary Ruth said.

'It's certainly an impressive document,' Alec agreed.

On the fifth of November, when they went to see Mr Field, they were no sooner seated than he asked Mary Ruth if she understood it.

'I think so,' she said, glad that they had spent so much time reading it. It was all out of her hands now: Mr Field was in charge. That's what Alec, and Tom who had been ringing regularly, had told her.

'You see, Mrs Findlater, I will need to find a barrister to represent you in the High Court on December the twelfth, but I must question you first in order to instruct—'

'I want to plead guilty,' she said, interrupting him. 'I've read everything including the amazingly long lists of goods stolen. I did it.'

'It is the business of the Crown to prove it, Mrs Findlater,' said Mr Field, who had begun to tire of Mary Ruth's amateurish attitude to the law at their previous meetings. He quelled his irritation and with a little smile which included her uncle he attempted a more subtle approach. 'I know the old joke about a professional being someone who tells you what you already know, but in language that you cannot understand,' he said with a wintry smile, 'but I really cannot allow any client of mine to make such a serious decision without making clear the consequences of such a decision.'

Mary Ruth, resigned to the necessity for a lawyer, suddenly felt sulky and didn't acknowledge his joke though Alec did and tucked it away for future use. He was hoping Mary Ruth would remember Kenneth's advice.

'I am a professional, Mrs Findlater,' Mr Field went on. 'You will have to bear with me.' Alec stared hard at Mary Ruth.

'Yes, Mr Field,' she said.

'You are indicted at the instance of the Lord Advocate,' continued Mr Field, 'and the case will come before the High Court in Inverness on Thursday the twelfth of December – five weeks and two days hence. The case is considered too serious for the Sheriff Court, because the Sheriff has limited sentencing powers. I need hardly tell you that the police have collected a lot of evidence from Carter's and Agostino's, from Millichop and Millichop and from Camfam too. This, together with the evidence from Balessie plus Lord Donald's statements, leaves little doubt of your part in the theft. There can be little likelihood of the case not being proved against you. Nevertheless,' he raised his voice very slightly as she began to draw breath and hurried on: 'I must explain to you that if there is anything in this indictment which is wrong, you must tell me now so that I can discuss it with the Crown Office and see if they will accept a plea of not guilty to that part of the indictment.'

'No, they seem to have got it all right,' replied Mary Ruth grudgingly. She was fed up with the whole business. She knew they could prove what she had confessed to doing. Jobs for the boys all this, she was thinking.

'Very well. I dare say all this seems like a lot of fuss for nothing to you, but I have to say that a plea of guilty will almost certainly result in a prison sentence, perhaps a long one. Prison is not brutal nowadays, Mrs Findlater, but it is degrading and most of the people in prison are deeply unhappy if not disturbed. You must not think it will be like being kept in detention after school, or being bored in hospital. These are not good comparisons.'

Which I am not making, thought Mary Ruth.

Alec laughed and added, 'You were never at public school, remember, Mary Ruth, the best training for life inside.'

Mary Ruth looked at her uncle in surprise. She knew she had to pay for her theft. Was he telling her to lie to the court? She was guilty, therefore she was going to prison.

Mr Field was glad of Alec's help. If the silly woman persisted she might get five years, especially if she got a hard judge. 'As we are both trying to tell you, prison is no laughing matter. It is a whole way of life and as a first-timer you will not know the ropes and you may well find it a humiliating experience. This in itself is a good reason for pleading not guilty, but it would be easier to demonstrate your motivation if you stood trial and could take the witness box and speak for yourself. This might earn you a shorter sentence.'

Mary Ruth was surprised. 'What has my motivation to do with it? I'm not even sure I know what motivated me.'

'You must have some idea,' said Mr Field politely, wondering if she was really as naive as she sounded and how he could use her simple manner to her best advantage. She must plead not guilty, he thought. The trick is to persuade her. 'You do realize that if you plead guilty, your defence will have to be based on your motivation, Mrs Findlater. It is important.' He waited for her to speak.

Mary Ruth suddenly remembered her first night in the real prison in Inverness when she had lain hugging herself and revelling in her triumph. I enjoyed robbing Lord Donald, she thought and what's more I'm proud of myself. I was angry that Mrs Joe and Kenneth were denied name and fortune and I was angry with Donald, he's careless of other people's feelings and as for offering me that North Lodge—

Mr Field cleared his throat and she realized that he was still waiting to hear her motive. Well, I'd rather be thought ingenuous than wicked, she thought. I don't want to sit in court and hear myself described as a bitter woman. I've never envied Donald and I have done something positive at last in answer to those harrowing appeals Angus kept bringing.

'I suppose,' she said slowly, choosing her words carefully, 'that I was upset when the visit was called off – we all were – and I was hurt when Donald didn't tell me about the sale of the house . . .'

The two men sat and listened in silence. Alec was thinking how much more use the contents of Fionn-glass were as food and medicine. Mr Field was wondering what the QC was going to plead if disappointment with her employer and his decision to sell his own house were all her defence.

Mary Ruth went on with increasing warmth, '. . . but it is evil, there is no other word for it, to let women hold their babies as they die for want of food, or because they can't have a measles jab, when we have so much.' She raised her head and looked at Mr Field and then at Alec. 'I know I have done wrong, but until the rich industrial countries of the world stop selling arms to the poorer,' she faltered as she tried to think of the right word, 'the poorer, agricultural countries, their women and children will have to rely on charity. I wanted to help the people in Ethiopia who were in danger of being forgotten because of the Gulf War.' None of this was any excuse for theft, she realized as she spoke and added in despair, 'I was tempted because I was in a position to help them.'

Alec took out his hanky and blew his nose. Mr Field did not say anything. Mary Ruth stood up and walked over to the window. She took a few deep breaths and turned to look at them both. 'I am pleased with what I have done and I'm prepared to suffer what consequences come my way.'

They were still silent until Mr Field said quietly, 'There are consequences for Lord Donald too, Mrs Findlater.'

'Huh!' said Mary Ruth. 'There's nothing coming over him.'

Ignoring this, Mr Field said hesitantly, 'Having heard you speak, Mrs Findlater, I really feel I must advise you to plead not guilty and go to trial, which means that you would be able to take the witness box, as I told you before.'

He had found her artless argument touching, despite his earlier misgivings. Nothing in his previous experience had prepared him for this straightforward, well-meaning and yet dishonest woman. He had to do the best for her. She was bound to receive some punishment, but five years in prison at her age . . . He sat for a while, sighed and went on slowly, 'You see if you plead not guilty then you could speak for yourself. You might win the day with your simple explanation.'

'Do you mean that if I plead guilty, I can't speak for myself?'

'Not unless you are going to conduct the case yourself and do without counsel.'

'That is not a good idea,' interrupted Alec with a sharpness in his voice which Mary Ruth hadn't heard for years, adding, 'There is no question of Mary Ruth conducting her own defence. At least,' he said turning to her, 'I hope, most sincerely, that you will not shame us all by such amateur exhibitionism.'

'Of course not Alec, I wish to plead guilty and get the whole thing over. I just wanted to know if I would be allowed to speak in court.'

'Not personally,' said Mr Field. 'Your counsel will speak in your defence. If you do plead guilty there will be no trial as it is generally understood. There will be a judge only, who will hear the Lord Advocate's case against you, and then your counsel speaking in your defence and then, although he may ask questions, he will pass sentence. There will be no string of witnesses to attest to your good character. It will all be up to your defence counsel to convince the judge that you should not be sent to prison for a long time.'

Mary Ruth thought back to her first meeting with Mr Field. She had been annoyed with him, and now she saw that he must have been annoyed with her. It was all much more complicated than she had realized.

Mr Field was speaking again. 'Mrs Findlater, I am concerned to help you. If you plead guilty you will have done the prosecution's work for them. It will be very difficult to offer a good defence for you.'

'Mr Field,' said Mary Ruth. 'I am guilty. I stole the contents of the house. I will not stand up in court and lie. The truth matters to me.'

'The truth matters to us all, Mrs Findlater, and no one is suggesting that you lie on oath but we are talking about the law, which is not concerned with hearing confessions, but proving cases. We are not in France. There, as you may know, the examining magistrate is primarily concerned with establishing the truth. Here—'

'Are you saying British justice is not concerned with the truth?' she interrupted him.

'There is no such thing as "British justice", as you call it,' he said, beginning to feel irritated again and trying not to show it. 'That is tabloid shorthand. We have an adversarial court system. It is up to the prosecution to prove beyond a doubt that what they accuse the defendant of is true. It is up to the defence to argue that the prosecution has failed.'

'How can they fail if I admit it?'

'Pre*cise*ly! A great deal of time, money and suffering will be saved, Mrs Findlater, if the judge can be persuaded to have a modicum of sympathy for the view that you took advantage of Lord Donald's carelessness and Carter's incompetence not to help yourself, but to help others. It is unlikely to set an example and he might sentence you to community service. I repeat, if you plead guilty you will not be able to speak for yourself.'

'If I stand up in court I shall tell the truth. How will that help me?'

'It will help in so far as it will give the judge a chance to hear you speaking about what you did and, of course, your counsel will ask the right questions.'

Mary Ruth snorted. 'What a fiddle! You mean I will not be asked if I stole everything at all?'

'Not in those words. No, but you will be cross-examined.'

Mary Ruth walked across the room and sat down. She sighed. 'I will plead guilty, Mr Field, I can do nothing else. The facts speak for themselves. I am not ashamed of what I did, though I am surprised that I shan't be allowed to speak.'

Mr Field sighed too. 'You don't need to worry about not speaking yourself. It's not necessarily a bad thing to be represented by counsel. You might find it daunting to repeat your motive in court. The judge will be used to hearing statements from barristers. Judges like things to be formal. They are not usually impressed by emotional appeals. They earn their living after all by paying regard to the law and there is no way we can pretend you haven't broken it.' He paused, then added: 'It appears that the opportunity to do good triggered your theft – no excuse of course, but it may serve.' He then sat in glum silence as he considered what the QC would make of it.

Alec said gently, 'Do please continue, Mr Field. None of this is easy, but we are listening.'

'Thank you, Mr Macleod.' Then turning back to Mary Ruth he went on. 'What I will suggest, if you are sure you wish to plead guilty, is that you give me a full precognition now – that is, a statement,' he added as she looked doubtful, 'and that I then send it to Mr Graham Affleck QC in Edinburgh with the other papers. I have worked with Mr Affleck twice recently and I have formed a very high opinion of his ability. If you agree to engage him then I suggest that you go to Edinburgh and see him as soon as possible and discuss the whole matter with him, with a view to his speaking in court on your behalf and presenting your side of the case in the best possible light.'

'I intend to plead guilty, because I am.' The rules of the game are becoming clearer, she thought and added, 'I'll give you a statement and I'll go and see Mr Affleck.'

'I think that's very sensible of you Mrs Findlater,' said Mr Field, though he thought her very foolish. No good ever comes of pleading guilty, he knew. 'It will be a great help to Mr Affleck,' he said to her, 'though you mustn't expect him to make use of every single thing you tell him. He will use his skill and experience to decide how best to present your case and which pieces of information to use.'

So Mary Ruth spent the next two hours answering Mr Field's questions, the answers to which he then dictated on to a tape for the precognition for Mr Affleck. Alec went off into town with an invitation to return at five o'clock to take Mary Ruth home.

When he returned they had tea and biscuits, brought in by the startlingly elegant receptionist. Alec was amused when he recognized her from Mary Ruth's earlier description. She may have become a thief, he thought but she's aye been a fine observer. He drank his tea and decided to ask Mr Field about the jewels while he had the opportunity.

'Kenneth, Mrs Findlater's son, and I were talking about the jewels,' he began. Mr Field looked surprised as he had forgotten about them. 'We agreed that I would ask your specific advice about them. I'm glad to have the chance to do so in the presence of Mary Ruth.' He nodded at her and she smiled. 'I understand that under the terms of Mrs Joe Findlater's will they were left to Mary Ruth to claim when she reaches sixty-five. If that is so, who owns the jewels now?'

'That's a very good question Mr Macleod,' said Field. He went over to his cupboard and after shuffling amongst the files in it he brought out a bundle of papers and put them on his desk. He sorted through the papers for Mrs Findlater's will. 'Ah yes, here we are,' he said and read to them.

> '. . . and I direct my Executors to hold my sapphire jewels for my daughter-in-law, Mrs Mary Ruth Findlater, and to

> hand the same over to her when she reaches the age of sixty-five years, declaring that the jewels shall not vest in her until she reaches the said age, and if she should die before taking a vested interest, then the said jewels shall immediately pass to her son Kenneth Findlater, whom failing, equally between and among his issue

. . . that seems quite clear.'

He went on. 'This is a case of postponed vesting, where the executors hold the jewels in trust either for you, Mrs Findlater, if you reach sixty-five years, or if you don't, for your son Kenneth. Right now they legally belong to the executors as I've said.'

'So does that mean that if Lord Fionn-glass found out about this will and the jewels being in your safe there would be nothing he could do about them?' asked Alec.

'That's another good question,' said Mr Field. 'Lord Fionn-glass has absolutely no title to these jewels at all, but that doesn't mean that he couldn't make difficulties. Suppose, for instance, that Mrs Findlater is convicted of this charge of theft of one point seven-five million pounds. Suppose also that she survives to sixty-five and inherits the jewels worth what – ninety-thousand pounds? What is Lord Fionn-glass going to do then?'

'But the jewels will belong to me,' put in Mary Ruth. 'You've just said so.'

Mr Field acknowledged that and went on. 'Yes, but put yourself in Lord Fionn-glass's position. You have been robbed of a very large sum of money and you can see the person convicted of the theft living in comfort. Regardless of where that person got the money, you're going to try and get something back, aren't you?'

Alec paid attention and nodded, but Mary Ruth didn't listen properly and when he had finished she said, 'I don't have anything that belongs to Donald Fionn-glass. Everything went to Ethiopia. It wouldn't be fair if he got the jewels. They're mine and one day they'll be Kenneth's. After all, he is the grandson of old Lord Fionn-glass. Lord Donald is only his nephew.'

'Well, Kenneth and I don't think he'll feel that way about it,' said Alec. 'He's cross enough now, and if there's a great deal of publicity about his uncle's "real" heir in the papers, he'll be even crosser. We think your best bet is to appear poverty-stricken from now on and hope he never finds out you've got any money, least of all his uncle's sapphires.'

'I agree entirely,' said Mr Field. 'Who else knows about your inheritance, Mrs Findlater?'

'Just Kenneth, of course, and my sister and you and your father.'

'Well, your secret is safe as far as we are concerned. You will be very discreet I'm sure, Mr Macleod, and so will Kenneth and your sister will, I presume,' he said turning to Mary Ruth, 'provided she is warned of the dangers. Do you think she will cooperate?' he asked, wondering how many other people knew about Mary Ruth's inheritance.

'Oh yes,' said Mary Ruth, 'when she knows what's at stake she'll keep quiet.'

'Well, let's hope so,' said Mr Field.

'I don't like the sound of all this,' said Mary Ruth after a pause. 'One minute you tell me the jewels will be mine when I'm sixty-five, and then you tell me Donald can get them back if he finds out about them. I have come to like the idea of having these jewels. My mother-in-law never had the good of them. I want Kenneth to have them. They were given to his granny by his grandfather. That must count for something.'

'Unfortunately it does not,' replied Mr Field. 'It's not the jewels Lord Fionn-glass can recover from you, Mrs Findlater. I agree they will be yours. It's restitution for his loss he'll be after. In my opinion, he would probably succeed if he knew the full facts and proceeded accordingly.'

'Well, I think that's downright unfair,' said Mary Ruth. 'I'm likely to go to prison for what I've done and I've always accepted that, but to lose what is legally mine and Kenneth's is monstrous. It means I shall be punished twice for the same thing. Some justice!'

Alec and Mr Field looked at each other.

'Mary Ruth,' said her uncle gently, 'you surely realize that Lord Donald has no easy way of getting back the value of the goods you have stolen from him. You told me yourself he only had them insured for a quarter of a million. Carter's were used to dealing with you and I suppose they will claim they did nothing wrong. It's unfair on him too.' Mr Field said nothing, but he nodded.

'His incompetence is not my fault,' said Mary Ruth. She remembered Mrs Inglis saying how they needed an inventory. She thought of the casual way Donald had let her know they weren't coming and the way she had heard he was selling the house, her home. She bowed her head and both men exchanged worried looks. She thought of her mother-in-law's long silence about the sapphires, of Joe and of her own husband.

Alec said, 'He may never find out, Mary Ruth.' Mary Ruth sat quietly for a moment and then she smiled at them both.

'I suppose he is justified in asking for their worth, but I'm going to make sure I keep them for Kenneth and my grandchildren. Do you know, Alec,' she went on cheerfully, 'I never gave Kenneth or you or any of my friends a single thought when I sold Donald's stuff. I just thought of all those people in Ethiopia and what a real difference a cheque for nearly two million pounds would make to them.'

'I know that. I understand,' said Alec.

'I never thought of all these problems. You've been so kind, Alec, and you too, Mr Field—'

'Ah, but I'm being paid, remember,' interjected Mr Field.

'Yes,' said Mary Ruth who had never thought about paying him, 'but there are others too, like poor Mrs Inglis who was humiliated by the police when she fetched my clothes. Whatever must you all think of me?'

'Speaking for myself,' said Alec, 'I made no judgements about you, but I support you in your present position. I hope you will be able to take possession of your jewels and use them to make your retirement comfortable and that ultimately Kenneth will have the good of them.'

'If it all comes down to keeping quiet then,' she said, 'so be it.'

Alec was relieved. She seemed to have taken the point at last.

To Mary Ruth's surprise, Mr Field then pointed out that she could renounce her interest in the will by deed of Family Arrangement, which would mean that the executors could legally hand the jewels over to Kenneth straight away, so that they would never have been hers, which raised her hopes. He then pointed out that it wouldn't necessarily be safer, because Lord Fionn-glass could still try to reduce the deed, if he should ever find out about it, which made her glum again. He finished by saying, 'You are not an easy person to advise, Mrs Findlater. If you are determined to plead guilty,' he paused, hoping she'd see sense even at this late hour.

'Yes, Mr Field,' she said, 'I am. I do understand what you have been saying and thank you for saying it, but I am determined.'

He nodded and reluctantly went on. 'Then the Lord Advocate will elaborate the indictment which you have seen and your defence will have to be your previous good character and the fact that you did not gain anything personally from the theft.' He stopped and folded his elegant fingers. 'When you have been to see Mr Affleck, it will all look clearer.'

'You have been most helpful,' said Alec rising. 'I will take Mary Ruth to see Mr Affleck next week. That's a good old Aberdeen name, by the way. Here's hoping he can persuade the judge that you are as good a woman as I know you to be, Mary Ruth. Thank you for all your help, Mr Field.'

They walked home without speaking and Alec held Mary Ruth's arm tightly all the way.

Chapter 22

On the twelfth of December and in the company of Alec and Kenneth, who had arrived the night before with hundreds of photographs of the baby, Mary Ruth arrived at the High Court in Inverness at half past nine. Mr Field and Mr Affleck were waiting for them. 'Hello, Mrs Findlater, Mr McLeod; the waiting is over,' the QC said, and smiled at them.

'This is my son,' said Mary Ruth, wondering why he was smiling. She felt sick.

'Kenneth Findlater,' said Kenneth holding out his hand.

'How do you do. Come over here and I'll explain matters to you.' They went into a corner and he told them what he was hoping to do, then he said to Mary Ruth, 'I must warn you Mrs Findlater to keep silent in court, no matter what is said. It is very important. You will antagonize the judge if you speak.' Mary Ruth nodded. Affleck did not mention his forebodings. He knew from previous experience the characters of the judge and prosecuting counsel.

At ten, the usher came and escorted Mary Ruth into the court. Kenneth and Alec went into the third row of the public benches to join Arthur and Martha Bold. Mr Field went to sit behind Mr Affleck. Seated on one of the front benches were the Chief Constable and Detective Inspector Sim. There was no sign of Police Constable Malcolm Malcolmson, but Colonel Fraser-Gordon was there.

'Court rise!' called the usher, and the judge entered. He bowed briefly to the court and sat down. He was wearing his red robe with white crosses and a wig with neatly rolled edges. The usher waved her fingers sharply at Mary Ruth who was still standing though everyone else had sat down. She sat, her mouth dry, her heart pounding and waited.

'How does the Panel plead?' intoned Lord Cook of Pentland who was a recently appointed judge. His meteoric rise to the Bench had alarmed liberal sentiment in Scotland.

Mr Graham Affleck QC stood up and said, 'I appear for the Panel who pleads guilty, m'lud,' and sat down. The clerk of court passed the written plea to Mary Ruth who signed it. It was then handed to the judge and to the prosecuting counsel to sign.

'What did he say, Alec?' asked Kenneth. 'What's the Panel?'

'Your mother. Technical term. Means the accused,' whispered Alec. Kenneth whispered to Arthur, who passed the information on to Martha.

'I know,' she hissed.

The usher gave them a slow and narrow-eyed look. They all sat up straighter and looked ahead. The judge turned toward Mr Rieval Wilson QC, who was appearing on behalf of the Lord Advocate. 'Well, Mr Wilson?'

Rising and after formally introducing himself the prosecutor explained: 'I am here to present the evidence for the prosecution in one of the most spectacular and cold-blooded cases of theft which has come before the High Court for a very long time.'

Martha sniffed and the usher looked up at her sharply.

The prosecutor then took the court through the formal procedures which had occurred. He referred to the discovery of the theft, the involvement of the police and the Panel's being cautioned and charged. The fact that she had said nothing when charged was emphasized by a significant pause.

We know she's guilty, thought Martha, because she's said so. All this is flannel.

As the QC settled into his speech, Alec nudged Kenneth as Lord Donald came in quietly and took a seat next to Detective Inspector

Sim on the front public bench. Mr Wilson was describing the long relationship of trust and friendship which had existed between the Panel and Lord Fionn-glass, emphasizing the closeness of Lord Donald to the Panel's husband and the many long summer holidays their two families had enjoyed. He spoke feelingly of the affection of their children for each other and the kindness of Lord Donald and his first wife to the Panel's mother- and father-in-law.

Lord Donald, who was listening avidly, nodded in agreement.

'In moving on to the events of early 1991,' Mr Wilson went on with a quick look at the judge, 'in connection with a proposed visit to Fionn-glass House, his Scottish seat, at Eastertide, Lord Fionn-glass of Fionn-dhruim had instructed the Panel to put through a sale of some silver cutlery at Carter's in Edinburgh, which occasion, m'lud,' he paused and sighed heavily, 'which occasion she used to worm her way into the confidence of one Miss Wauchop who was newly,' he paused again for a moment and then repeated, 'newly, m'lud, in charge of sales. Miss Wauchop has described this first meeting with the Panel as one of the most sophisticated pieces of confidence trickery she has ever encountered. She was left totally persuaded by the credentials of the Panel.'

Mary Ruth bit her lip. That's just not true, Verity was right.

'The deception of Miss Wauchop, Agostino's and the eminent legal firm of Millichop and Millichop had been meticulously planned and were spectacularly successful,' claimed Mr Wilson and paused again to let his words ring round the court. 'This trusted and hitherto utterly reliable family housekeeper's machinations resulted in the theft of the staggering amount of over one and three-quarters of a million pounds.' He looked up at the judge again and continued solemnly, 'Furthermore, m'lud, she channelled the stolen money to Camfam with such skill and cunning that Lord Fionn-glass has little chance of ever recovering more than a tiny fraction of his loss.'

Too damn right, thought Donald.

Mr Wilson then managed to highlight the burning of the letter from Millichop and Millichop by the accused as she sat in Constable

Malcolmson's car, much to Inspector Sim's delight. 'Yet another instance of the depths of deception to which the Panel had sunk,' he proclaimed and then whispered, 'Had the police learned the contents of that letter at that time Lord Donald might have been able to recover the money from Camfam before it went to Ethiopia.'

'Thank God for small mercies,' Alec muttered to Kenneth from behind his handkerchief, coughed a little dry cough and wiped his nose.

Winding up half an hour after he had begun speaking Mr Wilson concluded, 'Consider, m'lud, the thousands of people who are in positions of trust in this country and who are totally relied upon by other people. In particular those who guard the treasures of the nation. How would it be if they all helped themselves?' He paused again.

Mary Ruth had a sudden vision of the attendants of the National Gallery tucking portraits under their arms and sneaking off into the night. She couldn't believe the picture of herself just painted by the prosecution. It suddenly struck her that her defence counsel, Affleck, had only met her twice and that Mr Field had indeed had a point about pleading not guilty and going to trial. Her neighbours would have made her good character clear to a jury. This was unbelievable. She started to listen again.

'. . . consider too the distance from London to Fionn-glass House,' the prosecutor was saying, 'the impossibility of His Lordship being able to spot-check this housekeeper, who presented herself to him and to the community as the very soul of respectability even,' he paused dramatically to hiss the words, 'even selling plants at a stall at the church fête at the selfsame time when she had the valuer from Agostino's in Fionn-glass House assessing His Lordship's furniture for a totally unauthorized sale.'

He sipped at his water-glass. The public gallery was silent. Mary Ruth was disgusted. I manned that wretched plant stall in all kinds of weather for over thirty years, she was thinking as the prosecutor continued: 'Lord Fionn-glass relied also on his other staff, his cleaning woman and his gardener who had also been totally fooled. All the cunning that had been used to remove the stolen goods had been deployed so that these honest employees were away on holiday when the thefts actually took place.'

I did that to save them from blame, thought Mary Ruth. She was shaken. It was no fun sitting listening to this.

The prosecutor looked down at the lists gathered from the sales and said, 'I have never, never seen such cold-blooded, meticulous and determined organization in furtherance of a theft as this, m'lud.' He stood holding the lists before him in mute appeal. Lord Cook pursed his lips and made a small tidy note. There was obviously something coming. He waited.

Slowly turning over the pages of the list from Agostino's to find the already carefully marked place, the QC looked up at the judge and said solemnly, 'Even the stair-rods and their containing clips were prised up and sent to the auction rooms.' He then demanded in a thunderous voice, 'What more proof of malicious intent to rob her employer of every last possession could there be than that?'

Lord Donald shuddered and Douggie and Mrs Inglis, who had crept into the back of the public benches, exchanged looks of dismay.

'Your Lordship will hear a great deal from the defence about how the Panel sent all the stolen monies to charity, but in my submission this is irrelevant. It is not an acceptable proposition, to this court or to society, that theft of this magnitude, accompanied by the guile, cunning and deception we have witnessed here should be justified by the simple plea "I gave it all away, m'lud."' He paused for a moment. Like Mr Affleck, Mr Wilson knew Lord Cook's strengths and weaknesses.

'To allow such a plea to influence the sentence would blur the definition of the property-owning democracy in which we live. It would encourage self-appointed arbiters of morality to redistribute other people's possessions with impunity. It would place in jeopardy the very foundations of our way of life. It is the court's duty to punish deceit and dishonesty. I move for sentence.'

And with this ringing plea Mr Rieval Wilson QC sat down. The court stayed hushed for some moments. Then the public began to shuffle and cough and whisper. The Chief Constable wondered if Mr Wilson QC hadn't gone over the top by painting the crime as such a threat to civilized values, until he remembered the extreme right-wing reputation of Lord Cook, who had listened to Mr Wilson without interruption.

Donald Fionn-glass felt a brief glow of self-justification and hoped that even if he couldn't get his goods back at least Mary Ruth would get a long prison sentence. He was joined by Colonel Fraser-Gordon who had been sitting behind him, muttering, 'What d'you think?'

'Hard to tell at this stage. Judge could be a softie and take her age into consideration.'

'We miss her at church, I can tell you,' said the colonel. 'Sings up well.' Not for the first time Donald thought old F-G was losing his marbles.

Graham Affleck QC sensed the uphill task that confronted him and whispered to Mr Field and Mary Ruth, referring to the notes he had taken during Mr Wilson's speech.

Lord Cook waited patiently and looked round the court before asking Mr Affleck if he was ready to continue. Although impressed by the vigour of the prosecuting counsel's speech, Affleck realized that nothing new or unexpected had been said so he indicated his readiness.

'Please proceed,' said His Lordship.

'M'lud, the Panel has pled guilty to the charge of theft of some one point seven-five million pounds' worth of possessions of Lord Fionn-glass's and I appear to enter a plea in mitigation of sentence.' He looked up and turned his head slightly towards Mary Ruth who was sitting tall and perfectly still and upon whose hair a tiny and sudden shaft of sunlight was shining. She was wearing a dark green suit with a cream blouse and her red-brown curly hair was newly cut. Her pearl earrings gleamed in the sun and from across the court she looked both dignified and graceful. You never know, he thought, His Lordship might take a shine to her.

As the sunbeam disappeared he continued. 'It can seldom be that any court in Scotland has had to consider a charge of theft of this magnitude. My first intention is to direct Your Lordship's mind away from the emotive sentiments expressed by my learned friend relating to the possible breakdown of society should crimes of this nature not be dealt with by the full rigour of the law—'

'You are surely not going to suggest that theft is all right if you steal from the rich and give to the poor?' interrupted Lord Cook.

'Far from it, m'lud,' replied Mr Affleck, who hoped to do just that. 'My point is that a clear distinction has to be drawn between those thefts which are motivated by greed and those which are motivated by other factors,' he went on smoothly.

'Well, I will hear what you have to say,' responded Lord Cook, in the tone of voice which left little doubt as to his own views on that subject.

'What I have to do first of all is to correct some of the gross distortions we have heard in the last three-quarters of an hour from my learned friend. Distortion number one was to describe my client's relationship with Lord Fionn-glass as one of thirty-five years of friendship. They were employee and employer. If there were a closer bond between them twenty-five years ago when their children were young, that had much to do with His Lordship's first wife whom he left three years ago in favour of a younger woman, an Italian contessa, I am told.'

Lord Donald shifted restlessly in his seat at this jibe and the judge said sharply, 'The nationality and status of the victim's wife can surely have no bearing on this case.'

'My learned friend forgot to mention,' went on Mr Affleck as though the judge had not spoken, 'the reason why Lord Fionn-glass cannot recover more than a fraction of his loss. Distortion two, m'lud, was not to mention that he was so under-insured that he stands to recover only about a one-fiftieth part of the true value of the goods sold. It is no part of this court's duty to punish my client for Lord Fionn-glass's indolence and neglect of his own property.'

Lord Donald began to feel angry. Who was on trial anyway? Mary Ruth or himself? Kenneth and Alec looked hopefully at each other.

Mr Affleck went on to deal with Mr Wilson's other distortions. He argued that Mary Ruth's first visit to Miss Wauchop had been entirely innocent. He showed how Carter's had made everything easy by their negligent interpretation of Lord Fionn-glass's written instructions. He amused the court when he asked how much cunning or guile was needed to persuade an auctioneering business like Agostino's to handle a valuable furniture sale and he pointed out that his client had manned the flower stall at the church fête for over thirty years. Martha nodded her head at this fact. She was not impressed so far.

Affleck paused and Mary Ruth drew in a sharp breath. He hasn't mentioned my motive, she thought. She remembered what Verity had written to her after her arrest. 'Get the best lawyer you can and send me the bill. I can afford it, and I'm sure you and Kenneth can't.' Was this the best money could buy? Verity had also written, 'Don't panic when you hear the way the prosecution presents your case and whatever you do don't shout out in court. Leave it to the professionals. I was a barrister, remember, and a judge's wife. It's like a game of chess or snooker, is court, there's not much earnest seeking after the truth. All you can do is hope for the best.'

Reading this in the prison in Inverness Mary Ruth had smiled and thought how sheltered from life her cousin was, retired and tucked away in Bendaraloch, growing her own vegetables and mourning for her husband in her solitary, untidy house. She made a mental note to write and apologize for her thoughts. Verity knew the law.

'I turn now, m'lud, to the second and real question before this court, a question spectacularly ignored by the Crown. Why did Mary Ruth Findlater, housekeeper to Lord Fionn-glass, sell all the contents of Fionn-glass House and give the proceeds to Camfam for their Famine Relief Appeal earlier this year?'

That's what we'd all like to know, thought Martha.

Mr Affleck gave a concise history of Mary Ruth's life and asked again: 'Why did this sixty-year-old mother and grandmother, who has lived at Fionn-glass for forty years, whose husband was killed in the Malayan jungle in 1954 in the service of this country; a woman, moreover, who was a loyal and trusted servant of the Fionn-glass family entirely responsible for the management of the household and the estate for twenty years; why did she suddenly perpetrate this spectacular theft, which never did and never was intended to enrich her by one single penny?'

Kenneth's spirits rose. It was a good question. Mr Field sighed: this was mere rhetoric.

The judge looked at him without expression and said, 'Do pray continue, Mr Affleck. I'm sure we are all looking forward to your answer.'

'Is there anyone in the court who has not been saddened by the multitude of appeals to help the hungry which arrive by post so regularly?' Affleck asked. 'Is there anyone who has not felt pity for the starving like this good woman, the widow of a British soldier, a daughter-in-law of an exemplary kind, regarded by everyone in the community where she has lived for nearly forty years as a pillar of local society, a regular attender at her church, a woman,' he hesitated, glanced at his notes and then continued unabashed, 'a woman moved to pity by repeated requests for help for the unfortunate, an angel of mercy . . .'

'Steady the Buffs,' muttered Colonel Fraser-Gordon, who had a great regard for Mary Ruth and was enjoying the speech, 'she's not Edith Cavell.'

Donald Fionn-glass flushed with rage. What kind of rubbish was this? The bloody woman was a thief.

'. . . in the eyes of Camfam. She has admitted the theft. She has done wrong in the eyes of the law,' continued Affleck.

And in mine, thought Donald, thinking of the demand from Lloyd's lying on his desk in London. Six hundred and fifty thousand bloody quid.

'. . . but before she is sentenced, it is imperative that we understand her motive. I would remind you that she did not keep one single item from the house for herself. She did not make one halfpenny profit from the sales.'

What about the sapphires, thought Donald, who had spent over three thousand pounds trying to find them and was beginning to believe his former wife's suggestion that they had merely been painted into the picture.

'Not one halfpenny!' repeated Mr Affleck. 'She committed no violence against any person, m'lud. She took particular care to protect both Mrs Inglis, the cleaner and Mr Robertson, the gardener from any suspicion whatsoever. She did not involve her son, her uncle nor any of her many neighbours and friends, in the crime. She did it to help and help she did. Every penny went to the women and children whose plight has moved all of us as we have nightly seen the scenes of starvation upon our television screens.' He paused.

It is a pity, he thought to himself, that the local evening paper had printed that article last night. Poachers delivering salmon anonymously to pensioners and social workers wangling benefits for clients could perhaps be called modern Robin Hoods, but this . . .

Martha was thinking about the article too. 'Won't do her any good if the judge reads this,' she'd said to Arthur the night before. 'It's chicken-feed to what Mary Ruth has stolen. He'll want to make an example of her.'

'I too have been moved, Mr Affleck,' said Lord Cook leaning forward and fixing him with his eye, 'by scenes upon the television screen. Surely you are not suggesting that we should all respond in the manner of the Panel?'

'Indeed not, m'lud. What I am suggesting is that living in isolation, disappointed at His Lordship's last-minute cancellation of his long-expected visit at Easter, for which so much work had been done, followed by learning that the cancellation was due, not to illness as at first stated, but to a desire on the part of the young

Lady Fionn-glass to attend a ball in the company of royalty; added to which an arrangement to sell the house that had been her home for twenty years was made without her knowledge, plus the stress of the Gulf War – you may remember my client is a war widow—'

Lord Cook said, 'I made a note of that, Mr Affleck, the first time you mentioned it.'

'I'm very glad to hear it, m'lud,' said Mr Affleck and continued: 'I submit that the combination of these things caused a lack of judgement in my client. I believe she forgot all about the owner and thought only of the starving and the sick whom she has so greatly benefited. She is not and never has been a greedy or malicious woman. Mistaken perhaps, but she is not a dangerous criminal who needs locking up at great expense to the State.'

He paused to let the significance of this sink in. He was not feeling very happy. The judge had asked questions. Always a bad sign for a defence counsel in his experience. Furthermore, Lord Cook had listened with rapt attention to the prosecuting counsel. Another bad sign. He continued in what he hoped was a sensible manner.

'It is highly unlikely that my client will ever be in a position to commit another such theft and that, coupled with her selflessly giving all the money to help the starving is, I submit, m'lud, a sufficient reason for you to be clement and to dispose of this case with a non-custodial sentence. Her savings amount to less than two thousand pounds in a building society which makes meaningful restitution out of the question. My client, who is over sixty and is a first offender, will cooperate with any conditions of probation or community service which Your Lordship may wish to impose.'

As he sat down, the Chief Constable thought, He'll give her five years, will Cookie. Mr Field thought she should have gone to trial and Kenneth whispered to Alec, 'Wasn't he good?'

Douggie slowly shook his head and Mrs Inglis took out her hanky. She blew her nose and murmured to Douggie, 'He won't send her to prison, surely?' Douggie marvelled at women. So clever and yet nae wise.

Arthur sighed and caught Alec's eye. He smiled a sad little smile.

Colonel Fraser-Gordon said to Donald, 'Valiant effort, but she'll go down for at least three. Nothing else for it.'

Donald felt sickened. He didn't want her to be punished, he realized. She looked strained and lonely in the dock. Oh, Mary Ruth, he thought, what would Kenny say to me for bringing you to this? The war-widow line of Affleck had found its mark in one hearer. I don't want you to suffer, he thought wringing his hands, I only want my money back.

Next to him Colonel Fraser-Gordon wished Donald would stop wriggling. Bound to be an adjournment. Get to the toilet then. No self-control. Remembering his grandfather's old jest he smiled to himself. 'Pots of Potts money, put some backbone into the Findlater family,' he used to say. The colonel, whose thirty-thousand acre estate of Knockspindie was punctiliously run, sighed as he thought of the mess Fionn-glass was in.

The judge lifted his head from his notes. He glanced at the clock and said, 'It is after twelve. I propose we adjourn for lunch.'

Mr Wilson, the prosecutor, rose at once and asked for the Panel to be remanded in custody over lunch. The judge turned to the defence counsel. Mr Affleck nodded and so Lord Cook said, 'Mary Ruth Findlater, you will be remanded in custody over lunch. Court is adjourned until two o'clock.'

As he stood up the usher called, 'Court rise.'

Everyone stood. The judge bowed to the court. The court bowed to the judge and he left. Chattering broke out at once. The court duty police officer opened the dock for Mary Ruth, reminded her to pick up her bag and led her away to the cells, promising to fetch her some lunch from the canteen.

The Chief Constable and Detective Inspector Sim went down the stairs at once and through the tunnel in the basement under the road to the police headquarters. Colonel Fraser-Gordon looked at his watch. 'Come on, Donald,' he said, 'if we get our skates on we can have a decent lunch in the Grill at The Highland. It's not quite quarter-past. Hate rushing a meal.' Donald fell into step and they left the court smartly.

Mr Field and Mr Affleck assured Alec and Kenneth that there was always a chance Mary Ruth wouldn't go to prison and even if she did, her age would almost certainly keep her sentence light. They all went to The Highland for a bar lunch.

As Arthur and Martha Bold reached the court door she called out to Mrs Inglis and Douggie, who were waiting for them, 'Not much of a defence, was it? We all know she stole the stuff and gave all the money away because she said so.' As they went through the door she went on, 'He should have played up her mental state, her disappointment after all that work, said she was too old to know what she was doing. He should have made more of the stupidity of Donald Fionn-glass. He was always gyte. And made a lot more of the further waste of money putting her away. Anything to keep her out of jail. Men! They just love the sound of their own voices.'

'Sshh!' whispered Mrs Inglis frantically.

Douggie said, 'It was a lot of money, Martha.'

'They manage to keep finance directors who defraud big companies out of the jail,' Martha announced in a firm voice, to Mrs Inglis's further mortification, as they went into the street. 'And they steal millions more than Mary Ruth did. And they spend it on themselves.' Douggie couldn't help but smile. Martha's a Tartar, he thought, but she's right.

Arthur was wondering where they could get lunch. He also thought Martha would have put up a better defence for Mary Ruth if they had let her speak. He kept his thoughts to himself though, as usual and guided them all to the 'Kozy Kat Kafé' which he saw across the road. It stood up to a fierce scrutiny through the window by Martha, so when Mrs Inglis pointed out that everywhere would be busy soon as it was half past twelve, they went in.

At two minutes past two, Lord Cook came back into the court. He had lunched frugally at the Carlton Club as he always did when he was on the court circuit. Mary Ruth had eaten stovies and chips in her cell. The police officer had laughed when he saw her surprise and said, 'Don't you get chips with corned-beef hash where you're from?' He thought she was a Sassenach. She laughed politely, unaware of his meaning and when he had gone, ate it all. She remembered that Kenny had always said they had chips with everything in the army. The policeman gave her a Pandrop when he collected her plate, before he took her back to court.

Lord Cook was ready to deliver his judgement. He sat perfectly still, but raised an eyebrow towards the usher and then turned his eyes towards Mary Ruth, who was sitting thinking in the dock with the last of the Pandrop beneath her tongue. What had Douggie said, she was wondering. 'Jail's like the army', that was it, and she smiled a little as she remembered what the soldiers she had known used to say about the army. A hand wagging in front of her face surprised her. The usher whispered sharply, 'Stand up.'

'Mary Ruth Findlater, you have pled guilty to the charge of theft of over one and three-quarters of a million pounds. By any standards that is a very large sum of money and it is impossible not to take a very serious view of what you have done. However, I have listened carefully to what Mr Affleck has said on your behalf. I have allowed for your being a Malayan war widow and for your long record of service to the Fionn-glass family. In particular I have allowed for the fact that not only did you not benefit personally in any way from your misdeeds, but that your choice of beneficiary for the proceeds of your crime was one which has tended over recent months to attract sympathy from a growing section of the population. All these points have been well made on your behalf by Mr Affleck, but I have to say to you that no matter how persuasive he was, I cannot allow what he said to influence my judgement.

'It is clear that you pursued a course of conduct over a period of several months whereby you lied, deceived and stole. You lied to Carter's about Lord Fionn-glass's instructions, you deceived Agostino's and Millichop and Millichop as to your ownership of the goods, and when the cheques came in you stole the money from Lord Fionn-glass. You stole over one and three-quarters of a million pounds. As counsel for the prosecution has rightly pointed out, no self-appointed arbiters of public morality have the right to redistribute other people's wealth. I detect a growing tendency for people to think that they do have this right – witness the recent newspaper articles on so-called Robin Hoods. Nothing could be further from the truth. The law will protect whatever a man has legally acquired, and no one must have the slightest doubt about that. The nature of the good cause to which ill-gotten gains are directed has no bearing on the matter. Anyone who thinks otherwise must get it into their head that the court will not tolerate theft for so-called moral purposes any more than it will for immoral ones.

'Mary Ruth Findlater, you will go to prison for six years.'

Arthur burped. It was discreet, but Martha heard him. I knew that quiche at dinner time would make itself felt, she thought, with something almost of satisfaction in her heart. Pastry brings on his dyspepsia quicker than anything. Thrawn he was and is and always will be. So it's six years down the road is it, was her next thought, with one of those rapid switches of subject that had puzzled Arthur for forty-five years. He used to tell his cows about Martha's lightning mental leaps. He fancied they sympathized quietly as they chewed. He burped again.

A fitting comment in Douggie's opinion, who was sitting on his other side. Mrs Inglis was aghast. Kenneth had tears in his eyes, but Alec was plotting an appeal. He'd get on to Verity. She would know what to do. Six years. It was unbelievable. Something had to be done.

Kenneth and Alec were shown by Mr Field to a visiting room where Mary Ruth was standing. The policewoman who let them in said, 'She's in shock. Try to get her to sit down. I've sent for tea for us all. She'll be here overnight, it's too late for transport this afternoon. Has she got her night things with her?'

'No,' said Kenneth. 'We never thought, she hasn't got anything.'

'Well, if you pop round to Markies you could get her a nightie and Boots is on the corner so you could get her a washbag and a few necessaries. Get her some paper tissues, too. You can take her some photos when you go to visit. They give them clothes in the prison.' The policewoman was sympathetic and Kenneth was grateful. When the tea came Alec persuaded Mary Ruth to sit and drink hers.

'You'll be all right,' he said, 'they'll look after you.'

'I'll go to the shops,' Kenneth had said. 'You stay here with Alec, I'll be as quick as I can.' But when he came back Mary Ruth had been taken to the cells and Alec was sitting in the passageway. He looked white and shaken, and as Kenneth handed over the nightgown and washbag to the duty officer he said gently, 'We won't be long now, Alec. Where's Mum?'

'She's gone through there to the cells with the policewoman. She's gone away through.' The duty officer walked past them, picked up the bags for Mary Ruth and said kindly, 'The WPC will be back soon. I'll see this reaches Mrs Findlater.' He went through another door, assuming they were going to wait for the policewoman.

The two men waited ten minutes and when neither officer returned and Alec looked about to weep, Kenneth, confused and shocked at the day's events said tenderly, 'Come on, Alec, I'll take you home.' As they went through the street door WPC Martin returned and thought the absent duty officer had taken them to the cells. By the time Mary Ruth had realized what had happened they were halfway home.

'A guid greet will do her nae harm,' said the night WPC to her colleague as she listened to Mary Ruth's sobbing later that evening. 'I'll take her a cuppa at ten. Puir auld soul, eh? Didnae ken what she was lettin' herself in for, did she no?'

Heartsore, not speaking for fear of what they might say, Kenneth and Alec had driven home to Elgin. As they'd gone into the flat Alec had taken a piece of paper out of his pocket. 'The officer on the desk gave me her address,' he'd said. 'Visiting is allowed at weekends only, or by special arrangement. Here, you'd better make a note. I'm for a cup of strong coffee.'

On the paper was written *HMP The Valley, by Alloa, Clacks*.

Chapter 23

Friday the thirteenth of December was wet and windy. Mary Ruth sat huddled in the prison van. She had cried nearly all night because she hadn't been able to say goodbye to Kenneth. While Alec had coaxed her to drink her tea in the room behind the court, she remembered, Kenneth had gone off to buy her a washbag. He had never come back, though she got the bag and a nightie.

She had wanted to bring her own night things from Alec's flat, but Kenneth had said he was certain she wouldn't be sent to prison and it seemed tempting fate to take them with her after that. Tom had rung up the night before the court and said the same. 'No one puts respectable grannies in jail, no matter what they've done. There are all kinds of things now; supervision orders and community service orders. Lots of opportunities that don't mean prison.'

She smiled grimly as she thought about this. Tom couldn't come up for the trial because his wife was in hospital with a collapsed lung. He apologized for not coming, which moved Mary Ruth. The poor woman was deteriorating. Multiple sclerosis only gets worse. Tom was worried and unhappy and talking to him had made Mary Ruth feel strong and brave. She had always been fond of Tom and hearing his voice had been a great comfort to her. If only I'd married him when Kenneth went to Edinburgh, she thought, I'd have been safe. None of this would have happened. He'd offered to pay her legal fees, but she'd told him Verity had arranged to do so. As she had no money she had no option, but she felt slightly resentful of their charity. She was shocked at how her life was being taken over. It was humiliating. Mr Field had used that word. Damn know-all.

She couldn't get over the mess that had followed her trial. When will I see Kenneth again, she wondered for the twentieth time as the van roared through the pouring rain. How could that policewoman have let me down, she thought. I'll never forgive her, never. When she took me to the police cells under the court house, we left Alec in the passage to wait for Kenneth. When I asked to see Kenneth, she said that it would be all right and that she'd tell the duty officer. She had seemed a very pleasant woman, but I didn't see Kenneth again.

Lost in her sad thoughts she began to weep quietly in the stuffy van. The driver looked up sharply into his mirror. Mary Ruth saw his eyes. She didn't want him to see her weeping. She wiped her eyes discreetly, blew her nose and wished to God the journey was over. She thought bitterly of the other policewoman, coarse creature. She had brought her a cup of sugary tea at ten. 'Stop yer greetin',' she had snapped. 'An' get aff tae sleep.' Fat hope of that.

She had lain awake with burning eyes and a dry throat and had heard the town clock strike four before she'd dozed off. They had awakened her at half past five. Now, as the prison van drove through Alloa towards HMP The Valley, Mary Ruth, drained and frightened, looked through the rain-streaked windscreen at the few bedraggled shoppers in the high street. The van splashed its way past an old woman wheeling a cane shopper and Mary Ruth saw her look of resignation as she was sprayed by puddle water while the rain beat down on her head and shoulders. Poor old soul, she thought, she ought to be at home by the fire.

The van smelt foully of stale cigarette smoke. She was the only passenger. The driver had left the other two prisoners and their escort, all men, at Perth prison. They had smoked their hand-rolled pungent cigarettes all the way, leaving the tiniest fag-ends she had ever seen all over the van floor. She was thankful when they left. She had been given lunch at Perth prison, thin lentil soup, dry bread and the stickiest macaroni cheese she had ever tried to eat. The tea had been lukewarm and sickly sweet.

She had a sore head and her mouth was dry. Her few possessions were in a plastic bag by her side. No one knew where she was. She might as well be dead. She began to think what she knew about prison from books, but it was Abandon Hope All Ye Who Enter Here which came into her mind. She remembered how some wag at school had once pinned Dante's infernal welcome on the examination-hall door. She could see the brown varnished door clearly. The note-quote was not considered witty by some member of staff. It was removed during the morning and reference was made before the afternoon exam to the damage unlicensed drawing pins did to school property.

How humourless those undoubtedly good women were, she thought as the van bounced its way through the puddles. They were well-bred and well-read, but earnest and somehow – she struggled to find the right word – fearful. None of them was married. The First World War had seen to that, she thought. Lonely and soured by the latent Fascism in all schools, they had told the girls repeatedly, 'Work hard at school and you will be able to choose whatever career you like.' But what choice had they ever had? She turned her attention to Oscar Wilde. What was that about the prisoner who could only see the *little tent of blue, that prisoners call the sky*? He would have had a job today. Friday the thirteenth. Suddenly a great wave of misery spread over her. All her fears and tiredness combined and she was overcome with sorrow for herself and for everyone in prison, everywhere. No wonder St John's Revelations are so lurid and terrifying, she thought. Hadn't he been a prisoner in a quarry somewhere in Greece? Tears ran down her cheeks.

'Greetin' most of the way,' the driver was to report to the gate officer. 'Thought I didnae see her. Puir auld thing.' As she mopped her eyes with her wet hanky, Mary Ruth made a decision. She was not going to arrive in tears. Whenever she had to go somewhere new when she was a child she had felt nervous. Her mother had always said 'You'll be all right when you get there.' She'd always been right. This will be the first time I have lived exclusively with women since I left school. It will be interesting, she told herself firmly. She pushed her sodden hanky to the bottom of her bag, opened the box of tissues Kenneth had bought for her and blew her nose. Then she combed her hair, put on some lipstick, sat up and marshalled her thoughts. Her father who had encouraged all of his children to read as much as possible had always said, 'You'll always have your old friends, if you keep reading.' Robert Louis Stevenson and Goethe, he had meant. Well, she had kept reading and she'd go on doing so. There must be a library in the prison. 'The trick is to keep reading,' she said out loud.

The driver looked up sharply again. He'll think I'm a headcase, she said to herself and hunched into a different position, conscious that if she wasn't careful she was going to start giggling uncontrollably. She concentrated on trying to decide who her favourite writers were. Dostoevsky and who, George Eliot? What a joy Maggie Tulliver is, she thought. What about some of the Americans, Anne Ty—? The van slowed, turned sharp right and struck out into the broad, rain-swept, darkening strath on the road to The Valley.

She looked through the windscreen of the van. The road was narrow and the houses scattered. The windscreen wipers swept from side to side, making a clicking noise like an old-fashioned kitchen clock, and the rain tattooed on the roof of the van. The driver, perking up after the long drive, addressed her over his shoulder for the first time.

'There's the jile,' he said, and nodded to the right. She wiped a hole in the steam and looked out of the window next to her. She saw some flat roofs about half a mile away through the gloom and rain. Thank God we are nearly there, whatever it's like, she thought. It was nearly half past three and the headlights were on, illuminating the heavy rain and emphasizing the gathering darkness.

She tried to remember what the only prisoner she had spoken to in Inverness had told her. Cockie they called him. 'Only speak when you're spoken to and don't trust anyone,' he had said adding: 'To let you understand, don't trust the cons, the governors, the psychies, the padres, the teachers, but most of all the "friendly" screws.' He had winked and slipped her a chocolate biscuit. 'Nicked it off the governor's tea tray.' It was slightly sticky from his hand and didn't look at all appetizing, but she had eaten it there and then. She never saw him again.

The driver pulled up in the car park and unlocked the door for her. She scrambled down and they ran to the building to get out of the teeming rain. The glass-panelled door was opened by someone in the office behind the fortified window and they entered the lobby. Mary Ruth was desperate. On the right was a waiting-area with a toilet door in its corner.

'May I?' she nodded to the toilet.

The driver, who was lighting yet another cigarette, said, 'OK. Be quick,' and moved towards the grille to speak to the gate officer.

Mary Ruth darted through the toilet door. The first thing she saw was a hand-towel dispenser with Rentokil Cares For You emblazoned upon it. 'God help us,' she said and rushed into the cubicle. There was a sanitary-towel dispenser by the wash-basin and she thanked God fervently that she didn't need it any more as she washed her hands. How do they manage, the women, she thought as she dried her hands on the paper towel, if they have an accident? Dim memories of her own occupied her mind. She came out into the lobby to find the driver gone. A woman of about fifty in a white blouse and a navy blue cardigan and skirt was standing waiting for her.

'Mary Findlater.' It was a statement, not a question.

Mary Ruth faltered for a second, then said, 'Er, yes.'

Miss Laing reported later to her colleagues, 'That new wan's not up tae much. Didnae seem to ken her own name.'

'Folly me,' she said, nodding to the officer behind the glass. The inner-door lock was released. Miss Laing opened the door and they went into the jail. The heavy wooden door closed silently behind them. Opposite them across the inner lobby was an open door and Miss Laing took her straight through it. She then passed her a pile of clothing which lay ready on the counter. Judging her size and height with a quick look, she removed the jeans and fetched a larger pair from the shelf behind the counter.

'Shoe size?' she asked.

What a funny question, thought Mary Ruth as she gathered her clothes up. How does she even know who I am? 'Er, seven,' she managed to say. 'Or eight.' She added, 'I've a broad foot.' Miss Laing, ignoring this explanation, banged a pair of trainers on the counter. Mary Ruth scooped them up too.

'In here,' said Miss Laing, thrusting open a cubicle door. 'Here's a bag for your own clothes. Give me your bags.'

Mary Ruth stood in the cubicle and looked at the clothes. She could hardly move in the confined space. She took her jacket off. There was no hook on the door, so she laid it on top of the clothes. They all fell off the bench as she began to remove her skirt. The trainers looked huge. She struggled into the jeans and took off her cardigan and blouse, banging her elbow on the wall as she did so. The trainers were too big. She toyed with the idea of saying so to the officer, but decided that Cockie would have put this into the category of speaking when not spoken to, so she laced them up and rejoiced that at least they were not too small.

She was folding up her own clothes when there was a brisk knock on the cubicle door and Miss Laing said, 'We haven't got aw night. Aren't yous ready yet?'

'Coming,' said Mary Ruth stuffing her shoes in on top of her clothes in the bag.

'Your personal effects will be processed,' rattled off Miss Laing, who was off duty at four, 'and what you are allowed to keep will be delivered to your cell.' It was twenty to four. She took Mary Ruth's watch and left it on the counter. 'We go to the governor, now,' she said. She had received over three hundred prisoners that year. Going ahead of Mary Ruth up a narrow staircase and along the passage without speaking, she knocked on the door at the end of the passage.

'Come in,' called a man's voice. Mary Ruth was surprised, surely a woman's prison should have a woman governor. Before she had any more time to think, she was in the room and a pleasant-looking man in a grey suit who looked like a bank manager was walking round his desk and holding out his hand.

'Welcome to The Valley, Mary,' he said.

She stuck her hand out awkwardly and said, 'Good afternoon.'

'Good afternoon, Governor, sir!' snapped the officer behind her.

'—Guvnor sir,' repeated Mary Ruth, wondering whether she ought to tell him her name was Mary Ruth. He looked very kind and after motioning her to a chair he went back behind his desk and sat down. Miss Laing stood at ease behind Mary Ruth.

'Now you have had a long day, Mary,' said the governor, 'but I always like to meet new inmates on their arrival. You will be in Echo, as I'm sure Miss Laing will have told you.'

Ecco, thought Mary Ruth; sounds like a brand of petrol. Whatever does he mean?

'We will keep you there for a week or so, for assessment. That takes place in Cutting,' he continued pleasantly.

'Cutting?' said Mary Ruth involuntarily, with visions of having her hair forcibly cut off and hacking up carcasses with butchers' knives.

'Quiet. Wait until you are spoken to,' said Miss Laing, who thought the governor was a fool. Prisoners were not in prison to be humoured. They were there to be punished.

'Cutting out cloth, in the sewing shop,' explained the governor, kindly. 'That's where we assess our new inmates. You will find it easy work. You will be in Echo until you have been assigned a place. You'll probably move to Crocus next week and even Diamond in a few weeks.'

Mary Ruth thought, Diamonds. Crocus. Whatever is he talking about?

He leaned forward across the desk and said solemnly, 'Now,

Mary, you are not here to be punished, but as a punishment. We do our best to keep you occupied and to help you. My officers all wear a navy uniform and have their name-tags on so you will know how to address them. You'll soon pick up the women's names.'

Who are these women, thought Mary Ruth. Are there men here too? What does he mean?

'I know you are a first offender, Mary, and many of the inmates here have a lot of experience in manipulating newcomers,' the governor went on. 'Until you find your way I advise you to be very careful what you say and do not borrow anything even if it is offered in the nicest possible way. You may find the repayment expected will surprise you or lead you into trouble.'

Mary Ruth nodded. This made some sense.

'Is there anything you want to ask me?' said the governor.

'May I write letters?'

'Of course. Your hall officer will give you stationery on request.' He took his pen out of his inside pocket and reached for the pile of letters in front of him. The interview was over.

'Oh! good,' said Mary Ruth cheerfully, not realizing she was dismissed. 'My son forgot to buy me any stationery yesterday.' She was feeling more relaxed. Thank God she was out of that jolting smoky van.

'That's enough,' said Miss Laing. 'On your feet.'

Mary Ruth made as if to shake hands with the governor. He looked up from the letter he was signing and said, 'That's all, Mary, you can always ask to come and see me if you want to. I am always available. Go along now. Miss Laing will take care of you.'

As they went down the stairs Miss Laing said over her shoulder, 'The governor likes to tell every new inmate that he is available. Just doan be asking to see him, that's all.'

They went back into Reception where another officer, Mrs Stuart, was standing behind the counter with a large book in front of her, listing the contents of Mary Ruth's handbag which lay disembowelled in front of her. There was no sign of her washbag.

'What do you know about this?' said Mrs Stuart suddenly,

holding up a ten-pound note in front of Mary Ruth's face.

Mary Ruth said, 'Who me?'

'Don't try and pretend, Mary. This money. It was in your washbag, tucked inside the soluble aspirins.' She pulled the washbag up from behind the counter like a conjurer. Mary Ruth was beginning to feel light-headed. Mrs Stuart sighed and looked at Miss Laing. 'Never learn, dae they?'

'Answer Mrs Stuart,' said the caring Miss Laing in a voice of steel.

Mary Ruth turned round to look at Miss Laing, yet again standing behind her.

'Face the front!'

Mary Ruth swung round. Miss Laing went on, 'And don't come your airs and graces with me, milady. You may have sent lots of food to your little black chums, but their little black chums will have had the maist of it, Ah can tell yew. Ma brother's in the Merchan' Navy and he's seen them in Nigeria and tha'. They wiz carrying awa' stuff with Yewnited Nations stamped on it, let alane Merry Findlater's Food Parcel.'

'Gies a hale new meaning tae the expression black market, so it does,' cackled Mrs Stuart.

Miss Laing continued, 'An' whit makes yew so sure it hasn't been traded fur guns and bombs? They warlords are gettin' arms from somewhere. Nuthin's fur nuthin'. Ah suppose yew thought yew wiz helpin' they blacks. Well, I'll tell yew this,' she had glanced at her watch so her peroration was hurried, 'there's plenty here at home needin' help, so doan come the clever wan wi' me and answer Mrs Stuart.' It was five to four.

Mary Ruth was thinking about what Miss Laing had said. She knew there was bribery and corruption everywhere, but surely Camfam would have delivered the food by now to the starving women and children.

'When you're quate ready,' Mrs Stuart was saying, using her best English again, 'you can answer my question. What do you know about this money I found in your washbag?'

'I cannot tell you anything about that money you found in my washbag,' Mary Ruth answered. 'Everything in that bag was bought for me in a hurry yesterday afternoon, in Boots in Inverness, by my son after my trial.' She panted as she finished. This was the first proper sentence she had spoken since she and Alec and Kenneth had been talking on the way to court yesterday morning. Was it only yesterday?

'Are you saying your son put this money in the aspirin packet?'

Mary Ruth tried to think and so remained silent.

'Refusing to answer won't help you here,' Mrs Stuart said.

This is like school, thought Mary Ruth. She suddenly realized that Kenneth must have slipped the tenner in. Silly ass. Nae clyping, she remembered and kept quiet.

'You are not suggesting that I put it in, are you?' said Mrs Stuart menacingly.

I'm not such a fool as to suggest that, thought Mary Ruth, though from what I've seen so far I wouldn't put it past you.

'A sly wan tha,' said Mrs Stuart later to Miss Laing. 'She robbed some rich English bastard which is wan up tae her, but she's nae coming the clever wan over me. I really searched her stuff after tha', I can tell yous.' The few possessions of Mary Ruth not completely destroyed by this search reached her later in the evening.

Handing Mary Ruth a raincoat, Miss Laing took a huge umbrella for herself and led the way out of the room and round a corner. She opened the door which led into yards. Lit by neon lamps the glistening wet tarmac stretched away into the dark. The rain was falling in sheets.

Miss Laing set off grimly tucked under her umbrella and Mary Ruth followed her, pulling the collar of her raincoat up round her ears. The officer walked briskly and Mary Ruth hurried along behind her in her over-large trainers trying to miss the puddles. The top of her head was soaking wet by the time they reached Echo Hall.

Unlocking the door, Miss Laing motioned Mary Ruth to go in past her and shook her umbrella fiercely into the yard. Mary Ruth shook her head and took off her specs. She hadn't a hanky to dry them on so she undid her raincoat and dried them on the inside of her green sweatshirt. As she did so she looked around her.

Through a big glass window to the left she could see five girls sitting on a modern, smart three-piece suite in a large well-furnished and carpeted sitting room. At one end of the room the floor was covered with Vinolay and there was a round dining table and seven chairs. At this table sat a woman prison officer staring into space. Connie Francis was singing on the radio. As Mary Ruth waited for Miss Laing to close the door, she smiled as the words *Who's Sorry Now? Who's Sorry Now?* came belting out in the powerful voice of the old favourite.

In a small glass-walled office in front of her was a male officer. He was facing her. If he had turned his head to the right he could have seen into the big room. He was talking into the telephone and did not appear to have noticed their arrival.

Miss Laing indicated that she was to enter the office. She looked very hard through her still-misty lenses to see the name-tag on the seated man's ribbed pullover. She wanted to make a good impression. He put the phone down and Miss Laing said, 'Mary Findlater for you. She's brought the rain wi' her.' He looked up at her. He was about thirty-five. He had a broad face and dark hair, tidily cut. He did not smile.

He said, 'Uhu!'

Mary Ruth said, 'Good afternoon, Mr MacMeanie.'

Mr McMeny, looking up at her and narrowing his eyes, snapped, 'You English?'

'Oh! No! I'm from Edinburgh,' she said, amusement at his mistake and an unconscious pride in her voice aggravating the situation.

'Embra is it? Well Ah'm frae Glaas-go, Mary Findlater, and Ah doan care for funnies aboot ma name.'

'I'm sorry—' Mary Ruth started to say.

'Speak to an officer when you are spoken to,' growled Miss Laing and left them. He was speaking to me, Mary Ruth thought.

Mr McMeny said slowly and carefully and rather louder than before, 'Ma name is MacMany. Goat it? MacMany. It's no so verra difficult.'

And my name is Mary Ruth, thought Mary Ruth, and that's 'no so verra difficult' either, but I suppose I had better not mention it. 'Yes, sir,' she said. He stood up. He handed her a letter.

'This come for yous.' She pushed it into her jeans pocket. 'You're down here.' He went past her and out of the office. Turning left down the passage, he jerked a thumb to the left as they went. 'Ablutions,' he said. At the second door on the right he stopped. Selecting a key from his ring he unlocked the door, thrust it open, snapped the light on and went back to his office.

Mary Ruth went into the room. There was a metal wash-basin set in a small unit behind the door with a large empty cork board above it on the wall. There was a radiator under the window. The bed lay across the window and the radiator. There was a small wardrobe on the right. The floor was covered in Vinolay and one serviceable chair stood in the middle of the floor.

She took off her dripping mackintosh and hung it on the wardrobe door, then she felt the mattress tentatively. Not too bad, she thought and drew the curtains over the large small-paned reinforced window.

She had no spare clothes, nothing to unpack, nothing to read and she fancied a cup of tea. She moved to the basin, ran the water and rinsed her hands and face. Turning to look for a towel she was surprised to see a plump little girl who looked about fifteen perched on the end of her bed.

'Ah'm Cherry,' she said smiling at her. 'Yer towel's hingin' on tha' hook.' Mary Ruth reached for the clean white towel.

'Thanks,' she said.

'Yous are doon fur six, aren't yous?' said the cheerful Cherry. ''At's a terrible lang sentence fur a first offence, so i' is. 'At's whit the gurrels are sayin'.' Mary Ruth looked so surprised that Cherry went on. 'It wiz in the *Record* an' there's nae other wimin's jile in Sco'lan' so we've been expectin' yous, so we huv. 'At's why me and Sarah Anne made up yer bed, so i' is.'

'Thanks,' said Mary Ruth again.

'You're welcome. They doan tell yous nuthin' when yous first in here. Ah thought that little changing place was ma cell, ma first time. Ah screamed blue bloody murder. "Ah can't even lie doon in here," Ah said, "Ah'm no stayin' in a bloody rabbit hutch." They didnae like i'.' She sounded highly entertained at her own mistake, whatever panic she had felt at the time. Mary Ruth wasn't sure quite what to say, but she had no need to worry, Cherry enjoyed an audience.

'We're on Obs. in Echo,' she went on. 'They keep yous here until they're sure yous no goin' to top yersel', or if you come in high, until yous are doon. Whether yous are in fur the first time or the tenth, like Ferren, yous are here fur a few days then aff tae Crocus and then Diamond. They have proper chiny sinks there and duvays too, no jist blankets like in here and in Diamond there's carpets an' a'.'

She pulled up the bed cover with a contemptuous smile and showed Mary Ruth the blankets and tapped her foot to draw attention to the Vinolay floor-covering. 'When they upgrade yous in here, yous can see yous upgraded.'

'I beg your pardon?' said Mary Ruth who found the speed and the staccato delivery so difficult that she couldn't understand what Cherry was saying. 'I beg your pardon, I'm new here.'

'Ah can see tha',' said the friendly soul. ''At's why I come in. Wid yous like a cup o' tea?'

'Oh! yes,' said Mary Ruth. 'I've come all the way from Inverness in a smoky van and I'm buggered.' She used the word feelingly and it relieved her tension. It did more than that. It convinced Cherry that she was not 'toffee-nosed' and eased Mary Ruth into her new community quicker than anything else could have done.

'Whit d'they ca' ye?' asked the girl.

Mary Ruth hesitated, smiled and answered, 'Mary Ruth.'

'Well, come oan then Merry Ruth, we'll get yous a cuppa and Ah'll introduce yous to the gurrels.'

Chapter 24

Sitting quietly at the round dining table next to Pat, who had hardly touched her food and hadn't spoken at all since she had said 'Hullaw', and the elegant Fern, who smiled wryly from time to time as Cherry chattered on, Mary Ruth wiped up the remnants of the tomato and pasta bake with a slice of under-baked brown bread and thought longingly of her bed. She drank her hot, unsugared tea with relish and tried to keep her eyes open.

Opposite her sat Sarah Anne, nineteen and desperately thin, though she eats I notice, thought Mary Ruth. Sarah Anne had her sweatshirt sleeves pushed up and the series of scars on her arms, some pink and fresh-looking and some white, fascinated Mary Ruth. Maggy, next to her, was gazing absently at her cup of tea, her food growing cold on her plate.

'Eat up, Maggy,' said Cherry. 'It's no wonderful, bu'.'

Maggy straightened her back and picked up her fork.

'It's no bad, Magsie,' added Sarah Anne in support of Cherry. 'Look, I've eaten all mine, bu'.'

Maggy didn't look, but she did start to eat, very slowly.

'We are a crew,' said Fern. 'Cherry never stops talking, Pat never speaks, Sarah Anne would eat the plate and Maggy doesn't eat at all.' She smiled at Mary Ruth, 'and you haven't met Connie yet.'

Before Mary Ruth could speak, Cherry butted in to explain. 'She should be out tonight. She's on Lock Down, Body Dress, in Solitary.' She looked confidingly at Mary Ruth: after all, she'd befriended her first. 'They look in on yous through a peephole, high up, on the catwalk. 'At's humiliatin', so i' is, especially if it's tha' wee nyaff McMeny.' The whole group nodded in agreement.

'He's pure rubbish, so he is,' said Sarah Anne.

'I don't think he likes me,' said Mary Ruth. 'I called him Mr MacMeanie.'

'Tha's a compliment',' laughed Cherry. 'Tae whit we ca' him.'

'That wee nyaff makes yer boke, so he does,' said Maggy suddenly.

Anxious to regain Mary Ruth's attention, Cherry nodded across the room to a corridor leading off the main one. 'Solitary's doon there. Whan they scream it's awfu'.'

'Connie never screams wance she's in,' said Maggy.

'You should jist hear her while they're takin' her doon,' said Sarah Anne.

'She gets very upset occasionally,' said Fern, to Mary Ruth. 'Screams and throws things, including herself, all over the show, so they put her in the cooler in paper pants and an indestructible garment called a body dress, universally hated. They look like Mother Hubbards. Connie's putting a complaint to the Visiting Committee about having to have a visit in a body dress.'

'Whit's the use o' tha'?' asked Maggy. 'They Visitin' Committee's rubbage.'

'They are all we've got,' Fern said gently.

'Connie's right,' said Sarah Anne. 'If ye doan fight ye get nuthin' in this place.'

Fern smiled a wry little smile and went on, 'Anyway they've locked her up for a spell. She threw a wobbly at teatime last night.'

'She's awfu' guid fun is Connie,' said Cherry. 'You'll like her,' she added to Mary Ruth.

'You're tired, aren't you?' said Fern, looking at Mary Ruth and thinking, she's older than my mother. What a disgrace to put her in here. 'You should go to bed early. Just after six the gorgeous Miss

Duthie will be bringing your stuff when she comes on. Now there's a treat in store.'

Mary Ruth smiled at the sarcastic, so very English, expression.

'Actually,' went on Fern in her well-spoken English voice, 'she's not bad, though she'll be picking over your stuff as well as picking it up. Don't be surprised at the state it will be in.'

Mary Ruth nodded.

'I'm not sure she'll have much stuff left,' said Cherry. 'She told me Mrs Stuart found a tenner in her aspirins.'

'Tha' fuckin' cow,' muttered Maggy suddenly as she lifted her fork to her mouth. 'Tha' stewpot!' She chewed as she went on, little specks of food flying out of her mouth as she spoke. 'She ripped ma new bag to pieces. "Searching for illegal substances," she said. Why can't she ca' them pills, like everyb'dy else. They're called pills. Pills!' she said savagely, banged her fork down on to the rest of her food and began to weep.

Fern and Cherry looked round quickly and Sarah Anne put her arm round her. 'Don't cry, Magsie. You know it sends them spare. You don't want to be locked down. Come on, hen. Stoppit.'

Pat leaned across the table and said to Maggy in a venomous voice which made Mary Ruth shiver, 'Ah've telt yew whit Ah'm goin' tae dae tae 'at stupit bastard, when Ah get oot o' here. And Ah'll be daein' it fur yew too. Stop greetin'.'

This worked, and Maggy cheered up and tucked into her tinned pears and custard with enthusiasm.

After tea, Fern and Maggy sat and watched *Neighbours* on the television. Pat sat smoking quietly on her own, glancing at the screen every now and then. Sarah Anne and Cherry sat together in one armchair and talked to Mary Ruth about the prison. They were both nineteen and on their fourth sentence for drug offences.

Sarah Anne said, 'It's no verra posh in Echo, the maist o' the jile is OK, bu'.'

'Ah've never bin in Diamond,' said Cherry, 'bu' Crocus is aw right. Ye get tae cook fur yersel's in Diamond.'

'So ye do!' agreed Sarah Anne eagerly. They were like a pair of salesgirls in a cheap dress shop, thought Mary Ruth, determined you were to buy something and think you liked it.

What surprised her was the fact that there were only seven rooms and seven chairs round the table. In every film about prison Mary Ruth had ever seen there were hundreds of men roaming around vast halls and going up and down metal staircases. This was as warm and cosy as the sitting room in any old folks' home.

The curtains were drawn, there was a spider plant and a row of paperbacks on the shelf unit and the television was a big, familiar and comforting focus for the room. It was only the round, prison-made, unpolished wooden ashtrays that gave the game away. All the women were wearing jeans, but their sweatshirts were maroon, blue or green. Some were faded and some were new, some were worn with style over good busts and some were hanging loosely. The effect was not of uniformity, but of everyday life.

'Where are all the other prisoners?' she asked.

Cherry and Sarah Anne looked at each other.

'What d'yous mean?' asked Cherry.

Fern looked round and said. 'The whole jail is in units of seven, Mary Ruth. There's usually a Snow White on too and a duty officer in the office.' She nodded to the glass window where Mr McMeny was on the phone again.

'What's a Snow White?' asked Mary Ruth.

'Well, if you think about it . . .' said Fern, and waited for the penny to drop.

Cherry couldn't wait. 'Who's the Seven Dwarfs then?' She and Sarah Anne laughed delightedly.

Mary Ruth started to laugh too.

Pat snarled, 'Ah'm nae a fuckin' dwarf.'

Fern raised an eyebrow at Mary Ruth. 'There's a block of twenty-eight for remand prisoners, fourteen of us here in Echo on Observation, the others are upstairs.' She pointed. 'Then there's six blocks in Crocus which is a bit more comfortable and twelve blocks in Diamond, which is the jewel in the crown. They have learned something about women in the prison service, notably that we are not men—'

'We're not fuckin' dwarfs either,' burst out Pat and left the room. Fern carried on in her quiet voice.

'—and as we are women we behave properly if treated properly. On the whole. Some of the women here find it a haven compared with the pressures outside, believe me.'

'It's nothing like the jail in Inverness where I was.'

'It's nothing like the old women's prison either,' said Maggy suddenly, without turning her head.

Mary Ruth said, 'I've a lot to learn.'

'We'll look efter yous,' said Cherry. 'We know the ropes.'

'God have mercy on yous,' said Pat as she came back. 'With frien's like they two . . .' and sat down.

Fern smiled and said. 'You two chatterboxes should let Mary Ruth talk some sense into you. Here they are back again,' she went on, 'you'd think they'd no homes to go to.'

'Ah like the rest in here,' said Pat abruptly. Mary Ruth wasn't sure whether she was being truthful or criticizing the two young girls who were getting very excitable.

'They two wid gie yous patter aw night,' said Maggy. 'They doan know naethin'.' She never took her eyes off the screen as she spoke. She was worrying, as she always did, about her children in Drumchapel with her mother. '*She's no able fur them noo,*' she was thinking.

'They're only trying to make Mary Ruth feel at home,' said Fern.

'Aw stop talkin' about hame will yous, Ferren,' said Cherry, 'it's aw right fur yous.' She leaned towards Mary Ruth and confided. 'Ferren's family stay in a big huge hoose in the Lake District. Doan they?' she said turning to Fern.

'Do they?' asked Mary Ruth, looking at Fern with interest. 'My sister's in-laws live near Kes—'

Fern interrupted firmly. 'Don't tell anyone anything about your family and where they live, Mary Ruth. They'll not thank you if ex-cons start turning up on their doorstep. I can tell you. It happened to my mother and I didn't even know the woman who went. Word gets round. So keep stumm. Am I right, girls?' she asked the others. 'Or am I right?'

'You is right!' They all chorused, including Maggy who still didn't move her eyes from the television screen.

'Don't worry Mary Ruth, we'll look after you.' Fern smiled. 'I can tell you this, the first week is the worst. After that you get used to it.'

Cherry said, ''At's right, so ye dae. Funny that!' She leaned towards Mary Ruth. 'Me and Sarah Anne doan have nowhere to stay when we're outside, Merry Ruth. Tae let yous unnerstan', we've no proper homes. Sarah Anne was brought up a' the convent.' Sarah Anne nodded.

'You've got a mother, Cherry, I've seen her.' Fern said. 'Unlike my loving mother she does come to see you whenever you are here. Why can't you live with her?'

'Becoz she's shackin' up wi' a right bastard, that's why,' said Cherry. 'I canna stick him,' she said to Mary Ruth.

Sarah Anne laughed and added, 'An' he's no too fond o' yous either, is he? Stupit bastard. Bu' efter whit yous did tae him . . .' turning to Mary Ruth she said, 'Wait till Ah tell yous—' but she was interrupted by the arrival of Miss Duthie who called to Mary Ruth. She got up and followed the plain-faced, hefty woman down the passage to her room.

'Here's your stuff,' she said. 'Sign fur it,' and she thrust a book at her. She then went over to the bed and unloaded a bag she was carrying.

'I need my glasses,' Mary Ruth replied and went towards the basin unit to collect them.

'Ma Goad!' said Miss Duthie, turning and looking her up and down. 'Ah've been a prison officer here for fifteen years and Ah've never met naeb'dy who needed their glasses to sign the book. Ye sign wi' a pen, no wi' glasses, an' Ah've goat a pen. Stop messin' aboot.'

By the time this speech had been delivered Mary Ruth had put on her glasses, taken the pen offered and was ready to sign the book. Her father's words came back to her. 'Never sign anything without reading it first.' She looked at the list of her possessions written out in a neat copperplate hand. It began, 'One Washbag'. As she bent to sign her eye fell on the washbag, or rather what was left of it. All the inner seams had been cut open. All she could see inside it was a flannel with the hemmed edges cut off, her new toothbrush and some chunks of white plastic. She picked up one of the chunks and recognized it as soap.

'What's happened to my soap? Where's my toothpaste?' asked Mary Ruth as she looked into the bag. Miss Duthie picked up the book.

'Naethin' here aboot toothpaste,' she said.

'Well I had a new tube,' said Mary Ruth. 'It was new yesterday.' She looked again. There was no tube of hand cream either, but the face cream was there. She picked up the face cream pot and unscrewed the lid. It looked as if someone had dug their fingers into it, lifted out the cream and then smeared most of it back, which was exactly what had happened to it. The shampoo bottle was half empty.

'What's all this,' she said angrily. 'I hadn't opened the shampoo and someone's been digging about in my face cream.'

'Are yous making a formal complaint?' asked Miss Duthie. 'I wiz told this wiz your stuff. Ah've brought your claes over as it wiz rainin' whan you come in.' She pointed to the bed where a heap of clothing lay.

Mary Ruth swung round from the basin unit, but as she opened her mouth to speak, Cherry who had slipped into the room said, 'Sign the book, Merry Ruth, and come and huv a game of carts wi' me and Sarah Anne.' Mary Ruth hesitated, recognized the wisdom of the younger woman and signed. Next to the useless washbag was a box of cheap tissues.

'This isn't mine,' she said.

Mollified by her signature, Miss Duthie picked up the book and reached with her other hand for the box.

'Oh! it's hers, Miss Duthie.' Cherry said quickly. 'She told me she had some tissues, didn't you Merry Ruth? They're hers aw right.' She dug Mary Ruth firmly in the side as she spoke.

Miss Duthie, who was holding the tissue box by then, said sharply, 'Well, is it yours or no? Ye've jist signed fur it.'

'Er, yes, er, it is, thank you,' Mary Ruth stuttered.

Miss Duthie tossed the box on to the unit, said, 'Medical at eight-thirty. Change of clothes Tuesdays. Don't stick anything on the walls. Use the board.' And left.

Cherry looked at the soap and said, 'I'll lend yous some soap and toothpaste, till you get some more from the canteen on Friday. They think they're awfu' clever, but even they cannae get toothpaste back intae a tube. They must hae thought yous was smuggling something. Are yous?' she added, more in hope than expectation. When Mary Ruth was silent, Cherry said, 'They usually leave yous maist o' yer toothpaste.'

I owe this to Kenneth and his misguided tenner, thought Mary Ruth. 'Thanks, Cherry,' she said. 'At least I've salvaged some paper hankies.'

''At's cheap stuff, so i' is,' said Cherry. 'They bum all the guid stuff. Whit wiz yours? Tha' Anne-Drex?'

Mary Ruth smiled. The tissues had been Andrex. 'Yes,' she replied. 'Never mind. This'll do.'

'Come an' huv a game o' carts,' said Cherry. 'We doan play fur money, bu'.'

'No thanks, Cherry – I'm tired and she said I've got to have a medical at half past eight.'

''At's the morra. Doan take the cream puff. Come oan.'

So Mary Ruth calmed down and went to play gin rummy with Cherry and Sarah Anne until it was suppertime. She had a slice of bread and margarine and watery cocoa.

'We've ran oot o' mulk the day,' said Sarah Anne.

'That must have been my tea,' said Mary Ruth.

'G'wan!' said Cherry. 'The cow comes the morra.'

After using Cherry's toothpaste and having a quick wash, Mary

Ruth was locked into her room just after nine o'clock.

She put away her newly-acquired clothes and put on the pair of pyjamas. She put out her light and climbed wearily into bed. Just as she lay down she remembered the letter in the pocket of her jeans. She climbed out of bed again, turned on the light and fetched the letter. It was from Verity.

Bendaraloch House, by Lochfearn

Dear Mary Ruth,

I'm scribbling this in the post office at ten to four, on Thursday 12th, hoping to catch the post so you'll get it tomorrow when you reach the prison. Kenneth rang from Elgin to tell me the news. It's way over the top for a first offence, so don't worry, we'll get an appeal in hand.

I hope you are all right and not too frightened. All my women clients told me they were frightened at first in gaol. Mind you, they had mostly committed nasty crimes and were worried about the other inmates as well as the less attractive officers. I dare say I'll be too late with this bright advice, but I felt it was tempting fate to send you useful tips for surviving inside before you were sentenced.

Anyway, whatever you do, don't complain to the governor about any officer and don't tell tales about the other prisoners to anyone! Don't expect courtesy from the officers, but be scrupulously polite at all times to them. (VERY IMPORTANT). Don't be surprised at the kindness of the other prisoners, but don't tell them about your family, I mean where they live and what jobs they have, in case they go a-visiting when they get out. (Sounds like the ten commandments, doesn't it. So many negatives.)

I don't think I'll be visiting, but I'll keep in touch. Don't think you are forgotten and remember what you did for the people in Ethiopia.

Keep reading and keep a diary too. Your impressions of what it's like inside gaol should make interesting reading.

Must stop, I'll write again at the weekend.

Love,
Verity

Mary Ruth read it twice, then she got up and switched her light off again and went back to bed. I'll never get to sleep at half past nine, she thought as she snuggled down. I'll just lie and listen to the rain. She lay peacefully and her thoughts went to what she had done for the people of Ethiopia. And what was that, she wondered? Will I ever know? It was typically kind of Verity to have written so helpfully. It was a pity she hadn't written earlier, she thought. She did not feel happy about Mr McMeny though she was wrong. He had no sense of humour, but he was fair, she was to learn. He treated every prisoner with disdain, but that was no fault. He did not have favourites. The observation panel in her door swished open, startling her.

'Yous aw right, Merry Ruth?' came Miss Duthie's voice.

'Yes, thank you,' said Mary Ruth, adding quickly, 'Miss Duthie.'

'Ah'll bring you some toothpaste the morra. Ah'll charge it at the canteen fur yous. It only comes Fridays. You've missed it the day.'

'Thank you, Miss Duthie.'

'Goodnight, then.'

'Goodnight, Miss Duthie.'

The observation panel closed smartly. Mary Ruth sighed deeply, turned over on to her side and fell asleep. The rain continued to beat steadily against her window.

The taxi pulled up at Baltic Mansions and the driver twisted round and slid the glass panel across. 'Better pay me in 'ere, mate,' he said. 'It's a bloomin' clardburst aht there.'

'Thanks,' said Lord Donald, looking at the meter and waiting to hear what the driver wanted. The fare was always more than it showed in his experience. 'Keep the change,' he said and gathering up his overnight bag and his briefcase he opened the taxi door, leaped out into the pouring rain and, slamming the cab door behind him, made a bolt for the front steps.

It was half past eleven and the big storm door was locked. He struggled to find the right key and sighed with relief when he managed to open the door and get out of the rain. In the vestibule he shook his head, wiped his feet and unlocked the inner door. He went up the stairs two at a time to stretch his legs. What a journey, he thought. Typical bloody Friday the thirteenth.

As he opened his own front door he was calculating the chances of there being anything tasty left out for his supper. Not Dorinda's strong suit he knew, but he had left a message on the answering machine at seven before boarding the plane at Inverness.

The lights were all out. No one home yet. He couldn't see a snack left in the sitting room. The curtains weren't drawn and the rain was streaming down the windows. Shivering, he peeped into the dining room. Perhaps there was a sandwich there. The dining room was cold. He kept the heating turned low to save warping the good furniture and the picture frames.

He went into his study. Nothing. He drew the curtains, lit the electric fire, poured himself a whisky, took a good swallow and went to the kitchen. Since Dorinda had asked the cook to live out he could at least go into the kitchen without running the risk of her popping out of her cubby-hole and catching him raiding the fridge.

He made himself a cheese sandwich with chutney. Eating it and holding his whisky in the other hand he went back to his study. He was warming up. He put his glass down and lit his desk lamp. As he did so he saw an envelope on his blotter with *Donald* written on it. He picked it up, crammed the last of the sandwich into his mouth and reached for his paper-knife.

I don't know how to tell you this Donny, but I am leaving you. Tiger doesn't have time for Kitten any more and I haven't got a baby to keep me company and I never will with you. I am sorry for all your money troubles. My lawyer will be in touch. Your once happy, Dorinda.

Donald stood still holding the note. He couldn't think what to think. He put the note down on his desk and picked up his whisky glass, drained it, crossed the room, refilled his glass and sat by the fire. He was angry. Angry with Dorinda for her disloyalty. Disgusted with her reference to her lawyer. Her beautiful body had been less available to him since Julian's wedding. Once he had moved out and the cook had gone, Dorinda had been out very late almost every night and too sleepy to let him make love to her in the mornings. He had assumed she was disappointed about the Gstaad house and the Porsche which he had cancelled after all. Lloyd's would want money next year too, he'd been advised. He was a member of three syndicates. He'd bitten off more than he could chew. He'd sold the German pictures from the office and the family silver was going under the hammer in January. He had tried to explain to her, but she didn't seem to understand.

Perhaps she understands only too well, he thought suddenly. She's getting out before I go bust. Conniving little bitch. He read the note again. So her lawyer will be in touch, will he? Christ! He scrunched up the note and hurled it at the waste-paper basket.

Well, she needn't think I'm going to pay her a million pounds, he thought savagely. Mary was a loyal wife. She never left me to come home to an empty house in the winter without leaving me a sandwich if she'd gone to bed. She usually waited up for me anyway. She was a proper wife. She looked after the children. She wasn't a selfish ornament like Dorinda.

He looked at the clock. It was midnight. I need to talk to someone, he realized. Mary is the most sensible and after thirty-five years the first person, the obvious person . . . but she won't want me on the phone at midnight, if at all. He sighed. My mother will say it serves me right and I haven't spoken to my sister since I ditched Mary. What about the children? Not that I'm likely to get much joy from Lizzie, he thought, but little Kathy – but they have babies. I can't wake them up at midnight and the newlyweds aren't going to thank me for telephoning so late either. Overcome with self-pity he went to get another whisky.

That's it: I'll ring Bimbo Massingham. What are old school friends for. He reached for his address book and stopped with his hand stretched out. God. He was ill. Diabetes, they'd said. No wonder he'd been falling down all over the place. Freddie had rung to tell him. She'd found Bimbo in a coma and had sent for an ambulance. He was in the London Clinic before he came round. He was getting out today. Tomorrow. Anyway I can't ring him this late, he thought.

What about Giles and Marina? Mind you, she'd been a bit 'iffy' since Dorinda had told everyone that the beautifully preserved fifty-five-year-old Marina, groomed to perfection at all times, was 'the best-looking wrinkly Donald knew'. Dorinda had thought this was wit. Marina had not. He reached for his address book. It's worth a shot. Nichols-Gordon . . . he found the number and then listened to Giles's fruity tones.

'Sorry, we're not available. Friends, please leave a message after the blip. If,' he went on nastily, 'you are one of those idiots employed to ring up asking impertinent questions, don't ring back. You are not wanted on this line.' Donald put the phone down.

I must have been mad, he thought, not for the first time. Is there a male menopause and is that what's to blame? He switched on the answering machine and listened to his own voice asking Dorinda to make him some supper. 'The plane's late,' he heard himself saying. 'I'll be late.' She must have been gone by then, he'd been too late. It was all too late.

He smashed his fists down on his desk, then he got up and strode about the room. Suddenly he spun round and kicked the side table by his fireside chair across the hearth. It crashed into a small circular mahogany table, smashing a big cut-glass bowl of pot pourri. Another of Dorinda's ideas. 'Who wants bowls of dead flowers anyway?' he shouted. The dusty petals flew into the air and settled on the carpet with the jagged shards of glass. He felt better, briefly; went back to his desk, picked up the phone and rang his lawyer.

'I pay the sod enough,' he muttered as he stabbed at the keys, 'so why should he be fucking well asleep when I'm not?'

'Shackleton,' said the voice which answered the phone. It was a strong, confident voice. It didn't matter what Stephen Shackleton was doing when the phone rang – sleeping, shaving, screwing, he always sounded decisive and competent. His telephone voice was a valuable part of his stock-in-trade. His fees were exorbitant, but they were paid.

'Stephen, it's Donald here, sorry to ring so late.'

'Don't worry, old son,' said Shackleton, who had been changing the cat-litter trays. The three Persians were his and his wife refused to empty the trays or let their long-treasured competent cleaner do it. 'What's to do?' He's found out about Dorinda and the Eyetie cousin, I suppose, he thought. I hope he hasn't broken her neck.

'Dorinda's left me.'

'I'm very sorry to hear that.'

'I need to talk to someone.'

Oh, God, here we go, thought Shackleton. 'Fire away, old son,' he said and looked at his watch. He reached for the pad and scribbled down the time.

'I've been up to Scotland: Mary Ruth got six years. I stayed last night with an old neighbour. Spent most of the day tying up the loose ends from Fionn-glass. Paying off the staff, that kind of thing. They were very cold. I think they blame me for Mary Ruth. I'm so bloody confused about it all Shack, I do think I was right to prosecute, but as I saw her in court being sent down, I was weeping.'

Shackleton moved over to sit at the kitchen table. Portable phones have their uses. His wife put her head round the door. 'I'm going up,' she mouthed.

'OK,' he mouthed back, then he covered the mouthpiece and said, 'It's Donald Fionn-glass. Dorinda's left him and he's seen his housekeeper put away for six and he's sorry.' He raised his eyebrows. She pulled a face, pointed at the half-finished cat trays to remind him and tiptoed away.

Donald was saying '. . . the answering machine and we finally got airborne about an hour late. Awful journey, bouncing about, up and down, the tube was packed, had to wait for a taxi.'

Don't we all, old son, thought Shackleton, trying to read the evening paper headline upside down, without his glasses. It looked more interesting than Donald's story.

'. . . pouring down, soaking wet, getting a cold I shouldn't wonder, no supper . . . own sandwich.' He paused and Shackleton grunted encouragingly, noting that Donald had been talking for nine minutes, 'and then to crown it all I get in and find the note.'

'What have you done with it?' asked Shackleton, who had perfected the art of listening to a confused and repetitive client and grunting sympathetically. Once he had interrupted the flow and asked a question he was in control.

'Oh!' said Donald. 'It's here.' He looked over the desk desperately trying to see where it had landed. 'I've got it.'

'Read it to me.'

Donald tried to reach round to the waste-paper basket without putting the phone down. The crumpled paper had bounced off the edge of the basket and he pulled the answering machine off the desk as he stretched out to reach it. The noise made Shackleton shake his head.

'Still there, old son?' he asked. What on earth was Donald doing, he wondered. Donald was hitting his head on the desk as he bent to rescue the answering machine and by the time he was back in his seat smoothing out the note, Shackleton had noted twelve minutes on his pad.

'Sorry,' said Donald and read the note.

'Keep the note,' said Shackleton. 'Who's her lawyer?'

'Don't know.'

'It'll be Dobell and Stone, they act for her cousin.'

'Who?'

'Carlo, the Eyetie, the "safe in your bedroom" merchant. Ha! Ha!'

'What the fuck are you talking about, Shack?'

'Never mind. What has she taken with her?'

'Nothing, as far as I can see.'

'What about jewellery, clothes?'

'No idea.'

'Go and have a look, old son.'

Donald laid the phone down and rubbing his head, he went off to the bedroom. The little safe Dorinda had insisted on buying from cousin Carlo stood open. The picture which usually hung over it was on the bed. He looked inside. It was empty, but as he began to fume he saw the boxes of family jewels on the dressing table. Nothing was missing. The list for the insurance which she had paid was next to them.

The tiara which she was so proud of and which had caused so much trouble between them was in the House of Lords. He had paid a small fortune to have it remodelled for her as a birthday present. She had gone about telling everyone, including the papers, that it had been a present and that it was hers. Silly bitch.

He went into her dressing room. It was empty except for a few coat-hangers, a torn nightie and one pink furry high-heeled slipper. If she sells the lot, even at second-hand prices he reckoned, she'll have ten thousand quid. He went back to the study replenishing his glass before he took up the phone. It was half past twelve.

'Hello! Shack?' he called loudly into the mouthpiece.

The great man who was finishing the cat trays had hooked his receiver on to his waistband. 'Here, old son. Well?'

'No jewellery gone, except what was hers, but every expensive stitch of clothing which I bought her and a shoe collection to rival Imelda Marcos's have gone.'

'Right! Come to the office tomorrow and bring all the info you can about the cost of the clothes and shoes and presents you made her. Didn't you buy her a custom-made Porsche? That kind of thing. I'll need the value of the clothes so hunt out the bills, cheque-book stubs, receipts – you know the drill.'

'There must have been seventy thousand pounds' worth.'

'Well, you won't have to buy any more for her. Look on the bright side. Just bring me proof that you paid for it all.'

'What the hell for?'

'Question of joint estate. If she's had clothes worth seventy thousand out of the estate it's all the less for you to pay her.'

'I don't see why I should pay her anything. She's left me.'

'Donald, you are tired. Go to bed. Leave it to me. Just be thankful you didn't have any children. They don't come cheap either.'

Donald put the receiver down, turned off the lamp, the fire and the lights and went through to the bedroom. He took the jewel cases and put them back in the safe and rehung the picture. He started looking in his tallboy drawers for old bills. He couldn't find any. This is ridiculous, he thought, I know they're here somewhere. He pulled out a drawer and turned it upside down on to the bed.

The first thing he saw when he had put the drawer aside was the letter from Kenny Findlater, his boyhood companion and closest friend. It had reached him after Kenny had been reported killed in Malaya. He opened it and sat on the edge of the bed to read it by the light of the lamp. It was written on army-issue paper.

3/12/54 Malaya

Dear Donnie,

Sorry not to have seen you in London when we passed through. No time. We're off up-country tomorrow. The 'big push', they tell us. Mary will have told you our news, congratulations to you two as well. I hope our children will have as much fun together in the summers at Fionn-glass as we did. Look after Mary Ruth for me, if anything happens. She is more precious to me than any jewels, but she is an innocent. Because she is truthful she thinks everyone else is the same. Love to Mary,

Yours aye,

Kenny

Donald put the letter back into its envelope. Poor Kenny. Who would have thought all their high hopes would have come to this. I should never have prosecuted Mary Ruth, he thought. I was never going to get my money back. It's made me look a fool having a housekeeper who has robbed me blind and Mary Ruth is in some God-forsaken prison cell. Thank God Kenny doesn't know. He stood holding the letter and thought about Mary Ruth.

'If you have hidden those bloody sapphires away I wish you the good of them,' he whispered, though he couldn't believe she had stolen them. 'Oh! Mary Ruth,' he sighed. 'Oh! Kenny.' He began to weep. 'Oh! Kenny, Kenny!'

He looked at the mess on the bed, threw it off with one magnificent sweep of the duvet, undressed and got into bed. Well, he thought as he turned out the lamp, at least I'll never have to admire or pay for any more ugly, expensive fashionable clothing. That's something. Shack was right. He stretched out across the bed and, pulling the spare pillows into his arms, he cuddled up to them and went to sleep.

Chapter 25

'Well, that's the best birthday present I could have wished for,' said Alec to Kenneth, much relieved, as he replaced the receiver.

'Verity knows what she's talking about,' agreed Kenneth. 'I would never have known you had to write and submit notice and appeal within two weeks. I think that Affleck was a bit of a chancer. He didn't explain to us properly about appealing.'

'Never mind. We're on the way now,' Alec smiled. 'Funny old way to spend your eightieth birthday, trying to arrange an appeal against sentence for your niece. Poor lamb, we must let her know.'

'I'm staying until Wednesday, Alec, and then I'll go to see Mum before I fly back on Wednesday night from Glasgow.'

'And I'll write to her after supper,' said Alec.

Kenneth looked apprehensive as he waited, sitting by one of the six small tables scattered around the large, bare visiting room in the prison. One week today is Christmas, he thought. How terrible that Mum is going to be in here. He felt edgy and sick. He didn't like the smell of the place nor the young male officer sitting in the corner with his Walkman headphones on. He was nervous and his hands were clammy. The door opened and his mother came in. She was wearing a pair of jeans and trainers and a royal blue sweatshirt. Dressed in these clothes, all her comfortable maternal look was gone. She looked about thirty-five and greeted him with a beaming smile and a great hug.

'How wonderful to see you,' she kept saying as he questioned her.

'Are you all right? What's it like? Is the food all right?' he began.

'I'm fine, Kenneth. I was upset not to see you after the trial and the journey here was horrendous, but I'm all right now. How's the baby? Are you on your way home?'

'Never mind me. The baby's fine. What's the food like?'

'It's edible and sufficient. You men are always thinking about food.' She smiled, thinking how big and handsome he was and hoping there would be some other prisoners in for visits so he'd be seen. 'Honestly, Kenneth, the food is adequate, but the best thing about it is that it is organized, bought, prepared and cooked by someone else.'

Kenneth smiled a little at this and asked, 'What are the other prisoners like?'

'They are human beings, Kenneth. What do you mean, what are they like? Do you mean what age are they? What size and shape? What are they in for? Come on.'

'Well,' said Kenneth, 'I suppose I mean what, er—' he hesitated. The thought of *his* mother being locked up with the riff-raff of society made him inarticulate with distress. 'Er, I mean, what class of person are they?'

Mary Ruth looked at him in astonishment. 'What class?' she asked. 'What do you mean, Kenneth? You know perfectly well that the upper classes are kept out of jail.'

'You should have been.'

'That's what my fellow prisoners have been saying to me. "Yous a lady", they keep saying.'

'Well, so you are, Mum.'

'I'm a thief, Kenneth, and I'm not well connected enough to be waltzed off to an open prison.'

Kenneth shook his head. This is unbelievable, he thought to himself. She's acting as matter-of-fact as if she'd been drafted into the army.

'What time do you have to go to bed?' he asked.

'Nine o'clock is lock-up time, but I can read as late as I like. I usually put my light out at ten. Quite late enough. We're up at seven and work is from eight till eleven-thirty. Then we have dinner and exercise and at two we are back at work. I'm moving to Crocus next week. I'll be there before Christmas.'

'What the hell is Crocus?' said Kenneth.

'It's one of the upgraded blocks. Much more comfortable, and Fern is going too. She thinks we'll be in the same flat. I hope so.'

Not really listening, Kenneth missed the opportunity to hear about Fern who divided her life between drug raves in Edinburgh where she shared a flat with a distant cousin and spells in The Valley.

'I can't bear to think about it,' said Kenneth. 'This place is horrible.'

'It's a damned sight better than Inverness or Perth,' said Mary Ruth, pulling rank with great glee. She had to get something out of this visit. Prison had to be endured. Lists of questions to answer were no fun. She wanted news from outside. Most of all she wanted a radio of her own.

Kenneth thought his mother was far too cheerful. It must be terrible in here, why is she lying to me? 'What do you do all day?'

'Well, I'm in the cutting shop, where the hand-sewing is done too, not that I'm sewing much. I'm being assessed. Sentence planning,' she added, leaving Kenneth as ignorant as before. 'I hate sewing-machines,' she went on, 'and I'm hoping for a vacancy in the laundry. Connie told me after she came out of the cooler there was one due. She'd heard from one of the screws who has a soft spot for her. She doesn't want the job herself, so she told me about it. When I see the works manager I'll ask her for the laundry job, if it's still available.'

Kenneth, listening to her chatter, thought, She has become a stranger. Working in a laundry, in a prison, my mother. 'What did you do at the weekend? Did you go to church?'

Mary Ruth laughed. 'We don't go to church, Kenneth. A padre

comes to us. It was the Church of Scotland on Sunday, but he lent me a Bible and I'm reading the Psalms. Have you ever read Psalm twenty two, it foretells—'

The officer said, 'Ten minutes,' without removing his earphones.

Kenneth leaned forward and said, 'Never mind Psalm twenty two, please, tell me, are you really all right?' He caught hold of her hands.

'No body contact,' called the officer. Kenneth dropped his mother's hands. She smiled at him.

'Kenneth,' she said gently. 'I am all right. I'm not being beaten up. I'm not going hungry. My room is warm. The other prisoners have been very kind to me. So have the officers come to that. They all think I'm a poor old soul who has been given "an' affa' long length o' a sentence", so they dae. I want to hear about you and Alec, what you did for his birthday, what Verity had to say, and Tom? I want to feel I still have a life outside.'

At this point two tired women visitors who had come on the bus and walked the half-mile from the main road in the rain were shown in through the door from the entrance lobby. They sat down thankfully at one of the tables and dumped their bags.

Kenneth's eyebrows wiggled in their direction. 'Who?' he mouthed.

Mary Ruth leaned forward without turning to look and said quietly, 'Don't stare, Kenneth. They're someone's visitors.'

Kenneth continued to look at the women who were beginning to show signs of life. One had eased her right shoe off and both were slowly removing unsightly rain hoods, scarves and coats. As Kenneth watched, they slowly transformed themselves from tired old women into smart ones of indeterminate age.

The one with bright red hair peered into her mirror and coated her lips with colour. Her hair fluffed round her head, her skirt pulled straight and her frilled blouse rearranged, she gave herself a quick squirt of perfume behind the ears.

The blonde eased her high-heeled shoe on again and after brushing down her suit and pushing up her saucy curls proceeded to light a cigarette which she inserted into a long green holder. She crossed her thin legs elegantly and toyed with the wooden ashtray. Neither was smiling, but they were composed.

'Are you listening to me, Kenneth?' said his mother. 'And stop staring,' she mouthed. 'You're not at the zoo.' He shuffled round so he couldn't see the two visitors and saw the door behind his mother open. Through it came a smart young woman in tight jeans with a close-fitting, well-pressed maroon sweatshirt. As she passed behind Mary Ruth she cast a professional eye over Kenneth. Nae money, she decided. She sat down with her visitors and Kenneth, very aware of her, looked across at his mother open-mouthed.

'It's bearable,' she was saying. 'I miss my radio and Napper, but I can see it's going to be very boring after six years.' She felt hollow at the thought of six years of mid-Atlantic accents introducing pop music, of telly soaps, the calculated rudeness of some of the officers and the unguarded tongues of most of the prisoners. The jail, already familiar, was cheap and nasty.

She looked at Kenneth. He was in a state of shock, she realized. She leaned across the table and whispered. 'Kenneth, close your mouth, you look like the Laird of Udny's Fool.'

This made him laugh and respond with the traditional, 'And who's Fool are you?'

'That's more like it,' she said, 'now listen to me. Some of the women in here are so unhappy and have so little going for them it would make you weep. It does me, but they are not monsters. They make the best of things and so will I. I'm OK. Now, let's be practical. I need some money. By the way, did you slip a tenner into my washbag?'

Kenneth focused on his mother and grinned. 'Yes, yes. I would have told you if we hadn't made such a mess of it all after the trial. I just didn't know what to do. There was no one to ask and after ten minutes I really was worried about Alec. He looked so poorly, I took him home. I was glad I'd left the money for you. Did you wonder where it came from?'

'I wasn't the only one to wonder. It caused a right stushie!'

'I'm sorry. No permanent repercussions, I hope?'

'No, just underlined my amateur status in the prison.'

Kenneth smiled at her again, 'You look great.'

'So do you, you look wonderful.'

'I brought some money for a radio. Alec said he thought you'd go mad without long wave. I spoke about it to a woman in the office, where I came in—' He turned and pointed.

'That's the gate officer,' said Mary Ruth.

'Well, she said she would organize it for you. It'll be coming soon, she said. It'll be battery and mains. Verity told us to make sure of that.'

Clever Verity, thought Mary Ruth who had no socket in her room.

'Now, here's some photos of the children and one of Napper. I went to see Douggie. He said to tell you, Guid folk are scarce.'

'He told Malcolm to tell me that, when we took Napper to him,' Mary Ruth said fondly. 'He never paid me any compliments when I saw him nearly every day. He used to put me down all the time.'

'That's just his way. You must send him some word.' He smiled at her and she smiled back. Then he went on, 'Napper is thriving. He leaped up and down and licked my ears when he saw me. I think Douggie's very glad of his company now he's retired. Stella's still working at the builders, she sends her best. Ina said to tell you she was asking for you and I saw Colonel Fraser-Gordon in the shop too, and he said, "Tell your mother I'm sorry for what has happened and that we miss her at St Andrew's."'

'Did he really?'

'He did.'

'Bless him!' said Mary Ruth, surprising them both.

'It's nearly time. I've brought you some new novels which Alec and I bought for you and Mrs Inglis has sent you some Givenchy toilet water, for your Christmas. It must have cost her a week's wages, but she said you'd need something to keep up your self-esteem.'

'How thoughtful of her,' said Mary Ruth, catching her breath.

'I had to leave the presents to be checked, but you'll get them later. The cats have a life of ease and luxury beyond their wildest dreams in Mrs Inglis's house, I can tell you,' Kenneth was saying. 'They get to stay in at night too.'

The sight of Kenneth, the sound of his voice, the thought of presents and the messages from home were becoming too much. It was all Mary Ruth could do not to break down in front of him. 'I'll write to everyone and often to you,' she managed.

'Do that,' said Kenneth as he stood up to leave after a signal from the officer in the corner. 'Wonderful to see you. Keep smiling. Affleck will be here next week to see you. Monday I think and—' Here he found himself unable to go on. He wanted to wish her a happy Christmas, but how could he? Tears were stinging his eyelids. 'Take care, Mum. Abyssinia!' He hugged her fiercely and walked away.

Mary Ruth called, 'Happy Christmas!' as he went through the door, and burst into tears as soon as the door was shut.

The three women didn't look at her, but they fell silent.

The prisoner, Sharon, called across to her. 'See him, Merry Ruth. Ah cud go a bundle on him, so Ah cud!' Her visitors smiled tight little smiles to show their agreement. Mary Ruth wiped her eyes and nodded.

'Thanks,' she mumbled as she went out, 'Ah cud go a bundle on him masel'.' What an expression, she thought and what did Kenneth mean, Abyssinia. It was called Ethiopia nowadays . . .

On the twentieth of December 1991 Mary Ruth received twelve letters. It was Miss Duthie who handed them to her at dinnertime. 'Someb'dy's in luck, eh, Merry Ruth?' she said.

'Yes, thank you, Miss Duthie.'

The most interesting letter was from Lady Mary Findlater. After greeting her she wrote:

> Dorinda has left Donald and from what I hear from Julian he's going to be declared bankrupt. Donald told me in October

that Lloyd's wanted big money. He's never managed his affairs properly. Julian also told me that Dorinda is asking for £5,000 a month, to keep herself in the style to which she has become accustomed!

The good news is that Ffiona is expecting a baby in August. Fast work and early days yet, but she's over the moon – so is Julian, I'm glad to add. He seems to be settling down at last.

If there is anything I can do or anything you need, now or in the future, please let me know. The girls send their love. I've written to Kenneth and your uncle. Take care of yourself, Mary Ruth and keep in touch.

The other letters were from Dennis the rector, who assured her he was praying for her regularly, in private, which made her smile. From Martha Bold came the promise to keep an eye on Alec and a Christmas card with a Bambi on it. Verity had written to tell her about her appeal and what she was to do. Mrs Inglis wished her well on a traditional Victorian Christmas card and enclosed a photo of her cats in their new-found comfort. A long letter came from Ina, written between customers, with different pens, telling her that Sandy had been diagnosed as having a stomach ulcer. He was to have an operation and she hoped he'd be a new man after he came back from the hospital. She put a whole row of exclamation marks after these words. She continued with news of Fionn-glass:

The diggers are preparing the foundations for the lodges. The village don't think there will be much local work to come of it. The word is out that Filippinos are going to be brought in to run the place, when the building is finished.

Uncle Alec had written with a gracious remark about Martha's proffered help and sent a little Christmas poem he had written which she put up on her cork board, with the school photo of Malcolm Malcolmson's two boys. Helen sent her a long chatty letter about the doings at Knockglass, her niece Jean, still in the caravan behind the Mains and the widowed Donald Molloch who still came to have his dinner and tea. She wrote that the widows and single women of the neighbourhood were still looking askance at her for feeding him. Douggie's Stella sent a card with a big robin on it and wrote:

> A Happy Christmas. Douggie takes Napper everywhere with him. They are both well. Best wishes.

Mr Affleck had written to say he was coming on Monday next to talk about her appeal, and the last and largest envelope was from Angus, Bella and Uncle Angus. It was a card which unfolded so that three ships ten inches high came gliding up the Thames bearing gifts. Angus had scribbled on the back:

> I miss our little chats. Everyone is asking for you. Your hens have settled at Tibby's. Take care.

Cherry saw her mail as she passed her open door.

'The postie wull be worn oot, so he wull.'

Mary Ruth looked up and grinned. Sarah Anne appeared in the doorway holding her clothes, washbag, tape player and a box of tapes.

'Look whit Merry Ruth's goat the day,' said Cherry. 'It's a guid Christmas fur some. See her, see a tired postie!'

'Aw the nice!' said Sarah Anne who was moving to Crocus. 'Ah'll see yous gurls,' she said. 'Happy Christmas.'

'And the same to you Sarah Anne,' called Mary Ruth.

In the new year Mary Ruth like everyone else settled into the routine of prison life. Once Christmas with its family associations and memories was by, they all began to look forward, many to release. Most of the women had three- or six-month sentences and all considered Mary Ruth's six years a disgrace.

She was pleased to be placed in the laundry and found the work easy enough. The other women were no trouble to her. Fern had warned her to work at the same speed as the rest. She soon realized why and learned how to work just fast enough not to annoy the officers and just slow enough not to annoy the other prisoners. Fern also introduced her to Vi, who was the only other prisoner near her age. She was forty-seven.

'The Steamie's aye been popular wi' the wummen,' Vi told her one day when they were on exercise. 'Ye can press yer ain jeans.' Hers were pressed by Mary Ruth too after that. Little victories against the system like these made the day for them.

Mary Ruth's sister Catherine came regularly to visit her and brought her good books to read. The prison library went in heavily for romances, she had discovered. Her brother had sent her fifty pounds at Christmas, though neither he nor his wife came to see her. Weekly letters arrived from Alec and Verity and photo-filled envelopes came from France at erratic intervals.

'See her, see a tired postie.' Cherry's joke lived on after she had been released. Sarah Anne was released too and Mary Ruth thought she would never see them again. Connie went too, but she was only out for the weekend and was brought back on remand. She had flung a small oak table, a lamp and two metal chairs through the plate glass window of a shop in Sauchiehall Street. When arrested after some wild fighting she had been found with three ounces of heroin sewn into a pouch in her bra.

'See Connie, see a gallus wee lassie,' said Vi when she heard.

Mary Ruth met Maggy on exercise in the yards who said, 'See Connie, she made a mistake there.' Mary Ruth thought she was joking, but Maggy went on, 'She shud of hud the stuff in a bag. Naeb'dy's gonna believe even the Glesca polis sewed 'at stuff intae her bra. She must of bin plootered.'

'There's no doubt Connie is a spirited fighter,' Fern said, 'in both senses of the word.'

In March Mary Ruth was upgraded to Diamond and found the carpeted rooms and the private kitchen softened the day-to-day rigours of the jail. Vi was the appointed cook for the flat and the two women were glad to be together. They had little in common with most of the other prisoners, who were thieves or drug addicts and in and out of the jail. 'We're a cuppla wrinklies, Merry Ruth,' Vi said. 'They lassies need their airses skelpt.'

Vi had been in the jail for seven years and worked in the kitchens. She was friendly with the chief cook, who was a civvy. Their diet reflected this connection in the form of an occasional extra egg, or half a carton of cream. Vi was tiny and calm and had a lot of useful advice on everything. She helped Mary Ruth prepare her appeal. Mr Affleck was surprised at the worldly wisdom she had acquired.

Fern continued to be helpful without being particularly friendly. She had taught Mary Ruth how to make the most of her wages and told her to ask for help from the Visiting Committee when she was refused permission by a relief officer to write an Easter card to her daughter-in-law's family in her schoolgirl French.

"At wan's as daft as a ha'penny watch, so he is!' Vi said. 'Does he think yous are in M15 or whit?' They were finishing their pork chops in the flat at lunchtime.

Mary Ruth did get permission to write in French after Councillor Mrs Sibbald of the Visiting Committee intervened on her behalf. The card was six weeks late, but its despatch was considered a victory by all. Mary Ruth wrote to Kenneth:

> Without the other women I don't think I would ever have managed. They are magic. Fern has introduced me to the teacher and I'm going to go on the creative writing module in the autumn. They're all on at me to write my story under the title, 'How Lord McDoody Goat His Comeuppance' which I rather think gives the plot away! And Vi tells everyone new. 'Tha's some story, so i' is! She guv an English high heid yin his joatters.' I am getting the hang of the local patois, as you will see. I may have a go, it'll keep me occupied anyway.

Tom came every month, but the visits were a strain. His wife was dying and Mary Ruth didn't like talking about the jail. Their youth was long gone, the present was no topic for them and the future seemed another world.

'Are yous two gonny tie the knot, or whit?' asked Vi one day, after Tom had been to visit. Then, to hide her embarrassment at asking such a personal question added, ''Cos if you're no wantin' him, he'll do fur me.'

'Hope springs eternal does it, Vi?' Fern asked.

'She still believes Santy comes doon ra lum,' said one of the officers who was leaning on the wall and watching the telly, 'doan ye, Vi?'

Vi laughed. She was a lifer; she had killed her sadistic and brutal husband after twenty years by cutting his throat with a stolen butcher's knife, when he was drunk and asleep. Although into her eighth year she had no word of parole. She had regular visits from her three daughters and two granddaughters. Their pictures covered her room, even on the walls. No one told her to take them down. Fern had told Mary Ruth that the judge had talked a lot about Premeditation, the Cancerous Evil of Woman, before he sent Vi down.

Mary Ruth without thinking had asked, 'Was it premeditated?'

Vi was highly amused. 'Of course it was pre-fuckin'-meditated. He wiz sax-foot-fuckin'-two. An' Ah'm only four foot ten, so Ah am.'

When Mary Ruth, sickened at the stories of his bestial abuse of Vi and her daughters, asked her why she hadn't left him, the straightforward Vi had answered, 'Where cud I huv went?'

Where indeed, thought Mary Ruth. And with three children.

In September Mary Ruth was offered the librarian's job. She moved with pleasure, but she missed all the patter of the girls in the laundry. When she told Vi this, her speedy reply was, 'Come oan, Goad nivver shuts wan door, but he closes anither.' Mary Ruth smiled and said no more. Only at night did she mourn for her dog, her friends, her family and tried not to think about the crude or malicious remarks she heard so often. Her appeal was set for October the ninth.

She was conscious all the time of her surroundings and desperately sorry for the under-twenties. Cherry and Sarah Anne were back at the end of August. Mary Ruth was puzzled, for though complaining vigorously about the wrongs done them, they seemed happy enough.

"At's jist oor way o' life, Merry Ruth,' Cherry explained.

They had been on a spree to Leeds with five other women, all in specially adapted dresses. Cherry had also worn a wedding ring. This had tickled her. She had been caught coming out of Marks and Spencer's with twelve men's shirts stuffed into her pouch.

'Ah'm pregnant,' she had cried as she was arrested. 'Let me alane.'

Back in the jail on exercise she said crossly to the others, 'See Markies, if they's didnae use sae much packagin', I cud huv hud twenty in.'

'I don't think there's much hope of Cherry having half as much fun if she stopped thieving for drugs. She has a much more exciting life than I ever did,' Mary Ruth said to Fern and Vi as they walked around the perimeter wire together.

'You're the philosopher, Mary Ruth,' Fern replied.

'No, I'm not,' she answered. 'I lived alone for many years and I had a lot of time to think. Frankly, my life was safe and boring.'

'I don't know how you stood it all those years living alone in the country,' Fern said grinning. 'I think I'd rather be in here.'

Mary Ruth smiled at this. 'Don't let's be silly. I was used to being alone in the end. I like a bit of peace.'

'Well, yous'll no get tha' here,' Vi said. 'There's always someone at yer back.'

'Visit for Findlater,' shouted the duty officer across the yards.

Vi called after her, 'See whit Ah mean, bu'.'

Mary Ruth grinned back at her. It was Tom. His wife was dead. He talked about her for half an hour and then about his own misery for another half-hour. Then he asked, 'Are you all right, Mary Ruth?'

'I'm better than I have ever been,' she replied. 'I think I know now where I am going.'

'I wish I did,' said Tom. 'I can't live on my own, Mary Ruth. I'm going to be terribly lonely. I don't like being alone.'

You get used to it, thought Mary Ruth as she wished him farewell.

Chapter 26

'I'd wait until your appeal is over Mary Ruth,' Miss Whyte suggested, 'before beginning to write your story. Concentration in prison is difficult enough without all the excitement of an appeal hanging over you.'

Mary Ruth was more nervous than at her trial when she went to the Appeal Court in Edinburgh. Mr Affleck spoke vigorously about her age, her good behaviour, the lessons she had learned and then at some length about the expense to the State of keeping her in prison. The three Appeal Court judges looked solemn and Mary Ruth did not feel hopeful, but they cut her sentence by half.

'Thank God, I don't like prison,' she said to Kenneth when he came to see her in the waiting room after the court and before she went back to The Valley. 'Mr Field was right. I should have taken his advice and pleaded not guilty. It's a funny old world, isn't it? All this expense and misery because I told the truth.'

'Oh! Mum,' said Kenneth and hugged her. He was overcome and sat on the bench and sobbed. Mary Ruth sat down next to him and Mr Affleck who was very pleased with himself sat on her other side. As they waited for Kenneth to recover Mary Ruth chattered happily.

'I've only just over a year to go if I can keep out of trouble. I can hardly believe it. I feel like a bottle of champagne. In both senses.

"Ah cud fair go a pint o' foamin' ale!" as Vi would say, and I'm all bubbly inside too.'

'You're bound to feel flat after all the excitement of the court and seeing your son, Mary Ruth. The best cure, as I'm sure you know, is to keep busy. Now, will you try to get started on this story of yours?'

'I don't think it's of any interest, Miss Whyte.'

'Mary Ruth, you've had the whole jail by the ears for months. There's Maureen over there, she's been dying to ask you what you really did with the money and Senga thinks you should have given it to her.' Miss Whyte paused. She was a clever teacher. She knew no one would work unless they wanted to. Mary Ruth began to take an interest despite herself. Maureen and Senga pulled their chairs a bit closer to her and started in.

'Whit made ye dae it Merry Ruth?' Maureen asked.

'Why did ye gie aw the money away?' This was Senga. 'Ah cud huv been daein' wi' it, Ah can tell yous.'

'Well, I think it was a combination of all that stuff lying about unwanted – well, no, unappreciated – and the needs of the poor souls in Ethiopia,' said Mary Ruth slowly.

Miss Whyte put a sheet of paper in front of her. 'Begin at the beginning,' she said. 'What happened to make you even think of stealing it all? You'd been looking after it for years.'

'Well, I was the housekeeper for Lord Donald Fionn-glass.'

'Opportuni'y!' announced Maureen.

'And ye wanted to gie it to the starvin',' added Senga.

'Motive!' said Maureen firmly, "At's whit ye need. It says tha' in aw the stories Ah read.'

'Maureen is a great fan of detective stories,' said Miss Whyte.

Taking the paper back, Miss Whyte wrote: *Introduce yourself and your job.*

'Well, that's easy enough,' said Mary Ruth.

'When did it all start, the action?' asked Miss Whyte.

'Did yous get a mysterious letter,' asked Maureen, 'tellin' yous tae meet a masked man at midnigh' in the aul' Kirk yard?'

'No, but I did get three letters one day from Angus,' Mary Ruth said, smiling at Maureen's imagination and remembering the familiar short and portly Angus.

'Who's Angus?' the two girls asked eagerly.

'The postie.'

'Aw tha's no verra excitin', is it?' said Senga disappointed. 'Ah quite fancied the soun' o' him. Angus, a braw great Highlander with a kilt an' a sword.' Senga read romances.

Miss Whyte wrote: *Angus brings three letters.*

'Whit wiz in they letters?' asked Maureen scenting some news.

'Instructions to do a lot of work.' The young women laughed. 'And a promise of a visit from my son.' This time they shrieked with delight.

'See him, he's smashin', so he is. I seed him last time he wiz here,' sighed Senga. 'He's a right big stoter, so he is.' She affected a swoon across the table.

'And,' went on Mary Ruth, joining in the fun, 'an invitation to visit a lawyer, to learn something to my advantage.'

'Wiz naeb'dy helpin' yous?' asked Maureen, always eager to learn.

'Not with the theft, but there was with all the work.' Mary Ruth was quite enjoying herself. The enthusiasm of the two young ones was infectious. 'There was Douggie,' she continued, 'he looked after the gardens and the grounds and Mrs Inglis, who worked in the house.'

'Whit did they think, Merry Ruth?'

'They didn't know about the theft but neither did I, then. Douggie thought the intended visit was at a funny time of the year, but Mrs Inglis was delighted that we had something to prepare for.'

'Well, that's your first chapter then,' said Miss Whyte, finishing her notes with a flourish of her pen and turning the paper towards Mary Ruth.

She had written:

Introduce myself and Fionn-glass House where I am housekeeper. Three letters arrive. One is about work, one is about a promised visit and one is a mystery. Douggie is suspicious, but Mrs Inglis is supportive.

'Now you can get started,' said Miss Whyte.

She did, and became absorbed over the weeks that followed in remembering all that had gone on in 1991.

'Ah've never met naeb'dy like her in the jile afore,' said Maureen.

'Ah've never met naeb'dy like her at aw,' said Senga. 'Wiz she a skillteacher, or wha'?'

'Ah doan know. She's aw right bu'.'

The beginning of Mary Ruth's second year in prison was enlivened for her by a visit from her uncle Alec on his eighty-first birthday. She hadn't even managed a card for his eightieth, but this year she had organized a cake and they had a tea party in his honour in the bleak visiting room. Two other prisoners and their visitors were in and there was a lot of chat and teasing. Alec had a wonderful impression of the jail as a result. Tom had been up to Elgin to collect him.

'I've never been in a big Mercedes before,' Alec had said. 'Very comfortable. You could do worse,' he had muttered to Mary Ruth, nodding at Tom who was chatting to two of the other visitors. 'He's turned out very well, for a "rude mechanical", and he's very fond of you.'

Mary Ruth smiled and said, 'You look well, Alec.'

'I am, and I am grateful to Martha who is mellowing and if she wasn't I'd still be glad of her cooking. She's really an expert. I haven't eaten so well in my life. No wonder Arthur has indigestion.'

'I thought you were a little plumper,' said Mary Ruth.

Alec read the first part of her story. 'There's a lot of good social commentary here,' he said, 'though you're awful long-winded.'

'It's supposed to be a story, Alec. The girls don't just want the bare bones. They want to know what everyone wore and how their hair was done. I've been keeping it short!' They all laughed.

'If you tell them all about the jewels you might as well put an advert in the papers,' was Alec's next comment, 'or write to Donald about them.'

'They think I'm making that up. No one has shown any interest.'

'I wouldn't be too sure. Knowledge is power. Information can be sold. These girls, as you call them, have criminal connections.'

'Well, no one but the teacher really is reading it regularly, Alec.'

Alec shook his head. 'Well, don't say I didn't warn you.'

The following week Tom came again on his way south from Alec's. 'I managed to get an extra visit. I know you've told me they're a long way off conjugal visits, but a romantic connection obviously softens them.' He smiled at her.

Pleased as Mary Ruth had been to have an unexpected visit and glad as she was to see Tom and hear about home, she was slightly irritated at his implication of a permanent future with her. It was all very well to drop hints to ease his way through the regulations, but it would be all round the jail that he had been twice in a week as it was, without having them all thinking she was going to marry him.

'I'm sorry if I'm springing it on you, Mary Ruth, but I have to know what my chances are,' he was saying. 'I fiddled my way in again because I couldn't ask you in front of Alec. You know I have asked you to marry me before. Am I in with a chance this time?'

He sat four-square and humble on the opposite side of the table. His hair was turning white, but it was all still there. His eyes were dark brown and deep-set. His tanned skin was smooth. He is a good-looking man, thought Mary Ruth, and he's kind and he needs me. The question is, do I need him?

'I can't make any decisions for the future yet, Tom,' she said. 'I don't know where I belong any more.' He had to be content with that.

Thanks to Verity who had made it her business to find out what had happened to the Camfam money in Ethiopia, Mary Ruth received a letter from one of the Nursing Sisters of the Poor in Addis Ababa. She found the letter when she came back from work, three days before Christmas, but had no time to read it as she had to eat and then go to the performance of *Aladdin*, the Christmas pantomime they had been working on for the last two months. She was the prompt.

The show was surprisingly polished though the jokes were obvious. They had all had fun preparing it. Mary Ruth doubted whether the intended crushing satire was working when she noticed that the most cruelly satirized in the audience laughed the hardest. What would they think of this in Ethiopia, she thought. I'm enjoying myself.

The panto went well and was applauded by local dignitaries, the Visiting Committee, the governors and the prisoners. After it was over there was tea and Christmas cake and all the audience chatted with the performers. Mary Ruth was glad to be recognized by her one acquaintance on the Visiting Committee.

'You are doing a good job here, Mary Ruth,' said Councillor Mrs Sibbald. 'You're a very good influence on the younger inmates. Don't think your time here has been entirely wasted.'

'Thank you,' said Mary Ruth. Mrs Sibbald had a reputation for being tough. Her compliments and comment delighted Mary Ruth. She felt happier than she had for years as she went back to Diamond. Supper was ready and the women were excited. 'We guv 'em laldy the night, didn't we no?' Vi shouted from the kitchen where she was making hot chocolate. Mary Ruth was as excited as everyone else.

'I could see McMeny and Duthie laughing themselves sick, especially at Connie. God, she is funny.' It was in high good humour that they all retired. Sitting on her bed, Mary Ruth opened her letter.

It was addressed to her at The Valley, by Alloa, Scotland. There was no mention of the prison. It was from a Sister Elizabeth Mary who wrote that she had been trained in nursing in Edinburgh. She went on:

I can't begin to tell you, Mrs Findlater, what a difference it has made to our work here to have your money. We are particularly grateful for the promised Range Rover. Charities often help the local NGO's – non-governmental agencies. Would that they did it all the time and could persuade everyone to do the same. I'm afraid local government workers are too easily bribed or intimidated.

We run a big feeding programme here, a hospital which is mainly for amputees and a large nursery for orphaned babies. We would like to start up a school, though we are very short of materials and staff. There are six of us here. When I am home in 1995 I hope I'll be able to come and see you and I'll bring some photographs of our work and people. My eldest sister lives in Edinburgh and I shall be visiting her.

If you would like to come and visit us some day we'd welcome you. It is wonderful to know that someone somewhere cared enough about us to send help. Thank you. I wish you Christ's blessed peace at this tide and may his love surround you always.

Mary Ruth managed to keep busy and finished her story just before the teachers went off on holiday in July. Her sister and brother-in-law had come regularly to visit her and her son had been three times since her successful appeal. 'It must be costing you a fortune,' she had said to him.

'Worth every penny,' he had replied. 'It's wonderful to see you, even in here. You look younger every time and I'd never have seen so much of you if you hadn't been locked up.'

She had kept in touch with Lady Mary Findlater as requested, and with Verity and Alec. Fern was released and then re-committed, this time for four years. Mary Ruth didn't understand her any better, but still found her good company when they met. She and Vi were the old hands now in their flat. Vi had lost all hope of parole and lived day-to-day in a way that astounded Mary Ruth. I'd go mad if I didn't have a date, she thought more than once. Roll on December the twelfth.

She had a surprise on her birthday on the last Sunday in August. She hadn't expected a visitor and went into the visiting room with interest. Donald Fionn-glass was standing there. 'I hope you don't mind my coming,' he said, handing her a bunch of yellow carnations. 'Happy birthday.' She didn't know what to say. It was two years since they had last spoken in her kitchen at Fionn-glass House. She buried her face in the flowers and the scent of them made her feel giddy.

'Sit down, won't you?' she said at last, still looking at the flowers.

'I've been talking to Mary,' said Donald, sitting down and lighting a cigarette feverishly. 'She sends her love, by the way.' He was shooting little glances at everyone in the visiting room. 'The girls and their girls are well and Julian and Ffiona's twins were one on the twenty-first,' he muttered.

Mary Ruth nodded. 'Boys, aren't they?'

He nodded and hurried on. 'I have come to tell you that I am sorry. Sorry for being so cavalier about cutting our Easter visit out. Sorry for not being open about Mortimer-Desmond, but most of all, sorry for landing you in this place.' He shuddered as he looked around yet again and added, 'For all the good it did me, I might as well not have charged you.'

'It's not so bad when you get used to it,' Mary Ruth said politely, ignoring his last remark and wondering if the gulfs of misery and loneliness, the spiteful, unnecessary cruelties she had witnessed and suffered would mean anything to him. Would he believe the number of crude sexual remarks that peppered most conversations? Would he understand the boredom of listening to the constant talk about drugs, the buzz their acquisition gave, the ugly things the girls would do or suffer to pay for them, their cost, effects, side-effects, after-effects?

She had learned to keep clear of the eternal debate which went on between the supporters of the rival strategies employed by the two main local authorities. One supplied drugs to addicts to keep them out of jail and the other sent girls from sixteen upwards to The Valley for three months over and over again. Her age, and the fact that her family was so remote from the criminal classes meant she had been spared the pressure to have drugs brought in, but it was a knife-edge existence all the same.

As she looked at Donald she realized that he knew little and cared less about her sufferings. There was an unwritten rule that you didn't talk to visitors about the nastier side of life inside. It was like the conspiracy of silence women observe when they keep from the first-time pregnant the screaming pains of child-birth.

Oblivious of Mary Ruth's silence, Donald was saying, 'Mary told me particularly to apologize for my offhand suggestion that you could have the North Lodge. I went to look at it last week. It's awful. She was right. I didn't think, Mary Ruth. I'm sorry.'

He sat quietly. She was touched despite it all. She remembered how fond of him Kenny had been and the summers of long ago. Suddenly he stood up and said. 'I'll go now. I just wanted to speak to you myself. I didn't think writing was enough.'

'No, don't go,' she said. 'Please sit down again. Thank you for coming. Why didn't you tell me you were selling up?'

'I meant to that time in Edinburgh, but I couldn't. It seemed like the end of an era. I was thinking about Kenny and anyway, I apologize for that too.' Donald smiled briefly.

'I owe you an apology too. I had no business selling your property. I have suffered a great deal of worry about it. Not about the stealing,' she added with a little grin, 'but about whether it did any good. I am always being told that it's pointless giving anything to overseas charities. The received wisdom is that I am a bloody fool for not keeping it for myself and that the money I sent probably never got to the poor anyway.'

Donald looked at her with new eyes. 'Why don't you go and see what's been done with it?'

'I can't afford it,' she said. 'It's a long way to Ethiopia.'

'Couldn't Kenneth . . .?' he began.

Mary Ruth said, 'I couldn't ask him. He's broke visiting me as it is.'

'Me too. If I could only find those bloody jewels,' Donald perked up. Back on familiar ground he talked about his money problems to Mary Ruth. She's always been a good listener, he thought. '. . .So you see, if I could get my hands on the sapphires,' he went on to explain, 'I could buy myself a little flat near the girls and Mary. She's got all the money now and I think she might soften up a bit towards me if I could work on her from close quarters.' He smiled confidently and then pursed his lips. 'I'm kennelled in the attics at St John's Wood meanwhile, in the girls' studio flat. It's like a hen-coop. I'm working for Julian and handing over practically all I earn to that greedy little bitch Dorinda. It's humiliating. Those jewels were my grandmother's. I want them back.'

Mary Ruth thought about the jewels lying in the office safe in Elgin for the last sixty years. She should have made them over to Kenneth.

'Giles Nichols-Gordon has a venture on hand,' Donald went on again. 'He's leasing repossessed houses from mortgage companies and letting them to social security homeless. Nearly two hundred a week each. Bit sardine-like, but even Rachman in all his glory . . .' He laughed. Mary Ruth winced at the confused quotation.

'If only I had some capital!' Donald snarled, banging his fist on the table. He had nothing else to say to Mary Ruth. He thought he owed her an apology mainly because his ex-wife had told him so, but secretly he was hoping for news of the sapphires. 'If only I could get a kick-start, by finding the sapphires which I still think exist . . . Mary suggested they were painted on to the portrait. Never heard such nonsense! By God, if I could find them! Must be worth seventy thousand at least. I could invest them in Giles's company . . .' he paused, and Mary Ruth thought hard.

Alec and Kenneth and Mr Field had told her not to mention them to anyone, she remembered. She wanted to make up her own mind. What was all this Donald was talking about? Sounded dodgy. How would he react to learning the fact that Kenny was his cousin? He wouldn't like it, she decided, especially not the publicity. He would look a chump. Not even the direct heir to his own title. The tabloids would enjoy that. He had come to see her, admittedly nearly two years late, but he had apologized and he had loved Kenny.

She said slowly, 'Kenny was closer to you than you realized—'

Donald broke in immediately. 'He was my dearest friend. I never had a better. Even at Eton. Especially at Eton. It was his letter that has made me come here really. He wrote to me from Malaya just before he was killed. He asked me to look after you. I read it again that December when I reached home after your trial. I told Mary about his letter. Don't mind admitting it made me weep. I never minded his being the gardener's son, you know. I like to think that class distinction is dead.'

He paused and lit himself another cigarette. He didn't offer Mary Ruth one. 'If I'd had the sense,' he went on almost cheerfully, 'I could have saved Kenny from going to Malaya, you know. He had signed up for five years or something, but he'd decided he wanted to be a doctor when he was a year or two in. When he'd finished his term, just before he met you, he needed money to fund him through university. He'd been offered a place at Glasgow.' Mary Ruth was shocked at the hatred of Donald with his patronizing tone which was growing in her.

'I could have asked my uncle to lend him the money,' he went on confidently. 'My uncle always had a soft spot for him, for some reason. So when you met him he would have been a medic and he would never have had to go to Malaya. I feel terrible about it. I was the only one who knew. He never told his mother. She hadn't the money, he knew that. Well, obviously, she was only a gardener's wife, after all.'

With sapphires and diamonds you are never going to see now, thought Mary Ruth. To keep Kenny out of the army and to help him become a doctor, Mary would have managed to use those jewels. Joe would rather have had Kenny alive even if he had had to learn the truth about his fathering. She was breathing heavily.

You *stupit bastard*, she thought, you killed my lovely Kenny. You made me a widow and left Kenneth without his father. I'm glad I sold your stuff. You're never going to get those sapphires out of me now. She felt flushed and ice-cold at the same time and deadly certain of herself. She stood up and said, 'If I were as brave as Vi, Donald, I'd kill you.'

He looked up at her in astonishment. She turned, walked away from him, noticed the flowers still in her hand, turned back and hurled them at him. 'And you can keep your bloody flowers,' she screamed and ran out of the visiting room.

'Did me best,' said Donald to Giles Nichols-Gordon when he joined him at his London club for lunch. 'Apologized and all that. Screamed at me, she did. Flung all the bloody flowers I'd bought her at me. Women!' he added. They smiled at each other.

'I sometimes think they're a different species,' said Giles. 'What'll you have, old chap?'

'Another gin, thanks. A pity though. I hear she's going to marry Tom Wilson – Engineer, Channel Tunnel . . . air ducts. Plenty of the ready. Could have been useful.'

'Can't win 'em all,' said Giles.

Chapter 27

On Mary Ruth's last night in prison she was packing up her possessions when Vi brought her supper in at half past eight. 'Ah'm goin' tae miss ye Merry Ruth,' she said.

'I shall miss you too, Vi,' she replied. 'You are the bravest and most patient woman I've ever met.'

'Ah've never hud an educated friend afore,' Vi said. She dealt in realities. 'Ah like talkin' tae yous, I get sick fed up of they young wans goin' oan and oan about they drugs an' tha'. The jile's nae the same as it wiz.'

Mary Ruth smiled. 'You should go to the classes, Vi. Miss Whyte's all right. You could talk to her. I don't know how you survive in here.'

'What else is there tae dae?' asked Vi.

They sat in companionable silence side by side on the bed, chewing their scones and drinking their cocoa. Mary Ruth had been touched at the kind wishes from everyone that day. Even the staff who were not going to be in the next day had wished her well as they went off duty. She had met Mr McMeny just before noon after chapel as she walked back to Diamond.

'Ah hope ye can understan' the paa'er better noo?' he had said.

'Ah'm gettin' the hing o' i', Mr McMeny,' she had replied and been rewarded by a smile.

'Ah doan wantae see yous again,' he shouted after her which Mary Ruth interpreted as good wishes for the future.

'Will ye write me frae Ethiopia? Ah'd like fine tae know how yous are goin' oan,' said Vi suddenly.

'What makes you think I'm going to Ethiopia?' asked Mary Ruth turning to look at her in surprise.

'Ah doan know. Ah jist know yous'll never rest till yous know whit happened tae aw tha' money,' Vi said. She looked very serious.

Mary Ruth smiled at her and said gently, 'I will go Vi, I promise, and I'll write and tell you what I find out.'

Vi cheered up at once and said, 'So Ah wis right, so Ah wis.'

By lock down all the women in the flat had wished Mary Ruth a safe journey. Vi had triumphantly passed the word around. They all agreed she'd never rest till she knew what had happened. They know me better than I know myself, thought Mary Ruth, not for the first time, when she lay in her bed. She feared the worst had happened to the money she had sent to Camfam for Ethiopia.

'The only way to find out is to go and if it has gone astray, play merry hell with them,' was Fern's comment when she had tried to explain her fears to her a few days earlier. 'If a thing's worth doing, it's worth doing well, as my granny used to say.' She had grinned and added, 'I'm a thoroughgoing junkie. I followed her precept. She would have been proud of me, so she would.'

Mary Ruth smiled as she thought about Fern with her twisted sense of humour. I'll have to go, she thought. I've got to know. It wasn't enough just to give money. Wasn't that what the rector had said? Whether it counted if you gave other people's money was a good question. She laughed to herself as she snuggled down for the last time in a prison bed. It could be said to be my money if you looked at it in one way, she thought. Kenny was the direct heir to the line after all.

The following morning Kenneth and Tom came to the prison to collect her. Kenneth went into the gatehouse while Tom sat in the car. The two men had not spoken about the future, but both felt they knew what was going to happen.

Tom was excited. He had always loved and admired Mary Ruth. He would make it up to her for all the misery she had suffered. He would take her on a world cruise. He'd buy her anything she wanted. He was surprised to see her walk away from the prison as Kenneth came towards the car with her belongings.

Kenneth had told her Tom was waiting, but she had said she wanted to walk in the fresh air first before getting into the car. As she walked across the car park towards the exit she met Miss Duthie going to her work. 'Goodbye, Miss Duthie,' she said. She had grown fond of the bluff woman, she realized.

'Goodbye, Mrs Findlater, and good luck,' Miss Duthie replied.

Mary Ruth couldn't take her words in at first. She walked on, then as she turned into the road, I've got my name back, she thought. I can't believe it. I'm Mrs Findlater. I'm me. I'm free. She began to sing softly to herself:

> I'm a rambler, I'm a gambler, I'm a long ways from home
> And if you don't like me, then leave me alone.
> I'll eat when I'm hungry, I'll drink when I'm dry,
> And the moonshine don't kill me,
> I'LL LIVE TILL I DIE.

She roared the last line into the grey damp morning.

'Going our way?' shouted Tom out of the Mercedes window.

'We're going to a party in Edinburgh,' shouted Kenneth.

'East Windy, West Endy, d'yous mean?' said Mary Ruth, running round to the front passenger seat. She climbed in saying, 'Thanks Tom.'

'They're all dying to hear about the jail,' said Tom.

'Well, they won't hear anything from me,' said Mary Ruth 'That's all over and done with.'

'What's that you're clutching?' asked Kenneth.

Mary Ruth looked down. 'Oh, this is my story. Miss Whyte gave it back to me just now. I wrote it to please her and she's very taken with it. It's the Great House Robbery as seen through the villain's eye. She wants me to have it published, but I can't see who would want to read it.'

'Most of the *Sun* readers for a start,' said Tom. 'It was a spectacular piece of work. I bet they'd pay you a packet.'

Mary Ruth laughed. She thought he was joking. 'I don't think I ought to sell it. It might set a bad example.'

Kenneth said, 'I still marvel at your cunning, Mum.'

'It wasn't difficult, Kenneth. He was ripe for the plucking, like so many of his kind. Lazy and complacent. Greedy too, you should have heard him going on about the jewels when he came to see me.'

'What jewels are these?' asked Tom.

Kenneth leaned forward and said lightly, 'Some lost jewels which he's seen painted in a portrait. He thinks they're going to turn up in a secret drawer in a bureau some day.'

'And be posted back from the States by a simple-minded little millionaire who has bought the bureau I suppose,' Tom said and they all laughed.

At the flat, Mary Ruth was hugged and kissed and hugged again by Catherine and Allan and their children and by her brother Jim who had taken a week's holiday in order to be there. Kenneth's wife Marie-Claire came out of the kitchen smiling all over her face and she kissed her and hugged her until Tom rescued her with another hug and a glass of champagne.

Cards had arrived from Verity and Alec who had sent her flowers too. She was trying to unwrap them without damaging them, beset by many helping hands, when her brother Jim's wife Gillian, who had been setting the lunch table downstairs came into the room.

She was chic and perfumed and she held Mary Ruth at arm's length by the shoulders and looked hard into her face before she spoke. 'I only hope that you have understood my position, Mary Ruth. As a local councillor and a Justice of the Peace I hardly felt it proper to visit you, and frankly I dissuaded James from coming to see you because of his position. Civil servants have to be so careful these days. A shred of scandal can cause havoc with one's career.'

She kissed her cheek cautiously. 'I'm very glad to see you looking so well after your ordeal. I do hope the cheque James sent you arrived safely.'

'Thank you, Gillian,' said Mary Ruth. All four cheques had arrived safely, but she didn't say so. I've learned something inside, she thought.

Jim hugged her again then and said, 'Well played, Mary Ruth,' but whether for surviving prison or not telling Gillian too much she never knew.

Champagne corks were popping and hot vol-au-vents began circulating. 'Marie-Claire and I have prepared luncheon,' said Allan. 'We're very proud of it. Don't eat too many of these.'

'Why didn't you tell me Marie-Claire was here?' Mary Ruth yelled above the noise to Kenneth, hugging her daughter-in-law again.

'I tell him not to. I wish to be a surprise,' said Marie-Claire. 'Eat some more. You are too skeeny. Not like a granmothair at all.'

'The phone for you,' shouted Catherine over the heads of the company. 'Take it in our room.' She pulled Mary Ruth out of the throng.

As she went into the bedroom which had been her parents', she saw herself, flushed and pretty in the cheval mirror. Her hair had been set in the prison salon and the new dress her sister had bought for her suited her. It was the first time she had seen herself full-length for two years. I've lost weight, she thought.

'Hello?' she said.

'Mary Ruth? It's me, Mary, Mary Findlater. How are you?'

'I'm fine. Thank you for ringing. I've just arrived.'

'Well, I won't keep you now. I just wanted to welcome you back into the world and to tell you that we leave Paris for Addis Ababa on the first of February. I'll send the time and so on to you at Kenneth's. Don't forget to have a yellow-fever jab and start your malaria tablets and have all your other jabs. The doctor will tell you.'

'What do you mean, we?'

'I'm coming with you to Addis. Not for long. I've got you an open ticket which lasts for a year. I'm just coming for a few weeks. I want to see you safely there and have time to talk to you. Sister Elizabeth Mary knows. She sounds lovely, she wrote again last week. She says they have a visitors' room which is comfortable though the sanitation is basic and the new Range Rover is brilliant. From your money.'

'Oh good, I'm glad it's got there.'

'Oh Mary Ruth, you have become cynical, of course it's there. She sent a photo of it with all the sisters around it. She's the driver. I don't know what you thought a Nursing Sister of the Poor looked like, but Sister Elizabeth Mary looks like a land-girl with a nun's coif on her head and a crucifix hanging round her neck. Her letter is mainly about some corrugated iron she's been given by an Armenian friend which they are hoping to fix on the roof of the hospital before the rainy season. She comes from County Clare and did her nurse training in Edinburgh.'

'I know that much. She wrote to me, remember.'

'So she did. I think she writes as she speaks,' Mary Findlater continued, 'every second word is underlined and every third word is in capitals. She sounds great fun despite all the misery she works in. I feel I know her. I'm so excited about it all. How is everything there?'

'It's like Paddy's market; Jim's here and even Gillian, who went out of her way to explain that as she was so elevated in society she hadn't liked to acknowledge a sister-in-law in jail.'

Lady Mary Findlater laughed.

'Thank you for everything,' said Mary Ruth. The door opened and Tom came in, 'I'll go now. See you on the first.' She put the phone down.

Tom walked over to her, held her in his arms and kissed her. She kissed him and snuggled up to him. 'Who was on the phone? Are you all right? May I tell them the news? You are going to marry me, aren't you?'

She had a sudden vision of Martha Bold. All these questions.

'I'm going to Ethiopia with Mary Findlater. I've got to see for myself, Tom. I've been haunted by the fear that I may have done more harm than good. I want to know what has happened to the money. I promised Vi I would go too. You do understand, Tom?'

He was very still and quiet. 'Who's Vi?'

Mary Ruth paused for a second. 'A friend of mine,' she said. 'She's not free to travel at the moment.'

'Do you know when you are coming back?'

'No. Mary's not staying for long. My ticket is open for a year.'

'Well,' he said after a pause. 'This is news that must be shared. Shall I go and tell them, or do you want to do it?'

'Will you?'

'I will.' He kissed her warmly. 'I'm disappointed Mary Ruth, but you were always determined to have your own way. If I can, I'll wait for you again, but you know what an animal I am.'

'Go on,' she said. 'Tell them. Put them out of their misery. They think we're in here plotting our future.'

'We are,' he sighed and left. A moment later Kenneth came in.

'I hope you're not going to tell me I shouldn't go,' she said.

'Go where?'

'To Ethiopia.'

'Oh, I didn't know. Is that what Tom's announcing? I just came to give you a bear-hug.'

'You don't mind my going then?'

'Not in the least, and even if I did I wouldn't say so. You supported me when I wanted to go to art school.' He laughed suddenly. 'God, do you remember Aunt Connie? "There's no money in art." As if that was the point. What are you using for money?'

'I'm beholden to Mary Findlater for this. What with Verity paying Field and Tom paying Affleck, I feel like a charitable institution myself. I hate charity.'

'Ironic that, considering your recent activities,' said Kenneth. 'Is that why you are going yourself, to suffer a bit of heat and flies? I know you, you always do things properly. Don't drink the water and catch dysentery or cholera or typhoid.'

'Cheer me up, why don't you! I'm steeling myself with regard to the sanitation, which Sister Elizabeth Mary writes is "basic".'

'It'll be revolting, but you'll manage. That's what you used to say to me when I went away to school. "You'll manage", and I did.'

They hugged again. 'Come on,' said Kenneth, 'your audience is waiting.'

'I'll just tidy my hair,' said Mary Ruth. Kenneth left the room. Mary Ruth looked at herself in her mother's mirror as she brushed her hair. She heard her mother's voice. 'Oh, Mary Ruth, whatever are you up to now?' I don't want to get married, she thought. I don't want to organize cocktail parties in Poole. I don't want a second-hand existence. I want to work and at something useful. I'll write to Jamie and ask for ideas. He's a hospital administrator, that's a kind of housekeeper. It's all I have to offer, but I could drive too and garden and maybe they keep hens. 'Don't worry about me, Mum,' she said to the mirror, and went back to the party.

The delight at seeing Mary Ruth out of prison was tempered at first by the news that she was going to Ethiopia. The family sat round the lunch table enjoying Marie-Claire and Allan's *coq au vin* and shouting each other down. They argued the rights and wrongs of the venture, while Mary Ruth sat smiling and ignoring the many baits extended.

No one, however, liked to suggest they would all be happier if she would marry Tom whom they had all known so long and settle down. Gillian came perilously close when she remarked. 'Well, James and I have been married for over thirty years and we have never had a cross word.' The silence which followed this remark was broken by Kenneth and Allan rising simultaneously to offer more wine.

'Poor Jim,' Allan whispered to Kenneth later as they were collecting some more wine from the kitchen.

Kenneth grinned and pulled a face. 'Silly moo!'

Now it was Allan's turn to pull a face. 'Every family has one.'

At the table Marie-Claire was saying, 'My aunt has pray for you every day, and my mothair has say, a woman who permit her only son to live so far and not complain is,' she struggled for the word in English and then resorted to the French '*excentrique*. After that to steal from the milord and go to the jail is not surprising and she will say to go to *l'Afrique* when you are old is no surprise either.'

'Well, that's a relief,' said Mary Ruth, 'but less of the old. I'm a recycled teenager and I'm looking forward to going.'

'I understand,' said Marie-Claire. 'I tell you what my mothair say. I know you have a journey to go. You are welcome always in ours, *chez nous*,' she added as her English failed her again.

'Bless you,' said Mary Ruth.

Mary Ruth enjoyed her three days in Edinburgh with her family. Kenneth and Marie-Claire went with her to Glasgow as she needed a new passport and she managed to do most of her Christmas shopping. Tom had gone south already, but Jim and Gillian made a detour off the A9 to take her to Verity's house on their way home.

Jim wanted to take them out for lunch, but Gillian pointed out that they had a long journey ahead of them, so after a cup of coffee they went on and Mary Ruth, shivering with cold after her centrally heated prison days, borrowed two big sweaters from Verity and ate soup with her by the Rayburn in the kitchen.

They talked for hours. Verity was cross with her for not keeping a diary, but was mollified by being given the story she had written in the jail. She sent Mary Ruth out to walk down to the loch the next morning and read her manuscript in one sitting. She was not pleased.

'Very few articulate and observant people go to prison,' she said as she picked up a huge ladle and served them with the same soup for the third time. It had a curious texture which Mary Ruth couldn't account for. I suppose it's good practice for Ethiopia, she thought. Verity had many fine qualities, but she was no cook. As she chewed the heavy home-made brown bread and gulped the cloudy, lumpy broth Mary Ruth listened to Verity's complaint.

'It was your duty to write about it as I asked you. You have let me down. I have a connection, a cousin-in-law who would have been interested in publishing your prison diary. It is important, Mary Ruth, that the truth about prisons is known.'

'Well, I'm sorry Verity, but I didn't keep a diary. It's no good being cross. What did you think of my story about the theft?'

'What possible use could I make of that, unless you want to hand the jewels over to Donald Fionn-glass on a plate?' asked Verity. 'They are the thread that gives some interest to the thing.'

'Mr Field said I could make the jewels over to Kenneth.'

'Field is a fool. Donald could still get the value of the jewels even if you did give them to Kenneth. He won't get much change out of Carter's and Agostino's will have shipped the furniture to the States and it will have been sold on. It will take years to settle and he'll never get the full value back. The costs will be enormous. He'll be after anything you have, mark my words.'

'Why do you say Field is a fool?'

'Because he chose Affleck to defend you. Useless. You should never have been given such a long sentence. Any barrister with a shred of sense would have made a better job than this Affleck did. A first offence, too.'

'He won my appeal.'

'Anyone could have "won", as you call it, your appeal.' Verity was cross. 'Cousin Charles Grandsire was interested in your story. I write to him regularly and I've told him about you. It's not often that good women fall by the wayside so spectacularly, but it is the day-to-day prison detail which would have sold the book. I am disappointed in you. I was hoping for a lot of detail.'

Mary Ruth looked at Verity in astonishment. 'Verity, I don't want trumpeting all over the place. Tom thought the *Sun* readers would be interested, perish the thought.'

'Money is money, Mary Ruth, wherever it comes from. Don't be such a snob.'

Wisely, Mary Ruth ignored this. 'I wrote the story for fun, for something to do in prison, for the other girls – I am not interested in publication.'

'We shall see. Where are you going to live? What are you going to live on? Your State pension? You've nearly three years to wait for the jewels. Don't think you can go off to Ethiopia and hide from the consequences of your actions. I have had reporters here, here at Bendaraloch. They are itching to know what you got out of the whole business. People aren't stupid, Mary Ruth. Certainly not reporters. I suppose half the jail has read this.' She flipped the manuscript impatiently.

Mary Ruth sighed. Verity was hard work in person, although she was such a good correspondent and had been so helpful. 'Only the teacher and a few of the women read it, Verity,' she said.

'And you expect them to keep quiet, do you?'

'Alec made the same point. I don't know whether they will talk and I don't care. Those jewels are mine.'

'Mary Ruth, Donald Fionn-glass is legally entitled to reparation for the goods you stole from him and the women in the jail would be fools not to sell the information about the jewels if they could. We must just hope they won't be believed. This is the only copy I hope,' she added testily.

'Yes, it is. He may never find out, Verity.'

'Huh!' she said. 'More soup?'

'No thank you,' Mary Ruth replied placing her spoon over some grey, gristly part of a long-dead chicken which she had discovered quite early in her assault on the huge plate of soup she had been given.

Verity helped herself to another plateful. 'Have some more bread and there's some cheese in the dish. Mousetrap, of course. It keeps better.'

Mary Ruth smiled at this and discreetly cut the mould off her piece of cheese. Verity didn't seem to notice. She went on between great mouthfuls of soup. 'Furthermore, the people in Addis are poor enough without having to feed you. Had you thought of that?'

Mary Ruth had. She didn't want to think about food just then and she didn't want to argue any more. She decided to offer her apologies.

'I meant to keep a diary, Verity, but it's a bit like being in hospital. You make the most of every tiny incident and there's really nothing much to write about. I mean what's lumpy custard, or a letter coming a day late in the real world? Inside it becomes a huge issue. By the time we had all talked over some trivial incident, the last thing I wanted to do was preserve it for posterity. But I promise I'll keep a diary in Ethiopia. I know they are poor, but I intend to work while I'm there and I can live on very little now I have the experience of The Valley behind me.' Verity scowled, but she accepted Mary Ruth's apology.

On the Saturday morning Verity took her to Perth and saw her on to the train for Inverness. She warned her BR tea was expensive and handed her a large greaseproof paper parcel of sandwiches after Mary Ruth had lifted her case into the train.

Her parting words were, 'I'll see if I can cut out the stuff about the jewels from the manuscript and get Cousin Charles to look at it. Wire if you need money.' Crabby as she was, she was generous. Mary Ruth knew that she meant it.

She put the sandwiches made with Verity's heavy brown bread and fatty brisket into the waste bin in the lavatory.

Chapter 28

She arrived in Elgin at half past nine and after supper, which was Alec's special beef and beer casserole with smooth mashed potatoes and French beans, they sat and beamed at each other as they ate cheese and oatcakes and apples.

'How are you, Alec?'

'I'm in fair fettle. Martha is coming for lunch on Monday. She's bringing it and Arthur. She looks after me very well. She has a lot of questions for you.'

'She always has. It's her substitute for conversation.'

'Now, don't be unkind. It's sad that she lost her little girl. A daughter would have been a great comfort to Martha, especially as their boys are in Australia. She's tamed Arthur and she—'

'Now who's being catty?' Mary Ruth interrupted.

Alec grinned and went on. 'She has an over-abundance of energy, I agree. She should have had ten children.'

Mary Ruth groaned inwardly at the thought of Martha clones all asking questions. Changing the subject she asked, 'How are they all in Balessie?'

'Fine, so Mackie told me last week. I met him in the town and we had lunch together to celebrate my birthday.'

'Oh! Alec, I forgot.'

He smiled. 'Never mind that. Ina has been ringing me all week.

She says when you go to see Napper and Douggie, please will you call in.'

'Of course, I'll go on Tuesday. My plane leaves on Wednesday. I'm so anxious to see Jean-Marie Alexandre, but I want to see everyone here too. I have thought so much about them all, Alec. They must have known what I was doing. Certainly Mackie must have had an idea. He had all those Carter's people staying at the hotel and Mr Esau. Why didn't he say anything?'

'Perhaps because he was happy to think Kenneth was going to benefit. He is considered the true heir of Fionn-glass hereabouts.'

'Good heavens, did Mackie know that? He never mentioned it.'

'Of course he knew. All the village knew. You are still an incomer, Mary Ruth, after all. Mackie's parents ran The Commercial before him, remember. They were Joe Findlater's friends. Even now they are both gone no one talks about Mrs Joe passing off the old laird's baby as Joe's. I told you Kenny and Donald looked alike as boys, but it was the meetings in what our Shetland cousins call the "simmer-dim" plus the hastily arranged October wedding which gave the local intelligence the facts for its history.'

Mary Ruth sat listening quietly. 'So you think everyone must have known and didn't object? But I'm an incomer, why support me?'

'That's a good question, Mary Ruth,' Alec said smiling fondly at her. 'I don't think you begin to understand how pleased everyone was that you stayed with Joe and Mary and brought Kenneth up in their house after Kenny died. That's why you are so well-loved,' he added leaning forward and pouring wine into her glass, 'not for your wit and wisdom. The latter is under suspicion, by the by, not because you stole the money, but because you gave it all away.'

'That's what the prisoners said, except Fern who said it wasn't mine in the first place so giving it away was OK.'

Alec smiled at Fern's reasoning, though he felt much the same. It had been a relief to him when he learned Mary Ruth had not kept anything for herself. 'What makes you think they must have known?' he asked.

Mary Ruth thought. 'Well, on my birthday Angus said there wasn't much he missed and I had been getting a lot of mail, Alec, much more than usual, from Carter's and Agostino's and all the fine-art salesrooms sent me catalogues too.' She paused thinking back and remembered the fête. 'Mackie asked me straight out at the fête if it was to be Daldrum or Fionn-glass for time-share. I thought he had heard about it from Mortimer-Desmond, but I avoided answering.'

'Yes, he told me you dodged the issue. He worked it out when Mr Esau came from Agostino's because Mortimer-Desmond had been in one evening saying how thrilled his clients would be to have all the original furniture from Fionn-glass and there was Esau making another inventory of it. Tibby noticed the vans too. He told Mackie there was something odd going on because they kept going down the north drive and no one ever used it.'

'I was too clever by half obviously, and I didn't realize the family secret was local history.'

'Well, history is a funny thing, Mary Ruth. It's only as good as the historian and it's not all written down. To read about Columbus you would think he was a saviour, but not if you were the Indians who were raped and tortured and killed by the conquistadors. A certain selectivity has crept into many histories and sometimes it is written retrospectively, to suit the powerful of the day, but the history the ordinary folk know is a different matter. Trust the people.'

He paused and smiled at her again. 'Trust the people,' he repeated, 'in every sense. See how your neighbours in Balessie turned a blind eye to your activities and Mackie told me they managed to act the daft laddie to the detective inspector. They didn't tell him anything. He knew they must have known what was going on, he said as much to Mackie, but they didn't help him. They didn't tell that private eye Donald sent spying for your sapphires anything, either.'

'Surely they didn't know about them?' Mary Ruth was stunned.

'Be reasonable, Mary Ruth. Mrs Joe's estate was in the papers.

She left over fifty thousand, a lot of money for a gardener's widow. A muckle great portrait of the bejewelled former lady Katherine was the only thing you left behind at Fionn-glass. A private detective sent by Lord Donald is asking about some missing sapphires. Putting two and two together is an occupation we all enjoy. If not the jewels, certainly the worth of them had obviously been given to Mrs Joe and they all knew why, remember, but they never let on to the private dick. He was a fool anyway. Tried to suggest the locals would feel sorry for the laird and would tell on the housekeeper. Dear me! Mackie told me they had some good laughs over it all in The Commercial.'

Mary Ruth, who had not seen her mother-in-law's estate in the paper and had not heard it mentioned by anyone, sat silent. I knew nothing about my neighbours at all, she thought.

'People can keep secrets, Mary Ruth,' said Alec grinning at her. 'Joe never knew Kenny wasn't his son, Mary was never shamed, you were protected – all they know is that you must have inherited something from Mrs Joe, bless her.'

'Keeping the jewels a secret was not altogether good, Alec,' said Mary Ruth, and she told him about Kenny's wish to be a doctor and how Donald had not asked his uncle to help, 'though he said he had always had soft spot for him, but the worst of it is, Alec,' she added in a rush, 'if Mrs Joe had told Kenny about the sapphires she could have helped him. It might have saved his life.'

Alec sat quietly for a while. 'The only way she could have told him would have been to tell him the truth, Mary Ruth. Kenny was a happy child and a good young man, full of confidence, and he had a loving father in Joe. Do you think if he had known his natural father wouldn't acknowledge him, didn't respect his mother enough to marry her—'

'He gave her the jewels,' Mary Ruth said interrupting.

Alec looked at her and continued: 'And gave her jewels to salve his conscience which she couldn't turn into cash without breaking her husband's heart? Anyway, do you think that if he had known all this he would have had such a wonderful childhood? You can't put an unhappy childhood right, ever. Kenny was happy and he made us all happy. You'll have to remember that and not dwell on what might have been. Sufficient unto the day is the evil thereof!'

'Those Old Testament boys knew a thing or two,' said Mary Ruth. 'That's how Vi gets through her time. "One day at a time," as the song has it. I've heard a lot of country and western, down in the Valley-O! But it is how she survives.'

'So do we all,' said Alec. 'So do we all.'

They had a peaceful Sunday, only going out to the carol service in the evening. Once she had told Martha and Arthur at lunch on Monday about her trip to Ethiopia she found talking about the future was much more entertaining than her guarded remarks about prison life.

'Making yourself useful is the best medicine for the ills of old age,' said Martha as she served them rare roast beef.

'What ills?' asked Mary Ruth. 'I feel as fit as ever.'

'You're only young yet,' declared Martha. 'Use your energy while it lasts and see you boil your drinking water.'

Arthur said, 'Pay heed to what the locals eat too. You'll be all right if you're careful.'

'Arthur eats properly now,' said Martha. 'I've trained him at last.' She went to the stove to fetch the gravy.

Arthur smiled at Mary Ruth and whispered to her, 'I've no fancy for pastry any more and not so much indigestion. She was right all along,' he added rather sadly.

Mary Ruth went to Balessie on Tuesday and had a cup of tea with Ina at five when the shop closed. 'Sandy had his operation and is much better, though he's no more cheerful, he's away to the Cash and Carry. Eileen Malcolmson is helping Mackie in the pub part time, now her boys are at the school and it has cheered her up,' Ina told her in one breath, glowing with pleasure at her company.

Before Mary Ruth could speak she started again. 'Mrs Inglis is working at The Pitbee as housekeeper. She likes it fine. Miss Roland was in the hospital in August, but she's home again. She's not been gathered yet.' They smiled at each other. 'The work at

Fionn-glass is finished and the place is opening on the first of March. No one much local has got a permanent job there, but we hope there will be caddying and such.'

'Slavery, is what Douggie will call it,' put in Mary Ruth. 'I once said to him that perhaps the time-share developments would bring work to the Highlands, though admittedly the one we were talking about was funded by a syndicate of Germans . . .'

'That'd be popular,' said Ina, laughing.

'Exactly, "I fought in the war," he said, "and I didn't do it to see the buggers over here!"'

'He had a point,' agreed Ina and took up her story again. 'There's a new nine-hole golf-course by the river and all up behind the house. Tibby reckons they'll be wanting to buy some of his land to extend the course, if it takes off. He says it'll be better than set aside, less weeds.'

She drew breath, gestured at the teapot and as Mary Ruth accepted another cup of tea continued, 'Angus and Bella are well and Uncle Angus too. He's been to Toronto to visit his brother. Helen says they are all well at Knockglass. Donald Molloch is still being courted by the neighbouring widows, but he's sitting pretty and none of them has much chance against Helen's cooking. Jean is expecting a baby in April and they are higher up the council housing list this week. That list is a real mystery. They keep being overtaken by folk "pitten oot" of tied houses, all the estates are going in for holiday cottages now and the number of retired parents of white settlers who are moving in is becoming a scandal. The local young have no chance.' Ina paused, aware that she was wandering and said, 'Jamie was asking for you last night on the phone. We are all very happy for you, you know. You were very good to Mrs Joe. How are you?'

'I'm fine, Ina,' answered Mary Ruth, recognizing the oblique reference to her inheritance. Alec had been right as usual. 'Jamie was kind, he came to see me three times,' she went on. Ina smiled happily. The fact that her only son did not have his father's disposition was a comfort and a joy to her. 'He seemed so interested in the routine of the jail, but I don't think I was very informative. It's all like a bad dream now. I'm just glad to be out. I am going to Ethiopia to see what's what, but I'll keep in touch. I spoke to Jamie about my going to Ethiopia. He says an independent eye can be a great advantage to fieldworkers and encouraged me. I'm not really happy about charity, I now realize. Sending money to people is patronizing.'

'Helping people to help themselves is not patronizing, Mary Ruth. Those nuns need all the help they can get,' Ina said shortly. 'All that money from Fionn-glass is circulating at last, thanks to you.'

'I hope it's doing good.'

'Well, it wasn't doing any good gathering dust in the big house,' Ina said, and leaning forward she squeezed Mary Ruth's hand. 'Money makes the world go around, remember.'

'You're a real shopkeeper when it come to money, Ina,' said Mary Ruth. 'Mr Phimister always used to say, "Money must be made to work", when he finished his treasurer's report, at the Vestry.'

Ina nodded in agreement and said firmly, 'Money is a commodity Mary Ruth; it's how it is used that matters. What you gave Camfam is only a drop in the bucket, but it all counts.'

'Money counts, that's for sure,' said Mary Ruth. 'After what I learned in the jail I'm starting to think poverty *is* the only crime. Miss Roland would have a fit if she heard me say that,' she laughed. She put down her cup decisively and said, 'Tell Sandy I was asking for him. I'm sorry to have missed him. I really must go. I've a favour to ask Douggie.'

It took her another half-hour to get away.

Knocking on Douggie's door, she could hear Napper barking. 'Come away in,' said Douggie as Napper threw himself at her in ecstasies of excitement. 'I hear you're off to Africa,' he said as they sat down.

'I won't ask how you know that,' she said. 'I am, and I want to ask you a favour.' Napper was on her knee and licking her ears.

'Stella won't let me give him away anyway,' said Douggie. 'She blesses the day he came. She says I'd be a pest if I didn't have him to get me out of the house.'

'Well, that's all right then,' said Mary Ruth, putting the dog on to the floor and brushing his hairs off her skirt. Napper stood, his ears pricked, his tail thrashing, looking from one to the other. 'Where is Stella?'

'At the Kirk. The guild are cleaning it tonight, for Christmas. When are you off?'

'I'm going to Kenneth's tomorrow: we fly from Paris on February the first. I'm going with Lady Mary Findlater.' I wonder if he knows that too, thought Mary Ruth.

Douggie was able for her. He said, 'She'll not be staying though.'

'What makes you think I will be, Douggie?'

'Makes sense. You'd be some use there.'

'How do you mean?'

'Well, you're a housekeeper, aren't you? Thon places with umpteen orphans need housekeepers, I'd hae thought.' He paused and bent down to scratch behind Napper's ears. 'I'd not waste money on a stamp though,' he added as he straightened up.

'A stamp? What for?'

'A reference from your last employer.'

Mary Ruth began to laugh. 'Oh! Douggie! Would you say a request for a reference might rankle with His Lordship?'

Douggie looked at her with a mixture of affection and admonition in his face and then he said, 'I'd say it wis cheek.'

As Mary Ruth laughed and Douggie smiled to himself Stella came in and there was a great deal more hugging and more laughter.

'Did you make her a cup of tea?' asked Stella, looking for evidence.

'Nah, don't want to be spoiling her,' said Douggie.

After Stella had shaken her head, gone out, put the kettle on and returned she asked, 'Did he tell you about the private eye?'

'Nah!' he said. 'It's not our business.'

'Lord Donald sent him. He was asking all over the village about some—' she caught Douggie's eye and paused.

'Some what?' asked Mary Ruth.

Stella sighed. 'Douggie's right, it's none of our business and it was none of his, but I'm very happy for you and so is he,' she went on in a rush, nodding at Douggie. 'You deserve it.' She was blushing.

'I'm going to Ethiopia, Stella,' said Mary Ruth, touched at her words and anxious to smooth over her embarrassment, 'to see what's being done with all the money.'

'Now that is a good idea,' said Stella, 'it's always worth checking that a job's done right.' She went out to the scullery to make a pot of tea.

Douggie sat quietly across the hearth from Mary Ruth. The fire crackled and they could hear Stella humming happily to herself.

Mary Ruth patted her lap and Napper came at once, jumped up and made himself comfortable. As she sat by the fire stroking the dog she thought, I must get an international driving licence before I go to Addis.

'LIFE has been ONE whole lot EASier since we GOT Ras ROver, that's what the CHILdren call the RANGE Rover,' explained Sister Elizabeth Mary as she negotiated her way out of the airport and on to the main road to town. 'RAS means DUKE,' she added. 'We NEED a RELIAble VEhicle. We DARE not store TOO much AT the mission beCAUSE of the BANdits. We FETCH food AND medicines THREE times a WEEK from the TOWN.'

As they rolled along the broad road from the airport into Addis she pointed out ravines, eucalyptus, camels, donkeys; the Portuguese Mission which housed Dom Eugenio who came to give them mass every morning; numerous straw-roofed shrines, especially the one near the leper hospital to St Frumentius the Egyptian, who had brought Christianity to Ethiopia sixteen centuries before; distant high-rises, the new technical college funded by the

Italians; the tree-lined boulevard which led to the Centre for African Studies and the mud huts which stood between the villas of the merchant class and the public buildings.

'There are NEARly two MILLion in ADdis NOW,' she said in her ringing County Clare voice over her shoulder to Mary Ruth, who was in the back competing for space with six enormous cardboard boxes of vegetables. Mary Ruth was clutching an airport bag containing two bottles of Bushmills which she had presented rather nervously to Sister Elizabeth Mary at the airport. She had beamed at the sight of them and said, 'I see YOU are a PRACtical WOman, Mrs FindLAYter. Hold ON tight to them, FOR the love of GOD. The road aHEAD is BUMPy.' Now as she grinned over her shoulder she said, 'I do HOPE you are COMfortable. I colLECTed the VEGetables FROM an INDian friend in the MerCAto this MORNing, he's VERY generous TO us.' From where Mary Ruth was sitting she thought he was using the sisters as refuse collectors. 'We're a VERY ecumenical society here. THOSE are the PEAKS of EnTOto,' she said next, pointing to the mountains ahead. 'We're over EIGHT thousand feet HERE on the PlatEAU, but the PEAKS are fourteen THOUsand FEET.'

Surprised at the lack of flies and humidity Lady Mary said, 'The climate's lovely. I am surprised. We must be nearly at the equator.'

'YES, but we're NEARer to GOD too. It's the HEIGHT keeps us COOL. Down at the COAST it's TERRible, MosQUITos and ANTS in their MILLions, but HERE it is LOVEly, exCEPT when it RAINS. We don't SEE the HILLS for WEEKS which is dePRESSing.'

As they bowled along in the sunshine under a clear blue sky, Sister Elizabeth Mary kept up a monologue about the work of the mission hospital and their hopes for the future, interrupting herself to point out the roads to the Jewish slaughterhouse, a neighbourhood mosque, the international school and the new municipal sewage works, all of which seemed equally important to her.

'We're nearly THERE,' she said turning on the indicator and changing gear smoothly. 'We'd an OLD Morris, before RAS. One DOOR had fallen RIGHT off and it STANK of petrol and DID that

ROOF leak? In RAS we're able to HOLD up our HEADS, AND we'll keep them DRY in the RAINS.' She laughed heartily as they lurched across the mule and camel track that ran parallel to the road. She stopped and honked on the horn. 'Yacob and IsRAEL are our gateKEEPERS. I CAN open the GATES myself, but it's THEIR job,' she explained and sat patiently.

On either side of the wrought-iron gates, leaning against the wall or sitting on their haunches, were about a hundred children. 'That's the START of our LUNCH queue. MOST of them were THERE when I left at NINE to go to the MARKet and to collECT YOU. There are STREET children HERE in their THOUsands,' she said. 'Sister Benedict RINGS the bell at ELEVEN forty-five, we OPEN the gates and THEN we serve ALL who come. SOME of them TWO times I am SURE.'

'It must take a long time,' said Lady Mary.

'It does inDEED, but they ARE what we GODS-bodies are here FOR. They ARE the POOR. We need a SCHOOL and work TRAINing or they will ALL turn to CRIME and prostiTUtion and then DIE of AIDS,' she said. The two visitors sat silent, her matter-of-fact manner shocking them both.

She waited patiently while two thin boys in white cotton shorts ran to open the gates of the mission. Ten other children watched enviously from the steps of the house and the two women looked through the gates at the sombre house with dusty bushes clustered in front of it.

'It WAS a COPtic priests' SEMinARY. We WERE lucky. After seventy-four there was a MASSive reDIStriBUtion of property and Mother Serafina was alloCATEd this house. It's not BIG, but we DO have our OWN chapel. Thank YOU, boys,' she called as the two began to close the gates behind her. 'They're TWO of our ORphans. We've FORTty-two ORphan babies toDAY, we use the old reFECTory as a nursery. My first job EVery morning is counting EVeryone. We have thirty ORphan boys and girls, like THESE two. They all help WHERE they can. Our PAYtients are mostly REFugees from the CIVil war, AMPutees on the WHOLE. They STEPPED on mines as they FLED though some were SHOT and we have QUITE a few GIRLS who have LOST their babies. INfibuLATION is the CURSE of the COUNTRY girls here.'

'Sounds as though you need help rather than visitors, Sister,' said Lady Mary.

'Oh, visitors BRING us MUCH joy, Lady Mary. They're ALWAYS welcome. We do NEED another DRIVER though. ONly mySELF and Sister BernadETTE drive, she is OUR only DOCtor. She's in France at our MOTHER convent. Then she's going to PARis for a COURSE. Ah, here's Sister ZawDItu. She'll SHOW you to your ROOM. There's a WASHing place on the LANDing and DOWNstairs there's a TOIlet which flushes. When it's AWKward there's a BIG tin JUG and a TAP. Sister ZawDItu will SHOW you. She's only SIXteen. She's our FIRST novice. Mother Serafina IS looking forward to MEETing you at SUPPer. I MUST hurry now. I'm on FEEDing duty today, Sister BaTISTa YoHANNes is at the WOMEN'S hospital this MORNing She's LEARNing to REpair FIStulas. TheoDORus will be in CHARGE of FEEDing today. He is a WONDERful young man puts us ALL to SHAME conSIDering WHAT he has SUFFered.'

She parked the Range Rover, calling, Ibrahim, Asfa, Aisha, Wolete, Tadesse, Legesse to the children, who ran to help her unload the back of the vehicle. She hauled the boxes of vegetables out and gave them to the children and piled the sacks of flour and lentils on to a little wagon which Israel and Yacob had brought. Her little band went off to the kitchens across the yards, laughing and looking back at the strangers with big eyes.

'Why don't you grow your own vegetables and keep chickens?' asked Mary Ruth, picking up a box of vegetables which she could see were redeemable and following the children.

'No one to organIZE it,' said Sister Elizabeth Mary to her retreating back. 'I'm a FARMer's daughter, I'd keep GOATS too but first I'm a NURSE.'

She turned to Lady Mary and said, 'We are SO glad of the HELP we've HAD from Mrs FindLAYter through CAMFAM. SEE,' she said, and pointed to the side of the Range Rover, where *A GIFT FROM CAMFAM* was painted on its side. 'It's the SAME on the OTHER side TOO,' she added, propelling Lady Mary round to look.

Wondering if Sister Elizabeth Mary knew that all the help had been paid for from the proceeds of a robbery, Lady Mary said. 'You need a housekeeper, Sister.'

'We do inDEED,' Sister Elizabeth Mary said ruefully. 'But we've no MONey and no TIME to seek FOR a HOUSEkeeper.'

'Well, you've got one now,' said Lady Mary.

Sister Elizabeth Mary stood holding Mary Ruth's suitcase and said, 'What d' you MEAN?'

'Mary Ruth, of course. She's flexing her muscles already, just look at her. There goes a happy woman.'

The two women and the young novice stood and watched Mary Ruth walking across the yards chatting to the children and carrying her box.

'She's a housekeeper who needs a house to keep. That's why I brought her. She's willing to stay for at least a year and there's no need to worry about her pay. She has friends enough to see her right. She won't be a burden to you.'

'Beats me where she gets all her bloody money from. Goes off to Ethiopia with my Mary! Been there a month now. Mary's come home. Spoke to her yesterday. Says to me, if you please, to *me* of all people,' said Donald Fionn-glass to Colonel Fraser-Gordon, 'that she's doing the job she's best at. Taken over the bloody mission. She's their housekeeper. Last seen making a hen run apparently, with some Greek joiner johnny she'd met in the market. I ask you.'

The colonel sniffed at his brandy glass. Mary Ruth would find her level, of that he felt sure. The trim Filippino waiter poured their after-dinner coffee for them as they sat in the newly-opened lounge at the Fionn-glass Country Club and Time-share Complex.

'Fancy a cigar?' Donald asked. 'All on the house. Might as well make the most of the offer. I shan't be coming here as a paying guest I can tell you. Prices are bloody astronomical.'

The colonel accepted the offer of a cigar. I'll never understand Donald, he thought. Last thing I'd want is a meal in me own dining room, served by a foreign waiter. Not cheap either, he had noticed. Going for the big boys. He'd taken a good look at the rest of the diners. Not a Brit amongst them.

'You haven't answered my question, F-G. Where did Mary Ruth get the money to go to Ethiopia?'

'Not so loud,' said the colonel who found Donald, drunk and pettish, extremely distasteful. Should have refused to come, he thought, while acknowledging to himself that a sneaking interest in seeing the transformations at Fionn-glass House had made him accept the invitation.

'I think I know,' said Donald raising his hand to summon the waiter. He'd see if F-G knew anything about those wretched sapphires. 'See your cigars,' he said loudly as the man approached. 'I think I know,' he repeated turning to the colonel.

'So do I, so do we all.' Colonel Fraser-Gordon cut in. 'None of our business. Mrs Joe was entitled to leave her money as she liked.'

'What money?' asked Donald in surprise. 'She didn't have any money.' Really, he thought, the old boy's going downhill fast. 'Where would she have got money from?'

'No idea,' said Fraser-Gordon, embarrassed at talking about money at all. Not his way. It had been a mistake to come. 'Other things to do besides applying for the details of neighbours' wills,' he said briskly. 'It was in the paper. Lot more than you might think.'

The waiter approached and displayed the cigar selection to Lord Donald. He waved him towards the colonel.

'Make a note of that,' Donald said, and reached for the menu card he had brought from the dining room. He felt in his jacket for his pen. 'Tell Shack to check Mrs Joe's leavings, 'at's what I pay the bugger for,' he grunted as he pulled the top off his pen.

After their brandy and coffee Fraser-Gordon refused a nightcap. As they stood in the hall while the pretty receptionist fetched his hat and coat, the colonel said brightly, trying to please, 'Always had pretty housemaids here in the old days. Mrs Joe was the most remarkably pretty one of the lot. Remember her in the late twenties. Ten I was, when I first saw her. Fell in love with her at first sight.' He stopped abruptly as he recognized that he was prattling like a fool.

Donald smiled. 'The more things change, the more they stay the same,' he said with an air of great wisdom.

The colonel accepted his coat and shook hands with Donald. He was glad the evening was over and that Donald was not staying with him.

'Thanks for coming F-G, appreciate it,' said Donald. 'Bit of an ordeal, I'm afraid. Shan't be coming again.' His eyes were filling with tears.

'Goodnight. Thank you for asking me. Most interesting,' said the colonel, and left. What a fool Donald had been to accept the new owners' invitation to come, he thought and would that he had the grace to bear his troubles like a man.

Donald wandered into the bar which was in the little sitting room and drank five more brandies with the Swedes who were there. He told them a selection of his favourite stories about shooting parties of long ago, to which they listened courteously, and how Bimbo had fallen arse over tip down the stairs the last time he'd been i/c. One of the Swedes, a massive man who had a drink capacity far beyond Donald's, asked politely. 'What please is "arsoferteep"?'

Donald was shocked at this ignorance and found himself quite incapable of explaining. Stupid Neep, he thought. Typical bloody Swede. There was an embarrassed silence and Donald withdrew unsteadily and started up the stairs to his room. It was twenty past one. The pretty receptionist was waiting for him to come up to the top of the stairs. Good legs for a Chinky, Donald thought, holding firmly on to the banister and thinking himself a dignified figure in her eyes. Milord Fionn-glass of Fionn-dhruim, come home to his newly-beautified and warm mansion-house.

'I've turred your bed dow', Lor' Fearglars,' she said as she passed him to go down. 'Goo'ni'.'

Can't even speak the Queen's English, he thought and simultaneously wished he could take her to bed. 'A man needs his leg-over,' he muttered to himself as he surveyed his bed and began groping at his tie, 'only nachural. What's a pretty woman for, if not for pleasing her lord and master.'

Suddenly, clearly and completely, he understood. His uncle had sold the jewels to pay Mrs Joe, 'For services rendered,' he chuckled as he stood looking at his bed. 'The old devil!' he crowed as he fell across it. 'No wonder that stupid dick couldn't find the jewels – good ol' Uncle Donald had sold them and given the loot to Mrs Joe, the remarkably pretty housemaid, for services rendered.' He was too drunk to reason further, but as he struggled to his feet he knew one thing he had to do. He had to know how much actual cash Mrs Joe had left.

He stopped trying to undo his tie, had a pee, brushed his hair, went downstairs to the car park and started his Jaguar.

Singing merrily all the way down the drive he swung out on to the main road, ignored the valley fog, roared through Balessie and turned right without signalling into the Knockspindie driveway, hitting the left-hand gatepost a glancing blow with the nearside of his car. He pulled up in the driveway and sat holding on to the steering wheel.

Constable Malcolm Malcolmson, returning home from a road accident in the fog, saw the silver Jaguar surge out through the gateway of Fionn-glass House in front of him and heard it roar down the hill into Balessie. He alerted his sergeant, warm in the police station, that he was following an accident about to happen and pulled up quietly across the road from Knockspindie gates as the sounds of the collision were dying away. He ran across the road as the Jaguar engine pumped fumes into the fog. As he reached the car he was relieved to hear a voice singing,

'An' the ONLY ONLY thing, that he EVAH did WRONG,
Was to keep her, from the foggy, FO-Geee, DEW!'

He opened the door of the car saying, 'Please turn off your engine, sir.'

Donald did so, then he waved the menu card he was clutching at the constable. 'It's all clear to me now,' he said looking up at him happily.

'It's all clear to me too, sir,' replied Malcolm, recognizing Lord Donald. 'Will you step out of the car please, Lord Donald.'

'It's Constable-bloody-Happy-Birthday-Malcolmson, isn't it?' said Donald genially, hauling himself out of the car. PC Malcolmson leaned in and took the keys from the ignition.

'Are you hurt, sir?'

'Bit shaken; 'fraid I've given the old bus a bit of a knock,' Lord Donald replied and started to move around to the nearside of the car.

'Would you just blow into this for me?' asked Malcolmson politely. Lord Donald turned and looked at him with a puzzled face. Handing him a breathalyser, the constable smiled pleasantly and said, 'One deep breath and blow into here for me if you will, sir.'

'Not suggesting I'm over the limit I hope, Constable.'

'Of course not sir, just routine.'

Lord Donald blew energetically into the breathalyser and proudly handed it back to Malcolm. Now we'll see if I can hold my drink, he thought.

'I'm on my way to see my friend Fraser-Gordon,' he said decisively. 'I've worked it all out, I only need to ask him one question,' he leaned forward to confide in Malcolm, slowly lost his balance and bumped against his chest. 'Ooopsadaisy,' he muttered, leaning on the constable.

'I think it's rather late for a visit, Lord Donald. I'd like you to accompany me to the station,' said Malcolm, gently pushing him upright and taking hold of his arm. 'If you'll come over to my car I'll arrange for the garage to collect yours.'

'No need. My friend Fraser-Gordon will see to it. I insist that you allow me to call upon him.'

'No, sir. I followed you at over fifty miles an hour through the village and saw you swing across the road without a signal and hit the gatepost, and the breathalyser shows you are over the limit. You can see the colonel in the morning. Come along.'

'Now, look here Malcolmson,' said Donald pulling himself free. He was speaking clearly and standing upright. 'I know what's what. There are procedures to follow. I want to see Fraser-Gordon. I know you. You made a mistake arresting Mary Ruth so quickly. Unorthodox, that was. Cost me a lot of money. I know my rights . . .' He began to wilt, and Malcolm caught hold of his arm again and led him across the road. The menu card slipped from Donald's hand and lay on the wet tarmac. 'I know my rights,' he repeated as he sat in the back of the police car. 'I shall have to take this to a higher authority,' he added as the door was closed on him.

PC Malcolmson said softly, 'You do that, sir, but this time, I'm going by the book.'

More Compelling Fiction from Headline Review

TWO FOR JOY

A PERCEPTIVE NOVEL OF CONTEMPORARY FAMILY LIFE

AVRIL CAVELL

Avril Cavell casts an amused and occasionally rueful eye over the vagaries of family life in this engaging and absorbing novel.

'Twins, how lovely! Aren't you lucky?'

Delphine Dobson isn't so sure. Premature baby girls seem like double the trouble to her; and double the expense too – no joke when your husband is an actor long on charm but short of regular work.

And indeed life with identical twins proves tricky. Clover and Merrie are telepathically close and the best of friends until they are accidentally separated. When the longed-for reunion comes, the close and delicate balance of their relationship has changed. With the looks of angels and the temperaments of fiends, they chart the stormy waters of adolescence, bringing alternate despair and delight to their family. Until, eventually, they reconcile the pleasures and pains of their unique relationship in a surprising and satisfying way.

FICTION / GENERAL 0 7472 4324 7